ROOK

AARON MARQUIS / / ADAM KOVIC

First paperback printing October 2021
Cover design by Caleb Worcester
Edited by Rebecca Rutledge
ISBN: 979-8-9850926-1-5

Welcome and thank you for trying out *MindFull©*, the world's leading database of memories and experiences! Before we begin, we'd like to doublecheck that you've fully digested your anti-nausea capsule and have properly secured your complimentary diaper. If you have <u>not</u> received your complimentary diaper, please hit the large red panic button to your right. If at any moment during your memory-log experience you feel irrational emotions such as rage or suicidal ideations, please hit the smaller, magenta panic button, also to your right.

During your *MindFull©* experience, you may often feel a cognitive dissonance from that of your subject, and that's okay! Remember: *you're experiencing the personal memories of real, often complicated people.* Like most stories, these will be full of lies and half-truths that the subjects have tricked themselves into believing. But don't worry about that—you're here to enjoy the feelings of others guilt free!

Much of what you're about to experience has been artificially reconstructed from two halves of one brain. What does that mean? Well, there may be moments in which the experience can feel bi-directional. But never fear—that's just two parts of a big brain becoming one small, digestible bite for you.

If at any moment you feel the experience is lacking in contemporary story structure or relatable characters, please hit the giant crimson panic button on your <u>left</u>.

Throughout your chosen log, you may find gaps or missing moments of information. If such an occurrence befalls the user (you), stomp the burgundy panic button located directly <u>beneath</u> your feet. If no action is taken, one of our technicians will be more than happy to offer supplemental content until the rest of your selected memory is retrieved.

For this log, you have chosen the following: **doctorate reading level, heartfelt, with smatterings of mature themes.** Unfortunately, we were unable to find your desired request and have instead picked a fresh log at random. Please sit back, relax, and enjoy the story. And if at any moment you are not enjoying the experience, please scream into the scarlet panic cone located directly in <u>front</u> of you. Thank you. *—MindFull©* Team

LOG ONE

There's something really comforting about seeing a person whose life is more messed up than your own, I thought as I watched *RMZ Live* for the fifth consecutive hour. I'd been sitting in my apartment's Rig all day, completely sucked into the real-time virtual experience as camera drones buzzed around the war-torn Remilitarized Zone capturing the different shades of nutty escapades and drugged-out shenanigans of the lowlifes sentenced there.

"We're responding to reports of a rogue fleshie behaving oddly and attempting to vandalize a Canadian forward operating base." The narrator always sounded like it was Christmas Day. The image cut to a naked RMZ man with no teeth and a bundle of white gauze taped to his head. The man was trying to cut down a tree with his bare, bleeding hand. A drone moved in closer to interview him.

"What's going on here, sir?" The drone asked, shining a spotlight on the atrophied body of the lumberjack. His sore-riddled, sweaty skin and deeply lined face made guessing his age impossible.

He stopped chopping for a moment and stared into the lens of the drone, practically into my soul.

"I'm . . . cutting it down," he whispered, pointing with his eggplant-colored hand.

"Have you had any substances today, sir?" The drone asked.

The man gazed absently into the distant rubble with his black, dilated eyes, then eased them shut as he thought for a moment, letting himself bathe in the light of the mystical flying robot. He gently swayed, like an intoxicated summer sunflower.

"Are you the Doderer?" the naked man asked.

"Sir–"

"Am I the winner?"

"The winner of wha–"

A blur of skin bombarded my vision as the naked man sprang at the drone and knocked it out of the sky with his mangled hand. The drone lost visual for a moment as it slammed into the ground, causing a mild spasm in my body as my Rig's haptic feedback system shocked my brain stem to elevate the experience.

The *RMZ Live* narrator speculated about what hallucinogen/tranquilizer combo the man might be on as they switched to another event taking place just a few miles away.

Most of the residents—"fleshies," they called them—would be featured in funny situations—domestic squabbles, drug psychoses, insane stunts gone horribly wrong, things like that. They would never be punished, of course; they had already been sent to the RMZ.

The only time things got serious was when a fleshie wandered into a battlefield and found himself dodging the pulse artillery of warring bipedal Frames, fighting each other to secure their country's little piece of the RMZ. That's when I'd lose interest and let it play in the background while I did other things. Life and death just wasn't as fun to watch. I mean, it was still entertaining, especially if you were looking to take your mind off of your own miserable situation. Like I was.

It had been a week since I was placed on indefinite furlough by the plant, and I'd been dragging my ass looking for a new gig. I'd had a sharp headache since the "incident," so that was slowing me down, but

I'd also been hoping they'd do the right thing after reviewing my appeal.

For ten years, I'd kept my head down without ever causing trouble. When they asked me to surrender vacation and sick days, I gave them up. When they asked me to cut corners, I did so without asking questions. When I saw an assembly crane rip off Jacque's arm before exploding, I told investigators that Jacque threw his arm into the crane out of jealousy, causing it to explode. I'd been faithful to the company, and the loyal worm got the dirt, as they say. I think they said that.

DING! DING! The chime from my Rig was music from the gods. Finally, my appeal was ready. Peeling myself from my sweat-soaked Rig, I adjusted the *TeleTap*® on my temple, and walked the ten feet from one side of my apartment to the other, reaching beneath my door for the holographic envelope addressed to me. My letter opener was on the other side of the room, so I quickly browsed the online marketplace for another, closely inspecting each one until I found something that fit my nuanced and laid back personality.

"200 credits accepted. Thank you," my Rig said softly inside my head.

With a snap of my wrist, I summoned the knife. It appeared in my hand in almost the same instant, adorned with ancient Chinese symbols and a powerful chainsaw tip. I sliced the letter, accidentally ripping through some of the copy.

> From: **HR@NormanRobotics**©
> Subject: **RE: When can I come back to work??????**
> *Dear Mr. Lasker, after reviewing the circumstances of your recent termination, we have concluded our independent internal investigation. We have attached the following surveillance record that proves beyond a reasonable doubt that you acted carelessly and with ill intent.*

All right, not the best way to start off a correspondence, but that didn't mean I couldn't still come back to work. There was a file attached to the message after the first paragraph, so I tapped it with my forefinger. My Rig instantly transformed the apartment into a Virtual Reality Experience (VRE) of the robot production line with which I was so familiar, leaving me to stand there like the Ghost of Christmas Past, watching the action from only a few feet away.

There I was, alone in that lifeless concrete room, working the assembly line and overseeing the quality-control process. The QC scan showed signs of internal fracturing on a new batch of bipedal legs, so I sent it back down the line for inspection. For a moment, I got lost staring at Past Me, taking in how overweight and sad I looked. On the back of my too-tight work shirt was a patch of sweat that kind of looked like a disabled butterfly, and a breadcrumb was lodged in the corner of my mouth. Why hadn't anybody told me about it? I wondered how many people I'd talked to that day with bits of sandwich flapping on my cheek. A dull throb shot through my jaw as I grinded my molars at the betrayal.

Before I could plan my revenge, the room flashed red and an emergency alarm began to wail. The warm flush of adrenaline from the piercing noise felt hazily familiar to Present Me. Past Me looked around, confused, surveying the situation, then briskly walked to the emergency exit. I watched myself push the door release, but nothing happened. I pushed it again, then again. Nothing. I stepped back and threw my shoulder into it, letting out a small yelp as I collided with the steel door. Still nothing. The memory started to come back. *I remember being stuck, unable to escape, but then . . .* I couldn't recall. The memory was a swirling fuzz.

An oily damp fog started pouring in from the ventilation shaft above, and I watched myself blindly claw for an emergency kit on the opposite wall, but Past Me wasn't fast enough. He was already starting to cough and wheeze as blood began to roll down his chin. It was the gasps of a dying man, and the scene twisted my gut to watch. Somehow he got a second wind and managed to reach for a wall mounted gas mask, but passed out before he could get it on his face. Then he just lay there unconscious, probably in his own feces.

4

The scene then fast-forwarded—two hours according to the atomic clock—to a crew in thick yellow hazmat suits spraying the room down. Moments later I saw myself on a stretcher just outside the QC room, being talked to by a tall man in a silver suit.

I had no memory of any of this; seeing it unfold in real time was surreal.

"I'll ask you again. What happened here, Mr. Lasker?" The silver suit asked.

"Legs, working on legs. Door . . . broke. Door . . . bad." I wheezed.

"No, the door is working just fine. You *chose* to stay inside, didn't you?"

"I did?" The VRE playback dissolved and I was swept back into my dingy apartment, sitting in my Rig recliner as the final part of the letter began to read itself to me:

> As you witnessed, Null Lasker (you) admitted fault to our attorney by clearly saying, "I did." Therefore, we are upholding your termination for the following actions:
>
> > 1.) Inhaling company product(s), with possible intent to distribute.
> > 2.) Failure to manage a toxic waste zone.
> > 3.) Evacuation of bowels without written consent from a manager.
>
> While your actions were indeed negligent, we are also continuing to investigate whether your motives may have been corporate espionage. Any mention of the experimental biofume that you attempted to steal will be in violation of the NDA you agreed to by reading this letter. If you continue to threaten Norman Robotics© or its subsidiaries, we will be forced to pursue legal action against you and your next of kin.
>
> − Thank you for your time! The Norman Robotics© Legal Team

So that was it. I wasn't going back. For a moment I wondered if I should get a lawyer, but I quickly dismissed the idea. A trial would take too long, draining my account and my energy along with it. And just the thought of searching for an attorney, checking their reviews and rates, made me want to take a nap. Besides, if I did get a settlement, Norman Robotics© would probably just do the cheaper thing and have me killed. No, best to stay in my lane.

I could feel my skin starting to tingle as sweat poured down my back again. The stress was starting to get to me. I needed some comfort, some reassurance that things would be okay. I needed to talk to the only woman who ever loved me.

"Call wife," I said to my Rig.

The room went dark as Laya's WatcHer™ session loaded in. A glop of guilt began working itself through my gut as I waited for her sparkling face. The last few days I'd lied about my layoff, telling her I was out sick while I waited for the ordeal to sort itself out. But now I knew it was time to fess up and tell her everything.

She'd understand. Laya was amazing like that. Her levelheadedness was part of why I loved her. That and she could crush a cantaloupe between her thighs.

A virtual amphitheater swirled around me as I was taken to Laya's performance. Golden columns surrounded the endless theater, with velvet seats available for all those who attended. The ceiling, which had been opulent enough before, had been replaced with an open-air nebula.

I chuckled to myself. She had always talked about upgrading her workspace, but was waiting until she could afford it. Clearly she was having a fantastic month. I sat back in my favorite virtual chair, relaxing, but as the rest of the experience loaded in, I realized something was horribly off. The seat was sticky with fresh protein, and I was nowhere near my front-row center throne. Then it all became clear—I was in the nosebleeds, surrounded by anonymous, pantless avatars. This wasn't right.

6

Squinting, I could just make out Laya below, poised in a projection of her brightly lit living room, demonstrating the opening move of her daily YogaFu class. She was praised internationally for having the most authentic practice of the sacred meditative ritual, and it took only a few seconds of watching her strawberry blonde hair swaying against her see-through top to understand why. She was sensual, hypnotic with a hint of danger. Her transition from lotus pose to rear neck choke was powerful, yet graceful. Every raspy, monotone command seemed to rattle from the back of her throat, soaring above the crowd with its high-pitched lilt. As she smiled into the virtual spotlight, I knew she was happy, doing what she loved—making a room full of strangers rock hard.

"Ferry me to the stage," I commanded my Rig. "Laya must know that her husband needs to speak with her. It's an emergency." I waited a moment, but there was no response. "Take me to the fucking stage, ya piece of shit," I shouted. Still nothing.

For a moment, I'd forgotten that this was still work for her, and the performance was most likely set to do-not-disturb. I pulled up her info page to send a private message, but was met with an error prompt.

"Access denied to [Laya]'s personal inbox. Your account has been downgraded to freeloader," a friendly voice said.

"God damnit," I cursed under my breath.

"Shhh!" The avatar beating off behind me said, kicking the back of my seat.

My credit balance must have been lower than I'd thought. I knew that Laya would give me a guest pass while I was between opportunities, but without the credits, how would I get the message to her? I looked around the darkness for any roaming moderators. The stage wasn't too far, and if I was fast I could easily get a message to her. I waited for the climax of Laya's show—her infamous "Five Star Warrior Fist"—to make my move. As she slowly made her way into the pose, and I heard the rhythmic tugging of the crowd swell into what sounded like a million war drums, I sprang out of my seat.

"Going somewhere?" a giant moderator boomed, placing a heavy hand on my shoulder. He wore a thick, hooded cloak that concealed his face.

"No, I was just adjusting myself," I said.

"Yeah," he said. "You need me to read the rules to you, or are you good?"

I shook my head. "Right as rain."

The behemoth nodded, then eased into a seat a few rows down, watching me with a keen eye.

So much for that, I thought. But then, mid-move, Laya paused her performance.

"Ohhh, I almost forgot," she said, smiling. "I wanna give a big, loving message to someone who's always supported this nutty dream of mine. He's my partner and my husband, but more importantly, he's my best friend. I love you baby, wherever you are!" Laya blew a kiss into the darkened audience, practically right at me, as if she could sense where I was. My body melted into my seat.

"I luff you too, dar-ling!" a young, German voice chimed from a front row center seat. Laya's attention snapped to the voice, and her face broke into a wide, blushing smile.

"This next pose is for you, darling!" she said, cupping her massive breasts, squatting down.

Who the fuck was that?! I frantically searched the darkness, looking for the face of the sancho, then I pulled up Laya's stream status on my HUD, scrolling up the donor list. When I got to the number-one spot, my blood froze:

#1: Hymin Poündar, aka Husband <3

It couldn't be. There had to be some error or a miscalculation. Or maybe Laya was playing an elaborate joke on me as revenge for fibbing about work. But then I slowly realized that none of this was true. This was my new reality. I had to be a man and accept it—my wife had moved on.

I eased back gently against the headrest of my Rig and thought back to the moment I first met Laya. She was just a modest 24-year-old trying to make it like everyone else. Back then she only had half a million viewers a day for her performances, barely enough to make a living. But every day I'd watch her work, absorbing everything she ever put out—every performance, every status update, every nighttime thought—until eventually I *knew* her. She was my closest friend, and someone I could count on to make me happy no matter how bad things had been at work.

After a couple months, I mustered up the chutzpah to message her and solidify our relationship, which cost a small fortune, but I knew the risks. It started out with some light flirting—me sending a dozen messages or so, her pretending not to see them—until one day when lady luck decided to smile upon me.

Laya had been going through a particularly rough time, crying in the middle of a rigorous performance. Her mom had died or something and Laya had just come back from the virtual wake. That's when I felt it—that's when I knew she had to be mine. I pulled up my underwear, then pulled up her donation bucket, where I gave her as many credits as I possibly could. Her eyes were moons when she noticed the large contribution.

"What? Oh my god! Who—*Null Lasker*, where are you?!" She tried to laugh a little through her tears, but she was obviously still in pain. "That's the single nicest thing anyone has ever done for me! I'm yours, anything you want, name it!"

I remembered sitting there as I loaded into the front row of the theater, thinking to myself, *Was this the moment where a boy becomes a man?* It had to be. I went for it.

"Laya, will you marry me?" I said, standing up at the base of the stage. She paused. Her eyes searched the room for a moment before landing on me.

"I will. I do!"

And with those words began the happiest three months of my life. I shook my head at the memory, taking one last look at my now ex-wife. She was spreading coconut oil on herself, topless, performing a warrior pose. She always was a master of her craft.

"Treat her well, Hymin," I said under my breath. "She's more special than you'll ever know." I exited the amphitheater for the last time, lost in the haze of projected emotes, donations and masturbating avatars. *"ß'hend öväh ünt shöw me yoür smile!"* The thick German accent echoed throughout my apartment as the theater faded out of existence.

My heart ached and my head throbbed. *Probably just an empty stomach.* I tried to remember the last time I'd eaten a real meal. My order history instantly popped up.

> ***Yesterday: Phoking Great Pho©—One large Pho, two sides with one large drink and two sides—700 credits, 300 credit delivery fee, plus optional mandatory tip.***

Right. I needed to chew on something, get my mind off of things. Instinctively I pulled up a dozen menus, but decided against another night of takeout—I could barely afford the delivery, let alone a meal. So for the first time in a few weeks, I put on my cleanest floor clothes, and set about leaving my super high-rise apartment.

The heavy apartment door creaked, locking itself behind me as a cold gust of air blew by down the empty, dingy hallway. I placed my hands in my jacket for warmth, making my way towards the apartment lift to face society down below. Inside one of the jacket sacks I felt a few small metallic rectangles, perpetual hydrogen fuel cells I'd lifted from work. The haze of unemployment had made me completely forget the promise I'd made to my neighbor.

"You got dem! I didn't wanna bother you!" Juka's raspy voice echoed around the walls, only slightly revealing her island accent. I couldn't remember where she said her birthplace was, either the Mediterranean or the Philippines. Or maybe it was Hawaii. Someplace under about ten feet of water. Whatever, it didn't matter— hearing her always made me feel better. Her voice whisked me away to an imaginary sand dune in an ocean I would never visit.

"I was worried 'bout you," she said. "How are you taking the breakup?"

"You saw that? I guess everyone did. I'm okay," I said. "Been better, but fifth time's a charm, right? I was just heading out and wanted to give you these before I forgot." I handed her the small pile of energy cells. Her eyes widened and her entire body seemed to sag with relief. But just as quickly she shot back up.

"You want to see it?" she asked with a sparkle.

"Sure, why not?" I said. Juka gave my bicep a friendly yank and dragged me into her apartment, leading me to her dining table/kitchen counter/bath sink where a large object lay draped in cloth. Like a magician, Juka whipped the cover away, revealing the four foot-long plane underneath.

"Look at that pretty baby," she said, beaming.

I eyed the aircraft with its odd color scheme—a giant yellow "X" with green and black inlays. It had a sleek swept wing design with a fuselage in the middle that could store a cubic foot or two of whatever you wanted. Each wing had a typical turbine thruster, but also an aerodynamic cylinder I hadn't seen on Juka's previous versions.

"What's the cargo this time?" I asked.

"Same as always," Juka said smiling. She whipped open a cold locker and removed the storage containers inside, popping off their tops. "Sweet potato pudding, some fried plantains and a few Gizzada. With some pictures and a little note from me."

The glistening coconut pastries made my stomach gurgle, and Juka instinctively leapt on the noise.

"Here, have one!" she said.

"Oh, no. I'm fine. I'm actually full. That was a full noise."

"Ahh, okay," she said.

There was no way I could eat one of the pastries; they were specially made for Juka's family. All of them had been sent to the RMZ over the years—her brother, mom, uncle and other relations I couldn't recall had run out of chances and been whisked away to roam among the other outcasts. Last year they'd taken her fiance (he had been smoking brisket in his backyard without a license), leaving Juka alone on the outside. She hadn't heard from any of them—there wasn't really a way to—save for seeing her mom on *RMZ Live* five years ago fighting off one of the more interesting residents. So every couple months she'd scrimp and save all her credits to build another little DIY airplane to fill with pastries in an attempt to send a taste of home to the people she missed.

But the planes never made it. An engine would fail, or it would overheat, or RMZ air patrol would knock it out of the sky. Something always happened. This had to be the twentieth plane I'd seen.

"Twenty-eighth," Juka said. "But this one is gonna make it. Lookat dis." She tapped the mystery cylinder on one of the wings. "There's little flare pellets in there, throws off the surface to air. And see dat?" Her finger pointed to a copper jewelry box she'd soldered onto the interior of the fuselage, which contained circuitry and the spots for the hydrogen cells. "Gift from my pop when I was a girl. EMP can't penetrate copper."

"And the yellow "X" with black and green on the sides is camouflage," I concluded.

Juka raised an eyebrow. "That's the Jamaican flag, love."

"Right. Because . . . that's where you're from?" I said.

There was a long silence. "If ears were life vests, you'd drown, Null."

I shrugged. "When's liftoff?"

"Day after tomorrow," she said. "Gonna go to the roof with a bag of wine and some puff and let this baby soarrrrrr." Juka spread her arms out and glided around the apartment.

It was a long way from our highrise to the RMZ, and even if she flew that little plane at its top speed of two hundred, Juka was in for a thirty- or forty-hour flight. She wouldn't be able to sleep, and she'd have to keep the aircraft no more than a hundred feet or so above the ground to avoid counter measures . . . and that was before she got into RMZ airspace. There were so many obstacles, so many things to overcome. It always seemed impossible to me.

Juka could see me lost in my concern. "Life's just a big knot, you know?" she said. "Just gotta keep picking at it until you work one of the loops loose, then you *pull*. Before you know it, you'll have strings to tie into a bow!"

"Good luck," I said.

She blew me a kiss and I left the apartment.

Living on the 203rd floor of an ad-supported apartment complex came with a handful of pros and cons.

Pro: Actually running into a person was rare.

Con: The elevator took half an hour to get to the lobby.

Pro: Rent could be subsidized with only a few questionnaires and product reviews.

Con: Rent was so expensive it rarely made a difference.

"Lobby Level," the elevator chimed. I stepped out and was greeted by a large man dressed in black fatigues and a balaclava.

"Identification," he said through his modulated facemask.

I held out my palm. He latched onto my hand, forcing it downward. The grip buckled my legs.

"Calm down, we're almost done," he said as he twisted the skin and scanned my implanted ID chip. "Got any big plans for the weekend?"

"No," I said, holding back a scream. "Just grabbing a bite."

"Null Lasker, age thirty. One strike on record. All right, you're good. Carry on," he said, giving my arm back to me.

"Wait, what strike? I'm clean!" I said, rubbing the red burn on my wrist.

He sighed then started scrolling through his projected HUD. "Hold on, let's see. Yep, here it is. Multiple delinquent payments totaling one strike."

"That can't be right. I've only been—"

"Hey, not my problem! But a couple more of these and we'll be seeing you in the RMZ real soon. All right, move along." His eye caught another tenant entering the building. "Hey you! Let's see some ID!"

It was late. The sun had just slipped below the horizon and the city was bursting with 3D renderings of big-name ads: a translucent jet flying overhead, screaming the name of some airline I would never use; an attractive twenty-something peddling lawn aerating shoes; a simulation of what looked like my childhood dog promoting doggy biscuits that I ate sometimes when I couldn't afford food; and a sort of griffin creature asking viewers to support the local library.

Nobody paid attention to the ads. Everyone kept to themselves as they rushed along the sidewalk, avoiding eye contact. Everyone seemed nervous and on edge, including me. Whenever I was outside, I felt like I was exposed somehow, like those soldiers who used to hop the barbed wire and cross big open fields in Iraq, or World War II, or whatever war—I couldn't remember. It didn't matter, I just wanted to be in my bunker where it was safe. As I crossed the street, I accidentally brushed a woman's arm with my coat.

"Don't you fucking touch me!" she shouted, her wrist recoiling to her chest.

"Sorry," I said. "Thought I gave you enough space."

"Enough space?" she said, tapping her temple to start a new recording. "Whaddya mean by that?" A few other bystanders stopped suddenly and tapped their temples, too, waiting for the scene to unfold. I could hear murmurs of people asking what had happened, speculating on what I'd done.

"I . . . no," I said, turning on my heels, quickly walking away.

When I got to the Dicot Liquor and Deli, I scanned the provisions, trying to find something within my credit range. The ramshackle store was empty and fairly quiet except for an AI-generated news report playing off an old LED screen nearby, strung up in a corner by a couple pieces of twine and some hope. A fake shirtless man and woman with toned bodies sat in plush chairs, presenting the day's stories:

"An exciting upset today in the world of war as 184th-ranked Bhutan defeated China in what most commentators thought

would be a fairly uneventful battle. But early in day two of fighting, Bhutan somehow managed to penetrate frontline defenses and rush a small tactical nuke for seventy-five yards into China's forward operating base. There's speculation that there may have been help from guerilla forces inside the RMZ, possibly wanted unknown terrorist [Name], but it's still unproven. All 290 countries participating in the RMZ will convene for an investigation. If you were lucky enough to have credits on the battle, Bhutan paid twenty-four to one."

Loud explosions, rock guitars, and modulated war cries echoed through the TV's ancient, buzzing speakers.

"In manufacturing, Piece Industries reported lower-than-expected earnings due to decreased Frame output. However, a company spokesman believes interest will pick up as people sign up for the military sharing app SKIRM® to make extra money around the holidays. Piece plans to launch their new Bishop Frame around the same time . . .

I watched the slick new robotic Frame running around a battlefield in the RMZ, probably controlled by some asshole kid sitting alone in his bedroom, until my eyes drifted away. The hunger was starting to hurt. The analog list of edible items included grass-fed lab-grown burgers, meat-based chicken tenders and a hot dog—on sale. Playing it safe, I went for a pack of instant pasta and some ketchup. As the robotic claw gathered my cost-friendly dinner, I began to feel a sharp, foreign pain in my throat. I coughed a little, like when you swallow water the wrong way. It only lasted a moment, but then I went into a full fit, bracing myself against the glass.

The claw appeared to be concerned. "Will there be anything else?"

"Just—one second, I—" My response was cut short by a series of coarse, throat-ripping coughs. I tried in vain to keep my diaphragm from convulsing.

"One fry and a drink added," The claw parroted. "Two deluxe snack packs added."

15

My attempt to gesture "No, stop, no" was ignored. Green fuzz filled my vision as I felt my head break loose from its moorings. I pulled my hand from my mouth and looked down; it was covered in a crimson, muculent film. Terror seized what little breath I could gulp.

"Your order has been canceled. Have a good day," The claw said cooly.

I stumbled back to my place, leaning on anything I could for balance, stopping every few steps to cough and hack the fluid from my lungs. I tried to keep myself together, keep from screaming so onlookers wouldn't think I was a junkie or a nutter. My right calf started to sting, and then it went numb. Oh god, no. Involuntary whimpers croaked out as I hyperventilated. After twenty minutes or so I finally made it back home, just as my other limbs started to sizzle; soon they went limp. The fat tears swamping my eyes made seeing anything besides my death hopeless.

My Rig had a basic body scan function, so I crawled toward it, hoping I could call up an online doctor to help. I desperately combed through my contacts, looking for a doctor in the network, but a new volley of personalized ads made it impossible to navigate.

"Feeling down? Slurp up a cool KavaJava™."

"Need to feel like a real man? Try CaffaKava™! Now free with purchase!"

Adblock wasn't working—another subscription lost to my dwindling credit balance. I fought through a barrage of vacation packages, dating sites, and recruitment tools, until finally landing on an affordable clinic, *Mr. Doctor™*.

"Welcome Null," a sweet-sounding voice said. "It looks like you only have enough credits to use our subplus, ad-supported menu! Please nod if you agree with our terms of service."

I moved my neck as far as my failing body would allow.

"Thank you! Before we begin, would you like to take a quick survey?"

"N—"

"Would you like to know which one of these famous actresses had surgery? The answer might surprise you."

"NO."

"Okay then! Are you ready to begin—"

"Yes!"

"—A new life abroad on a fabulous three-night cruise taken from the comfort of your own home?"

"NO! Cancel, I need to talk to a doct . . . Eeerrr." My speech began to slur.

At that moment an actual doctor's face popped into view, and I was now virtually sitting in their exam room. Product art and slogans were slathered on every surface around me, making it hard to maintain eye contact.

"Welcome to Mr. Doctor™!" The twenty-something doctor said cheerfully. "Your session has begun. How can we help you today?"

"Can't. Move." I whispered. My throat was shrinking, collapsing into itself.

"I'm sorry, I didn't quite get that."

"Paralyzed . . . it's . . . spreading . . . help!" I squeaked out, slamming the projected touchpad of my Rig. The doctor stared at me smiling, watching me die.

"Unfortunately there is nothing we can do for you at this time. In the event that your symptoms prove fatal, we have dispatched an on-site practitioner to secure your organs. Thank you for your time!"

The exam room faded away. I sank to the floor and lay there, paralyzed, fighting to keep my eyes open as the room started to spin into a whirlpool of darkness, sucking me into the void.

The reverberations of a power tool drilling into my head woke me up. I reached with a trembling hand to massage my bloody, pulsating scalp, feeling what seemed to be a piece of my brain sticking out of the side.

"Hey bud, no touching for a day or two." The stupid voice ping-ponged around my skull.

"What . . . what did you do?"

The sloppily dressed paramedic looked back at me as he packed up his dirty tools. "Standard brain plug. Added in a cortex stimulator myself. It's the same thing we give all the preemies uptown. Oh, and don't worry about payment. I went ahead and set up your subscription."

"What's the damage?"

"Standard. First month is on us, but it'll be 2500 every two weeks after that." He got up to leave.

"I meant physically. What happened?"

"Oh. I dunno. And honestly, I don't wanna know. Just gonna say you're lucky I got here when I did. Motor skills look fine, but your brain stem is fucked. I'd avoid hard math problems and crosswords for now." He thumbed through his work padlet. "Alrighty, you're all set up, Mr. Lasker. You have yourself a nice day, okay?"

"Sure."

He stopped and looked around my bare apartment, no doubt noticing the lack of digital art. "And uh, you should probably set up auto-renewal ASAP. Always a shame when people go into shock and croak just because they forgot a bill."

"Yeah, thanks for the tip."

He slammed the door without looking back. I immediately scratched my drill hole. A sharp pain shot across my scalp and I jerked my hand back, noticing the chunky beige pus under my fingernails. I looked over at my Rig and sighed. Guess it was time to find a new gig.

The job board was crowded and noisy. It always was in the early afternoon, when the army of the unemployed started to wake up. In the morning I could at least read the job description before selecting it, but now it was just a mad dash to get whatever I could. I snatched a handful of postings, then took a peek at my catch and started contacting potential employers. The first dozen rejections came quick, without even an explanation. The rest were just scams to get my vault info. Then, after thirty minutes of going down the list, I was contacted by the first job posting that looked genuine:

SUBSTITUTE PRIMARY SCHOOL INSTRUCTOR

Lower credit school districts need someone to fill in for science teacher who is about to pass away (students must not know). Limited A.I. assistance available. No formal education required. Public speaking skills are a plus.

I pinged the school and was immediately greeted by an invisible voice.

"Hello, is this Null Lasker?" the person asked.

"Yes, it is," I said, straightening up in my chair.

"Congratulations. You've got the job."

"Wha—?"

Without warning, I was patched into a classroom, and sitting in front of me were hundreds of child avatars, all sending emotes and carrying on separate conversations that made a wall of sound. One by one they started to notice me, their projected substitute teacher ready to expand their minds.

"Who're you?" one of the students in the back demanded.

"I'm your sub for today," I said, trying my best to smile as I glanced at the lesson plan projected in my field of vision. "It says here you guys were learning about carbon. Who here already knows what carbon is?"

"Show us your plant!" another voice shouted.

"My what?"

"Plant!" a bunch of voices said.

"I'm not showing you my—"

"Why? You don't wanna slap with us?" a rough-looking boy said.

"I didn't say tha—"

"Wait. So you *do* wanna slap with us!" an older girl hissed.

"No! I want to teach carbon!"

A younger boy up front turned back to everyone. "HE WANTS TO SLAP WITH US!"

Hundreds of voices chanted in unison, "PEDO! PEDO! PEDO . . ."

I terminated the connection, arriving back inside my safe and childless apartment. The job search felt more hopeless than before, and I was considering just giving up for the day, but then I remembered a special VRE I had purchased and had yet to watch. I knew it would be the perfect pick-me-up, so I blinked twice, loading the digital experience.

A few seconds later I was sitting in a plastic chair beside a large swimming pool inside an ornate room. The ceilings were twenty feet high, covered with fancy Persian tiles all painted with gold swirls and accents. On the table in front of me was an AK-47 and a crimson beret—my size. My olive green fatigues were well fitting, but also well worn.

"The convoy has left," a voice behind me said.

I turned and saw Raphael Calabrese, the five-time neo academy-award winning actor, approaching the table dressed in the same fatigues and beret. He plopped down in the chair across from me.

"The head start should be enough to get him to the bunker, God willing." He nervously touched the end of his thick moustache. I'd seen him in a hundred VREs, but this was the first one where he had facial hair. He was such a chameleon. A true master of his craft. And someone I could only dream of being.

"Something wrong, comrade?" he said, noticing my mood.

"I'm—I'm having trouble finding a job," I said, fidgeting with the butt of the assault rifle. "It's feeling a little hopeless."

"Null," Raphael Calabrese said, as sentimental music began to play, "You have to push thoughts like that out of your head. They do nothing but stain the spirit. Besides, I need you to be strong right now. I can't do this without you."

I nodded, doing my best to chin up.

"There you go," he said, grinning. "I want you to always remember: there's no such thing as a hopeless situation." At that moment he looked out the window at the advancing division of American soldiers and tanks. "Now, how about you and I buy our leader some time and give these foreign devils a taste of death?" He jutted out his hand and I grasped it.

I backed out of the VRE just as the first tank shell blasted through the wall, turning my head into a thick mush of hair and jawbone, feeling reinvigorated. Time to take care of business. I blinked another two times, opening the job queue back up.

QUALITY CONTROL ASSOCIATE

Fortune 50 company needs QC associates. Up to 0.5 Credits Per Minute, depending on ability. Must have an IQ of 70 or higher.

I pinged the manager and was immediately patched into her office to the seat across from her desk.

"QC applicant?" she asked, not looking up.

"Yes," I said. "The best you'll ever hire."

"Please complete the following cognitive test," she said.

A prompt appeared in front of me: *Say as many words starting with the letter "S" as you can in thirty seconds.*

"Begin," she said as a counter started.

"Um," I said. "Snake . . . sunflower . . ." I paused a second, thinking. "Soap . . ." I tried to come up with more words, but at that moment my mind went blank. Nothing came to me. For the remaining twenty-eight seconds I sat silently, staring at the woman. Then the timer dinged.

"Wow," she said, staring at me for a moment in awe, then the office swirled out of view and I found myself back in my apartment. I closed the job board and sat for a while, not doing anything. Might as well go back to sleep, I finally thought. As I made my way over to my bed, I noticed there was a message hovering above my table from my brother Aarau telling me to call him.

"Null!" Aarau said moments later with a sideways smile. He seemed to have a fresh tan, probably from one of his many vacations during the year, and his hair was immaculate—the dense, wavy locks of a man who rarely worried. "Saw the community board. Your job search is magma."

He shared some videos that strangers had made of me failing to name "S" words, re-cut into memes and dance music videos. As I watched the surveillance footage of my fat ass spilling over the interview chair, I appreciated how quickly they made them.

"Anyway," he continued, "I thought you could come over and help me figure out this new security system, then I'll feed you."

The last thing I wanted to do was work for my brother, but my stomach was killing me.

"Yeah, okay," I said.

I hailed an MTV so I could make my way over to the south side of the city, but had to pick the "pool" option so I could afford it. For two hours the automated car circled the same few blocks around my apartment, picking up as many people as it could, then when it was full, it drove me the five miles into the planned developments and stamp-formed houses of my brother's suburban haven. I tried to take my mind off of breathing in the diseased exhales of my fellow passengers by focusing on the scenery swooshing by outside. There were the thousands of synthetic trees full of carbon filter leaves, still green because they hadn't been switched to Fall yet. A little further down was an enormous, beige fulfillment center full of goodies waiting to service its corresponding subdivisions. Past that was *Willie's Wild Wings*, a trendy buffalo wings restaurant whose parent company was the same as the fulfillment center's and the trees. A part of me was always jealous that the suburbs had a single parent company running every business. It meant you only needed one account for everything, which was really convenient.

After we went through a couple of checkpoints and most of the other passengers had been dropped off, I arrived at my brother's house. I plodded up his walkway and knocked, immediately hearing the shrill bark of his mini Great Dane, its useless nails scratching on the other side of the door.

My brother shouted, "Motley, you bastard! Keep it up and I'll pull your last tooth!" The door slid open and my brother was standing there smiling, gently holding the pooch. I looked at its grey fur and milky eyes.

"Jeez, Aarau. How old is he now?" I asked.

"He'll be twenty-nine in a couple of months, right, Motley?" My brother gave him a pat on the chest and the dog hacked. My brother looked guilty a moment, then his face twisted with concern as he eyed the device drilled into my head. "The hell is that?" he asked.

"Had an accident at work," I said. "No big deal, it's temporary."

"Does it hurt?" he said, peering carefully around the seeping plug.

"Oh yeah," I said.

"Okay, well, let's figure out this security system," he said.

A few minutes later I stood in the middle of the front lawn while Aarau fiddled with a breaker in the house.

"Anything?" he yelled out.

"No," I said, looking at his neighbor's houses tightly packed together, their slate silicon exteriors reflecting the crimson haze of the evening sunset. When Aarau and I lived here with my dad as kids, the lots had been so much bigger. But over the years as prices went up, they had been split in half, then in half again, until everyone had their own expensive little postage stamp to live on.

"Strange," Aarau said. "Should be getting power." From my spot on the tiny lawn, I watched him through the front door as he shuffled some equipment around. "So what's the plan? Gonna look for the same kind of gig, or . . . ?"

"I dunno, may—"

"Y'know, I don't even think I know what you did. Robot stuff, right? Assembly?"

"Kind of, yeah," I said, remembering the countless times I'd told him about my job.

"So you're looking for something like that?" he said.

"If I can. Those jobs are hard to find. I only got that one because I was lucky. That's why I stayed so long."

"Gotcha, so maybe just find something to hold you over. Actually, you know, you're a whiz with machines and all of that—a lot of people around here need help with little maintenance stuff. Maybe you could be a mobile handyman."

"I can't live off of that," I said. "I'd still need to work two or three other jobs."

"That's tough," Aarau said, digging through a box of tools. "Three jobs, working to live. That's what Dad did."

"Except I'm not him, so—"

"I didn't say you were," he said tensely. "Also, it's not a put down."

"Yeah it is. Saying I'm like a guy who was suffocated by a Zooka's waitress in a motel."

"*Accidentally* suffocated," Aarau said, getting angrier. "And you know what? You don't even—"

At that moment, an MTV hummed up to the house. Aarau's partner, Paris, stepped out and sent it back on its way. She trudged up in her meticulous executive fall wear, pausing only to yank off her high heels and throw them in her bag.

"Hey, Paris," I said.

"Null!" she said, her face breaking into a huge smile. "I didn't know you were coming over. Have you eaten?"

"We're gonna feed him. It's part of the deal," Aarau shouted. Paris looked confused.

"I'm helping set up the security system," I said.

"Secur—? You don't have to build things to eat with us," she said, looking back at the house with a frown.

"Did you see Null's memes?" Aarau yelled from inside the house. He giggled to himself and mumbled something I didn't catch.

Paris leaned toward me. "You doing okay?"

"Yeah, I'm fine," I said.

"Listen, anytime you want to just stay here and get away from things—doesn't matter how long—just say."

"I don't really want—"

"Just think about it, okay?" she said, walking up to the entryway. "It's good for you and Aarau. I can tell."

"Anything yet, Null?" Aarau yelled again.

"No," I yelled back.

"You know," Paris said, stopping in the open doorway. "Maybe you should look into what your nephew's been doing for work."

"What's that?"

Aarau shouted, "Lynd's been gigging for SKIRM® during the evenings, after he finishes his school work—Anything, now?"

"No!" I said. "The fighting app?"

"Mhmm," Paris said, "They let you pick whatever country in the RMZ you want to fight for. It's pretty cute. Lynd says he made a couple thousand credits last week working as a . . . damn, what was the name?"

"A 'Pawn'!" Aarau yelled. "For the Indian army."

"You have a good Rig, right?" Paris asked.

"Sort of yeah, but not for that."

"Why not?"

"Because gigging for militaries is for kids and losers."

"I think it may be the way to go, Null," Aarau chimed in. "What else are you gonna do?"

"Aarau!" Paris shouted into the house, embarrassed.

"I dunno," I said defensively, "but there's gotta be something. I can do things besides assembly stuff. Maybe there's a skill I could pick up, or even if there's, like, a trade mentor—"

"Oh, here we go," Aarau yelled. I heard the click of a solenoid switch. An intense pulse shot through my lower intestine, vibrating it like a fault line, and I suddenly doubled over in agony as my bowels emptied. The energy wave stopped; I crumpled onto the grass and curled into a fetal position just as Aarau came out to investigate. Paris bolted into the house and returned a few seconds later with a couple of plush towels.

"I think we're good to eat," Aarau said. "And lemme give you Lynd's referral code while we're in there."

"I'm not signing up for SKIRM®," I groaned.

LOG TWO

Congratulations, Null! You've successfully signed up to be a SKIRM® military contractor! Before you start fighting for the world's most convenient provider of military personnel, you'll need to watch our orientation modules. Once you complete them, you'll receive your fighting certificate of excellence and be all set to earn! Choose ACCEPT when you're ready to proceed.

I shuddered and hit accept, then swirled into an off-white space with no beginning or end as classical K-Pop music bounced around blissfully. High above me, different word phrases flew in a circle formation. But before I could read them, I felt a presence lurking behind me and spun around to see who it was.

It was an androgenous humanoid with a buzzcut. "Hi, Null! I'm Drew!" they said. "I'll be walking you through your orientation modules!"

I took a swing at their head, but there was no reaction. Low-level A.I.

"Let's start with our first module!" they said. A phrase swooped down and hovered inches from my face: HOW SKIRM®WORKS.

A fog rolled into the room and swept the words away, and I found myself standing on the edge of a soggy battlefield, watching a man in a plaid skirt on horseback address a thousand other men in plaid skirts as a sweeping orchestral score swelled from . . . actually, I'm not sure where.

"For millennia," Drew said, "the best and bravest have taken to the battlefield to fight for just causes . . . "

At that moment, the plaid-skirted horseback man shouted to his troops in a thick accent. I think it was Australian.

"For those feeling fear in their hearts," the Australian man said, "remember this. Every man dies, but not every man truly lives!" The plaid-skirted army roared with cheer, then raised their huge swords and charged down the battlefield toward a bunch of puny guys wearing metal hats. Right as steel clanked against steel, the world swirled, and Drew and I were now watching a battalion of malnourished blue soldiers fire seven-foot-long rifles at grey soldiers with bushy mutton chops. The music continued.

"For some soldiers," Drew said, "their cause was to save a Union."

BOOSH! A cannon on the other side fired, sending a cast-iron ball whistling past us and into a wagon of ammunition, which exploded so forcefully it knocked us off our feet and into . . .

Sand. We were now lying on a desert floor. Out of nowhere, an armored Humvee with an old-style American flag launched over us and raced toward a bunch of bearded men in robes, firing machine guns.

"For others, their call was to liberate oil-rich countries from brutal dictators." Another Humvee raced into view and slid to a stop next to me.

"Hey, soldier!" a lieutenant wearing performance shades and manning a machine gun shouted. I looked over my shoulder, but there were only shrubs and sand.

"Me?" I said.

"Yeah, you!" he said. "Guess who we just nabbed?"

"Who?" I said.

He grinned. "The Ace of Spades, Motherfucker!" He reared his head back and laughed, letting the machine gun sing as the Humvee roared off toward the setting sun, a rooster tail of sand spraying to heaven. I stared at the awesome display, half-wishing I was riding shotgun, but my coveting was interrupted as I was swallowed into the sand and spit out into . . .

A barbershop. A dozen young men sat, having their hair indiscriminately shaved by humorless barbers, while a dozen more waited their turn, forming the head of a long line snaking its way outside.

"But whatever the cause," Drew continued, "the glory of being a hero was always ruined by one thing: *commitment.*"

I watched a man with giant puffy hair frown as a barber buzzed a valley right through the center of his head.

"Joining the military always meant long-term contracts and multiple tours away from family," Drew said. "Do you have a family, Null?"

"I had a wife, but she's fucking some Germ—"

"And could you imagine being away from that? Awful. What's worse is what happened to those poor souls who tried to get out of their commitment early." Drew pointed behind me.

I turned to see what he was pointing at and found my nose practically touching a cold concrete wall. When I turned back around again, instead of seeing just Drew, there were ten uniformed men with rifles pointed at my face. Drew was in the center, adjusting their gun sights.

"The penalty for desertion was death, Null. And an ugly death at that."

Staring down the barrels of those old guns unnerved me. I'd had enough. "Rig, quit SKIRM®."

There was no response.

Drew smiled. "Oh, you can't leave," they said. "You made a promise to us."

"Rig, force quit SKIRM®," I repeated.

"Any last words, comrade?" Drew said.

"RIG, QUIT NOW GOD DAMNIT!"

"FIRE!"

BOOM! BOOM! PFFFFT! POP! POP! POP! I winced and jolted at the noises. But then after a moment, I slowly opened my eyes, and saw I was curled up in a ball in front of a few hundred smiling people, all posed in front of SKIRM® headquarters as fireworks exploded overhead. It looked like they were about to take a company photo.

"At SKIRM®," Drew said, emerging from the group, "there's no such thing as desertion because there are no contracts. You fight when *you* want to fight. Simply choose the mission you want from our bounty board, and complete your objective. That's it. Earn all the credits and glory you want, with none of the annoying downsides of traditional war. Stop and start whenever!"

Drew walked over to me as the world spun and morphed back into the off-white space. "Now, let's move on to your next module."

Another word phrase flew down into view: CHOOSING YOUR FRAME.

The letters broke apart into billions of little metal pieces and reassembled in the center of the room, forming a lean, bipedal robot with glowing blue eyes.

"Before you start accepting missions for SKIRM®," Drew said, "you'll need to first purchase a fighting Frame that's in good working order." He strolled up to the Frame and gave it a pat on the shoulder. "For example, this is a Pawn. It's our entry-level Frame and what most new SKIRMERS® use."

The Frame waved at me, and I instinctively waved back like an idiot.

"It's the least powerful Frame in our lineup, but it's also the lowest priced. Our other options are a Bishop, a Knight, and a Rook, which get stronger and more expensive in that order. Sort of like chess."

"Aren't Knights and Bishops considered even?"

"Knights look cooler! Plus they're invisible. And please, save all stupid questions for later. You control the Frame remotely from your at-home Rig. You see what it sees. See?"

Suddenly I was patched into the Frame next to Drew, staring at an overweight piece of shit. *Oh god,* I thought. *Is that me?* There was a huge green stain underneath my belly, extending beyond one of my folds, visible to everyone but me. I was quickly patched out and back to my body.

"The type of Frame you have determines the missions you can accept from the SKIRM® bounty board," Drew said. "For instance, if you had a Pawn like Daniel here, you'd probably want to take a mission with a simple objective, like being a sniper distraction."

"I'm kind of expendable," Daniel said.

"That's right, Daniel. You are," said Drew. "Now, if you had a Bishop or a Rook, you could take on missions with more specialized objectives. And higher pay."

"What about a Queen? And where's the King Frame?" I asked.

"Whoa whoa, Mr. Questions! Let's run before we fly, okay?" All at once the room lifted and we were in the middle of what looked like a showroom, with thousands of powered-down Frames. "Now," Drew continued, "Frames must be purchased through SKIRM® and SKIRM®-approved vendors, and are stored at SKIRM® supply facilities when not in use. Attempts to purchase black market Frames or manipulate software will result in banning and imprisonment."

"Besides," Daniel the Frame said, "You don't know what kind of junk some of these shady dealers are selling." Suddenly one of his eyes exploded and his arms and legs fell off, leaving him a helpless torso on the ground. He strained his titanium neck to turn and look into my eyes. "Remember me, Null," he said as his blue eyes faded to black.

Drew looked at the pile of Frame, crestfallen. Then they smiled at me. "Next module!" they said. Another title swooped into view: ACCEPTING MISSIONS.

The title flew back up to the top of a giant board that looked like an airport departure screen, but with hundreds of different names on

31

it like "OPERATION TINY TRUMPET (CHINA, BISHOP)" and "BATTLE FOR SECTOR 12 (USA, KNIGHT)".

"This is the SKIRM® bounty board!" Drew said. "This is where you'll find available missions along with a description of what they entail. Every mission has the country you're fighting for and the level of fighter required. You'll have ten seconds to make your decision on missions. If it sounds good to you, simply accept and get to work! SKIRM® will transport your Frame to the required fighting area."

The bounty board fizzled into a fine mist which twirled into a cyclone that spread itself all over the floor of the room, forming what looked like a map beneath us. Then Drew and I were lifted from our feet and made to hover like buzzards above it. Words appeared over the detailed map: LEARNING THE RMZ.

"As a SKIRM® contractor, you're expected to know the boundaries and rules of the World Remilitarized Zone, or RMZ," Drew said. They pointed down at the map. "The RMZ is divided into numbered sectors, but almost all sectors have their own nicknames. For example, see that one over there?"

In the upper left corner of the map was a sector with two big mountains squashed together, each with a protruding observation tower at the top.

"That's Sector 20, but contractors will often refer to it as 'The Rack.' Be sure to learn the location of all sectors and their nicknames, in your off time."

"Okay," I said, eyeing the thousands of names and numbers on the map. In a few areas of the map there were greyed-out patches. I saw one labeled "Desolin."

"Why's that sector grey?" I asked.

"That's a community of RMZ prisoners, or fleshies, as we call them. Those areas aren't your concern, only battle zones. Exploring off-limit areas can result in a perma-ban."

"Pure," I said.

32

We flew around the border of the RMZ, and I took in the fences and security measures that separated it from the outside world as Drew pointed out SKIRM® features.

"We have excellent customer service, bonus incentives, and our secure high-speed network ensures zero latency connections and super fast logins so you spend more time killing and making money. Just make sure to always log out properly, and your experience should be seamless!"

"Does my account lock if I don't log out?"

"Sort of!" Drew said. "Due to the nature of our network, failure to log out correctly can result in corrupted files, delayed payments, and Frame Brain."

"Frame—"

"Brain, yes," Drew said. "Oh, look at that!"

A sector below us started to blink rapidly. It displayed the French and Swedish flags next to each other, then in an instant the French flag was replaced with the Union Jack.

"Allegiance change," Drew explained. "In the RMZ, country allegiances change by the hour, so be sure to know which countries are allies and which are enemies at any given time."

I nodded.

"To help anticipate allegiance changes, we recommend studying the socio-economic history as well as the political and cultural zeitgeists of all major foreign powers in the world—in your off time."

"Right." There was so much to take in. I was overwhelmed, but also pumped. I had already forgotten the nicknames for sectors 20 and that place I wasn't supposed to ask about. Would I need to learn Mandarain or would they supply a basic translator? Suddenly I got hungry. I wasn't sure if I wanted chow mein, fried rice or half and half.

Drew shot me a grin. "You ready?"

"For wha—?"

We dropped from the infinite white ceiling, falling toward the map. I could feel my jowls rippling as we hurtled toward the ground, but stopped right before the moment of impact and our feet settled firmly on the dirt. We'd arrived at the next module: PROVIDING A 5-STAR FIGHTING EXPERIENCE.

"What separates SKIRM® from other military fighting apps, besides our monopolistic size, of course, is the level of service we provide," Drew said, motioning to the Frames around us charging toward a base of some kind. "When a country wages a war, they don't want surprises when it comes to their fighters. They want predictability. They want *consistency*. That's why we have our rating system. It ensures our contractors are the best a country can get." We strolled around the battlefield, watching Frames fighting alongside human counterparts, both getting blown apart in the chaos.

"Wait," I said. "Why are those fleshies helping?"

"Many reasons!" Drew said. "Credits, commuted sentences, or just for the fun of it!

At that moment, a concussion mortar landed at the feet of a fleshie, blowing him into the air like a rag doll.

"Now," Drew continued, "our fighters are rated on four important criteria: Punctuality, Courteousness, Diligence, and Cleanliness."

"Cleanliness?" I said.

"Yes! At every battlefield, there are multiple cleaning stations for Frames," Drew said. "Here you can wash off the well-earned grime of a successful mission, at your own expense. Failure to keep a clean Frame can result in a lower rating."

"I don't get it. What's it matter if your Frame is clean?"

Drew laughed. "Cleanliness is next to godliness, Null. And a war without God is unwinnable!"

I was getting tired of Drew's attitude just as a familiar sensation of giving up began to creep down my back. I shook the feeling; I had already come this far. So what? I would have to clean up after myself once in a while. Maybe it would be a nice change of pace for me. The clouds parted and a ray of sunlight warmed our faces as we were sucked back up into the heavens and the off-white room.

"Last module!" Drew cheered, as the only word I cared about hit me: PAYMENT.

Drew stepped in front of me and displayed a plain calendar. "Your pay period goes from Monday to Sunday," they said. "On every Monday morning, you'll receive your payout minus Frame fees, subscriptions, and other associated costs. And that's the orientation. Any questions?"

"Wait, that's it?"

"Almost," Drew said, smiling. "There's someone very special who wants to say something to you."

An enormous man stepped out of the shadows, probably six-five, three-hundred and fifty pounds, with a noticeable limp. Sweeping trumpet fanfare heralded his arrival. I had no idea who he was.

"Hi, I'm Henry Oakley," the giant man said, "SKIRM® Hall-of-Famer and one of the fifty greatest fighters of all time. On behalf of SKIRM®, welcome to your new home, Noole. You're gonna see a lot of stuff in the RMZ—countries givin' it their all, weapons of mass destruction, unnamed terrorist masterminds—but at the end of the day, know that you're always comin' home to the best family in the business: the SKIRM® family. So get out there and give 'em hell, and maybe one day you'll be the one givin' this speech. And be sure to check me out on *INSIDE SKIRM®* with Michelle, Terry and Beef as we give in-depth coverage on the biggest fights in the RMZ, every night at seven on *SKIRM® TV*."

Another voice boomed from above, "Congratulations Null, from the entire SKIRM® team! Now go out there and make some money!" The room went dark, and then I found myself back in my barren apartment.

I was tired. Between flying around with Drew and listening to their stupid lessons, a nap sounded pretty good, so I leaned against the headrest of my Rig. Instantly I recoiled, rubbing at the still-tender site of my stimulator implant. No naps for the poor.

I loaded back into my Rig and opened the SKIRM® app. War drums faded in as opaque Frames and other needless propaganda filled my view. A military training yard came into focus, and soldiers jogged in formation in the distance, chanting in unison.

" . . . When my daddy was 95,
He did SKIRM® to stay alive.
When my daddy turned 96,
He did SKIRM® just for kicks.
And when my daddy turned 97,
He flew up straight to heaven.
He met St. Peter at the pearly gates,
Said, Gee, St. Peter I hope I'm not late.
St. Peter said it ain't your turn,
Drop down daddy and hit the SKIRM®."

A message popped up in my HUD: *Please purchase a Frame to continue.* Four Frames appeared in front of me: a Pawn, Bishop, Knight, and a Rook. My inclination was to go for the Pawn, the cheapest and weakest option, because that's what I could handle, and it seemed more my speed anyway. When I hovered over it, a prompt popped up telling me it was two thousand credits, which I knew was probably more than I had left in my vault. I moved to buy it, but stopped short for some reason, looking at the Rook.

Couldn't hurt to see what it was about. The prompt for the big, sleek Frame popped up with a list of features and animations branching off from its rotating body. After the slick sales pitch, it was kind enough to finally let me know it was ten thousand credits. I laughed. No way I could even touch that thing. I went to switch back to the Pawn but another prompt popped up: *Finance your Frame today with SKIRM®'s Low-Interest Loan Program. Guaranteed Minimums! Flexible Payback Periods!*

The thing Drew said about "specialized missions" and "higher bounties" popped into my head. Maybe a loan wouldn't be so bad if I was making more money. I mean, I wasn't going to be a weekend warrior in this thing—this would be my job. And what's the point of doing a job if you don't get the right tools? A Rook seemed like a smart investment.

Confirm purchase (10,000 credits) of ROOK Frame ver.2.07.90 (OR similar)?

I confirmed.

Suddenly, an electric bomber drone buzzed the deck and I jolted, like I was on the edge of sleep and free falling. That's when I looked down and noticed my hands weren't flesh, but a shiny alloy, and my skinny white legs were replaced with slightly less skinny, actuated ones. I gave myself the full up and down, fully taking in the Frame I was controlling, then tried taking a few steps forward in my new purchase. Immediately I got vertigo and lost control, smashing through a tall hedge and sending stick splinters everywhere.

"That's right! You show that shrub who's boss!" A voice behind me said.

I wiggled out and turned to see another Frame watching me. It was another Rook, casually standing with his weight on his right heel. I got the feeling if he had back pockets, his thumbs would be hooked into them. "Don't worry, man," he said, "if anybody asks, I'll say it drew first blood."

"Thanks," I said, standing up on shaky legs.

"These things take a sec to get a hang of," he said, "but once you do, you're quicker than a two-credit peep show." He raised his arm slowly, rotating his hand, then closing it into a fist, then extending his thumb up from the fist to make a thumbs up. "I'm Bartok, by the way."

"Null," I said. "Is this the training?"

"I mean, that's what they said. Supposedly we gotta do this before we start claiming bounties, but I've been waitin' in this goddamn lobby for twenty minutes for other people to queue. I tell ya, this always happens to me. Anywhere I go, if I sit at a full table, the fuckin' people clear out."

"Weird. Me, too," I said. "I always wondered if I had halitosis or something."

"Nah, your breath's nice, Null," Bartok said. "If I had to guess, I'd say it's your personality."

"Figures," I said. "So what've you been doing in here for twenty minutes?"

"Well, eighteen of it was spent scratchin' my metal ass, then the last two I spent learnin' to juggle. Check it." He picked up three rocks and started to fling them into the air. All of them veered from their arc and smacked his head with metallic clanks.

"That's pretty good," I said.

"Nah, wait a sec, hold on. Normally I got terrible coordination, but look here—Hey SKIRM®! Load up that profile, Albert Lucas, the juggler." Bartok's gaze drifted. His Frame emitted a few beeps and boops, then an audible confirmation chimed to indicate his file had been loaded. He picked the rocks up and resumed juggling, but this time he didn't miss a single one.

"Look at that!" he said, launching the rocks higher and higher. "More! Throw some more!"

I bent down and picked up some concrete pieces, hefting them into his rotation as he grunted with joy at his expanding ten-foot juggle.

"Yessir! YES. SIR!" he said as he did a shimmy. "I am a bonafide freak of nature! Now you, Null!" He used one hand to launch the pieces out of the arc and toward me. I instinctively dodged them, covering my face and genitals. He stopped.

"Ah, sorry 'bout that. I shoulda let you load a personality profile with some goddamn huevos!"

"Personality profile?"

"Yeah, man! It's actually pretty pure. I had some time to poke around the system settings and found out that all SKIRM® Frames come with this *licensed database* of enhancements based on real-life people. Take a peek."

I entered the Frames submenu, hidden in the corner of my vision. I navigated to the *ENHANCEMENTS* tab and a waterfall of optional programming greeted me: Combat, athletics, language, pole vaulting, CSS++ coding, sculpting, auto repair, jacuzzi maintenance . . . the list went on and on. My heart began racing as the list of potential options streamed past my iris two dozen at a time. A hundred million years worth of experience just a tap away. I could feel my self-doubt fading like soapy water down a steep driveway.

"Nice, huh?" Bartok said.

I nodded, half-listening, lost in a sea of people I could choose to be at any moment.

"Hey, so nobody else is loadin' in this thing and I'm tired of waitin'," Bartok said. "Let's just do the training together without the herd."

"Can we do that?"

"Why not? Help desk said there'd be a full class, but I could start whenever I wanted. I just figured if nobody else was here I wouldn't be motivated, ya know?"

"No, I get it, I'm the same way. Let's get this thing over with." I said.

"Pure! Okay, let's hit up combat training, I heard that's the easiest one to do first."

We pulled up a pre-loaded map and strolled in the general direction it said to go, taking our time and absorbing the compound. From what I could tell, we were somewhere on the outskirts of some sector in the RMZ. I could hear the faint thunder of ordnance and, when the wind was right, the buzz of drones. The sky was sort of green and orange, like the tornado skies of Los Angeles and Portland, probably due to the constant weird changes in atmospheric pressure from explosions and projectiles.

The actual training grounds were well kept and mostly sterile. The entire compound stretched for miles with no beginning or end in sight. Frames would load in and out as dozens of drones zipped around picking them up or dropping them off in a brilliant ballet of coordination. There was no greenery or color of any kind, and we seemed to be constantly treading on fine grey dirt, like the kind people bring back from the moon.

"Damn. This dirt is drier than my grandma's pu–" Bartok quickly scanned my face, trying to gauge my reaction. " . . . meatloaf," he said.

"Sucks for your grandpa," I said, grinning.

"Ha! Nice!"

We both chuckled, and in that moment Bartok reminded me of someone. But who? I couldn't put my little metal finger on it.

We came to a set of squat buildings with a half-dozen obstacle courses outside and started with basic maneuvers first. I'd gotten the swing of mobility earlier with Bartok, so we moved through the section pretty fast. Weapons training was a little trickier, and it took a bit of practice to aim the rifles at the holographic targets (which were all Chinese, for some reason), but eventually we could make nice groupings. Mine were in the heart, Bartok's in the crotch.

Next we made our way over to another building for hand-to-hand combat. The facility's interior resembled an old boxing gym, complete with the simulated smell of sour, musky sweat pumped into my Rig so I could get the full experience. I looked around and saw other Frame models spread about, some conversing with one another, others lifting heavy weights.

"Why are they working out?" I said. "Do they need to work out?"

"Look," Bartok said, "you get a robot body, you wanna see how much you can lift. It's just natural."

"Huh, I guess that makes sense."

"You two, get in here! You're late!" a loud voice boomed through the gym. Over in the center ring was an actual flesh-and-blood man, pointing at us. He was enormous, red faced and bald, with a thick vein popping out of his forehead. He was strongman thick, proudly displaying the scars that filled out his bulbous physique. Bartok signaled a *shrug* emoticon to my HUD. I replied with a *flex* and a *wink*.

"Out in the RMZ you're going to run into all kinds of crazy shit," the instructor said as we trotted over. "Convoys, bi-peds, tri-peds, suicidal pigeons with strap-on explosives—you name it. I've seen a lot of boys and girls and theys get soft out there, too reliant on their piece. And forget Frames. They'll get their skulls crushed in by fleshies half their size." He grabbed a perfectly ripe peach from his pocket and crushed it between his hands.

"You, Slim!" he said, gesturing to Bartok. "Get over here and show me your moves!"

Bartok eased over to him "Look, sir. I don't wanna have to fuck you up–"

The instructor snatched his head, slammed him face first into the ground, then maneuvered him into a rear-naked chokehold. Bartok squirmed, looking for an out but finding none.

"Gonna fight back?" The instructor asked.

Bartok tried to roll to one side, attempted to get an arm up, but nothing worked. He tapped.

"You see? What good are you in a Frame if a regular grunt like me can take you to the ground?" The instructor released his grip and Bartok quickly got back to his feet, looking embarrassed. "All right, Slim, you're done," he said. "It's your boyfriend's turn."

I shrugged off the instructor's archaic relationship stereotyping and hopped in the ring, tagging out Bartok. The human callus pointed his giant index finger in my direction, then curled it backwards, beckoning me to participate in his great human-pretzel experiment. I felt panic heat my nape as he stalked toward me—this was going to be the first fight of my life, and I was going to lose. But then, when he was almost an arm's length away, I remembered the personality profiles. I quickly searched, saying the tags "greatest fighters," "KO," and "crazy." A personality list with a dozen names came up, but I didn't have time to read, so I picked a random name as the instructor closed the gap. Suddenly my Frame took an aggressive, staggered stance, and I raised my fists in front of my face, leaving only a little daylight to see my opponent. The instructor's eyes widened and he looked genuinely thrilled. We circled one another waiting to see who would throw the first punch, then he stomped forward with a quick left jab, but I ducked, swinging my head under and back up faster than I could process. It was *instinct*.

"Oooohh, very good," the instructor said, his eyes twinkling. I stayed focused. I could tell his words were the distraction meant for me to lose my foc–

SMACK!

His rear leg low kick nearly took me to the ground, but I caught myself and readied up. He followed with a quick hook to my temple that I backed out of in a flash, his hairy knuckles just grazing my forehead. I responded with a quick jab and uppercut combination, sending his chin to the ceiling. I saw his pleasant glimmer quickly snap to anger as he lunged towards my torso, throwing jabs into my side hydraulics. I blocked as many hits as I could, but he was getting some serious work in. Each strike sent a shock through my system that caused me to lose focus and stamina. Then, in the middle of the punishment, an inspirational quote I'd never heard in my life suddenly popped into my head:

Kill the body and the head will die.

In a blink, I side-stepped his next jab and he missed, stumbling off balance. I seized the moment and threw all my power into a punch to his kidneys. He yelped and tried to counter. But in the same instant time seemed to slow down; I could see his punches before he threw them, his own muscle twitches giving away his every move. I dodged one swing after another, making him pay for every miss with my own bullseye gut torture, until he started to slow down, breathing harder, slower.

I was winning. I couldn't believe it. As he leaned on me, grappling, I knew a few more well placed punches would take him out. But as I was about to push him off of me so I could finish the job, a weird impulse jumped up my spine, too strong to resist. Before I knew what I was doing, I took the instructor's ear into my metal jaws and chomped down as hard as I could.

"AAGGGHHHH!" He clutched his head and stumbled backwards in the ring, blood squirting from his ear flap onto the mat. He felt around where his ear should have been, then checked his bloody hand. He looked at me and Bartok.

"You're crazy! You're both crazy! He ran out of the gym screaming.

A chime in my HUD indicated that all of stage one training had been completed.

"Damn, that was pure!" Bartok said, running up to me.

"Your perthonality profileth thaved the day!" I said.

"Ah, hell! Of course– Wait, you have a lisp!"

" . . . Theriouthly?"

As I turned off the profile, a message scrolled across my HUD: [*incoming video message*]. A surly-looking man in uniform popped into frame.

"Congratulations, new recruits, on completing phase one of basic training. All continued training is optional and should be completed in your free time. You're now ready to accept SKIRM® missions! Please check the bounty board for available assignments. Best of luck, soldiers! We're all counting on you!" [*end of message*]

I looked over to Bartok. "Should we check it out?"

"I didn't do this just to watch you eat people," he said. "Let's war, baby!"

LOG THREE

B artok and I stared at the last three available jobs on the bounty board:

☐ RMZ Sector E-432 Patrol (UK, Rook) [easy] - 2000 credits

☐ Intel Gathering (Australia, Rook) [moderate] - 4000 credits

☐ Intel Retrieval (USA, Rook) [intense] - 6000 credits

My eyes darted between the last two. What was the difference between gathering and retrieval? Maybe chumps gathered and heroes retrieved. But then I remembered that hunters gather and dogs retrieve, so I didn't know what to think.

"Second one looks pretty pure," Bartok said. "Payout's good, and I've been labeled 'moderate' by a few ladies in my time. Plus, if we get in a tight spot, you can just start chompin' ears—"

"Let's do number three," I blurted.

He looked back blankly, not saying anything, oddly still. For a moment I thought he had logged out.

"Bartok?"

After a beat, his body jolted. "Yeah, man! I'm in. Lucky number three."

A bird's-eye map of the training grounds popped into our HUDs, highlighting a path that led to a landing pad a half mile away. We could see a live satellite image of a "Vertical Take-Off and Landing" (VTOL) craft standing by, and a readout told us it was waiting to take us on our first mission. We marched through the grey dirt toward the spot.

"Hey Null, can I tell you something?"

"Yeah, sure."

"Well, I know—" he dipped his head, avoiding my eyes. "I know I talk a lot and um, and make jokes, and most of what I say is bullshit, but if I'm bein' honest, I'm a little nervous about all this. I need it to work, ya know? I need the credits."

"Porn's free, Bartok."

"I'm serious, man."

I paused as he mustered up the words.

"I got two little ones at home. I'm raisin' them alone," he said. "And lately my health's been on the slide, so good gigs are hard to come by."

"Sorry, I didn't—"

"Ah, you couldn't have known. And I'm not tryin' to make you feel bad. What I'm tryin' to say is that I'm in this thing to tear these jobs apart, ya know? Whatever it takes. Whatever it takes to get paid and take care of my boys." He stopped in the dirt and looked at me square. "This Rook cost me everything. I lose it, we don't eat. I should be more nervous, but, I dunno—knowing that someone like you has my back—I feel like it'll be okay."

The words sat on my chest like an old house cat. "Anything you need, Bartok," I said. And then that strange wave of familiarity swept over me again. I stared at Bartok, trying to connect the cosmic dots, but I must have stared a little too long.

"Don't make this weird," he said.

We resumed marching through the compound. Thousands of drones zipped around above us, dropping off dirty, war-ravaged Frames at a storage facility, then latching onto other users' Frames and hauling them off to battle. The spectacle was a beautiful ballet of chaos, but if you unfocused your eyes a bit, it looked sort of silly, like a swarm of 'copter cats ferrying their Frame kittens around by the napes of their necks. It was efficient, though, and the only way SKIRMERS® could fight for Poland on one side of the RMZ in the morning, then battle for Iceland on the other side that night. Meeting the drones in the hazy ash skies of the RMZ were other VTOLs taking off and landing, all with shrapnel scars from surface to air flak.

To our right was an alluring market where users bought the latest munitions and customizations for their Frames. An ad popped up in my HUD telling me that for the next ten minutes I'd get ten percent off there, and I was tempted to stop, but I didn't want to hold us up. Another quarter of a mile and we came to the landing pad, where we were met by two other Rooks who definitely looked in charge.

"Soldiers, I'm lieutenant Gatzun and this is sergeant Luiz." The second one barely nodded, keeping his chin so high it seemed like he was staring down his nose. "You two will be providing crucial security on this mission."

Bartok leaned in and whispered, "Pure."

"When we land," Gatzun continued, "you two will guard our parachutes to ensure no one steals the fabric while Luiz and I go and complete the objective."

"Oh," Bartok said.

"Okay," Gatzun said, "The LZ is a thirty minute ride out, so let's move. We're burning credits." He jutted his thumb behind him, pointing us to the back of the VTOL. We made our way up the ramp as they lit the engines, a deafening spin of the four giant blades that made our eardrums weep, and each took a jump seat—Bartok and I sitting next to each other, Gatzun and Luiz across from us. The aircraft lurched upward and my stomach dropped into my perineum.

47

I settled in for what I figured would be a boring but profitable couple of hours. The two Rooks were discussing something, but the roar inside the hollowed-out cabin was too loud for me to hear much. All I picked up was "RMZ" this and "RMZ" that, so for the hell of it, I pulled up my search function and looked up "RMZ." Growing up, everyone learned about it for two minutes in school, and it was a staple of the news every day, but I'd never actually stopped and read up on its history.

Remilitarized Zone

"RMZ" redirects here. For the sexually transmitted infection, see *RMZ (2023 Pandemic)*.

The **Remilitarized Zone** (RMZ) is the name adopted by the World Trade Organization, NATO and the Reunited Nations to designate an Earth-based region that serves as a persistent, highly profitable, and inescapable war zone. Today, the RMZ most often refers to the landmass in Russia, where 189 countries participate in the ongoing war effort.

Notable past RMZ locations include Liechtenstein, Назарово, and Yellowstone National Park.

Visiting

The RMZ can be found in the eastern half of Russia, bordering Mongolia. While tourism is encouraged, most civilians are not allowed to enter the RMZ unless escorted or detained. Most choose to observe the war-torn region from state-sponsored and network streams, such as *RMZ Live* and *INSIDE SKIRM®*, often inviting romantic partners over for *"War and Piece."* [*citation needed*]

History

The RMZ was originally conceived as a method to combat prison overpopulation while simultaneously boosting the war economy. Historians still debate the exact timeframe in which the idea of a dedicated combat zone developed, but many point to the following as important building blocks in its creation.

The 20th-century philosopher George Carlin suggested during one of his televised sermons that the United States should create "prison farms" in Colorado, Kansas, Wyoming and Utah where society's top-performing criminals would be allowed to roam free. He further suggested that the farms be televised, and that once a month prisoners be allowed to attempt escapes. The idea was never executed successfully during Carlin's lifetime, and some historians believe his proclamations were made in jest.

Next, in 2013, Hollywood (the center for 21st century film production before The Great Quake of 2030), released The Purge. In the film, citizens could commit any crime for exactly twelve hours, once a year. The hit movie franchise was used as an example in a 2035 senate debate, wherein Senator Tiff Cortez suggested that the U.S. adopt a similar strategy to alleviate the ongoing problem of over incarceration. Many senators surprisingly agreed, despite the fact Cortez was making social commentary to highlight the country's willingness for cheap and quick solutions. In spite of his own pleas to not go through with the plan, the idea gained momentum, and in 2036, Purge-Mas officially became both an American holiday and national disaster. Hours of operation varied from state to state, and some residents were free to opt out of the experience if they desired.

Ultimately, American citizens found the rules confusing and obtrusive, which stopped many from fully embracing the holiday. And while the economy saw a slight boost from small arms and baseball bat sales, city services were overwhelmed by the countless fires and wounded citizens. The abundance of small claims court filings that followed also nearly crippled the American legal system.

Sen. Cortez resigned later that year, accepting no responsibility for his actions.

Despite this initial failure, public opinion of Purge-Mas grew more favorable as time passed. Anonymous surveys in the summer of 2038 showed that the public preferred a more dedicated location for those seeking a violent outlet. Small, walled-off sectors started popping up around the U.S. and parts of China, wherein participants were granted two full days to commit any crime they wished. However, the experience favored rich, big-game hunter types over lower-class citizens, and violent offenders found the experience to be hollow and boring.

While smaller purge startups gained their footing, violent protests and riots were reaching an all-time high. Historians believe this to be in response to the countless rigged elections and law enforcement-related beatings around the world, but official records insist that it was due to people wanting to purge. Prison populations also began to reach record numbers. Nations around the world had to adopt a two-strike system in an attempt to quell the growing unrest, but ultimately the system only led to further arrests and lifelong sentences.

On the world stage, the Declaration of Peace was completed and signed in 2039 by every nation on the planet except for Sri Lanka. Tensions rose around the world as the Coalition of Nations grew uneasy with the silence of the secretive island.

A decision was made to send every available tank, warship, drone and soldier to invade the uncooperative nation. The attack, known as the <u>World Wide War</u>, lasted only two minutes and left the entirety of Sri Lanka in ruin. It was later discovered that Sri Lanka had never been invited to the Declaration of Peace Summit, as their communications had been destroyed weeks prior by a record-breaking hurricane season. After the defeat of the terroristic island, the world rejoiced, entering the <u>Age of Peace</u>.

One month later, the Age of Peace ended when Russia accidentally invaded itself. The bloodshed prompted confusion as to which country was invading who and where. In addition, troop allotment could not be properly tracked, resulting in record-high friendly fires and defections, even though most soldiers claimed to be "just following orders." Russia, admitting both victory and defeat, demanded an emergency meeting with the Coalition of Nations to address the problem with peace.

The RMZ Summit

A week-long event took place that same year in <u>Johannesburg, South Africa</u>. Experts were called in to offer solutions to the problem of peace and overpopulation. On the seventh and final day of the conference, as no solution had been agreed upon, the summit came to a close. Just as the attendees were being dismissed, the then leader of Russia, <u>Vlad Nikolaev</u>, made a surprise announcement.

In a joint collaboration with the <u>EU</u>, <u>Middle East</u>, UKS, and China, Russia would donate a large, uninhabitable piece of land which they called the RMZ. Originally used for weapons testing and prisoner rehabilitation (before the <u>melting of all permafrost</u>), every country, no matter how big or small, would be able to buy a base of operation. From there, the war effort could continue between nations, staying separate from the rest of the world. It was also proposed that any prisoners, regardless of sentence, would be invited to the RMZ to save on inmate costs and alleviate budget shortfalls. Russia cited an overall reduction in crime-related activities after they tested the two-strike rule on their own citizens by shipping them to the closed-off region. The offer was extended to all participating members of the Coalition of Nations, new and old. Just as before, the former island of Sri Lanka had not been invited and was invaded one last time the following week.

On January 1st, 2041, the RMZ officially opened for business. Private prisons saw a 94% reduction in both inmates and staff as they transitioned from a rehabilitation to a transportation-based model. Initially only eight countries claimed operational control of the felon-infested, open land mass, but by 2053, over 129 nations had joined the RMZ. Russia would go on to win sixteen Nobel Peace Prizes for their contributions, and be offered a 10% founders fee for all transactions made within the RMZ. As of today, the Russian States of the World maintain the highest GDP and prison population of any country in the world.

Modern Warfare

As the RMZ continued to grow and flourish, foot soldier recruitment fell to an all-time low, partially because of unbearable outdoor temperatures, but mostly due to combat becoming increasingly drone-based. Most countries embraced the change primarily because drones increased spending budgets and would result in far fewer unit casualties.

Unfortunately in 2065, the nonprofit news network, *Inside the RMZ*, was purchased by the FOXTEL® Corporation, an entertainment conglomerate that was focused on creating content for a new and burgeoning audience. Programming

MARQUIS / / KOVIC

blocks included pay-per-view battle highlight events, infomercial-based news, human dramas focused on local residents, and reruns of *Friends*. FOXTEL® executives immediately put pressure on nations and companies fighting in the RMZ to "sex up" the slate:

"People don't wanna see planes or drones or whatever shooting each other all day—they wanna see heads pop, bodies bleed." — *FOXTEL® CEO, Jorg Hustain, internal investors call.*

In response, the military contractor Shirov® LLC, a subdivision of the SKIRM® Partners group, unveiled plans for a new bipedal robot. Known simply as the Frame, it was designed to replicate the ground forces with which audiences were familiar. At a press conference held in New York City, CEO Dennis Yarland debuted not one, but six Frame models. "War is a game of chess and we intend to build upon that idea." The units, initially bulky and fragile, were created with mass production in mind. Each Frame was designed to address multiple facets of ground combat: Pawn, frontline; Bishop, backline; Rook, heavy; Knight, cloak / tactical; King, base; Queen, WMD (classified).

The state-of-the-art technology was an instant hit with soldiers and audiences alike. At one point, it was suggested that the clunky warbots wear the skin of their kills, but this idea was—

"WAKE UP, NULL, FOR CHRISSAKES!"

I jolted from the page. Bartok was screaming in my face over the roaring wind as dense smoke fumes enveloped the damaged cabin. A giant hole was in the fuselage. Outside I could see that two of the engines were on fire.

"This is Lady Three declaring an emergency!" Gatzun shouted into his comms. I searched for his partner, but couldn't see him.

"Jesus! Where's the other guy?" I yelled to Bartok.

"Uh, he said he left his stove on and walked out of that hole in the plane," Bartok yelled back.

Somewhere deep inside I had a feeling my new ten thousand-credit Rook wasn't far behind him.

The VTOL shuddered violently as heavy flak exploded above and below us. Outside the hole I could see ground-to-air tracer missiles whizzing past us and upwards into the dusk sky.

"Should we jump?!" I screamed over the barrage.

"And land where? We don't even know where we are!"

"Yeah! But it won't be long before one of those missiles–"

Everything flashed white and I was yanked backwards. The shockwave was such that I didn't even hear the explosion. I was in muffled darkness for a moment, not aware of anything outside of my violent womb, then my vision slowly came back into focus and I saw I was in freefall, racing the flaming wreckage of our plane to the ground. My HUD refreshed as my Frame automatically oriented me, revealing emergency landing procedures. Multiple green circles and red x's filled my vision. My eyes focused on what looked like a tire yard in the middle of a trash compound, and I fanned out my arms and legs, like a sugar glider made of titanium.

Ten seconds to impact.

I frantically searched through hundreds of diagnostics, emergency protocols—anything to dampen the blow.

OPTIONS//HELP//FREE FALL//LOW ORBIT//**CANOPY**

Five seconds to impact.

I managed to right myself, legs pointed downward. A complex series of artificial muscles and shocks expanded then contracted as I prepared for impact.

Four . . . Three . . . Two . . . One . . .

A confetti explosion of waste and rubber filled the sky as the left knee and right fist slammed the ground. Diagnostic scans began immediately, and information floated around me indicating my Frame had taken minimal damage. Standing up, I could feel the shock through my system via the neural network connection. I knew it wasn't real, but it sure felt like it was. Overall, I felt okay, just had a little headache, a small price to pay for keeping my new purchase intact.

I took in my new surroundings. Just junk as far as I could see, and small burning bits of wreckage from our VTOL. Then after a moment I realized something: Bartok was nowhere to be found. I sprinted between the mounds of trash, searching for signs of an impact, but there were none. For a moment I listened for anyone calling out, or the stomping of a Rook's feet, but I only heard the far off volleys of artillery. Maybe he had landed a ways off because of the explosion. Then I thought maybe he never made it out at all.

INCOMING MESSAGE

"Anyone there? This is Commander Ironside." An officer with fiery eyes and a deep-lined face popped into view on my HUD.

"I'm here." I said, my head still throbbing.

"All right, let's see here," the commander said. "Okay, there you are. Null Lasker. You're a . . . *new* recruit? And this is your *first* mission?"

"Yeah, I was supposed to guard fabric. But I guess there's no parachutes. Wait . . . shit, am I not getting paid now?"

"This is a mistake. This was a classified mission for elite members only. Jesus."

Ironside muffled his mic and chewed out some unlucky lackeys. I waited around awkwardly until he stopped his tirade.

"All right, Null. Listen here," he said. "Normally, I'd boot you from the system and let the poachers pick your shitty little Frame of all its tin, but as it so happens we don't have time to launch a second mission. I'm gonna need you to finish this fight."

"What fight?" I said. "I don't even know what's going on!"

"A few days ago, a very important man named Dr. Shavanka was abducted from a U.S. compound by German mercenaries," Ironside said. "He's a key asset to our war effort for reasons I won't go into here. Right now he's being held a couple of kilometers from your position, but Southies are on their way to . . . well, *extract* things from him. We can't let that happen."

"And I'm supposed to do what?" I said. "Break him out by myself? I can't even juggle!"

"We don't have time to send backup, Null. We need you."

"I don't know . . . "

A lackey offscreen whispered something into Ironside's ear, but he shook his head. Then they pressed it and he finally gave in. "Look, if you do this for us and survive, you'll get the entire mission's bounty. All four credit payments go to you."

"Really?"

"And we'll heavily discount a replacement Frame if this whole thing goes tits up."

Suddenly a strange tingle swept up my lower back to my fingertips. Something I'd never felt before in my life, the feeling of being *needed*.

"Okay, I'm in," I said.

"Sending you the waypoint now. Get moving, we're running out of time!"

The small yellow indicator popped into view, but it was obscured by mounds of junk towering all around me. I needed to get to higher ground. A few yards away there was a towering maintenance building surrounded by a fifteen-foot fence. I ran toward it at full speed without a real plan, but when I got there I found myself scaling the metal barrier easily and launching myself onto the roof before I knew what was happening. For a moment I stood gobsmacked, looking down at where I'd come from, then shook it off and scanned the horizon. A few kilometers away in the simmering evening haze was the midrise that was my target, but between me and it was a bombed-out warzone.

"Hi, uh, Commander Ironside?"

"Yes, Null? What is it?" he sounded panicked.

"I need a weapon. And probably something better than the crap we had at training."

It was silent for a moment. "Copy. There's a weapon depot location nearby. We'll send you something special."

Another beacon popped into view, not too far from the marked objective. I made my way out of the landfill into an open road with a clear shot to the waypoint. It was only a few kilometers away, so I started a light jog, which was an odd feeling because I hadn't done that in real life in probably thirty years. Just as I started to gain some momentum, another tutorial message came into view.

"Sprint-mode now available. WARNING: Overuse can overheat system." All at once the Frame's legs started to morph, the knees bending backwards, until I resembled something more animalistic and pure looking. Yes, I could see it now—an *ostrich*, a big feathery bird of prey, charging at full speed, feet barely touching the ground. My pointy toes launched me further and further ahead with every thrust.

As I came upon the beacon, my Frame started to slow down instinctively. I made one last giant leap, turning and digging my feet sideways into the dirt road, sliding thirty feet to just outside of the weapon cache dropoff. I stood there a second in the kicked-up dust, hoping I could watch a Mark—the saved snapshot of my synapses from this moment—when I was done with the mission. An enormous green holographic ring appeared on the bombed-out area ahead of me, then a message scrolled across my HUD: "INCOMING CARE PACKAGE. STAND CLEAR."

There was a strange whistling high above, growing louder and louder, and I darted to a burned-up tank drone, jumping behind it for cover. I glanced up just as three orange parachutes deployed, and what looked like an old refrigerator drifted to the ground twenty yards away, crushing a patch of wildflowers.

After checking my surroundings to make sure no one else was around, I ran over to it. A security screen on the container read "Verify Identity".

SECURITY QUESTION: What was the name of your first pet?
I typed in "Pookie."
USER VERIFIED.

The door depressurized and opened, revealing a custom assault rifle, a red and white paint job accentuating its immaculate design. As I picked up the gun, a diagnostic readout described it in full detail.

Song Of Prophecy// DMR || ASSAULT VARIANT ||
RARE ★★★★☆
Hollow point, armor-piercing tracer rounds
Infrared, night and body heat sensor
Grenade launcher attachment
Comfort Gel Grip
Runsitter & Associates™

I picked up the rifle, admiring the weightiness and expert craftsmanship, then noticed a small engraving on the side: "aut viam inveniam aut faciam." My HUD auto-translated the dead language:

I SHALL EITHER FIND A WAY OR MAKE ONE

I was in love.

"Hell-o, friend!" A man with a thick Russian or Ukranian or something "-ian" accent yelled from not too far away. I spun and saw a lone figure concealed by battleworn armor and a weathered hood, standing next to a mud-caked motorcycle. I snapped the rifle to my shoulder and pointed it at him. He shot his hands up. "No bad! No bad!" he said in a friendly tone.

"What do you want?" I said.

"We help!" -ian said.

"We..?"

Just behind me, two more dirty fleshies were scanning my empty care package. Their eyes widened at the readout, then they turned and stared at my rifle, speaking in hushed, excited tones to one another. I heard dirt crunching and spun to see -ian moving closer to me. I set my sights on his chest and he froze.

"You and your guys back off. No one has to die." My voice auto-modulated to sound extra intimidating, which scared me.

"Yes, yes. No die. We help." He crept closer, one step at a time, ignoring my orders.

I brought up my comms. "Commander Ironside, you there?"

"Yes, Null! Are you near the compound?"

"I'm close, but I have a problem. Just ran into some local, uh, people here and I'm not sure what to do."

"Kill them."

"I don't think they're armed, sir."

"Null, you listen and you listen good. If someone's in the RMZ, it's not because they kiss puppies and wear undies made of pink frosting, understand?"

"Not really . . ."

"They're the worst of the worst. KILL THEM."

I cut the comms and addressed -ian. "Look," I said, "I'm not here to hurt you. I'm just passing through on my way to save someone. Okay?"

"Yes! Save! Okay!" -ian said, stopping his advance and relaxing.

"Okay. I'm going to go now," I said, lowering my rifle.

"Yes! Go!" he said. The two others by the empty container relaxed, too. I eased up, and adjusted the grip on my new gun.

"You all have a nice day," I said. -ian smiled and waved me off as I turned to head towards my objective, feeling pretty damn pure.

WHACK! My rifle slid across the ground, knocked from my hands by two other fleshies hidden in my blindspot. One of them swung an electric baton, connecting with my head and bringing me to my knees.

"напад!" -ian shouted. They all rushed me at once. The two by the care package produced a net, and the other two mercilessly laid into my Frame with blow after blow. But then suddenly, time felt like it was slowing down. The HUD indicated that reflex-mode™ had been initiated. I dodged the next electric rod swing, delivering an upper cut to the fleshie that launched him violently backwards. His friend jumped on my back, trying to rip at anything on my Frame that he could. I grabbed him by his thick skull, and in one motion pulled him over my head and threw him into the net of the two advancing lackeys. The force of the impact yanked the two scavengers together and slammed their foreheads, knocking them out. I looked over at -ian, who was now all alone.

"No, bad!" he said.

"Yes, no bad," I said. I picked up the electric baton of the unconscious scavenger, and before -ian could react, I hurled it at him, striking him square in his rubles. His scream ripped through the air as he fell to his knees, clutching himself.

I surveyed the pile of fleshies around me. Some were unconscious, others moaned; all had been dispatched by me. Alone. For a second I stood there trying to think of something clever to say, but I couldn't come up with anything. Then I pulled up the personality profiles and searched "hero," "one-liner," and "foreigners." I picked one of the names that came up and suddenly I had my line:

"Welcome to Earth," I said.

I decided not to think too much about what it meant and set off running toward the beacon, but before I got too far, something caught my eye: -ian's motorcycle. It seemed with his new groin injury, I'd be doing him a favor by borrowing it. I saddled up, squeezed the synthetic grips, and raced off to save the doctor.

Twenty minutes and two pretty bad crashes later, I pulled up a few hundred feet away from the distress beacon. It looked to be coming from a newly constructed, four-story modular unit. A quick scan with my HUD told me that the building was actually a King—what countries called their forward operating base. Interesting. I switched my rifle scope to thermal and scanned for any signs of life. The bottom floor was guarded by a half dozen human conscripts in constant patrols. Moving up, the second and third floor appeared far less defended, just a handful of soldiers and engineers taking apart large machinery. At the top floor I could faintly make out what had to be Dr. Shavanka, strapped to some kind of suspended crucifiction rack. Directly across from him was a large man gesturing angrily. The thermal scan indicated that he was at least seven feet tall and weighed three hundred pounds, and that two additional guards were there to back him up.

"Commander, this is Null."

"Go ahead, we're here."

"I've arrived at the compound. I think I see the doctor."

"That's great, Null. Quick update from intel: we just learned that the insurgents are now interrogating Dr. Shavanka. His heart rate is skyrocketing and he appears to be losing blood and other fluids. You need to move before it's too late."

The doctor's vitals popped up on my HUD.

"Right, I got that. But there's a lot of security in there, so I might need some more time to figure something out."

"There is no time! If you can't do it, we'll go with the backup option," Ironside said.

"What's that?"

"Protocol states we destroy any intel the enemy may find. We'll fire on the area until all remaining targets are properly dealt with."

"You're going to kill your own guy?! Just like that?"

"Shavanka's work is far too important to be intercepted by the enemy. Letting that information out could cost the research department trillions of dollars," Ironside said.

"Well, I'm already here. So bombing isn't necess–"

"Negative, Null. HQ has just determined you lack resolve. Option two has been initiated."

"What!? I didn't say anything!"

"You had a tone."

"There wasn't a tone!"

"We're done here," Ironside said. "You have six minutes to leave the area or you'll be destroyed with the compound. You tried your best, but it wasn't good enough. Goodbye, Null."

I sat there, deflated. No credits, Bartok was gone, and nothing I had done mattered. I gazed out over the pockmarked vista, figuring out a good path to take to get free of the blasts. A westerly route seemed pretty pure. As I righted the bike to get moving, I stopped and looked back at the compound. The King.

"Eh, fuck it," I said.

I revved the electric motor and launched off toward it, accelerating the cycle as fast as it could go. Shrieking voices flooded my comms telling me to turn back, but I ignored them. A thousand meters until impact . . . six hundred . . . three hundred . . . one hundred . . . twenty. Time slowed; I could feel the Frame tense for action, perched on the seat ready to spring. The sentries barely had time to react, getting only a few shots off before I was at their door. Right before the bike slammed into the building, I lept off and onto the third-story wall, reaching for anything I could grip. Pulling myself up was a struggle; the smooth surface made it a losing battle. I slipped down helplessly. Then I felt my bottom half latch onto something, then my hands. Thick, razor sharp talons had emerged from my feet, and claws from the tip of my metallic, nanocarbon fiber fingers. I didn't question it and made a break for the roof, skittering upwards, trying to get there before the conscripts had time to react. But when I popped up over the ledge, I found three guards waiting for me. With a single shot I gave one of them their first helping, but the other two had the drop, pinning me down behind a water tank. I tried to pop up for a shot, but the guards sprayed a wave of suppressive fire, sending shrapnel and water from the tank everywhere. They kept up the barrage until one of them had to reload. I shifted to get off a shot, but then I heard a loud CLINK and felt a stab in my arm as I spun around and off my feet. From the other side of the roof, a half-dozen shooters had appeared up the stairs and were peppering everything around me. Sandwiched between the two advancing units, I crawled to a space further inside the leaking water tank to escape the crossfire. I popped the Song of Prophecy around a corner and used the thermal scope to take pot-shots. A couple of guys took cover, but another took aim. KRRSH! The rifle flew from my hands to the ground and I scrambled for it. The moment emboldened the two sides and they seemed to all shoot at once in a constant stream—I couldn't even hear the space between the shots. The soldiers moved in closer and closer as I lay on the flooded ground and covered my stupid alloy head, realizing I'd mucked up. Should've headed west when I had the chance.

Suddenly, an explosion rocked the roof. For a second I thought I'd been grenaded, but when I saw I had all my robot-y bits in one piece, I spun to face the stairwell side. The five guards were gone, and a sixth was on fire, screaming and running around amidst the debris. None of it made sense.

"That was loud!" a familiar voice said. I turned to the ledge as a figure hopped over into view. I couldn't believe it.

"Bartok!" I said.

"Tis I!" he said, putting his hands on his hips. The other two guards spun to him. "Oh, shit!" he said, hitting the deck as they opened fire. He army-crawled to my cover through the rising puddle to shake my hand. "Nice to see you!"

"How'd you survive the fall?" I said.

"Fell into a compost heap," he said. "An old one, too. Real soft and shitty."

"Pure."

"So, what's the plan here?" he said.

"The plan is to rescue this doctor before the entire area is bombed in a few minutes."

"WHAT."

I started to scan the roof's layout and composition. "Damn, we could've gone down that stairwell, but . . . " I pointed at the collapsed rubble where the exit used to be.

"Sorry 'bout that."

"Don't be," I said, taking in the cheap roof structure made of American steel, and the standing water from the tank. "I have an idea."

I picked up the Song of Prophecy and checked my options, finding what I needed. The nitrogen-fused grenade loaded with a satisfying click, and I fired at an angle toward the remaining guards. It plonked over and exploded at their feet, peppering them with instant ice shrapnel. The remaining liquid nitrogen spread across the soaked roof, deep freezing the water and making the entire structure brittle. I checked the timer on my HUD. Two minutes until the military flattened this place.

"Let's go!" I said, pulling Bartok up. We ran across the roof until I saw the perfect patch of ice. I jumped up and Bartok followed. We landed with full force and shattered the ground, falling clumsily through to the floor below and drawing immediate fire from the handful of fleshie and Pawn guards on duty there. Bartok and I tag-teamed lighting them up in a sort of violent interpretive dance, jumping and bending around each other, until they were all put down.

"Okay," I said. "The doctor should be at the other end of the floor."

"Hope he takes walk-ins!" Bartok said.

We got up charged through the haze, carefully checking rooms for any stray heroes. But as we rounded a corner, I heard a quick burst of shots and felt hot pieces of metal and carbon ricochet off my side. I instinctively pivoted and fired at the movement in my periphery, taking down the shooter.

"Where'd he come from?" Bartok said.

I looked down and saw Bartok splayed out on the floor. One of his arms was missing below the elbow, and only a few strands of fiber-optic held the torso of his Frame to his bottom half.

"Bartok!" I knelt down and accessed the damage. Besides all the major body failures, a scan showed that his power pack was punctured and he was losing energy. His Frame was about to die. Bartok held up his severed arm and studied it a moment.

"And I never got to play the trombone . . . " he said, easing back against the floor. "What a let down. Thought I'd get to finish the mission with you."

"I wouldn't be here if it wasn't for you," I said.

"Nah, you're crafty. You're one of the smartest people I know, Null."

His compliment hit me deeper than it should have, for a reason I couldn't explain.

"Now," he said, his voice starting to crackle, "You go and save that Doctor and make me proud. I'll see you on the other side, okay?"

I hesitated, thinking on the word proud—it felt good to hear.

"Go!" he said, snapping me out of it. "Make those credits! But also . . . do it for SKIRM®!"

"All right!" I jumped up with new purpose and raced my way over to Dr. Shavanka. I could see in my HUD that he was unconscious now, his heartbeat slow but steady, though none of that would matter if we all got shot up in a minute.

I burst into the holding room and found the doctor still strapped onto the interrogation table. He stirred a little at the noise, then went still again. I used a jagged piece of steel support beam to cut through his rubber restraints and slung him over my shoulder.

"We're getting out of here, Doctor."

CRACK!

A metal stool connected with my chin and knocked me off my feet, sending the doctor plopping to the ground. The overhead light was all at once eclipsed by an Everest of sweaty skin and scraggly hair. Oh, right—the big guy.

Rising to my feet, I faced the seven-foot wall of muscle. His nametag read "Albert." That's sweet, I thought. In a flash I reached for my rifle, but he was too fast, knocking it from my hand.

"Fight for real, tin man." Al said with a thick accent. His crusted, bleeding lips spread wide across his war-torn face.

"I really don't have time for this." I swung for this head, hoping for a quick knockout, but I missed. He returned the favor, blacking out my view momentarily with a swift jab. His knuckles were bleeding, but he appeared unfazed.

"You think you're first tin man to come after me?" he said, showing me his oozing hand. The torn flesh was hiding a kind of metallic, reinforced bone modification. "Your head will make lovely trophy for wall. Give it here!" Albert lurched forward, grabbing for me. I rolled behind him and reached for the rifle. For as big as he was, he moved like a rabbit. He countered my roll and stomped a heavy boot on the Song of Prophecy, snapping it in two.

"No guns, fight like men."

"Fine."

I offered a quick headbutt, disorienting him just for a moment as I lifted my leg and dropped it on his sixteen-inch foot. He gathered himself, smiled, then snatched me up in a crushing bear hug. The pressure made my alloy tink and groan, and I knew it was becoming too much for the Frame. I had to think fast.

"That best you have, tin man?"

"No . . ." I coughed out. He let out a booming howl of a laugh as he squeezed tighter, and that's when I saw my chance. I jutted forward, taking his ear into my mouth and biting down as hard as I could.

"AGGHHH!"

I spat out a chunk of cartilage as the talons erupted from my foot, piercing through whatever bone modification Al had. He let out a high-pitched shriek that pierced the walls as he released his grip. Then I took his big fat head in my hands and unretracted the claws, digging them deep into his thick skull. The razors punched through the metal plating like rice paper, paralyzing him. He convulsed on the ground, screaming in agony.

I grabbed Dr. Shavanka and slung him over my shoulders, moving back to the building's skylight for our escape.

"Commander Ironside, I have the doctor," I said.

"We can see that, Null. Great job."

I could hear the VTOL overhead, its electric blades whipping the air. A rope dropped through the hole in the ceiling, coiling on the interrogation room floor. I snatched it up and tugged, letting them know we were good to go. As we rose from the ground the rope began to retract, pulling us into the cargo bay. When we were inside, I took a seat and eyed all of the other soldiers catching a ride around me. I tried to decompress for a moment, but then–

"I've never seen that before, Lasker."

Off to my right was the man himself. Commander Ironside, in the flesh.

"Sir?" I said.

"This was your first go, yet you completed a classified mission intended for four veteran Rooks. And you survived without a scratch."

"Almost," I said, looking at the graze on my arm.

"Almost," Ironside said, smiling. "Null, I want you to be a part of SKIRM® Elite™."

"Really?"

"Really. I know talent when I see it. And the best deserve the best around them. It's only a year contract, and you'll get preferred access to bounty boards, weapon upgrades, cleaning stations, everything you need to be all that you can be."

It was all too much to process. I couldn't believe it. "Hell ya!" I said. "Sign me up."

"Excellent, we'll take it from here, soldier. You have yourself a good rest of your day, and we'll see you tomorrow. Bright and early." He saluted me, then the entire plane rose to their feet, clapping and chanting my name.

"NULL . . . NULL . . . NULL . . ."

The echoing voices faded as I logged out, finding myself back in my apartment. I immediately checked my credit balance and saw it was back in the black. Big time. I exhaled, a wave of relief sweeping over me.

After a moment the adrenaline subsided, and for the first time I could feel how exhausted I was. My lower back ached from sitting upright and tensed in the Rig for so long, and when I pressed a finger into my thighs, I couldn't feel anything.

I had just enough energy to crawl to my mattress and pass out. That entire night I dreamed of my new life in the RMZ.

LOG FOUR

It was around one in the afternoon when I awoke to gentle licking on my hand. I looked down and saw the small quokka's glossy black eyes staring up at me, hoping that this time it would be enough to get me up. I gave Pookie 2's fur a petting for reassurance, and wished it felt as soft as it looked in the pictures, and not like a cheap hairbrush.

I'd always wanted a quokka, ever since I saw one in that old documentary on Australia, *Uninhabitable,* where they were transporting animals off of the continent to shelters around the world. But I never had the funds, and the little cat-sized marsupials were expensive to buy and expensive to keep. That changed though when I walked away from my first mission for SKIRM® a week before with twenty-three thousand credits and a hero's thanks. After picking out some new clothes and buying Juka some high-end parts for her next airplane (#28 hit a microburst and was lost a hundred miles from the RMZ), I messaged everywhere I could looking for one, and after a few days, I found Pookie 2 at a mum-and-pop pet store on the other side of the city. The girl at the pet store showed me the special-order hibiscus plants I had to feed him, his skincare regime, and all of the prescription medicines I had to give him once a month, and then I gave her five thousand credits—the first of six payments—for my little buddy. And now here he was, practically smiling and demanding more special leaves. The cuteness was too much and I didn't want to forget the feeling of the moment.

"Rig, make a *Mark*, please."

A gentle *bloop* noise sounded as my Rig took a snapshot of the neurons and synapses firing in my brain, and uploaded the file to the cloud and social media. That was going to be a good memory to revisit, but it also reminded me to make advance payments on my cloud storage sub. It was crazy to think that I'd almost lost all my Marks when I got canned from the plant.

I ran my hand over Pookie 2's hair again and frowned. The pet store clerk told me that there was a rare expensive horse hair conditioner I could get to soften up his coat a bit, but I hadn't gotten around to buying it yet—there had been so many other purchases that it got lost in the spree. In the week since I saved Dr. Shavanka and lost Bartok, I'd been taking it easy, getting my life back on track. I was SKIRM®'s Golden Boy, part of the SKIRM® Elite™, and for the next year I was contracted to win big for them— a fact they hadn't let me forget since I'd logged out. Every couple of hours I got messages begging me to take on a mission, but every time I snoozed them. I'd log back in eventually, but for now it was *me* time. A lot of the little things I'd been meaning to take care of the last couple of years—buying new house sweat clothes, getting my back hair lasered, replacing my teeth—were checked off my list. On top of that, I'd met a new girl. Which reminded me . . .

I dumped some hibiscus flowers in Pookie 2's bowl, hopped into my Rig, and adjusted my *TeleTap*®. Slowly, I faded into a silky crimson holding room where I gave my authentication code and was asked if I wanted to join the current experience.

"What's on the menu?" I asked.

"Attack Of The Fifty Foot Woman," an automated voice purred back.

"Yes!"

All at once I found myself on a city street with people screaming and fleeing all around me. Everywhere I looked there was chaos and mayhem—cars burned, people were flattened into the pavement, and a few skyscrapers were leaning at dangerous angles. Then I heard the sound . . . BUM . . . BUM . . . BUM . . . like a thousand bass drums hitting at the same time, every beat throwing me off balance and sending bits of building tumbling to the street below. I stumbled around a bit, but regained my footing just in time to look up and see her.

She rounded the corner, using the twentieth floor of an apartment complex to swing herself and make the turn a little tighter. She was wearing an old-fashioned microkini, though I could tell that she'd once been wearing a shirt and shorts by the bits of thread that still clung to her in vain. Her perfect, sinewy legs flexed everytime she took a step in her three-story heels, and her swaying bob cut made its own wind gusts. Enormous perfection.

"Take her right flank, we'll take the left!"

At the other end of the street, a man in his underwear was leading three dozen men in various states of undress, all with some sort of weapon in their hands. Some had big hedge clippers, others had machetes or chainsaws, but the traditionalists had scythes. No matter the weapon though, their goal was the same—remove all articles of clothing from the giant woman before the time was up. It was a classic experience, and no one did it better than Angelina.

She saw the naked little men and instantly pivoted, her heels destroying the asphalt and bursting water mains as she fled. I chuckled, but then as all of the men took off in pursuit, I had the urge to talk to her. Technically our date didn't start for another five minutes, but I didn't care; she'd be happy to see me. I pulled up the options, but didn't see any way to talk to her directly. Then I saw that Angelina had listed a jetpack for a thousand credits in the item menu. A pretty valuable tool if you're trying to cut the clothes off a gargantuan woman, but of course none of these guys had bought it because they were duds who didn't have the credits. I accepted the purchase and the jetpack appeared at my feet, then I strapped in and took off zooming toward my love. As I approached her head from the south, a gust of her perfume blew past me, and I could feel a tingling warmth in my stomach that began to spread all over my body. I remembered our first date a few days before, and the electricity she made me feel. There was no woman like her. Her existence was effortless, and she made me feel like– JESUS!

Her giant hand swatted at me, just barely missing. The turbulence sent me into an uncontrolled gyration that I desperately tried to correct. Up was down, right was left, and every control input did the opposite of what I wanted. A patch of thick air let me right myself . . . just in time for the next swat. This one hit the pack and ripped it from my body, sending me free-falling toward the ground.

"ANNNNNGEEEEELLIIIIINNNNNAAAAAA!"

The wind roared by my ears as I hit terminal velocity, but then right as I was about to liquify on the pavement, everything went dark and I wasn't in freefall anymore. I looked around, seeing if I was back in the waiting room, but then I realized I could still hear the muffled sounds of the street chaos and Angelina. Also, it was *really* humid and smelled like gonads.

All at once it was bright again, and as my eyes adjusted I saw two blue eyes the size of swimming pools, and I realized I was sitting in the palm of Angelina's hand.

"Null!" she said.

"Hi, Angie."

She looked at the broken straps on my back. "Awww, you bought a jet pack?"

I nodded. "I wanted to be close to you."

She tilted her head and smiled. "That's really sweet," she said.

A grappling hook shot up and wrapped itself around the clasp of her top, then started furiously tugging. Down below, ten men were at the end of the rope in the struggle of their lives.

Angelinia looked down at them, then back to me. "Hey, so I'll be done here in a few," she said. "See you then?"

"Pure," I said.

She blew a kiss, then crushed me with her hand, sending me back to the waiting room.

A few minutes in the plush crimson room later, and slowly everything swirled until I was sitting in a ferris wheel car at dusk, making my way to the top of the arc. Below me, people casually strolled along the boardwalk, occasionally stopping to play prize games or buy something fried, and out to my left was an endless ocean, its tide slowly creeping up the beach.

"Hey *you*," a sweet voice said.

Angelina was next to me now. Gone was the microkini, traded for a light blouse that seemed to catch all of the neon from down below and make her shimmer.

"I've been waiting for this all day," I said. "You're the first thing I think of when I wake up in the morning. Just the thought of you makes the entire rest of the day so much better."

She beamed. "Aww, thank you. That's nice."

"Have you been thinking about me?" I asked, taking her hand.

"Oh, definitely," she said.

Those two words sent me flying. I intertwined our fingers and scooted closer.

"I want to tell you something," I said.

"Okay."

"Ever since I met you a few days ago, I've had this feeling that I can't get over. And . . . well, you're perfect in every way to me and . . . I'm in love with you."

It took her a moment, but then a smile spread across her face and her head tilted to the side again. "Aww, Null. Me, too."

"Anything you want, it's yours," I said. "I want to give you everything."

"No, Null. I want to give *you* things," she said, scooching closer. "There's actually something I've wanted to give you since I first met you."

"What? What is it?"

She stared deep into me. "I want to give births," she said. "And I want you to be my first."

I couldn't believe it. "Angie . . ."

"I've thought a lot about it, and it just feels so right. You're such a nice guy and a gentleman. I can't think of anyone I'd rather try this with." She leaned in so that her lips hovered millimeters from mine. "And so you know I'm serious . . . I want you to have fifty-percent off the normal price."

I felt my body get heavy. "When?" I said.

"Now. Just let me get the equipment." I nodded, and after a moment my world went dark and I was prompted by an automated voice.

"Would you like to 'birth' with Angelina for two thousand credits?"

"Please," I said.

My account was debited, and I found myself in an even darker place, surrounded by calming warmth, lying in the fetal position. I couldn't move, but I didn't want to. This was the only place I needed to be, and nothing outside mattered. The constant and reassuring heartbeat that vibrated through my soul lulled me into a lucid state, and the only thing I could feel was love.

But then . . . a sliver of light. Right above my head. It beckoned me to wriggle toward it with promises of an even higher acceptance.

"Would you like to crown?" the same voice from before asked.

"Yes," I said.

My account was debited, and I found myself drifting upward, the light expanding and becoming brighter, until I breached and was overwhelmed by the sights, sounds and smells. Everything around me was crisp and vibrant, washing me with a euphoric connectedness. Then I was lifted and carried over to awaiting arms, which bundled me in a blanket, cradling me.

"Hi, Null," Angelina said, looking down at me. "I've been waiting for you."

I smiled up at her, then let my eyes close a moment so I could soak everything in. I felt weightless in her unconditional love. Then, the same automated voice from before spoke up.

"Would you like to suckle?" it asked.

"Yes," I said.

My account was debited . . . and then declined. I tried to authorize the purchase again, but it was declined just the same. Breaking from my trance, I checked my vault balance and saw it was firmly in the red with new overdraft fees.

"Is everything okay?" Angelina asked, covering herself up.

"Oh yeah," I said. "I just forgot . . . I have an important mission starting in a few minutes."

"For SKIRM®?"

I nodded. "The entire thing was planned with me in mind. They needed the best for this one."

"Wow. That's something," she said.

"Will you wait for me, darling?" I said. "It won't take long, I promise."

"Yeah, sure." she shrugged.

"I love you," I said, running my small infant hand across her clammy skin as I left the experience and faded back into my apartment.

I quickly pulled up SKIRM® and was greeted by the familiar boot clomps and cadence call as I made my way to the SKIRM® Elite™ bounty board. My plan was to pick a mission for a lot of credits that was easy—but not *too* easy—that I could finish quickly so I could get back to Angie.

The board loaded up and I scanned it for a good mission. There were dozens of them, but none of the bounties were more than two or three hundred credits. This couldn't be right. I scrolled through page after page until I got to the end. Nothing. All of it was scrap. Maybe it was a slow day or something.

I thought about it for a second, feeling thankful I was SKIRM® Elite™and not a typical for-hire soldier. Who knows what kind of junk bounties they were seeing? I'd just have to do a bunch of little missions in a row to make up for the lower bounties. I looked again and found one to start with:

☐ RMZ, Sector F-232, Patrol (UK, Rook) [easy] - 300 credits

The objective was to "investigate a suspicious tunnel outside of the squadron's forward operating base." Sounded simple enough. I brought up the weapons store and perused the offerings until I landed on a pure-looking Directed-Energy Weapon, or a DEW as they called it, with a translucent blue finish and a carbon barrel. It was five thousand credits, but as an Elite I could get it for four thousand and pay it off for eighty-four months. Not that I'd need that long.

I loaded in with my new DEW, and after a minute or two found myself on a shoddy track vehicle rumbling across the warzone toward the base. I examined the ancient tank with its corroded metal sides and missing seats. It was filled with scrap metal and chunks of concrete, as if someone had used it as a dumpster while tidying up their yard, and I was the only Frame inside. *Oh well.* It was no VTOL, but you travel however you can during war.

The vehicle eventually stopped outside of the UK base and I got a message telling me that I'd arrived at the drop-off. A beacon popped up on my HUD telling me where the suspicious tunnel was supposed to be. Then the vehicle's stairs dropped down, which I thought was amusing because it couldn't have been more than ten feet to the ground. I pulled myself up and hopped over the side, landing hard on the dirt, and collapsed.

"What..?" I looked down at my right leg and saw the buckle in the alloy and the fluid leaking out. A status report on my HUD popped up, which told me that the fall had critically damaged the leg and that it would only work at about fifty percent of its ability.

It was only ten feet, I thought, gathering up my fancy DEW, limping toward the beacon. As I shuffled over the terrain, I couldn't help but notice that everything felt sluggish. When I turned my head or made any movement, I didn't feel as one with my Frame; it was like

I was drunk or something. My cognitive facilities were there, but my body wasn't listening.

I was maybe a quarter of the way to the beacon when I came upon an overturned bus in the middle of the road. As I went around it, a stringy man with deep circles under his eyes and open sores all over his body suddenly appeared with a large baton and stood in my way.

"Give me the gun," he said.

"What? No," I said.

Behind me and to my sides appeared some of his scraggly friends, maybe seven or eight of them. They all had the thousand-yard glassy stares of people who get most of their nutrition from pipes.

"Give me the gun," the stringy man repeated.

I ignored him and pulled up my personality profile database, searching for "hero," "outnumbered," and "intimidating." The database searched for a few moments, then I stared in disbelief as the results that came back were greyed out and unavailable. I turned my attention back to the guy and tried to improvise something heavy. "You, uh . . . should have some more of them," I stammered. "These guys, I mean. Your gang."

He eyed me, confused.

"Look," I said. "We both know you can't win this. Why don't we save time and just pretend like it never happened?"

The guy shook his head impatiently, then motioned to one of his friends who quickly stepped in with a rifle and shot off my arm at the shoulder. Both gun and arm landed at the guy's feet. He casually picked them up, tossing the arm aside as I looked on in horror.

"Ooh, I like this," he said, hefting the weapon. Then he looked back at me. "Uh, just do whatever with him," he said to the others.

They swooped in. I tried to counter the rush, but my movements were too slow. One of them did a flying leap with an EMP baton, knocking me to the ground, then four others used a net to hold me as another came in with a plasma saw. He lowered the blade to my neck and proceeded to cut off my head in a shower of sparks and smoke. He pulled and yanked at it until the last little bits of wire holding it to the body snapped.

As a severed head, I watched the rest of them scavenge the body, which now couldn't fight back, for any useful parts. Then as my power started flickering out, I found out why the fleshie holding my head was probably in the RMZ in the first place. He examined my face closely, then plucked out one of my eyes, pulled down his pants, and began humping. The last thing I saw was his pelvis smashing against my nose as everything faded to white and the words "Mission Failed" burned into the background.

I shivered in the white void as a VRE phantom pain shot through my shoulder. What had just happened? No way was that the same Rook I'd used the other day. There had to have been some error during my deployment. In my field of vision, two options appeared: *Re-Deploy* and *Help*. The first option was greyed out, so I went with the help menu, but it just redirected to a FAQ page.

I am having too much fun. Is making all this money bad for me?

No! But be sure to stretch when you can.

Should I sign up for a SKIRM® high-yield interest loan? I've heard negative things.

Yes! Don't believe anything you see online. Never pass up a good deal!

Can I cancel my account?

No. Contact customer support for more details.

I scrolled through the long list of questions and buttoned-up answers until I found the entrance to the complaint department. A translucent, almost invisible progress bar appeared, loaded, then the white world faded into an unfamiliar crowded oblong room. I was back in my avatar body, sitting in a hard, out-dated plastic chair next to a stack of ancient looking books with creased matte covers. When I tried to stand the VRE wouldn't let me. I was furious at the lack of answers and mobility, but the tap on my free-flowing anger began to close as a relief twisted its steady hand. The artificial pain from earlier subsided. I reveled in the comfort of having two working arms again and a head free of molestation, even if it was in a simulated space.

The numbness in my limbs vanished and I felt a gentle tickle in my palm. I opened my hand and saw a slip of paper the size of a cracker, shaped like an arrow. The number *514* flashed with a faint orange glow. I tossed the meaningless trash aside and focused again on the room. The walls were adorned with a train of retro monitors showing off a SKIRM® slideshow of new recruits and top ranking bounty takes. The endless snake of rectangular LEDs wrapped around the room, broken up every few feet with black scoreboards that read "Now Serving 009." My hand pulsed again. Another slip had appeared in my palm with the number *514*. *Guess I'm going to be here for a while.*

The waiting room had an uneasy stillness to it. Dozens of recruits sat in silence, digitally glued to their chairs reading, or just staring off into space. After a few minutes an elderly man across from me groaned loudly, cursed something in a language I didn't understand and then evaporated from his chair. Past him I could see the help desk where a faceless avatar behind a window was assisting a young woman who's eyes bulged as she spit out her complaint.

I decided to check out some of the literature lying around and to my surprise I recognized a few of the relics. My great-grandpa had hundreds of them and I hadn't seen one in years. We called them "rustlers." I remembered the artistic images inside the floppy books, and excitedly picked one up, only to be disappointed that it was full of SKIRM® recruitment ads. I tossed it aside and turned my attention back to the woman at the help desk, who was now jumping as she screamed at the sentient mannequin.

"Whaddya mean you can't get my Frame back?" the woman yelled.

"Sir or madam, please calm down," the faceless person said.

"No! I wanna know who has it!"

"I apologize, but your Frame has been confiscated by terrorists."

"Terrorists? You assholes! All these trillions of dollars you make and you still can't catch [Name] and her rejects?"

"If you could just—"

"I'm not the only one pissed about losing Frames, buddy. A lot of SKIRMERS® are mad. There's gonna be a bunch of people quitting this thing, lemme tell ya."

"Please take a seat while we go over the mission logs."

"Suck my ass." She stormed out of the cramped office, her avatar digitally fading from existence.

"Have a nice day! Number ten, please approach the window now."

The thought of my Frame in the hands of terrorists made my stomach bubble, so I rifled through the stack of outdated rustlers to distract myself, picking up a SKIRM® Monthly 2089 Holiday issue. It had some article about a limited-edition Bishop model along with a sneak preview of the 2090 Rook refresh. After reading a few sentences, I got bored and glanced up at the numbered LED. There were still 503 more until they got to me.

I thought about leaving, but figured I should get things settled while I was there. They'd probably see their mistake pretty quickly, give me a sincere apology deserving of my rank, then I'd get back to the RMZ—and back to births. I flipped more pages, but found only ads, so I tossed it aside and found a rustler of something called *Newsweek Geographic Time*™ that was only a couple of months old. The headline read "SKIRM®: The Future of Tomorrow, Today!" with a pasty old man, the CEO or president, I guessed, standing before silhouettes of newly unveiled Frames.

"Number 514, please approach the window now."

I double-checked my paper, the numbers now a calming blue, flashing erratically. The chair's invisible grip loosened allowing me to stand. Probably better not to ask questions. As I approached the window, I could see the digital avatar behind the glass window staring back at me with a newly projected cheerful, yet soulless smile.

"Hi there! How can we help you today, recruit?"

"Yeah, hi. So I died but it wasn't my fault. There was something wrong with my Frame and—"

"Fault admitted and logged. Thank you for your assistance! Would you like to apply for a SKIRM® loan today for a new unit, or would you rather it be deducted from your next paycheck automatically?"

"What? No. There was a problem, I need you guys to give me the Frame I used last week."

"Okay! Let me check our records, one moment please!"

Its face morphed into a big toothy grin as his eyes slowly drifted from side to side.

"Good news!" the avatar blurted. "Our records indicate that you failed. In that failure you allowed company property to be destroyed and fornicated by enemy combatants. We can have a reconnaissance team retrieve your mutilated unit for a nominal fee. Would you like us to do that for you?"

"No. Listen, I want the Frame I had last week, not that toaster you gave me today."

"Okay! Please have a seat while we process your request!"

I sat back down, trembling with rage. Why were they doing this to me? I was an Elite member! Were they not aware of my rank? Stories of my mission had to have spread throughout the entire RMZ by now. Probably even had highlights on that sports show *INSIDE SKIRM®*. Some of the mission's high points flooded back to me, and I remembered the hesitation I felt, the euphoria of winning, the pain of loss, and . . . Bartok! I almost forgot. I brought up my contact list, but his online status showed him as away. I hoped he wasn't going through the same thing as me, stuck in some waiting room after having his head humped by some riffraff.

The room suddenly stretched even longer, and more chairs appeared as recruits arrived to get help. I snatched up another magazine, *Monthly Metacine.* The cover featured a topless doctor with some tips to slim down for the summer.

"Can I take a peek at that after you're done?" An elderly man to my left asked.

"Oh here, you can have it." I handed him the rustler, meeting his shaking hands halfway.

"Thank ya, young man. What's your name?"

"Null, nice to meet you, sir."

"Pleasure's mine. Call me Cal. You a new recruit, Null?"

"Sure," I said, unable to hide my curtness.

"Ah. That's cool. Always nice to meet the fresh ones. How are you finding the experience? I know it can be a lot for a rookie."

I felt insulted by the comment, but quickly forgave him. He didn't know about me.

"What's your name again?" I asked.

"Cal."

"Right, Cal. You know, at first I wasn't sure about the whole SKIRM® thing. Thought it was going to be just another low-paying circle of hell. But turns out it's pretty lucrative. Well, if you're a prodigy like me, I guess."

"Oh. Is that so?" Cal said.

A few heads turned as some of the people in the waiting room tuned into our conversation.

"Yeah," I said. "I can't really talk about it, but during my first mission I did something that really impressed the top brass."

People in the group looked amongst themselves, then a mousy man with a bowl cut spoke up.

"You saved Dr. Shavanka?" he asked.

"How did you—" I started to ask him, but realized it was a stupid question. Of course details about the mission had leaked by now. "Yeah. That was me."

There was a moment of silence. "Wow," the bowl cut man said, looking to the others. "Can I make a mark with you?"

Cal raised a hand. "Maybe let the hero have his space."

"No, it's okay," I said, feeling a little embarrassed. I never thought I would have a fan. "Mark it."

The man smiled and winked at the group, saying, "Rig, mark this moment with the hero who saved Dr. Shavanka, please." I nodded my appreciation to him, then straightened up, trying to look heroic for the mark.

"Okay, I'm ready," another man in the group said, as he took the same heroic pose as me. "Mark away!"

"Idiot, he's talking about me," a young boy said, now also posing.

"You're both wrong." A young woman stepped forward, grinning. "You all know I saved Dr. Shavanka from that underground base."

"Underground base!" A few of them looked to each other incredulously.

"When I saved him he was in a cabin in the middle of a forest fire!" a kid off to the side said. This set off everyone talking in a maddening cacophony.

"I'm not lying," I shouted. "I'm really Null Lasker! I saved him!"

The talking stopped as they focused back on me. "We know," the mousy man said. "That's what makes it so precious."

Cal grimaced and shook his head.

"We all get our little hero moment," the bowl cut said. "That's how they get you."

"What're you talking about?" I demanded.

"Null, why don't you come with me?" Cal said gesturing towards the exit.

"Look at Coddlin' Cal over here!" mousy man said. "He's going to find out anyway!"

"Find out what?" I said.

"Stop," Cal begged.

"None of it's real!" the mousy man said. "It's all designed to make you feel like the hero so you buy into all their stupid perks. I swear this shit wouldn't happen if people just did some fuckin' research before they join. I mean, I know they censor all that stuff but if you use a TOR with a secondary VPN and backchannel off your neighbors—"

"They also unlock all of your Frame's abilities," a woman said. "Make you think it's that good from the *start*. They call it a 'potential preview'."

I searched the faces of the crowd. All seemed resolute.

"No, it couldn't be a setup," I said. "I fought a gang and infiltrated a building and—"

"Killed a big fat guy?" mousy man said.

"Yeah! Wait. Oh, no . . . "

"Uh huh," he said. "He's just some poor fleshie for hire. At least, he was . . . *murderer*."

They all laughed. I felt sick.

"Don't worry, we've all killed a big fat guy," the woman said. "I think SKIRM® uses pedos. Or tax evaders. I dunno, one of those. They live, they get a shorter sentence and a commission from whatever you're suckered into buying from SKIRM®. They die, well, they're dead."

"But there were two of us," I said. "I met someone and he helped me."

"Met someone?" Mousy man looked confused, racking his memory, but nothing came. People in the group were similarly baffled at the anomaly. My chest inflated with hope. I knew what I'd gone through was real. No way had I been baited into whatever sick scheme they were trying to torture me with.

A woman in the group gently touched the man's arm. "Bartok," she said.

My shoulders slumped.

"Oh, right," the man said. "Everyone gets a Bartok. **B**efriend, **A**ssist, **R**eassure in **T**andem. **O**bserve then **K**aptivate. It's always personalized to play you like a kazoo."

"They use your background and search history to model its personality," the woman said. "He could be a celebrity you like, an animal, an old college friend . . . or if you had a lonely childhood and grew up with no self-esteem, they might model him after—"

"My dad." I fell back into my chair.

"If it makes you feel better, it happens to everybody," mousy man said. "And if there was some way I could warn others without SKIRM® grinding me into dust, I would. But if "ifs" and "buts" were credits and nuts, I'd be wearing a giant gold jockstrap."

My head floated from my neck and bobbed above my body. All of my limbs felt like long pieces of taffy. Everything sounded like my ears were loaded with water, but muffled war stories still vibrated through . . .

"So the second time I signed up, I wanted to see what would happen if I just kinda . . . you know . . . let the doctor die. Like, what was SKIRM® gonna do?"

(A volley of questions from the crowd)

"If you wait long enough, they just come and pick him up and commend you on your negotiation tactics. Even after that they still try to make you sign up for their stupid Elite program, like I'm gonna fall for that"

"And if you clear the second floor there's an antimatter grenade you can find in one of the lockers that'll suck that fat guy's head inside out."

"Aww, I had to use his shoelaces to choke him!"

"You know what I would've liked to dig my talons into?"

"What?"

"NULL LASKER!"

I snapped up and saw that the digital assistant was waving in my direction, beckoning me to come over.

"Hello Null Lasker, good news," the assistant said. "We have retrieved your Frame. There will be a four hundred credit repair fee. For your troubles today, we have applied a two percent discount. Thank you for being so patient. Have a pleasant day!"

"But . . ."

"Now serving 515, please approach the front desk now."

The waiting room was now a convention hall, hundreds of seats with mountains of magazines piling up. I moved for the exit, head down, when I felt a frail arm slink over my shoulder.

"Still feeling down there, bucko?" Cal said gingerly.

"No, I'm fine. Gotta go work some things out."

"Doing anything for lunch?"

"Um, no."

"Join me, would ya? My treat."

I searched for any excuse not to dine with the stranger. Cal sensed my hesitation.

"Hey, no pressure! First week is always the best and worst part of the job. Feel free to add me to your buddy list if you ever wanna talk shop."

"I'm not exactly in the buddy mood. Sorry, Cal."

"I read you loud and clear. Most of my kids aren't in high spirits at first. Just wanted to say that I see some potential in you. I think you got some big things in your future, Null."

I paused, taking in his words. He seized on it.

"Do you like Italian?" he said, smiling.

Minutes later we were loaded into a VRE, sitting in a faux leather booth that was far too big for the two of us. I noticed that some of the restaurant's art had failed to load, but what did appear was abstract Italian imagery of coasts and countrysides. Classical guitar music played distantly in the background as parents at other tables sat with their overweight children glued to small tablets watching cartoons, perusing the menu. Some patrons were enjoying a post-meal mint and desalination IV drip.

"What is this place?" I asked.

"A relic of a simpler time." He chuckled.

A young waiter approached us, looking down at his padlet. He made a couple taps with his right thumb and pocketed the device.

"Hey, welcome to Tomato Terrace™. I'm Ronnie, what are we having today?"

Cal hadn't even looked at his menu. He was beaming,

"Aren't you going to tell us about the specials today?" he said, winking at me.

"Specials?" the waiter said, raising an eyebrow. "Oh right, let's see. Today we got pasta. Red, white, and mixed. Breadsticks are two for one, and the chickparm comes with a free slice of lasagna birthday cake."

"Oof, well, I think we need some time to decide. Can you give us a couple minutes, Ronnie?" Cal said.

"Sure, take your time." He pulled out his padlet and walked off.

Cal was soaking in the atmosphere; this was clearly his home away from home.

"How are you feeling, Null?" he said with a therapeutic softness.

"Fine," I said. "Sad, but hungry. I dunno, this place is weird."

"I meant about SKIRM®. I've been in the game for a while, so I forget how intimidating this whole war thing can be for new recruits. It was pretty barebones when I started."

"How long have you been doing this?"

"With SKIRM®? Only about four years. But I was in an outfit before that. Been gigging for the military twenty plus years now. Not that it's always been this way. Believe it or not, it used to be a lot worse."

"I really don't see how."

"Well," Cal said, "before the network improvements, you'd have to be stationed out in the RMZ strapped to some uncomfortable chair in a shipping container. Back then, any remote work had to be done in close proximity. The guys I worked with were part of a more well-financed outfit, but we always heard the horror stories. Log outs back then weren't as quick either, so if you lost a Frame and the enemy found the base you were working out of, well . . . the ones who didn't eat a bullet probably got Frame Brain. Wasn't pretty."

"Maybe they were the lucky ones," I said, not knowing if I actually meant it.

The simulation wafted in the aroma of freshly boiled pasta and imitation cheese, but the sharp sting of garlic killed any appetite I may have had.

"I get the sense that you're feeling a little in the weeds," Cal said. "Let me guess: kids are growin' up, you gotta pay for a fancy school, and you saw SKIRM® as a quick buck."

"No, no kids. Been married a couple times but it never got that far."

"Second sex change?"

"No."

"Loan sharks? I could see someone like you having a gambling problem."

"No."

"Hmm, racial reconfiguration? I know a few boys who got it done. They love it, got all the inbreeding flushed out of 'em."

"No."

"Workplace-related accident, not your fault but you got blamed anyway? Tried a few odd jobs, nothing stuck, so now you're trapped with SKIRM® because you were sold on a lie?"

"That's oddly specific."

"I'm telling you, I've seen it all," he said. "Years of being out in the muck, scrapping for every last credit—it's given me a keen eye for talent. How big of a loan did they get you for?"

"Ten."

Cal leaned back and lifted his hands as if to push the idea away. "Oh, that's nothing," he said. "You'll be fine, son. You had me really worried for a second there."

A nearby table started clapping and cheering as a distorted voice echoed over the restaurant's PA: "In honor of Trishi Ping's 89th birthday, all drinks are on us. Saluti!"

Bags of house wine dropped from the ceiling, suspended by thin, translucent tubes. Mariachi music began to play and the waiters began dancing erratically. Cal appeared unfazed, pouring the bagged beverage into his water-spotted cup.

"You're a straight shooter," he said. "I like that about you, Null. So I'm gonna be straight with you. I mean, your actual aim is horrendous, but we can work on that if you join up with us."

"What do you mean, join up? I'm already stuck with SKIRM® for a year."

"SKIRM® is just the tip of the pyramid. Listen, I want you to join my Line: *Cal's Pals.*"

"You want me to what your what?"

"Think of it like an exclusive club that anyone can join. SKIRM® calls them 'Lines.' Other PMCs call 'em Clans or Subsegs, but the idea is the same. Too many Frames out there for SKIRM® to manage, so a few years into the program they created Lines. We're just a close circle of friends, looking out for one another."

Ronnie the waiter had returned to take our order, his white shirt splattered with crimson. "Ready?" he asked, not looking up from his padlet.

"I think we'll just have the unlimited breadsticks creel. By the way, the wine is excellent today."

"Okay," Ronnie said, taking our menus without looking at us as he disappeared into the void of Tomato Terrace™.

"How many of these 'lines' or whatever are there?" I asked.

"Oh, hundreds," Cal said. "Maybe thousands. Most are just little rinky dink clubs, then on the other side there's the flashy big dogs like PsiWarriors and BroCalibur. But you don't wanna go with them."

"Why not?" I said. "Flashy sounds like money."

"Flashy is trouble," Cal said. "Remember, Null—you want safety. *Stability.* When you take away all of the glamour and youth and the obscene credits and the sex from an outfit like BroCalibur, you don't have anything. With us, you get *mileage.*"

"What's the catch?" I asked.

"It's simple really. You sign up with my Line and we make sure you're taken care of. We have union dues once a month, but it's only .01% of whatever you bring in—you won't even notice it. Plus, we guarantee health benefits, co-workers, and minimum bounty board takes."

"And none of that's against the rules?"

He looked away from me to the floor, then back. Smiling, always smiling.

"Let's just say it's not worth SKIRM®'s time. They have a war to keep up, and investors barking at 'em every which way. As long as we don't cut too much into their bottom dollar and keep the family happy, they leave us alone."

Ronnie the waiter arrived with a laundry basket full of breadsticks. He dropped the horrific bounty of simulated carbohydrates on the table and walked away. Cal breathed them in, then plucked one up, examining the buttery gleam and chunks of sea salt. He sighed with bliss as he sunk his teeth in.

At the table across from us, a father sat with his two sons, and in the middle of the table was a salad bowl the size of a satellite dish. He was struggling with the cheap tongs to pinch the foliage into his boys' bowls.

"Where I grew up, this place was the only game in town," Cal said. "For years my dad used to take us here for family nights. Not often, maybe every few weeks. But even that was too much for me." He took another bite of bread. "I hated it. Hated the food, hated the way he tried asking me how school was. All I wanted to do was go back home and play online." He laughed as he brushed salt off of his shirt. "At some point he started to pick up on my indifference. So we started coming here less and less, until one day we didn't go at all. I didn't even notice, really. Then I moved out and started my own life with all the extremely important things that come with that, of course." He shot me a grin. "We'd talk online enough, but we never really saw each other in person. Then I think I was in my forties when he started asking me if I wanted to go again. We'd try to meet up, but plans just seemed to fall through. Then after a few years we just stopped trying."

Cal finished the last bite of bread and grabbed for another, but instead of chomping right away, he stared at it a moment.

"They say there's a delay between your brain and stomach," he said. "See, your brain doesn't tell you to stop eating until you've eaten a dozen too many breadsticks and you start taking on water like a grounded schooner. But I think it goes the other way, too. You don't know you're starving until your stomach has a big dull ache." He took a thoughtful bite. "Sometimes you don't realize you need something until it's too late."

"Listen, Cal," I said. "I don't think I'm ready to sign up for anything extra just yet."

He snapped out of his long stare and focused on me. "Hey like I said, no pressure, son. Last thing you need right now is another obligation. Believe me, I know."

"Thanks, I just have a lot to think about right now and it's probably not the best time for me to be making decisions."

"Good for you! Thinking like a real life a-dult. Listen, if you change your mind, just accept my invite, it'll be in your private messages or spambox. The Cal's Pals is a contract-free Line and everything we do is off the books. It's probably one of the only places that enforces the honor system on this damn planet."

"That sounds nice, actually."

"And Null . . . sign with me, don't sign with me . . . just be smart, okay? A lot of crooked guys with easy paths looking to get theirs at the cost of yours." He stood up and extended his hand. "It's been a pleasure talking with you. We hope to hear from you soon." He winked, put on a cowboy hat, and sauntered out of the restaurant, digitally fading as he turned the corner.

Ronnie shuffled over, plopping down another bread pile and leaving the bill where Cal had been sitting. I picked up the tab and opened the black check holder. It was paid for, signed *The Cal's Pals*. I thought about what Cal had said, then took one of the parmesan-ladened bread spears and sunk my teeth in. At home, my Rig pumped a gelatinous paste into my mouth, simulating the taste of whatever Tomato Terrace™ wanted me to ingest. It wasn't bad, it wasn't good. It just was.

That night I lay awake as Pookie 2 scratched at my feet. Everytime I tried to close my eyes, I thought back to my failed mission and saw three inches of defeat going in and out of my eye socket. Maybe my personalized inbox could distract me until I fell asleep, I thought.

I was met with a short blurb about a new leaked celebrity sex experience up for limited pre-orders.

Next.

Western European Provinces Fail to Establish New Artificial Coastline to Counter the Ongoing Hurricane Season

Next.

Breaking News: *You're going to die! Watch now to find out how it happens!* Three images of my face on three different outcomes with giant question marks were projected behind a fake-looking news anchor, gleefully waiting for me to proceed.

Next.

Aarau's face appeared. "Hey, so I just got this at-home distillery kit," he said, standing in front of a copper still and a bunch of clear tubing. "Thought we could make bourbon tomorrow and talk about your new gig. Let me know if you—"

I closed the message. The last thing I wanted to do was sit around with Aarau talking about how SKIRM® was going. He'd know right away that I screwed up, and if by some miracle he didn't, I'd either have to fess up or sit around all night lying. My stomach was starting to twist nervously. Maybe the messages weren't a great idea. I thought of another distraction.

"There's fresh dung just through there," Raphael Calabrese said, shoving aside some branches as he trudged back to our spot in the forest. "That bull couldn't be more than a couple hundred paces away." He took off his bush hat and ran his fingers through his perfect hair.

We were near the end of the VRE I'd purchased a few days ago, *The Big Grey Invisible Ghost That's Also Unfindable,* a 19th-century period piece about hunting the last African grey elephant in existence. The buzz was that Raphael Calabrese was going to clinch another award for this one, and it was clear why. Every time he spoke it was liquid poetry. Especially that monologue of his when we found that elephant graveyard. I couldn't remember what he said, but it was more about *the way* he said it.

"Everything all right?" Raphael Calabrese asked in an Australian accent. Or maybe it was Scottish.

"No," I said. "I messed up pretty bad with SKIRM®. And my vault is negative because I spent too many credits. I don't know what I'm going to do."

"Null," he said, "You're going to be okay. You're crafty. Resilient. If there's anyone who can dig themselves from a hole and pop out without a speck of dirt, it's you." He smiled.

"Thanks, Raphael Calabrese."

"Of course," he said. "But if there's something to learn from this, it's the power of sacrifice and conservation. We must have the foresight to recognize when something is limited, and take the steps necessary to preserve what's left."

I nodded.

"Now," he said, checking the rounds in his elephant gun, "Whaddya say you and I go and show this beast what it means to be *endangered*?"

"I'm in!" I said, hopping up. "Maybe if we can get it in a crossfir"

A violent stabbing pain shot through my skull and ripped me out of the VRE. One of my legs went numb and my head started shaking as the brain stimulator began to pulse. My inbox flashed red and a message flagged "urgent" popped into my view.

From: info@normanrobotics©.go©
Subject: Upcoming Late Payment

Dear Null Lasker,

*We hope that you are enjoying your newfound health! We wanted to remind you that your bi-monthly payment will be due tomorrow. Looking at your account, we have noticed that you will default unless funds are refilled **immediately**. We have disabled your rehabilitation rod for the next thirty seconds. Failure to comply could lead to your death. With this knowlege,* *you will willingly be committing suicide. Suicide is punishable by fine and can result in a fine to your next of kin or closest friend. Have a nice day!*

Best,

Norman Robotics™ Inc. a S&P™ Walt Disney® Company.

The stimulator kicked back to life with a friendly chime. I breathed heavily in my Rig chair, slowly regaining my motor functions. Sand-like tingling sensations made their way through my body.

"Rig, launch RMZ." I slurred out, my speech still reeling from the temporary shutoff. I was transported to SKIRM® HQ and chose "deploy." Four blank Frame silhouettes stood to the right of my mangled Rook, which showed a status of *56% Repaired.* I was presented with a list of options—I could either pay extra to speed up the repairs, sell my current unit, or rent a SKIRM® Certified Pawn. My SKIRM® Elite™ status offered a one-time discount of five hundred credits for the loaner. It was crap, but would be enough to keep me working until they flushed all the fleshie spunk from my Rook.

With a heavy sigh I agreed to the terms, which resulted in an error message: *Insufficient Funds.* I logged out and stared at my ceiling, where a picture of the Beijing skyline began to blink out as my account continued to overdraw. Then the glowing image disappeared, throwing the room into darkness.

I rolled to my side, trying not to think about it. Trying to push out everything. Then my Rig chimed with another SKIRM® notification.

"CONGRATULATIONS! You have been pre-approved for an additional SKIRM® Elite Loan! SKIRM® Elite™ offers a wide range of credit lines for its exclusive members. Consolidate your debt with us today to lock in our introductory interest rate of 25%. Low minimums guaranteed!" Without thinking I smashed the 'Accept' option.

Another error.

"Your account is currently 10,000 credits negative. Please reduce your current debt to 5,000 credits or less before continuing."

I pulled back out and desperately looked around for something to cancel or sell online. I pulled up my purchase history. Everything was either past the return date or ineligible for a refund . . . except one item.

Pookie 2 rolled to his side and stretched, smiling up at me.

LOG FIVE

"*Sbrigati! Macchina terribile!*" A heavyset Italian man in makeshift armor splayed his sausage fingers at me as I loaded up my paint gun. "You paint like-a old people fuck!" he said in his Italian way.

I poured the red paint in as fast as I could, but I'd lost feeling in my fingers and was just guessing how far I needed to move my Frame's hands. Half the paint went into the hopper, half spilled onto the floor.

"*Pezzo di merda!*" The man swatted my alloy with a *clank* and stomped off, muttering to himself and throwing his hands to the sky.

I bent over to scoop the red paint from the can on the red floor into the red hopper on my spray gun so I could get back to painting the facade red.

Technically the color was called *Rosso Corsa* in Italian, or *Racing Red* for those of us who no speak-o. It was the color Italy used to paint its race cars back when racing was a sport. So when war became the sport of all sports, it seemed natural that the Italian military would adopt the color.

But 'adopt' was an understatement. Everything was Rossa Corsa. The uniforms, the vehicles, the weapons, it was all so red that if you took a mission fighting for the Italians, your vision was completely green for days after logging out of SKIRM®.

And nothing was more Rossa Corsa than the building I was currently painting, the Italian forward operating base, or as SKIRM® called it, their King. Construction had finished on the base earlier that morning, four days after it started. These bases were crucial to whatever campaign a nation fought against their enemies; they functioned as the epicenter of military response and logistical support to the war effort.

But not for the Italians. All of that was secondary to the *form* of the building. The Italians insisted the building had to look like an absolute work of art, so it might inspire in their enemies a feeling called *countach.* Basically, this meant when a soldier or whoever saw the Italian base for the first time, they were supposed to be rendered speechless and feel a fizz in their perineum. Great pains went into the building's aesthetics in order to achieve this bit of psychological warfare, hence the meticulous painting.

But this came at the expense of more practical architectural considerations. The building's construction was garbage. In every campaign the Italians had fought, going back many years, their base was destroyed within the first few minutes of fighting. This was the fourth Italian forward operating base I'd painted in the last month, and in a few hours they were starting a campaign against the Costa Ricans. I sprayed the wall, knowing the building would likely collapse before the paint dried.

I checked my clock. 4:58 p.m. Thirteen hours so far today, and if I was lucky in the next couple of minutes, it would end up being about sixteen. I peeked around the corner and saw that my supervisor was gone, probably off terrorizing somebody else. Quickly I pulled up my SKIRM® menu and went to the bounty board, checking to see if new missions had been released. It was still almost bare, with just a few jobs that had been sitting there unclaimed for a while because they paid crumbs.

The last few weeks had been like this. Nobody in the community knew why. The wise vets had plenty of guesses, of course. Some thought SKIRM® was updating its spectator and betting interface to bring in more credits and make the battles more exciting for the public. Others figured this was one of those freak lulls where a majority of nations were at peace and had no imminent need for war, which of course wasn't good for anybody. And a few had proposed a more disconcerting theory: that SKIRM® was trickling missions out so their contractors would get desperate and accept the same jobs for lower rates when they were released. While nobody could settle on the reason, everyone could agree on one thing: SKIRM® was releasing their big daily batch of missions in the afternoon now, around five o'clock. If you weren't lined up at the trough at the precise moment of the slop dump, you went hungry that night.

My HUD popped down as I went back to absently spraying the wall, checking to make sure I was still in the clear. Outside the window, my supervisor was fussing with some fleshies and Frames about the landscaping. Perfect. I went back to the bounty board to wait. I'd calculated weeks ago that between my rent, subscriptions, food, and the brain stimulator, I needed to average six missions a day just to break even for the month. This project was my fifth for the day, and if I didn't squeeze one more in, I'd have to do seven tomorrow, which meant I'd be extra tired for the six I'd have to do the next day. And the next.

Maybe next week I'd buy some stims from the pharmacy, do twelve or fourteen missions in a row then take a day off. I remembered reading that Hitler fed the Nazis amphetamines and it worked pretty well. I couldn't remember if they'd lost or just agreed to a cease fire.

DONG! An alert sounded and the bounty board began populating with tons of missions. Right on time. A rush of warm adrenaline flooded my body as I frantically scanned the bounties, looking for what I could claim. There were hundreds of them, but as soon as I found something promising, it would disappear as the thousands of other contractors simultaneously claimed their stake. It was Christmas with the Devil. Suddenly a batch of missions sprang up that were right up my alley, and I wasn't about to let anybody claim–

"What is this?"

I flew out of the bounty board and found the Italian man staring at my idle Frame. The paint gun had used up its *Rosso Corsa,* and was now just shooting air at the wall, creating a bald patch of concrete.

"You screw this up!" he shouted. "You fix!"

"My mom just died," I said. "I need to talk with the disposal people . . ."

"I don't care! You fix now or I don't pay. Then I report!"

Every millisecond I wasn't on the bounty board meant a dozen lost gigs, but losing this gig meant no dinner tonight—and the Italians banning me from future jobs. I didn't have a choice. I did as I was told and loaded the paint, spraying over the bald spot and evening out the rest of the wall as he watched. Inside I burned, feeling like nothing but a forgettable utensil to serve others. When he was satisfied, he pointed his finger at me and disappeared around the corner of the building. I rushed back into the bounty board to claim what I could, but there was nothing left. As I closed the board, I fell to my metal knees and placed my head into my hands. For a while I sat in a curled ball, breathing heavy breaths.

When my painting was done, I logged out of SKIRM® and sat silently in my Rig. After a moment, I got up to go to the kitchen and immediately face-planted into my wall and ricocheted onto the floor. As I rubbed my bloody nose, I looked up at the seven rows of dried blood spots and cursed myself for leasing out part of my apartment's space three weeks before. Fifty square feet hadn't seemed like that much, but when I signed the deal with my neighbor and the wall started to move inward, it just kept going and going until it compressed my bed, making it bow in the middle. Now when I slept, I had to throw my body over the hump, like it was a giant shoulder and I was an injured soldier. But the extra credits my neighbor paid me for the space meant I could eat.

The taste of copper ran down the back of my throat as I searched for a sock to plug my nostril, but after looking a while, I remembered I didn't own socks anymore.

//Sub Entry Sept.08.2090   #OU812

My back arched in a violent spasm from a fifty thousand-volt shock sent through the controls of the giant land excavator I was supposed to be driving. The sleep sensors had detected my brain entering into delta waves and decided to remind me to focus on my task. I saw I was drifting right, so I yanked the wheel with my left arm, but nothing happened—I'd lost that arm in a battle that morning, I remembered. I corrected with my right, straightening the machine out as it finished digging the last pass of ground.

I'd started cutting an hour of my sleep every night so I could get into SKIRM® earlier, meaning I was down to just four hours a night—two complete REM cycles and an hour of tossing. My body still hadn't adjusted. Maybe it never would. Scientists said that anything less than four REM cycles shortened life expectancy by an average of ten years, so at least there was that to look forward to.

I glanced over my damaged shoulder at the latrine pit I'd just dug. It was about thirty by thirty meters across and seven or eight meters deep. Militaries used them as treatment pools for all the fluid and solid waste from fleshies and Frames at bases and on the battlefields. My shoulder stub and its useless servos hummed and grinded, trying to move a limb that by now some scavenger was probably using as a back scratcher.

I hadn't had time to fix my Frame since the battle. After every mission I had to rush to the bounty board to claim whatever I could—scrap work, decoy, suicide charges, janitorial, and now digging this latrine pit. The pace was brutal, but I was behind on every bill save for my brain stimulator. And if the automatic withdrawal didn't go through for that, I'd have a violent seizure and die with my back arched like a dinosaur fossil. I tried to not think about it, because if I did my heart would kick at my sternum until I worked myself into a full-blown, sweaty panic attack, then SKIRM® would automatically log me out. I pretended to ignore my fear of death and pulled up my comms.

"This is Null Lasker to Amber Five. I've finished the latrine. Over."

"Copy that, Null. Get outta there and we'll fill her up. Over and Out."

I reached down and pushed the start button on the excavator so I could drive out of the pit, but nothing happened. I pushed it again. Still nothing. I pushed it over and over, doing it progressively harder until I was punching the button.

POP!

The button went through the console and disappeared. I stared at the empty space for a second, then started looking for some sort of override to fire up the machine. As I groped the console for salvation, I heard a noise.

The four drain pipes hanging over the latrine pit started to groan and flex, and a low roar began to crescendo. *Oh God.* My spine instinctively straightened and I felt a surge through my limbs. I hopped out of the excavator and dashed for the ramp, but someone had already retracted it. I ran to the nearest wall and started clawing at it with my one good arm, but I only managed to climb a couple meters before I lost my grip and crashed back down. I tried again, then again. It was too slippery, too high. There had to be another way. Maybe I could use a piece of the excavator as a climbing axe. I ran over to the machine to find something to break off, but then the sound came rushing.

Glug! Glug! Glug! Glug!

I craned my neck just in time to see all four pipes blast out waste like a blunderbuss, torrential waterfalls of murky horror that quickly filled the floor of the pit and knocked me off my feet. Back home in my Rig, my nose was pumped full of whatever combination of chemicals is needed to produce the smell of hydraulic fluids and shit. Maybe it wasn't chemicals. Maybe they were pumping actual shit into my nose. I tried to swim, but it was hopeless with my damaged Frame. Slowly, as the level rose, my Rook fizzled, then did an automatic safety shut off. As SKIRM® returned me to the home screen, I was presented with a birdseye view of my Frame as it floated lazily with the rest of the turds in the pond.

//Sub Entry Oct.15.2090 #OU812

Fifty of us sat bobbing on a ground transporter headed to Sector 8H, where a platoon of fleshies had mutinied and sealed themselves off in a Canadian base. I tried to go idle a moment and rest, but I was too tired to sleep. The SKIRM® app detected my lethargy and pounced. A familiar face shoved into my field of vision.

*"EARN CREDITS! WATCH THE BEST IN PRE- AND POST-WAR ANALYSIS WITH THE AWARD-WINNING **INSIDE SKIRM®** CREW, ONLY ON SKIRM® TV!"* Drew, the annoying orientation AI said. *"HOW ABOUT IT, SOLDIER?"*

"Sure."

I was swept into a sleek titanium studio where three men and a woman sat at a giant desk. Dozens of three-dimensional projections of battle replays slowly rotated around them as they spoke.

"Welcome back to *INSIDE SKIRM®*," the woman said. "I'm Michelle Shawg. With me as always is "Lord" Henry, Terry "The Drone" Jones, and of course, Beef." Beef nodded his enormous head in acknowledgement. I recognized Lord Henry from orientation when he'd introduced himself as Henry Oakley and said that nonsense about "joining the SKIRM® family." He had gained a few pounds since they shot the orientation bit.

"We've got a pretty packed show today," Michelle said, "so I guess we'll get right into it. How about that brushup between China and Mexico last night?"

"That was a *long* war, Meesh," Lord Henry said. "Felt like I was watching Beef do math." Terry "The Drone" Jones snickered.

Beef lifted his paw and pointed at Terry. "Keep it up. First I'mma knock you out," he said, then pointed at Lord Henry. "Then you."

"What did I do?" Terry said.

"You laughin'!" Beef said.

"Anyway, it was twelve hours and two stalemates before Mexico eked this one out," Michelle said as the battlefield swept into view. The battle replay that flashed in front of us began with a Knight Frame on the China side charging through his own Pawn grunts and fleshies to spray the Mexican enemy with rifle fire.

"Xi Lee went eleven for three thousand last night, his lowest shooting percentage since his rookie year," Michelle said as the same Knight Frame continued to shoot indiscriminately at the Mexicans.

"That's just awful," Lord Henry said. "If I'm the Chinese commander and my Knight is shooting point-three percent, he's sittin' down and I'm puttin' in a reserve player. I don't care if he's a star."

"Beef?" Michelle said.

"I disagree with Hank," Beef said in his baritone. "Yeah, if you're a Mao Chang or a Zhibin Chow or some other role player and you miss a few hundred shots—"

"Few thousand," Lord Henry interjected.

"I said thousand!" Beef shouted. "Anyway, yeah, you gotta sit. This is war and you gotta fight at a high level. But Xi Lee is a star fighter and even if he ain't knocking down enemies, he's making plays away from the main battle and gettin' soldiers involved."

"If by involved you mean killed," Terry "The Drone" Jones said, raising an eyebrow. "Look, I was one of the best shooters in the RMZ. Probably still am."

"Here we go," Lord Henry said.

"All I'm sayin'," Terry continued, "is that if my gun is that cold and I'm missing opportunities, then I gotta sit and reset. Maybe even do a little calibrating."

An enormous Mexican Queen appeared on the battlefield, silencing Xi's firing and systematically eliminating the entire platoon of Chinese Frames. I'd never seen a Queen in action before. It was frightening to watch as it moved with its ungodly speed, like a roach skittering from target to target.

"Man, that Queen's something else," Lord Henry said, transfixed. "Look at that."

"War ain't pretty," Beef said. "Some nights you get Champagne, some nights you get Real Pain."

"Well put, Beef," Michelle said. "And how about that BroCalibur line lending their legendary lashing skills to the Croatians the other night in their rout against New Bosnia?"

Rook Frames covered in gold flake paint and the crest of BroCalibur charged into a small outpost and slaughtered everything in sight with a mix of pulse rifles, melee weapons, and hand-to-hand combat. Frames and Fleshies were strewn everywhere. The Bros were hypnotic to watch, and so damn stylish.

"You can't watch this line and not get excited," Lord Henry said. "They're smart, they fight hard every night, and they do something special every battle. Like, look at this kid right here, Brannen8008–"

The VRE flashed to a lone BroCalibur Frame as it climbed to the top of a three-story wall to look down, eyeing an enemy New Bosnian Frame and a Fleshie as they eased toward a blind corner. Brannen8008 jumped from his perch and landed a foot directly on each enemy's head, shoving them into the ground like tent stakes.

"Look out below!" Beef said, laughing.

"This kind of play is why we love BroCalibur," Lord Henry said.

"Well, interesting you say that," Michelle said, "because as we all know by now, the Reunited Nations is considering new rules of engagement in the RMZ to even out warfare and I wanted to get your thoughts on—"

"They're stupid," Lord Henry said.

"Well, we know you think that, Hank, but–"

"They are! 'Cushions of engagement', 'hand-to-hand checks', no flagrant kills—it's stupid. Look, Michelle, people wanna see soldiers fighting, not dancin' around each other sippin' tea."

"Beef?" Michelle said.

"I agree with Hank. You can't be babyin' on the battlefield. When me and Hank and Terry fought, we went in and fought hard. Nobody was cryin' 'bout cushions and all that."

"We actually have proof of that," Michelle said.

"Ah, I know what this is," Terry "The Drone" said.

A projection popped up of a younger Beef and Lord Henry controlling Frames on a battlefield in the middle of a firefight. An announcement sounded that the battle was over and Beef's country had won. The firing stopped, but Beef taunted and puffed out his chest at Lord Henry. Lord Henry threw a chunk of concrete at Beef's head, barely missing. Beef sprang at Lord Henry with a glancing punch and tackled him, which led to a massive brawl between both sides. The projection ended with Henry on top of Beef, but getting his ass kicked by everyone else. "Man, how many times you gonna show that?" Lord Henry asked.

"'Til it stops bein' funny," Beef laughed.

"It stopped bein' funny ten years ago!" Lord Henry said.

"You just mad 'cause you lost the fight."

"I was on top! The winner of a fight is whoever's on top!"

"You didn't win. I missed your head on purpose 'cause I know your momma—"

I closed the show and collected my credits. All the talking was making me anxious, and I could feel my brain stimulator heating up.

//Sub Entry Oct.24.2090   #OU812

It was sometime around five a.m. and I was claiming bounties as the *INSIDE SKIRM®* Battle Day Special played in the background. Lord Henry (Hank) said everyone should put their credits on Finland to win over Denmark because Finland knew what it took to win a war and Denmark didn't have any heart. Then Beef accused Hank of not knowing what it took to win a war because *technically* he had never won one, despite being one of the best SKIRM® fighters of all time. Then Hank got up and the two had some words. Hank rushed Beef, causing them both to stumble and crash into one side of the desk, crushing it, which made Terry "The Drone" Jones shake his head condescendingly like he always did, while Michelle tried in vain to get them back on track, as she always did.

A prompt sprang up asking me if I wanted to bet on Finland or Denmark. I had a hundred credits to last me till the end of the month, and I needed every one of them if I wanted to eat. I put it all down on Denmark.

After claiming a dreggish security mission, I had some time to kill, so I navigated over to the SKIRM® clubhouse. SKIRM® didn't devote physical space to a clubhouse in the RMZ, but they did leave a few gigabytes on one of their pre-quantum servers to host a VRE simulation of one, which was nice of them. The clubhouse was infinite and beige, with a bar in the center above which hovered a twenty-inch screen broadcasting SKIRM® TV. There was a pool table off to the side, but it had no balls or sticks.

It was pretty packed with avatars when I got there. Islands of arguments floated everywhere, about RMZ rules, country predictions, point spreads, and just about anything else you could think of.

"Brazil is strong this year. I think they're the one to watch," a moustached man named Duff said.

"I don't wanna hear one word about those cheaters," said another man named Robin2.

"Cheaters?" Duff said. He scoffed and threw back his drink. His avatar somehow raised both its eyebrows.

"The president sentenced more than half the country to the RMZ to inflate their numbers," Robin2 said. "They got Fleshies crawling all over the place."

"Oh, don't give me that," Duff said. "They were scum! You ever been to Rio?"

"Nice beaches," another man said.

"Everyone's a criminal there," Duff continued. "Even the kids. One time I was standing in line for a caipirinha when all of sudden this toddler gets the jump on me and stabs my calf with a screwdriver. Then he runs off with my flip-flops. My FLIP-FLOPS! Not even whole shoes!"

"They should connect those women's uteruses directly to the RMZ with a big tube," a man at the far end of the bar said. "She pops one out ... THONK! It gets sucked into war, with all the other degenerates."

My eyes drifted to the screen in the middle of the room, where a bunch of battle footage was cycling through, including my Denmark versus Finland match.

"I tell ya," a woman named GaiaGoddess said, "if I don't start getting some real payouts with," she mouthed the letters S-K-I-R-M-®, "I'm going to be the one stealing flip-flops."

Head nods all around.

"I hear they're getting rid of all discounts soon, too," a woman named MaryHELLa said. This tensed spines throughout the room.

"What! Where'd you hear that?" someone asked.

MaryHELLa shrugged. "I dunno. Just heard people talking."

Speculation exploded. Voices trembled as they spoke about rumors they'd heard and how changes to the system would make it impossible for them to earn a living. I noticed that conversation always dissolved into this sort of bubbling panic when SKIRMERS® got together, probably because their waking (and non-waking) lives were devoted to the company. Plus, there was something warm and comforting about being in a room with people whose lives were also in a perpetual state of ruination.

Back at the screen, a company of Danish Bishops was overrunning a Finnish base and chaos was everywhere. The Finns were starting their retreat.

"Pretty packed today," a voice said.

Next to me a tall man with sharp blue eyes and an immaculate hairline simpered. "Who are you going for?" he asked, motioning to the screen.

"Denmark," I said.

"Solid bet," he said. "Let's hope Finland doesn't get some of that *Sisu* going, though."

"Sisu?" I said.

"It's a Finnish word. Sort of like courage. Extreme courage. Basically you go beyond what the mind says is physically possible. It's weird stuff."

"It sounds like a soup," I said.

The man laughed and looked around the room at the anxious SKIRMERS®. I followed his gaze, absorbing the sunken eyes and deep-lined faces.

"God, if their avatars look like this," he said, "what do you think they look like at home?"

"The same as you and me," I said.

He nodded and chuckled again. "Been tough on the bounty board lately."

"Yeah, it has," I said.

"Seems like as soon as you get a rhythm going they change the rules. I hear they're getting rid of discounts."

"That's the word around here."

"Bastards."

Back to the screen. I squinted, trying to process what I was now seeing. An entire company of Denmark fleshies and Frames was destroyed. Thousands of Finn Pawns were running up the sides of another Danish company, distracting the Danes as a platoon of Finnish Knights pushed their way up the middle.

"Well, look at that," the man said.

The Finns charged through the enormity of the Danish army, unblinking and unstoppable, until they finally overran the Denmark Queen and won the battle—and I lost all my food money. I sank to the ground and sat on the floor.

"Sorry, guy," the man said.

"I can't do it anymore," I said.

"Can't do what?" he said.

"This. SKIRM®. I don't have enough time, enough skill. Enough money. I'm never going to catch up. I can't do it."

He absorbed my words, then let his eyes drift around the room at all of the others in their hunched-over conversations, hissing and seething about their troubles. He started taking a deep breath, but then cut himself short, probably trying to not inhale the toxic green cloud emanating from the people.

"There are ways to get an edge in SKIRM®," he said.

I craned my neck to see him. "Yeah?"

He nodded. "There's a clocking tweak. *Mantis.* You know it?"

I shook my head.

"Mantis overrides the processing and energy throttling in your Rig and SKIRM®. It's like opening up a dam and letting all the water flow through. You're faster, more connected. You can use your energy more efficiently."

"But—"

"It's illegal. You use more SKIRM® processing power than the individual allotment they allow, and you react faster than they're comfortable with. They catch you and you're banned. Probably worse than that. Plus it pushes your Rig pretty hard. Could make things unstable."

He checked the screen. A post-battle analysis of the Finland/Denmark fight was ramping up.

"Anyway, it's there," he said. "If you ever wanna be an outlaw."

"Thanks," I said, "but I don't think I can afford to risk it."

He smiled. "Smart man."

An alert sounded that my mission was two minutes from starting. I nodded to the man and left the clubhouse.

//Sub Entry NOV.02.2090 #OU812

"Mission Complete, great job!"

I had just finished my eighteenth straight hour laying fiber for the ever-expanding SKIRM® HQ. I was beat, ready to punch out for the day. I started my logout procedure, but something was off. The HUD called out to me, "You've been matched with a nearby job, accept now and receive .5x bonus credits!"

It was tempting—I needed the work—but my joints ached and my eyes felt like they were covered in ash. I turned down the offer and began to log out again. "Mission Accepted. keep it up, Null!" I was too tired to be angry at another glitch. This time I tried to force quit the Rig, but nothing happened. My only choice was to take the Frame to maintenance and do a forced logout. Slowly I made my way in the opposite direction of the HUD's suggested route, heading for the inspection depot. Only a few steps in and my head yanked backwards toward the mission start area. I fought it, but it was like the Frame was being led by an invisible tether. I reached for whatever was pulling me, finding nothing but cold air. A quick jerk of my head only made the line stronger, and suddenly I found myself fighting whatever was pulling me towards my marker.

I dug my heels into the concrete, reaching for something to stop myself. My feet began to leave the ground, and I felt myself yanked skyward.

That's when I saw my hands. They were my human hands, not Frame hands, and I could see I was back in my body, naked. As I thrashed, attempting to free myself, my jaw started to stretch and dislocate. The invisible force pulled me up faster, past the clouds into space itself. There were no stars, only darkness. I felt a vice-like grip around my body, my left eye nearly bulging out of its socket.

Two hazy, giant silhouettes appeared, the taller one holding me in its grasp.

"Great catch, buddy. Biggest one of the day."

"Can I bring it home?"

"No, we gotta release it so there's enough for everyone else. Let's send him back home, okay?"

The smaller giant ripped the invisible hook from my face, my jaw now only hanging by a small bit of flesh.

"Oops, gotta be gentle, son."

"Oh, no . . ."

"It's okay, they don't feel pain." The faceless creature eased its grip, letting me fall back to the ground below.

//Entry NOV.10.2090 #OU812

No sleep again. The stims had been keeping me going the last however many weeks, and my brain just wouldn't shut off at night. Bounty boards kept resetting at different times on different days. There was a pattern, but I wasn't seeing it. I brought it up to my SKIRM® therapy group. The current rumor was that a rival PMC to SKIRM® was flooding the system with ghost accounts, taking jobs and dropping out mid-mission, but no one knew why.

"I don't understand, these guys take our jobs and then just leave them?" I asked Kalum, my therapy partner, during one of our sessions.

"It's probably more complicated than that," he said. "It's just another layer of the fight. They call it corporate warfare, but we're the ones getting hurt. Just another casualty, ya know?"

"How do they do it?" I asked. "Use our system better than we can?"

"I dunno. I imagine whatever it is, it isn't legal."

I thought of what the stranger said back at the bar about getting ahead—Mantusk or something. Could it be the same thing that was being used against us?

"If everyone is cheating, then no one is," I said under my breath.

"What's that, mate?"

"Nothing."

That night I was feeling especially down so I popped an anti-d chewable and switched on *RMZ Live* to feel sorry for someone else. The show's drones gave me a view of RMZ security forces encircling what they claimed to be a drug lab hidden beneath thick brush.

"You can take the RMZ out of a fleshie, but you can't take a fleshie out of the RMZ." The presenter said with greasy smarm. I wanted to make sense of his adage, but before I could, a missile from a security drone fired on the structure below. Fireworks rained on the dry branches, igniting fires all around the area. Ground forces moved in, circling the half-destroyed building. From the wreckage emerged a single figure, wearing dark clothes and a heavy coat.

"Hands up!"

"Nice and slow!"

The figure appeared calm, especially for just having had his hideout blown up. With raised hands he moved towards the Pawns and deputized fleshies—"leeches," they called them. Half a dozen soldiers had him surrounded, shouting conflicting directions while their fingers grazed their triggers. The *RMZ Live* feed switched to a closeup of his sad and disheveled face, blasted white by a security drone's spotlight. I perked up in my Rig with anticipation. Anything could happen. I wanted to see the drones burst his body like a water balloon as much as I wanted a peaceful resolution. I hated myself for enjoying the show, but at the same time, I couldn't look away.

"Another successful takedown, ladies and gentlemen," the *RMZ Live* narrator said. "We're now moving to—wait. What's that?" The camera pulled back on the suspect, who stoically raised his hands high above his head, forming them into some kind of sign, bracket-like shapes holding an invisible word.

"Get them out of there!" The pilot screamed but it was too late. The entire region flashed from night to day, vaporizing everything in an instant.

The shock blew away my brain fog for a moment and I felt unsettled. I hadn't expected to see that fleshie form the sign of the terrorist [Name]. How many of those little devils were hiding in RMZ bushes, I wondered? My synapses relaxed. Rubbing my eyes, I leaned back in my chair and let sleep take me away.

//Entry NOV.24.2090 #OU812

"CAR TO CROQUE?" A distant voice screamed. My vision slowly came back. I found it was filled with dirt and I was on my back staring at another Frame, his hollow eyes searching mine.

"Are you OK?" he yelled again. Another explosion to my right jolted us off balance. The Frame grabbed my arm and pulled me to my feet. Must've passed out mid-mission again, I thought. A quick check on my HUD told me that I was on my 68th consecutive hour—another four and the system would do a mandatory logout so I wouldn't hurt myself or get "Frame Brain," or whatever it was.

Pausing for a moment, I let my Rig inject another stim, feeling a shiver run its course up my spine. A quick shake and a hop, and I was back to work. Me and two other Pawns were running munition restocks for a week-long assault on an outpost rumored to be protecting the right-hand man of the terrorist mastermind [Name].

The second-in-command's handle had escaped me, partially because I hadn't slept in three days, but mostly because they used a convoluted card system to identify levels of wantedness. He was the Ace of Clovers, maybe? Or the King of Jewels? I didn't know—I'd only seen a deck of cards once in an antique shop. All I knew was that he was bad and SKIRM® wanted him dead. He could be called Billy Bob Joe Frank for all I cared. The only thing that concerned me was that for once in too many weeks, I was going to make a decent-sized bounty from a mission. When this one was done, I could catch up on some bills and then take a six- or seven-hour nap before I'd need to get back to work. Just the thought of that made me want to collapse and happy cry.

Another explosion in the distance spiked my adrenaline, shoving me back to reality. Off to my side I saw an ammo crate that I had dropped, but wait—no, it wasn't mine. It belonged to another guy, what was his name? I couldn't recall. His Frame was toast either way, though, and the more ammo I delivered the more I got paid, so I snatched it up.

"That's cold, Rook. At least wait for Tully to log back in before taking his stuff," one of the Pawns remarked. Tully, that was his name. Tully was a jerk. I didn't care. I looted his metallic corpse and took what I needed.

"Friendly bombardment detected," my HUD chimed. I could just make out a faint whistling in the distance, steadily getting louder. It was SKIRM®. They were firing indiscriminately from the backlines, not caring that some of us might be in the crossfire. Hazard pay, as far as I was concerned. And what was another nick or two on my Frame? It was starting to look like an old quilt anyway.

With the crate slung over my shoulder, I ran as fast as the extra weight would allow, my feet protesting with every step. But I was too heavy and slow to outrun the aerial deathstrike. The whistling was almost on top of me. I abandoned my crates and sprinted toward cover beneath the depot. But it was too late. There was a bright flash and a smell of sulfur. The words "Mission Failed" clouded my view.

My nose slammed against my apartment wall as I ripped myself from my Rig chair. I bounced off onto the floor, face planting into the film of filth usually reserved for my feet. My legs were numb, asleep from three days sitting, and the apartment smelled like old onions and burnt hair—a byproduct of two showerless weeks. All around me were enormous SKIRM® ads in place of the art I originally had. Reminders of the deal I signed for a one percent discount on my sub fee. When I could finally stand, I snatched an old cereal bowl and hurled it at the ad above my bed, shattering it and throwing a spray of image dye against the wall. Then a quick kick brought down my bed shelf and all of the used take-out containers on top of it. I fell to my knees, looking up at my ceiling.

Incoming Message! My Rig chimed. A quick glance told me it was Aarau, but when I went to silence it, I accidentally accepted.

"Where the fuck have you been?" he demanded.

"I can't right now, Aarau," I said.

"Whaddya mean you can't right now?" he said. "I haven't heard from you in months! You can't give me five seconds?"

Had it been months? How many? How long had I been here?

"Sorry," I said finally, trying to think but only finding haze and fuzz. "I meant to message you back the other day, but I got busy—"

"Just stop," Aarau said. "I don't want to hear that bullshit. I really don't."

"It's not bullshit—"

"If you want to be a flake, be a flake. I don't care," he said. "But don't lie to me saying you were going to message. It's a waste of time."

"Okay," I said. My body was melting into the floor.

Aarau paused, taking a second to look me up and down for the first time since he'd appeared. "Man, look at you, Null. Your hair's greasy, you're not taking care of yourself. You look like a bum. What's going on?"

"I'm fine. It's just . . . Work's been a lot."

"You can't keep going like this," he said. "You're gonna kill yourself."

"I'm gonna be fine," I said flatly. "I don't need you telling me what I can do."

"It looks like you do," he fired back. "Because no one else is going to. I'm telling you, you remind me of—"

"Shut up!" I snapped. "I'm tired of you saying I'm like him."

"But you are! It's weird. You're going down the same path he did, and work killed him—"

"No, his dick did. Dad was MIA, then he was an insurance check. A small one. That's it."

Aarau's spine stiffened. "Are you really that stupid?" He said, his eyes burning. "Maybe you are." He shook his head. "Maybe you're just too stupid to deserve better."

"Fuck off," I said, reaching to end the message. Aarau's face twisted with regret.

"Wait, Null! Stay with me and Paris—"

"Bye." He disappeared and the room went dark.

I needed to get away, so I took a piss, jumped back into my Rig, and loaded into the SKIRM® clubhouse. It was nearly empty, only a few users hanging out near the dart board with no darts and the video poker machine.

At the bar I ordered a beer, something cheap that carbonated water could simulate convincingly, then took a gulp. It was mostly tasteless but I didn't care. On the screen above the bar, *SKIRM® News Now* was doing another story on the recent bounty shortage ahead of the holiday break. I rolled my eyes and blinked twice, changing the channel to *RMZ Live.* A subseg calling themselves the *Lone Wolves* was out hunting a group of recently deployed fleshies after their transport was shot down by enemy forces.

"My dad used to take me hunting before it was banned," a familiar voice said to my right. It was the blue-eyed stranger, sipping a fancy cocktail.

"Yeah?" I said. "How was that?"

"Tedious."

We both turned our attention back to the TV. The *Lone Wolves* had come upon a nest, a dozen or so fleshies crushed beneath a fuselage, unable to move. The Frames flexed and posed, taking marks next to the screaming sycophants as they begged for help.

"He wanted me to know what it meant to take a life," the stranger said, savoring another sip from his glass. "But even then, it always felt like cheating. Something about sitting on a heated pad above the treeline in a camouflaged tent just didn't feel right."

"Maybe your dad had the right idea," I said, watching one of the Frames strap an explosive paste to the fuselage. "We earned it, didn't we? Climbed out of the ooze, ran from monsters for a million years until we got our place on top of the food chain. Survival of the fittest, right?" The stranger looked away from the TV to meet my gaze, nodding.

"3 . . . 2 . . . 1 . . . Fire!" The fuselage exploded into a million bits, the fleshies along with it. "Oh well, can't save them all, right boys?" The *Lone Wolves* began howling as human bits and metal fell from the sky like chunky raindrops. The TV turned off and I noticed the club was now empty. Only the stranger and I remained.

"Seems like you've been thinking about this a lot." The stranger said, smiling. "Rough week?"

"Something like that," I said, wanting to laugh, but not finding the energy to. "I could use a little help."

There was a long pause as the stranger read the lines in my face. "Yeah?" he said finally.

"Yeah."

He nodded again. "You know," he said, "once you start, that's it. No going back."

"Survival of the fittest." I said, taking a final swig of my virtual beer. "Tell me about Mantis."

LOG SIX

The stranger raised his glass to his face and paused to stare at the final sip beyond the end of his nose, then quickly downed it.

"Not here," he muttered under his breath. "Follow me." He eased off his barstool and led me to the far end of the bar, where he knocked on its oaken top in a seemingly random series of spots. A hidden partition appeared on the blank beige floor next to us and slid open, revealing a long, wooden stairwell descending into darkness.

"Watch your step," the stranger said as he started down the winding, dimly lit stairs. I gripped the walls for balance, following behind as closely as I could.

Soon the wooden steps turned to concrete as we entered what looked like a secret war room. The walls were lined with red leather couches that surrounded an antique Formica conference slab in the center. The stranger moved over to the table and flipped a switch underneath, bringing up a holographic readout of the RMZ. The display blipped out for a moment, then returned after he gave the table a swift kick.

"Junk," he grumbled.

"What is this?" I asked, surveying the dingy room.

"Somewhere SKIRM® can't hear us. Old but safe," he said, scrolling through the 3D terrain.

"Yeah, I get that," I said, "but how can you have a hidden room in someone else's virtual space?"

The stranger looked at me like I was stupid. After a long silence he finally spoke, "With code?"

"Okay," I said, not wanting to press further. I pushed down on the collapsed cushion of one of the couches, hearing the spring protest. "So, this is where you install Mantis? How do I do it?"

He snorted, laughing to himself. "Not here. *Here*." The holomap zoomed out, revealing a highlighted location deep in the RMZ nestled within some mountains, further than I had ever been before. The area was deep in the uncontested region, an uninhabitable wasteland that most avoided. Finding transpo would be tough, which probably meant a week-long trek on foot alone—a good way to make yourself vulnerable in the middle of the RMZ.

"No way," I said. "I can't make it out that far."

"You'd be surprised what you can do when you really want something," he said.

"You'd be surprised what a fleshie can do with an eye socket." I glanced back at the map and made a Mark, saving the coordinates to the Mantis location on my Rig. "Thanks anyway, though. Maybe I'll run into you again sometime." As I made my way to leave, I got an error message about the Mark I had just made. When I pulled it up, the memory was a scrambled mess and the map a blur.

"Funny how quickly we forget things," the Mantis Man said, chuckling.

"All right," I said, turning back. "How much?"

"Ten."

"What? I can't pay that much. How do I know it even works?" I felt like an idiot for getting my hopes up, like I'd tried on a nice pair of shoes without checking the price tag.

"Don't be stupid," he said. "Here, look at this." The holomap flashed, transforming into the familiar heads-up-display I had grown accustomed to on my Rook. The simulated HUD accessed a SKIRM® bounty board, going through the long load times and typical sluggish menu.

"What's the most important thing to have in the RMZ?" Mantis Man asked.

I thought about the question, and after a moment it clicked.

"A clean Frame," I said.

"*No*," he said, looking at me sideways. "That's not even—" He cut himself off, shaking his head. "*Speed.* Speed is everything. Speed kills, you follow? Mantis makes your experience go from this, to *this*." The HUD split into two identical displays, SKIRM®'s clunky overlay and Mantis's modified OS. The difference was jarring, as if the Mantis system was fast-forwarding and SKIRM®'s was paused. Bounty boards loaded instantly, flying by with their credit amounts, while the SKIRM® side chugged along. Mantis even highlighted the bounties that were the most rewarding according to their risk.

This is it, I thought. *This is how people are getting bounties so quickly.* All that waking up early and being first to the boards was never going to matter—I needed Mantis. But I still had financial issues to figure out.

"I still don't have the credits." I said. "Unless you have a sale going or something."

"You're not the first to show up with light pockets," he said, smirking. "People don't look for shortcuts if everything's going to plan, do they? So here's what I can do. Give me what you have right now and we can put the rest on your tab. I'll only charge you twenty percent interest. Deal?"

Another loan, great. But now that I'd seen the good stuff, I couldn't go back to how things were. It's like tasting expensive champagne or wearing a really nice suit—you're forever changed, disappointed any time you have to settle for less. Not that I'd never experienced either of those things. The closest comparable I could think of was that one time I got a free week of *Spunk Premium* on VRE. For a month after, my penis looked like an over-boiled hotdog.

"Where do I send the credits?" I asked.

I studied the waypoint one last time, committing it to my actual memory, then started combing the day's bounty boards. The mission didn't need to pay particularly well, it just had to be something that got me as close to the Mantis location as possible and back in one piece. It was still early in the day, but pickings were slim. Russia had a FOB close to where I needed to go, but it was still a two-day walk through Chinese territory with no ride home. Was China still fighting with Russia? I couldn't remember.

I swapped over from the freelancer section to the subseg / line listings and saw they weren't much better, with most of them either too full or unable to provide transpo. But just as I was about to close out, a familiar name caught my eye. The pay was practically nothing, just a simple satellite repair job deep in fleshie territory, but it was right where I needed to be. If I was careful, I could slip away and not have to deal with—

"Cal! Remember, Null? Hey!" Cal yelled from the front of the parked halftrack. I gave him a wave and nod, trying my best not to engage. I took my seat in the back and looked the other direction, but that didn't deter Cal and his rusty Bishop from climbing over seats and other Frames to come greet me face-to-face.

"Had to see it with my one good eye to believe it, Null Lasker! So you finally decided to join the *Cal's Pals*?" the chipper old man said.

"Just for today. Still feeling things out, you know how it goes," I replied.

"I do, I do. No pressure, of course, but I'm tickled you came. How's everything else going? I see you've still got that old Rook. Always liked the classics myself." Something metallic shook loose and fell from Cal's neck and hit the floor. He didn't seem to notice.

"Everything's great, thanks," I said. "Really looking forward to the mission today, can't wait to get started. Now." I just wanted him to disappear.

Cal beamed, nodding excitedly along with his hands on his hips. It took him a moment to feel the awkward silence.

"Things are going good for us, great even," he said, unprompted. "I mean, not great but good. Did you hear? We're the last independent subseg at SKIRM®. Real honor. Yep. Last of our kind."

"Oh, pure. Congrats." I said, flatly.

"It's not good, actually. The whole thing kind of paints a big target on our back. A lot of the lines are trying to shut us down, but we're not giving up! Right boys? The *Cal's Pals* are free and clear!" he screamed to the crowded halftrack. A Frame near the front coughed and someone else hooted, but it was unclear if it was in response to Cal or not.

"Yeah, well. It was good seeing you, Cal," I said, breaking eye contact to stare at the back of a Frame's lopsided head in front of me. Cal looked down at his bare metal wrist.

"Guess we should get going," he said. "Buckle up, everyone! *Cal's Pals! Cal's Pals!*" Cal continued chanting to himself as he made his way towards the driver's seat. Another Frame coughed, louder this time.

The ride was awful—six hours of jagged terrain and washboard roads through RMZ wasteland—and Cal somehow figured out a way to get us lost three times, despite the halftrack having auto-pilot and laser-guided GPS. I passed the time by taking apart and reassembling my AR, but Cal's horrendus driving made the zen-like exercise a total pain in the ass.

When we finally arrived at the busted satellite array, Cal broke the squad up into groups by way of team captains. Team A would work on repairs, while Team B would guard the surrounding area. From what I could see, Cal's leadership style was focused around not hurting feelings and his own social anxiety, which led him to assign roles that best fit everyone's comfort level and mood. After forty-five minutes of double checking that everyone was happy with their job titles, Cal finally gave the OK to get to work.

My Team B guards consisted of three Pawns, two Bishops and another Rook, Gordy, who had lost his lower half in a previous battle. Cal provided him a box dolly that we were instructed to drag him around on. I positioned myself on a nearby hillside as close to the

Mantis coordinates as I could get without breaking comms, and with Gordy by my side, we dug in and began securing the area.

According to the mission log, the satellite repairs were supposed to take no more than two hours, but we were already running behind schedule. *Jesus*, I thought. No wonder the Cal's Pals were the laughing stock of SKIRM®. It didn't matter. I was where I needed to be and just moments away from escaping the perguratory of entry-level bounties. I made my move.

"Hey, did you hear that?" I asked Gordy, looking down the scope of my AR.

He looked up at me lazily. "I only hear good out of one—"

"Damn, fleshies on our six," I said. "Stay here, I'll go check it out. Keep me covered." I shoved a rock under one of Gordy's wheels so he wouldn't roll away, and before he could grunt out a confirmation, I was en route to the Mantis coordinates.

After I'd walked a couple hundred meters, the hill dipped into a valley where I found a small gorge masking a hidden bunker overrun with vegetation.

Carefully, I poked my head inside. My eyes took a few seconds to adjust to the dim space. At the far wall, I could just make out a hooded figure standing with their back to me, working on a makeshift bench with an assortment of tools. Without looking at me, they pointed over to an ancient chrome barber's chair bolted to the floor.

"Sit," the stranger said in a thick accent, removing their hood. It was a fleshie, but not like the others I had fought with in the RMZ. This one was clean shaven. Strange, but I didn't have time to question it. I sat down in the cold and uncomfortable chair. The fleshie flipped a nearby switch, and the low hum of large batteries filled the emptiness of the bunker. My Frame tensed as I was sucked firmly against the chair.

"What the hell—" I said, struggling to move.

"Magnets, very powerful. Try no moving. Protect me, not you." He pulled out a large drill, then removed a thin plate from the side of my head. A warning message splayed across my HUD as everything flashed red.

WARNING UNAUTHORIZED ACCESS DETECTED
INITIATING COMBAT RECOVERY PROTOCOL

I was no longer in control. My Frame was being overridden, trying to attack the fleshie using some sort of fight-or-flight mechanism, but the magnets held me in place.

"Heh. Always feisty," the man said. "Okay, what we got here?" He attached a data cable to my head then swiped a finger, making adjustments on his AR display. "Shouldn't take long, I make fix."

My Frame went into shutdown mode. The flashing error message disappeared, leaving me paralyzed in complete darkness. A warm flush of fear filled me up as I sat locked in my own body, every second feeling like a hundred. In the darkness, random bits of code began to scroll across my HUD. A moment later my vision came back online and I could see the fleshie looking into my face like a peephole. His lips were moving, but I couldn't make out the sound; my sensors were only giving me partial information.

The familiar SKIRM® OS readout welcomed me back, but now it was accompanied by an opaque logo of the stylized 'Mantis' insignia. The fleshie then placed his hands on both sides of my head, forcing me to stare into his eyes. He began speaking again, again in his native tongue but more slowly, carefully enunciating every word. The Mantis software began to translate his mouth movements into a text-to-voice pattern that sounded robotically British.

"Are you hearing [me] now?" The translation spoke and displayed across my HUD, adjusting keywords to help me better understand the live dictation.

I nodded.

"Good, [the] root worked," he said with his Oxford voice. "Install this after the software update." The fleshie held up a small circuit board, no bigger than a box of matches. He turned around, pointing to the lower part of his right buttcheek just above the thigh. "Here."

One by one, different parts of my Frame began coming back online, but the magnets still held strong. The more I struggled, the harder the chair pulled me in.

"OS [is] still updating," he said, placing the chip down on the table next to me. "The chair will release shortly. Good luck, Rook." The man collected his belongings, and before I could say goodbye, he was gone.

After about ten minutes, the Mantis update finished and instructed me to insert the chip provided by my handler. The hum of the batteries faded, followed by a loud *SNAP* just as the magnets disengaged. My Frame felt more sensitive, more responsive, but I wasn't sure if it was the software update or just a side effect of having been strapped in a chair for thirty minutes. First I reached for the Mantis chip then started looking for the service slot the fleshie had instructed me to use, and suddenly felt an uncontrollable acceleration in my arm. I punched myself in the ass, buckling my Frame on impact, dropping the chip and sending a shockwave across the metal which hurled me to the floor. Instinctively I threw my hands out to brace my fall, but instead of cushioning myself, I punched two enormous holes through the wooden baseboards. Dust floated through the air as I tried to get a handle on my new physics. Everything I did felt fast and jerky, like I'd spent my entire life with weights strapped to my limbs. Moving as delicately as I could, I picked up the Mantis chip off the floor before standing back up on my feet.

The Frame's service slot was in an awkward location tucked behind some reinforced plating , so I had to bend backwards, stepping onto my tippy toes, to reach it. With the chip between my thumb and forefinger, I tried sliding it into my service slot, but it didn't fit. I flipped it and tried again. Still no luck. Then I flipped it a third time and like magic, the chip was in me.

MANTIS v.53 UPDATE INT.

My Frame went into shutdown mode again and froze in place while the final update ran its course. Each module came back online much more quickly than during the first install. During my temporary paralysis, I poked around the expansive submenus and other custom options, and could see just from a quick glance that over half of the Rook's strength was locked behind a software patch. It had potential I'd never even known about, much less had access to. I felt a surge of anger at SKIRM®. I had paid for this Rook, but I had never really owned it, and that's the way they wanted it.

While I stood like a statue, gazing at my new display, something else caught my eye—thirty-seven missed messages in the past hour. *Shit.* They played back, limited to just audio:

Hey Null, just checking in. Cal out.

Everything okay up there Null? Just seeing how you're doing. It's me, Cal.

Null, I'm here with Gordy. He says you went to investigate something. At least, I think that's what he said. Check in when you can. This is Cal.

NULL! COME IN NULL! OH MY GOD OH GOD, I CAN'T LOSE ANOTHER ONE!

(inaudible) Hang in there, Null! We found your signal, we'll be right there!

Suddenly there were footsteps just outside the bunker. Cal must have brought two thirds of the regiment to find me.

"In here, he's in here!" Cal said. The Mantis update finished right as he busted in, seeing me standing alone, frozen, with my ass sticking out.

"Null, are you hit?" he shouted.

127

I waited a moment, then turned around. "Cal? Oh thank god. Did you see them?"

"See who? What were you doing—"

"The fleshies, they hit me with an EMP and ran off. Are you sure you didn't see them?"

"No, the place was empty. Null, you weren't . . . no, you wouldn't—" Cal started, but cut himself off. The rest of his squad came lumbering in, tripping over one another, weapons drawn.

"Found him!"

"Secure the area!"

"Gordy!" said Gordy.

"Something you want to ask me, Cal?" I asked, narrowing my gaze. The old Bishop looked unsure of himself, lost.

"No, just glad you're OK, son." Cal's tone was noticeably somber. "False alarm, everyone, let's get back to work."

When I left the bunker, following Cal and the others, my eyes burned. The sky had never looked so vibrant. It almost felt like I was there in person looking at the RMZ. The software automatically lowered a polarized visor, instinctively protecting me. Before Mantis, my retinas would have just taken the abuse, because no one cared if I went blind. My Rook felt like a whole new Frame. I was excited to see what it could do.

"Oh no, not again!" Cal screamed from ahead of the group.

The satellite had been overrun with heavily armed fleshies, thirty-one of them, according to my HUD. And the Frames Cal had left behind to work on the dish were lying in a pile of scrap, picked apart by their attackers.

"There's too many!" Cal cried. "Retreat while you can! Preserve the Cal's Pals at all costs!" He spun on his heels, huffing it back the way we had just come, tail firmly between his legs. As each Frame followed their fearful leader and deserted the mission, their readouts changed from a green "Active" to a red "AWOL", and each of their payouts moved from one Frame to another until it was all in my name. What was once a small bounty split up twenty ways was now a single pot ready for the taking. When all the Cal's Pals were out of the way, I moved ahead with the mission. Alone.

"He's crazy!"

"Leave him!"

"Gorrrrdy!"

Later that night I relaxed on my bed while INSIDE SKIRM® droned on in the background. My eyes started to feel heavy looking past the projected flatscreen on my wall. I wanted to sleep, but my adrenaline was keeping me up. *One last time,* I told myself. Tomorrow was the beginning of a new Null. I replayed the RMZ footage of my fight near the satellite again, choosing for a cinematic interpretation. I lay there in awe, watching myself fight off the armor-clad fleshies five at a time. The camera pulled out for a sweeping shot across the mountainous terrain as I fired a shock round into the back of one last fleshie, tagging it for reeducation camp, netting me an extra 5k bonus on top of the already generous bounty. It was the single purest thing I'd ever done in my thirty years on earth.

As I sat lost in myself, a familiar voice said my name somewhere far off in the background. It took me a moment to process, but then it slowly hit me. *No way.* I jumped to bring INSIDE SKIRM® to main view, and saw Beef presenting his famous segment, *Beef's Grade A Play of the Day.* I raised the volume as loud as it could go.

" . . . and then, my man Null says 'where y'all goin?'," Beef said, showing the Cal's Pals fleeing from the fight with silly saxophone music playing in the background.

"Like roaches with the lights comin' on," Hank said, laughing.

"You right, Chuck. But Null ain't having that." As I started clashing with the fleshies and Frames, Beef imitated my voice, giving me a suave accent that sounded nothing like me: "Y'all may be Beeferoni, but I'm Prime Rib," he said, as various highlights of my fight flashed through, set to an heroic string-hop orchestra.

"Ooh, damn," Lord Henry said. "I'mma need a cigarette after watching this."

"That's the last thing you need," Michelle said. "All right, next up, big trades coming in the RMZ as countries look to do some shakeups—"

I turned off the feed, still shocked. It felt like I was looking at myself from above—this couldn't be my life. As I went to remove my *TeleTap*® for the day, a few messages floated to the top of my mailstack. I sorted through the spam, a message from Aarau, another from Juka about the newest mods for plane #30—typical needy noise. Then something caught my eye. The digital projection was in an unassuming envelope, but unlike the rest of the junkmail, this one had an amber glow emitting from it. I summoned the letter to my hand and opened it up. A pleasant-looking avatar projected herself to the foot of my bed.

"Mr. Lasker, on behalf of BroCalibur and Associates, we would like to invite you to our annual open enrollment one week from today. Your recent battle report caught the eye of our top recruiter who is very excited to meet you. We look forward to seeing you at the tryouts."

The digital projection blipped out of existence. I sat a moment and let the small victory wash over me before watching my battle replay one last time.

LOG SEVEN

Over the last few days I'd learned how to say "Holy Shit!" in nearly thirty languages. There was that Bishop Frame I chased down and trapped in a gully who yelled, "ариун новш!" (Mongolian) right before I lit him up with my plasma rifle. Then when I breached that forward operating base in the scuffle with the Chinese and surprised all of those Pawns, they said "อุจจาระ" (Thai) as I shredded them with mine frags. And when I landed on the roof of that MTV transporting a platoon of Rooks from the American Sign Language Society, they signed their thumbs into their closed fists over and over so hard that sparks shot out. Turns out the Mantis wasn't just a way to get ahead; it was educational as well. The way I figured it, the more ass-kicking and word-learning I did before my BroCalibur tryout in three days, the better.

I'd only been using the Mantis hack sparingly, when I really needed it. Like when I was claiming bounties in the morning, trying to beat out the millions of others who were scratching for the same jobs, or when I was on a mission and knew I needed just a little extra something to finish it out. As soon as I did what I had to do and got my credits, I would throw the Mantis' kill switch and go back to being a nameless, worn-out cog on SKIRM®'s wheel. I was making a ton of credits, which

I used on countless software and hardware upgrades. It was a tedious process, but I could feel my Rook starting to work like it had during that first scam mission. Plus, with another few thousand I could upgrade to *Server-Preferred®*, a faster access point into SKIRM® where the Frame movement felt much more natural—not as good as Mantis, but better than what I had now. Then I could use the hack less and less until finally, after a few months of killing it on these missions, my debts would be cleared and I could afford the surgery that would rid me of the brain plug.

And I couldn't get that thing out of my head fast enough.

Since I'd installed the Mantis system, my drill had been acting up, randomly heating to unbearable temperatures or temporarily shorting out, causing me dizzy spells and little blackout seizures. Apparently the stress put on my Rig from the Mantis, plus the upgrades I'd been buying for my Rook, were causing some serious problems. A worrier might even say they were *life threatening*, but I didn't really have time for that. I'd seen another *Mr. Doctor*™ who told me that it was a relatively common procedure to repair my brain stem. Apparently my condition wasn't as unique as I'd thought, and many of the SKIRM® recruits—mostly out-of-work parents or bedridden blue-collar stiffs with no other VRE training who were running out of disability checks—had similar experiences to mine. Regardless of their ailment, the consensus was the same: "Get that thing out of your head before it kills you."

Right. So the plan was:

Use the illegal program to destroy my enemies.
Join BroCalibur.
Buy Food.
Get my life-saving brain operation.

Simple. I always felt better when I made lists; it was like half the work was already done. I logged back into SKIRM®, excited to start the rest of my life. But instead of the familiar cadence call, a message shoved into view:

A SKIRM® REPRESENTATIVE NEEDS TO SPEAK WITH YOU IMMEDIATELY. DO YOU ACCEPT?

My heart punched the back of my chest as that sickening dizzy feeling that honest people never have to deal with swept over me. I re-read the sentence and wondered what would happen if I just ignored the prompt.

CONNECTING YOU NOW.

SKIRM® must have detected that I was staring at the question. Suddenly I was face-to-face with an expressionless young woman. I couldn't tell if she was an avatar of a real person who was dead on the inside, or an AI simulation that was never alive in the first place.

"Good afternoon," the woman said. "With whom do I have the pleasure of speaking?"

"Null Lasker."

"Hi, Mr. Lasker. My name is Linda and I'm with SKIRM® technical security. Per protocol, I have to let you know that our conversation is currently being recorded. How are you today?"

"I'm fine." I searched her face for cues.

"That's great. Do you have a moment to answer some questions for me?"

"Well, actually, I . . . uh . . . yeah, I guess I can."

"Great. Your birthdate is February 7th 2040, correct?"

"Yes."

"And you've been a member of SKIRM® for about twelve months, correct?"

"I . . . that sounds right."

"Can you confirm you were using SKIRM® on the following dates: Monday, November third, Tuesday, November fourth, and Wednesday, November fifth?"

"I'd have to check my calendar, but yeah I think—"

133

"Great. Do you share your Rig with anyone else, Mr. Lasker?"

I paused, thinking on the question.

"Mr. Lasker?"

"Yeah."

"Yes, you do share your Rig?"

"No. I mean, I don't think so. I mean people have access to my apartment, but I haven't seen anyone else use it. But maybe someone could—"

"But have you seen anyone use it or do you know of anyone using it?"

"No."

"Great." She made some notes and read something silently in her HUD.

"Sorry, what's all this about?" I said.

"Unfortunately I don't get details about what this information is used for. But I can tell you that it's somewhat common to collect it from users."

"So you ask people this stuff all the time?"

"That's correct."

"Oh." I let my shoulders relax. "Didn't realize that. Good to know."

"As a matter of fact, we're done here, Mr. Lasker," she said with a stiff smile.

I straightened up, feeling like I could breathe once again. "Okay, great. Happy to help."

"One more thing. Can you confirm your address is 127 Broadway, apartment 23331?"

"That's right."

"Fantastic." She disappeared.

KNOCK! KNOCK! KNOCK!

I spun to the door.

"Hello?" I said, my voice wavering. There was no response. I checked the view on my Rig and saw a man in a silver suit standing there, motionless. Slowly I made my way to the door, my hand hovering over the release button. I took a deep breath and pressed it.

"Hi there, Null," he said.

"Hi."

"I'm Gene, your SKIRM® Ambassador. I just wanted to stop by and introduce myself."

"Ambassador?"

He laughed. "I know. Sounds pretty grandiose. SKIRM® assigns ambassadors to users who are particularly prolific in the system. Ambassadors handle technical issues and upgrade needs on more of a *personal* basis. Just think of us as your own guardian angel."

"But aren't there millions of contractors using SKIRM®? How do they give everyone an ambassador?"

"Oh heavens, no. There's only one ambassador for every couple hundred top-tier users, and I'm yours. I gotta say, you've really been doing some impressive work."

"Oh . . . thanks."

"Not a problem. Just acknowledging your explosive efficiency and effectiveness on these missions."

"Well, I'm not *that* efficient. I have my good days and bad days like everybody else."

"No. No, you seem to always have good days, Null. It's interesting. Sort of like a guy who wins fifty straight hands of blackjack," he laughed. "If I was a pit boss at a casino, I'd be watching you *very* closely."

He spied past my shoulder at my Rig.

"Ah, there's where the magic happens," he said. "What model is that one?"

"It's uh . . . the EV-Quantum2."

He nodded his head and looked thoughtful for a moment, then beamed a smile again.

"She stock or have you made any upgrades?"

Was that a trick question?

135

SKIRM® didn't own my Rig and aftermarket upgrades weren't illegal. So maybe it was just small talk, but maybe it was a leading question. I'd made a few tweaks to compensate for Mantis overheating my system, but that was it. I played it safe.

"I'm really not much of a tech guy, I just use what came with the place."

Gene smiled. Did I give something away or was he bored of the conversation?

"Well, Null, I should be moving along. Lots of meetings today. But I'm glad I could stop by and introduce myself."

"Yeah. Me, too."

"If you need anything, don't hesitate to call. We're always just around the corner."

I nodded.

He smiled then pivoted on his heels to disappear down the hall. I waved until I could no longer see him, then slammed the door and leapt back to my Rig, pulling it out of the battery pack and shutting it down immediately.

"Lights off!" I said, as I jumped into bed backing myself into the farthest corner I could. I just sat there in the dark, replaying both conversations again and again, analyzing every word. The SKIRM® lady had said it was common to ask for that information, or wait— she'd said it was *somewhat* common. So it wasn't rare, but it wasn't regular, either. And did they always ask those things before an ambassador made a house call? Or was that a coincidence?

It couldn't be coincidence. They were messing with me. Or were they? I thought about how calm Gene had been with that self-assured smirk, almost like he knew something I didn't.

The Mantis hack would have to go. If they found out what I was up to, or if they even *suspected*, I'd be thrown in a bag and dumped in with all of the other fleshie rejects, doomed to fight and shovel shit with tin soldiers. I threw open the access panel to my Rig and started digging around for the factory reset switch. I'd still have to comb through my Rig's operating system for any traces of Mantis, then take the module attachments out of my Rook manually . . . and then . . . and then . . . and then . . . I found the reset switch, rubbing my thumb on the thick plastic breaker. I tried to make myself activate it, but I couldn't.

If SKIRM® knew I was hacking, then another day or two wasn't going to make me *more* guilty. It wasn't like I could be double-banished. Plus, if they didn't know already, the odds of them finding out in a couple days was slim. I was confident that I could make it into BroCalibur on my own, but I didn't want to jinx it. I closed the case of my Rig and turned the lights back on.

Two days before orientation and I continued to work, taking on a bounty list as big as a bad Chinese menu. Or a good one. First I had to drive a platoon of fleshies and Pawns to a hotspot where a couple of countries—I couldn't remember which—were tearing each other apart. Then I'd have to help construct a barebones forward base for Frames to recharge and Leeches to shit in. And while I worked construction, I'd also help coordinate a supply caravan with another contractor for the upcoming offensive. It was a lot to keep straight, and I hadn't really slept since the visit from the Ambassador, but I shook it off and let the adrenaline take over, reinforced by a handful of stims.

"Platoon 51, load up! We're leaving!" I shouted to the squad. They poured into the transporter while I went over the task list one more time. But suddenly something caught my ear. A buzzing somewhere overhead. I looked up and saw a solitary drone hovering a hundred feet above, perfectly still. It had no identifying markings of any kind and didn't look like any I'd seen in the RMZ before—it was bright yellow and unarmed.

"Hey, SibRiggs," I shouted to one of the Frames boarding the transporter.

"Yeah, what's up, Rook?" he said.

"You ever seen one of those before?" I said, motioning to the drone. He looked up.

"One of what?"

I snapped my neck skyward. The drone was gone.

"There was a drone," I said. "There, just hovering."

"And?" he replied. "There's lots of drones out here. Was it friendly?"

"I dunno. It was small and . . . *yellow*."

SibRiggs tilted his metal head. "And?" he said.

"All right, never mind. Let's go."

He shrugged and hopped in the transporter. I followed, plopping in the driver's seat.

The autonomous transporter hummed along, rising and falling with the bombed-out terrain. I did a quick scan of the instrument panel, looking for high temperatures, warning lights, etc, before I quickly pulled up my HUD and scrolled through my calendar, eyeing the BroCalibur tryout. For a moment I stared at the entry, letting my mind drift into fantasy, imagining how my existence would finally go from day to day to quarter to quarter, which was always the dream. *A three month cushion of credits*—as good as retirement for my generation. I smiled at the thought, but my bliss was interrupted by a familiar sound overhead.

The drone was back. It was flying parallel to our transporter, sitting at our two o'clock like an oil painting, not trying to evade or hide. Was it SKIRM® TV? No, it couldn't be. Nothing was happening here. And if it was an enemy drone, our comms would have picked it up. This was something different.

Think of us like your guardian angel.

I grabbed the controls and disengaged the autopilot. The transporter swerved left as I corrected, trying to get a feel for the machine.

"What's going on?" a voice in the back yelled.

"Nothing. Everything's fine," I yelled back. I saw a deep ravine and threw the transporter towards it, maxing the throttle. Everyone lurched forward in their seats.

"Hey!"

I slalomed around giant boulders, clipping every one of them with varying degrees of severity, all the while looking up through the window at the drone. There it was, just casually keeping pace. Ahead, the ravine opened up to a dilapidated industrial complex outside an abandoned military outpost. I raced towards it, trying to find cover.

"We're way off course!" a Pawn had made his way to the front and was shouting over my shoulder. "Where are you taking us?"

"New orders," I said, flailing around the controls. "There's an incoming pulse strike. Gotta get clear of it."

"We didn't hear about any—"

"Because it's secret information!" I yelled. "Do you have magenta clearance?"

"Well . . . *no.*"

"Then sit down, soldier! You wanna die? HUT! TOOP! THREEP! FOURP!"

The terrified Frame ran to the back of the transporter as I continued weaving the vehicle around buildings and through debris. I squeezed the transporter through every tunnel or bridge or overhang I could manage, sending sparks flying as the titanium scraped the structures. I craned to the window to see how my drone was keeping up. But it was gone. The sky was empty.

It couldn't be. I scanned all around, forward, to the sides, then stuck my head out to check behind us. Nothing. It was gone. I stared at the sky for a moment, enjoying my small victory, giving myself a moment to appreciate my impressive driving skills. I guess I was a natural. Never would have figured–

"HOLY SHIT!" a voice screamed. The transporter clipped a power transformer nestled in the ground and launched into the air, rotating slightly and landing on its left side, sliding for a few dozen yards before coming to a dusty stop.

It took us an hour to get the transporter righted and running, which made us late building the base and setting everything up. Everyone was furious with me and I almost lost my bounty for the mission. I blamed the drone, but no one else had seen it. I started to wonder if I had imagined it.

That night I slept less than thirty minutes. and in that little window I had a dream I'd had regularly since I was a kid: I was a prisoner in a maximum security prison, carefully making my escape over the razor wire of the outside wall, all while sirens blared and people shouted at me. I always made it over the wall and into the woods, running as fast as I could as the drones and marshals closed in. Then something would block my path, a river or a cliff or something, and they would catch up to me. But I'd always wake up before I was actually caught or killed. In my post-dream haze I would reason that maybe I managed to get away.

But this time I didn't wake up. The Marshalls cornered me and all fired at once. As I slumped to the ground, I suddenly found myself looking at my dying body from above, realizing it was all over and I wouldn't have another chance at life.

When I awoke from the nightmare, my head was pounding. The brain drill felt like it was on fire, and it was making a grinding, whirring sound I could feel in the tips of my teeth. I massaged the side of my head, clearing some of the pus that had become matted in my hair. *Soon,* I thought. *Soon everything will be better.*

During my bounties the next day, I didn't look up at the sky. Didn't question if someone was looking at me for too long. Didn't pick apart any coincidences. I just kept my head down and did what I needed to do, only stopping occasionally to check the time. On my final bounty, I shot cover fire over a retreating division of Hawaiian soldiers, and every volley of the seventy-five caliber cannon felt like an old piece of me disappearing into the horizon. When my ammo was spent and the leis had been dispensed, I checked out of SKIRM® and collected my credits.

The next morning I logged into SKIRM® and made my way over to BroCalibur's HQ for my scheduled orientation. But when I tried to enter the waiting room, a hulking moderator appeared and told me I'd have to complete an entrance exam. It didn't make sense. Why would BroCalibur invite me to join just to make me take a test?

"Welcome back, Null, good to see you again!" Drew, the digital eunuch said, teleporting from behind me. "Before new recruits are enlisted to a subseg, they must first complete a standard issue tryout. Failure will result in a ten-month ban of eligibility and demotion in rank. Do you accept?"

"Wait, what?" I said. "The recruiter didn't say anything about that."

Drew returned my frustration with a big, stupid smile. "It was all in the terms of service that you agreed to. This is your final chance to accept."

"Fine, where's the party at?"

The SKIRM® training course was crowded with potential BroCalibur recruits. I suddenly felt less special. There wasn't a Pawn or Bishop among the group, just Rooks. I felt even less special.

"You'll do three modules today testing your skills in analysis, agility and reflexes. Is everyone ready?"

No one reacted.

"All right! Let's begin!"

A wall of words shot into our HUDs:

MODULE ONE: ANALYSIS

"Assessing threats is crucial in the RMZ," Drew said, as a projection of a bungalow zapped into view twenty meters to the right of us. "You're told that there may be enemy combatants in this building," he said, motioning to the hologram bungalow. "When I say 'proceed,' please address the situation using proper SKIRM® protocol! Proceed!"

The hypothetical was stupid—War 101 type of stuff. I instinctually pulled up my thermal imager to see if there were hostiles, but before I could scan anything an enormous roar came over the field as half the class started firing at the building. I hit the deck and watched as the holographic building flickered from the projectiles. A recruit on the far edge spun violently as a pulse of plasma blew through his shoulder. After a few more minutes of firing they stopped, and when it was completely silent, bold red X's appeared above the culprits with a loud buzzing noise. Drones approached on the horizon to haul away the failures and damaged Frames.

"Fantastic!" Drew said. "Next module!"

MODULE TWO: AGILITY

"Moving around the RMZ takes some grace, and your Frame isn't exactly a ballerina!" Drew said. His neverending cheer made me want to squeeze his neck and pop his head off like a zit. To the left of us, a start/finish line projected into view. "When I say 'go'," Drew continued, "finish the obstacle course and return here as quickly as possible without stepping out of bounds! Go!"

We all sprinted toward the start of the course. The first obstacle was a simple man-made ravine which everyone tried to jump as a herd, causing some to crash into each other and fall into the pit. X's and buzzes floated behind me as I made it across and pulled ahead of the flock, pumping my legs. I was doing great, moving perfectly in sync with my Rook without feeling the need to activate Mantis.

Next was a set of cement pylons to weave through, which I made quick work of as the others bashed them to pieces. More X's and buzzes. Faster, faster. I rounded the checkpoint and had just turned back toward the finish line when I came upon a double line of old tires in the ground. My feet double-time stomped through the center of each one. As I cleared the last one, an alert of a hidden landmine appeared in my HUD. I located it and skipped over it in a flash. Running through the home stretch, I listened for what I knew was coming behind me . . . BOOM! Pieces of my less observant Rook colleagues shot into the sky as I crossed the finish line, pushing myself harder than I needed to but not caring—this was my only chance to prove myself.

Then I felt a surge in the back of my head, as if a jet of water was rushing around my skull. Colors and light bloomed around me and time seemed to slow down. But before I could make sense of what was happening, the moment passed. I felt normal again. There was no time to think about it; Drew appeared again for the final module.

MODULE THREE: REFLEXES

"You've done so well, class!" he said to me and the six others remaining. "But analysis and agility aren't everything! You'll need great reflexes out there in the RMZ!" Ahead of us, a target range two-hundred yards long and fifty yards wide lit up. "When I say go, shoot as many hostiles as you can in thirty seconds without hurting any innocents! Go!"

Holographic enemies sprung up all over the range, and the other Rooks and I started lighting them up. I made quick work of the targets, popping one after another. *This is too easy. What's the catch, you soulless, holographic monster?* Then I froze when I registered a specific target, a woman carrying a shopping bag and holding a child's hand. *Why in the hell would a–* BLAAM! The woman and child exploded as a classmate took them out. An X and a buzz for him. I went back to furiously firing until the timer beeped a five-second warning. Another mother popped up, but this time her baby was holding something—an explosive. I did a quick scan. The mother came back as an undercover SKIRM® operative, but the baby was blank. There was only a moment to respond, so I made the sensible decision. I shot the baby's arm off, giving it a 68% chance of survival. It was the best I could do.

"Congratulations, class! And congratulations, Null Lasker! You're the first soldier to see that infants can also be threats. Size isn't everything, soldiers, remember that!" Drew said. "In fact, only three of you didn't completely wash out. For the rest of you, the drones will be here soon. Now, you three, report to BroCalibur HQ for your assignment. Good luck!"

The orientation was to be conducted through VRE. So we could do it while our Frames were being cleaned up, Drew had pointed out, and also to give us time to get "better acquainted with everyone face-to-face."

God, I hated Drew. But it made no difference. I just wanted to get it over with.

I was transported out of my Rook and into my avatar, eventually appearing outside BroCalibur's compound. A restless crowd already milled about, talking loudly over one another, near the high steel gate at the compound's entrance. BroCalibur was even more popular than I had thought. I guessed the interview process was going to be one of those group things, which was awful, but then I looked around a little more and noticed a lot of the people were holding signs and tagging the outer walls of the compound with digital graffiti. A man next to me had his shirt off, and written in black on his chest was "SHUT DOWN THIS!" with an arrow pointing to his crotch.

"Null?" a familiar voice said behind me. I pivoted and saw Mr. Breadstick himself. Cal seemed stringier than before, his eyes darker, but the hopeful grin was the same. "It *is* you!" he said. "I can't believe you came out. This is great!"

"Came out? Wait, what is this?" I said.

"It's the protest!" Cal said. He waited for recognition in my face, but it didn't come. "The protest of BroCalibur? Those BC brats shut down the Cal's Pals, didn't you hear?"

"I guess I didn't."

"They said we were sniping too many of the big bounties, so they went to papa SKIRM® and cried. Then SKIRM® told us we needed BroCalibur to rescind the complaint and that their hands are tied until someone makes a move. It's a mess."

"Sounds like it," I said reflexively, thinking that it didn't really make sense. SKIRM® was always authoritarian when it came to decisions, and they didn't let contractors decide their fates. I looked back at the impressive BroCalibur compound, with its ten-story columns supporting the overhang of the golden rectangle structure.

Cal's band of merry men out front was an eyesore. They looked like they belonged under an overpass giving handys for cans of beans.

That's when I realized why they were probably shut down: BroCalibur was fun to watch, and the Cal's Pals were not. It made sense to give the popular kids as many bounties as they could handle and draw in the eyes and bets of the outside world.

"Hold on . . . why *are* you here, Null?" Cal said.

Before I could answer, the gate to the compound opened and a few of the Bros appeared.

"Where's my orientation people?" a man with high cheekbones said.

"Right here," I said, stepping toward the gate. Cal placed a hand on my shoulder.

"Oh, no. Null, c'mon."

"Hands off, Cal!" Cheekbones said. "You know the deal. You can look but you can't touch."

"Null, join the Cal's Pals," Cal said in a rushed whisper, letting go of me. "We can match anything they offer."

"I don't know, Cal," I said, looking at the Bros in the gate.

Cal's eyes darted from me to the Bros, then he suddenly jumped in between us.

"I didn't want to do this!" he shouted, ripping off his shirt and revealing a bag of manure strapped to his chest. He pulled the detonator from his pocket. "Now we're gonna have a conversation," he said, his eyes wild.

I eyed his bomb, realizing I'd never actually seen one in a VRE before. Trolls always used them as a last resort when bringing down a VRE, because if someone could prove you used one, you were sent to the RMZ automatically. No questions.

"Now you send out a negotiator," Cal said, easing forward, little bits of shit falling out of his chest bag. "And I want some pizza for my boys—"

A projectile shot from a fence pillar. It knocked the detonator out of Cal's hand, exploded, and encased him in a giant clear bubble. As

Cal tried to process what happened, the lead Bro casually walked over and scooped up the detonator. Cal's shoulders slumped as he looked back at me.

"Please, Null," he pleaded. "Tell them to lift the complaint. Without the Pals, I'm back to where I started. I'll have nothing."

"I can't, Cal. I'm sorry," I said, walking past his bubble and into the gate. Behind me, the Bro with the detonator chuckled at him. "I'm sorry, too." The bro pressed the button, then the inside of the bubble was coated with bits of Cal and manure.

Inside, BroCalibur's home base was monumental. A two-hundred foot vaulted ceiling hung over the marble floor, and everywhere you looked there were statues of Bro members and awards for battle. It was a cathedral, a place to worship the holy trinity: kicking ass, taking names, and cashing checks. And I was ready to be baptized. I made my way over to one of the medals hovering above its podium. It was a crystal shark, and underneath it read:

BROCALIBUR: SUBSEG OF THE YEAR, 2089

"IN A SEA OF FISH, YOU WERE THE SHARKS.
WITH YOUR BLACK, DOLL-LIKE EYES,
YOU TORE INTO THE FLESH OF YOUR ENEMIES
AND TURNED THE OCEAN BURGUNDY.
A HUNDRED MILLION WENT INTO THE WATER IN 2089,
BUT ONLY ONE SUBSEG CAME OUT ALIVE."

"That's so fuckin' pure," a voice behind me said. A young man with pink hair was reading over my shoulder. He shot me a grin, then turned around. "Hey, uh, Timm?" he shouted to another young guy over at a statue. "You see this one?"

Timm, dressed head-to-toe in form-fitting black clothes, sauntered over in thick-soled boots and stuck his nose right up to the plaque to read.

"Sharks," he said in a deep baritone. "No more swimming backwards for me."

"What's your name, guy?" The first man asked me.

"Null Lasker."

"Null, I'm Moe Reeves. Guessing you didn't wash out today. You looked good out there."

"Yeah, thanks," I said.

"But not *that* good," Timm said, sizing me up.

"We'll see," I said.

"Timm almost tackled me out there, thinking I was a protestor," Moe said, laughing.

"You were chanting, waterhead," Timm said.

"Yeah, so? It looked fun." Moe said. "I love protests."

"Maybe you protest better than you fight," Timm said.

"Oh, I guarantee that's not the case, friend," Moe replied with a smile.

"I guess I'll have to witness it for myself," said Timm.

"You will," said a bald woman in a crisp military jacket standing off to our side. "In about five minutes." We looked at her and she smiled, raising her arms. "Welcome to BroCalibur, soldiers! I'm Captain Shalita and I'll be your point of contact today. You have been selected out of millions of recruits to try out for the most coveted subseg in the RMZ."

"Take me, momma!" Moe shouted. "I'm ready to sign!" Timm shot him a scowl.

"That's wonderful," the captain said. "But to join BroCalibur you must first complete a monitored field mission in SKIRM®. Based on your test results we're throwing you boys into hell feet first. I assume you're all familiar with the terrorist [Name]. [Name]'s organization has been showing increased activity with Frame tech. We need you three to figure out what that is."

A 3D map projected around the room indicating multiple hot spots and potential landing zones. Captain Shalita cleared her throat and continued.

"For today's mission, you'll be retaking an enemy compound in the Northeast quadrant of the RMZ." The map moved behind her, highlighting the base. "It's a research facility that was once under the control of the East Indian Republican Guard, but is now overrun with [Name]'s guerillas. Once you capture the base, additional instructions will follow. We expect heavy forces, so be on alert. You will be judged based on how well you operate in the field as a unit, but your individual performance will also be closely monitored and scored." The map disappeared and her eyes narrowed. "Lastly, there is only room for one new recruit this cycle, so please try your best."

The three of us looked at each other.

"Complete the mission and report back," Captain Shalita said. "Your Frames are being transferred to the takeoff point now. Find out what [Name] is working on or don't come back." She disappeared into the floor.

The VTOL shuddered violently in the thick air as we flew fast and low over the RMZ. I stole glances of Timm and Moe's Rook Frames strapped in their seats. Both of theirs were so much newer and sharper than mine. I looked down at my Frame and noticed the messy spot-weld on my leg I must have missed. It looked like a stress crack was starting to spread. I quickly moved my hand to cover the blemish.

"So I think we can all agree," Moe began, "that the situation is . . . not ideal."

"Is that how you feel?" Timm said with a chuckle.

"*And*," Moe continued, ignoring him, "I think we can also all agree that we won't be able to finish the mission without each other."

Timm and I nodded.

"So I propose we all do this the right way with no bullshit," Moe said. "The best man wins, plain and fair."

"Fair is what got me here," said Timm, smiling.

"Me, too," I said.

"Good," Moe said, pleased with himself. "Glad we got that out of the way."

We slowed sharply and the nose pitched up, meaning we were over the landing zone. As the VTOL made its descent, we suddenly heard a burst of fire, and then dull metallic thuds as flak hit the craft.

"Oops," Timm said.

An alarm screamed. The VTOL spun toward the ground, pinning us in our seats with the g-forces. *Why do these things always crash?* Our virtual stomachs hit our throats, then SMACK! The VTOL pancaked and my world went dark.

When I came to a few seconds later, I saw the VTOL had split in half, exposing us. Moe and I were still strapped in our seats, and he was still buffering. Some firing off to our right caught my attention, and I looked over and saw that Timm had left us for cover nearby. I wrestled Moe from his chair and dragged him by his leg to another patch of cover, waiting for his Rig and Frame to resync. Suddenly a dozen fleshies burst out of a relief tent and rushed toward us with plasma torches. I aimed with one hand while pulling Moe with the other, pushing my Frame hard. The strain was giving me a migraine, but I knew I was being scored, so I shook it off and fought through the pain. A few of the fleshies fell, but soon the rest were on top of me and I was going hand-to-hand. I swatted at one with my rifle while another went for Moe's head with a torch. Without thinking, I swung Moe as hard as I could into a small group of fleshies, flattening them against a wall. "Again!" Moe screamed. I was still lightheaded from the last one but I nodded, building momentum for another swing and—

It's Sunday afternoon. I'm walking out the front door to the driveway. The sun is blinding. Dad is underneath the car. Aarau hands him something through the engine bay. If Dad doesn't get the car fixed by tomorrow morning, he can't get to work. He has no choice. I ask if I can help, but they say no, it's okay. This is Dad and Aarau's thing. I don't have a thing. Aarau always went with Dad. I went with Mom. But she's gone. I head back inside. Close the door to my room. I get on the Internet to find something to do—

"Heads up!" Moe shouted.

My vision came back right as a steel beam smacked my face, spinning me around. *What the hell was that?* The fleshie culprit was off to my side. I rushed him, planting a kick square in his sternum, then tried to shake off whatever had just happened. Had I gone offline for a second and daydreamed? Or maybe there was some interference from another Frame. But that hadn't been another person's memory; that was *mine.*

The hostiles around me were thinning, while Timm and Moe's kill count was growing on my HUD. Suddenly, Moe looked at me with burning eyes and pointed his rifle at my head. I threw up my hands, attempting to plead with the insane Rook, but before I could say anything, he fired. I ducked just in time for the burst-fire shot to miss and hit the fleshie sneaking up behind me.

"You're quick," Moe said, smirking.

I shot back up and met his twinkling eyes. He looked like an apex predator toying with his prey. I ground my teeth as I realized I'd have to watch my back with this idiot.

"Great work, soldiers." Captain Shalita appeared on my HUD. "You have completed phase one of your mission. The Indian Guard is mobilizing back to your area. Get to the research station before they do."

"I'd like to see that," Timm said over comms.

"I like your attitude, recruit. But even with three of you, you'd all be dead in minutes. I'm sending coordinates to the main research center. Retrieve whatever [Name]'s forces were looking for and get out. Keep up the great work, well, most of you." She disappeared.

The coordinates led us to a freestanding research station with reinforced steel doors.

"I got this," Moe said, gripping one of the metal doors.

Continuing the teamwork farce with Moe felt gross, but there wasn't time for honesty or confrontation. I had to suck it up and play pretend.

"No, let me." I jumped in front of him. I needed the points. The stainless steel door thundered as I rammed my shoulder into it over and over, snapping the latch mechanism. We pushed inside.

The research station was clean, not a trace of dust anywhere within its towering walls. Work terminals took up most of the space, with a couple of sealed-off areas near the far side of the room. We made our way through, following the only power signal still active within a hundred meters. Something moved, alerting each of our motion trackers. With Timm and Moe behind me, I entered a small conference room with a large oak desk taking up the center. The light on my rifle illuminated as I peeked under the table. A thin man was huddled underneath staring back at me, his hands up, showing he was unarmed. As I pulled him up he started speaking in his native tongue for just a moment before the HUD's translation software kicked in.

"Are we safe?" he stammered. "Am I going home? Did you kill it?" He looked malnourished, as if he'd been locked away for days or even weeks.

"We're looking for something, the secret you are working on here. Where is it?" Timm said, choking his gun grip.

The man stared back at him, confused.

"Intel. Secret project. Anything?" Moe chimed in.

Nothing.

"Can you show us where you work?" I asked gently.

He looked back at me, finally understanding what we wanted, and the color from his face vanished. He shook his head aggressively looking at the floor. I put a hand on his shoulder and spoke again.

"We just want to see your work. We can help you leave after—"
BOOM!

Moe lowered his sidearm as the researcher's body hit the floor.

"Why'd you do that?" I screamed.

"Didn't need him, just this." Moe reached down and pulled a silver drive from his pocket.

"Yeah, but why did you shoot him?" Timm demanded. "He wasn't hurting anybody."

151

"Everybody hurts somebody. Also, if I'd shot him in the foot he would have taken *forever* to die. Come on, let's go." Moe said, turning to leave the room. Timm and I looked at each other. Moe was the real deal, a true psychopath. Any more time associating with him and my conscience would pack its shit and get a separate apartment.

Timm and I followed our sick compatriot, but a noise stopped us. It sounded like a million nails tapping on a desk.

"What was *that*?" Timm said. We searched around in the dark, then he turned his light on the far wall and we saw them. A hundred Bishop Frames, staring back at us. But they weren't individual units—they seemed to be combined in one reptilian entity. When one moved, it rippled across all the others like a wave, and it constantly seemed to be adjusting its shape. The head, made up of a dozen contorted units, opened to reveal sharpened "teeth" made up of Frame appendages and electrified melee batons.

All at once, the horde lurched up, standing tall and arching its back, like a cobra ready to strike its prey.

"Move!" Moe screamed as he dove into me, pushing the two of us outside the room. The horde snapped forward, crushing Timm instantly from the massive force. Moe and I sprinted for the exit as I twisted to spray whatever it was with some pulse shots to slow it down, but it was worthless. The thing was gaining on us.

Moe made it out before me, turned around and hit a control panel outside.

"Have a good time, Null," he said over our comm channel as blast doors slammed in my face.

Plain and fair, he'd said. My heart plopped to the floor.

Behind me, the horde was perched, ready to strike again. The head punched forward like a cattle gun, grazing my shoulder and shearing titanium as I dove out of the way. I unclipped a grenade from my belt and stuck it to the side of the beast, rolling into cover as the explosion took off half of the Frames that made up its head. It stopped a moment as the Frames moved around, reorganizing themselves into a scorpion-like formation. It was smaller, but it moved even faster. I swapped to armor-piercing rounds, then incendiary, then high impact. I couldn't tell if I was hurting it or just making it angry.

The horde started to morph again, this time into what resembled a fifty-foot-tall carpenter ant. It raised its head and unleashed an ungodly screech before ramming into me at full speed. I hit a wall and blacked out for a moment. Then I found myself on my knees, staring down at the floor. My Rig was struggling to keep up. Malfunction errors clouded my view. I dismissed them, trying to focus as the room started to spin. I was sweltering. I felt my eyes bulge as one of the horde's massive pincers squeezed my neck and lifted me off the floor. *It's a school night. I'm trying to finish Algebra. Aarau is reheating leftover spaghetti for us. He's been on edge all day; something is on his mind. Midnight comes, but Dad isn't home. Usually he would have been home two hours ago. I go to sleep. Aarau doesn't. He wakes me up in the morning. A cop is outside with Dad's friend Dave. Dave needs to tell us something. My chest freezes as he talks, and all sounds mute. My eyes unfocus. Aarau and I travel in car after car.*

Later we're in Grandma's kitchen, and she's in the living room on Facetime with someone. "Of course it happened like this. Pathetic little perv suffocating—"

The beast's head was only a yard away. I could see my fading reflection in its immaculate alloy skin. Its jaws slowly opened, as if it wanted to savor the meal. I swung my arms wildly, connecting with nothing. Everything I did was useless, weak. Defeat was coming and it made me burn. What a waste—I'd come this far just to lose everything I'd worked for.

But wait a second. No. There was another option. If Moe wasn't going to play by the rules, why should I? *Survival of the fittest.* I initiated the Mantis bootup sequence.

Forty-five seconds to reboot. Thirty seconds. I could see the beast's gullet, but now I was unable to even squirm. *Fifteen seconds.* I felt its cold mouth grasp my ankle.

```
5 . . . 4 . . . 3 . . . 2 . . . system
offline
```

Aarau and I are sitting at a conference table. So much yelling in the next room. A woman in a suit briskly walks from behind us toward the screaming. "Just another few minutes, I promise," she says, smiling as she enters. I catch a glimpse of my Grandma and some family I haven't seen in a while. More shouting. Aarau stares at the wall as I cross my arms on the table and rest my forehead against them. Bits of conversation float out. "Doesn't it take effect immediately?" "It was still in underwriting." "What about the paperwork you gave him?" "That was a quote draft." "But he already had a policy!" "Higher limits still have to clear underwriting. The coverage wasn't bound when he passed. Look, thirty-thousand is still something." Aarau gets up and goes to the bathroom.

The world turned white.

"Mantis Protocol Installation: Success."

I awoke to the back of my head throbbing and the horde slowly chewing on my ankles, bringing me into its private club, but a surge of energy pulsed through me and the Rook suddenly felt more powerful. In my upgrading spree I'd forgotten to configure the Mantis properly, and now everything was in overdrive, allowing me to see sound, feel color. Time itself became a clear path, branching into multiple streams of impossible and possible, running parallel in a neverending mobius strip. Then, I saw something in the metallic beast's core—the first Frame, the assimilator, the hive mind. My Frame's outer layer began to harden. *It could do that?* I reared my right arm back and punched downward, then again with my left. Bits of Bishop exploded like confetti as I dug deeper, eventually finding it—a small Pawn with a unique heat signature. It tried to fight back, everything inside of it working to protect itself, but I was too strong. With one final punch to the core, the collection of malformed Frames fell to the floor.

I'd won the fight, but there was still the matter of the mission. *There is only room for one new recruit.* No way was I going to let a brat like Moe win. My head was exploding with pain now, but I knew it was only temporary—just a few more minutes and it would all be over. I pulled up Moe's ID and found his coordinates immediately. He was heading for the exfil spot with the intel in hand. I pried open the steel door and made my way toward him as fast as I could, faster than I'd ever moved before.

My Rig was at max capacity; the nitrogen tanks cooling the quantum processor were moments from splitting like sausages. I was pushing my luck, but with the Mantis reactivated, I felt like I was making my own. *You're almost there, just a bit further. Get the drive, kill Moe, be happy.* There he was, the Rook that had left me to die. I was trailing him by only a few meters, moving so quietly that he hadn't noticed me yet.

When I was three strides away, I long-jumped with one rigid leg locked forward and slammed on his heel, snapping his left leg in half. Moe fell, rolled onto his back, and started firing blindly from the hip. I dodged the rounds, knocked the rifle from his hand, and caved in his ocular sensor with my foot. We were only a few hundred meters away from the extraction point and free of any security feeds. I had him all to myself.

Moe managed to pull his head up as I removed the silver drive from his satchel. I hefted it in my hand and felt my chest swell. The spot was as good as mine.

"Null? How the fu-ck?" His audio feed was distorted and crackling.

"It's just a bad dream," I said. "You'll wake up soon enough."

I kicked in his head, using only half strength. I wanted him to see my foot in his face at least two more times before his Frame shut down.

A VTOL buzzed overhead, the rushing wind from it kicking up bits of Moe and dirt. It landed over the horizon, occasionally flickering and glitching in my vision. The back of my head pounded and I felt an intense searing behind my eyes, but I was here in one piece. And I looked *good*. There was no way BroCalibur would pass me up, partly because there were no others to choose from, but mostly because I came and conquered. And now as a bit of icing, I'd hang on to the side of a VTOL and get lifted out of a battlefield. I couldn't let this memory slip away.

"Rig," I said. "Mark this momen—

LOG ERROR

LOG EIGHT

// Log Could Not Be Found.

// Please enjoy the following article while
we attempt to reconnect.

The Founding of Amazon®'s Dream City

From Wikipedia Britannica, the world's oldest free encyclopedia

This article is about Amazon.com, Inc.'s attempt to create a master-planned community. For the documentary about the extinct forest, see <u>The Fall of Amazon's Last Tree</u>.

Background

In early 2029, the CEO and founder of Amazon.com, Inc., Jeff Bezos, announced that he had created the *Prime Company*, a subsidiary of Amazon® that would spearhead the development of the world's first "perfectly engineered city" from the ground up. The city would be a "modern utopia," with a diverse society, revolutionary government, and complete technological integration.

Though technically The Walt Disney Company had created their own dream city, *Celebration,* in Florida thirty years prior, Bezos described the effort as a "Mickey Mouse operation," and went on to say that "Florida is where dreams go to die." It was noted at the time that Bezos' second ex-wife was from Florida, and he frequently had to visit the state for legal proceedings.

A month after the initial announcement, the name and future location of the city was revealed to the public. *Prime Town* would be situated on 5,000 acres (20.2 km²) of industrial wasteland to the southeast of Amazon®'s Seattle headquarters. Work began immediately on the city.

"Day 1" in Prime Town

Bezos firmly believed that all companies experienced the following five life cycles or "days":

Day 1: Start up
Day 2: Stasis
Day 3: Irrelevance
Day 4: Excruciating, Painful Decline
Day 5: Death

At Amazon® he instilled the mentality that "It's always Day 1," and intended to do the same with *Prime Town*. This meant "getting big fast" with explosive growth due to "high-velocity decision making" and "eagerly adopting external trends."

Following this mantra—as city architects and contractors built the road system and erected the city's commercial buildings in the spring of 2029—Jeff Bezos sent out a tweet to his followers that simply said "Who wants to make history?" with a link to a *Prime Town's* available real estate and a winky face emoticon. Prospective residents had to put down a $10,000 deposit for one of the 1,500 home plots and 500 condos. Inventory sold out in three minutes.

Next, the city's initial charter and laws were drafted. Bezos took on the task personally, insisting that the documents be simple to avoid "bureaucratic bullshit that inhibits Go Time." Essential to the city's "Day 1" strategy would be zero government officials and the use of Amazon®'s proprietary voting app, *Votable* (free to Prime members, or $4.95 monthly). Every citizen would have a say in the drafting and passing of new laws, making *Prime Town's* democracy pure and efficient.

When Bezos released the finalized charter and laws to the public, people were quick to note that there were similarities to *Federation Law* from *Star Trek,* a popular science fiction series. In a *New York Times* interview, Bezos strongly denied plagiarizing the show. However, when the journalist pointed out an odd law that forbade the trading of Tallonian crystals to Ferengi, Bezos abruptly ended the call.

One of the final pieces of the "Day 1" strategy was to jumpstart *Prime Town's* economy so that it was booming from the beginning. To do this, Amazon® would locate a new fulfillment center in the city, which would provide hundreds of jobs and millions in tax revenue. But because *Prime Town* was classified as an "unincorporated development district," all property and business tax revenue from the Amazon® center went to the Amazon® company, which then sent the money to its offshore Cayman Island holding company.

After months of rapid building, residents and businesses were allowed to move into *Prime Town* at the end of 2029. A massive ribbon-cutting ceremony was held in the town square. Jeff Bezos was in attendance, sitting in the backseat of a hired Mercedes. At exactly noon, he rolled down his window and unveiled the city's official motto:

Plant Roots. Live Well. **Make History.**

The Dream Meets Reality

In its first months, *Prime Town* far exceeded the expectations of even its most fervid supporters. The city had zero percent unemployment, a negligible crime rate, exponential GDP, and a Twitch following that was comparable, according to one analyst, to that of "any heavy-chested female gamer."

Participation on the *Votable* app was nearly one hundred percent, leading to quick passage of policy improvements and new laws. The city was constantly in the headlines, and catapulted to the top of the "America's Best Places to Live" lists. The Amazon® board, most of whom had been initially skeptical of the venture, praised Bezos for yet another slam dunk.

But around month six, the tide of the city began to ebb. Voter participation decreased as people grew tired of constantly making decisions, and many complained that the two-step authentication of the *Votable* app was too burdensome. The feature was removed, yet voting still declined, with one resident saying, "Well, you know, it's still a *whole thing* to use it."

Lower voter turnout soon led to passionate fringe groups and trolls having their say with legislation. In one busy week, both speed limits and vaccinations were outlawed in *Prime Town.* Three months later, an outbreak of Chickenpox and HPV swept through the city, infecting nearly every resident. When people attempted to buy calamine lotion online from Amazon®, they found the prices had risen 500%, so they took to the streets, racing from store to store. Over fifty people died in the subsequent car crashes.

Crime also began to rise in the city. There was no police force in *Prime Town*, only a Neighborhood Watch group ill-equipped to investigate the string of burglaries, vandalism, and other crimes now occurring. In a bit of 21st-century ingenuity, the group attempted to solve the crimes using Amazon®'s facial recognition software and Internet message boards. In many of the cases, the perpetrator was identified as Gabriel Day, the city's only African-American resident. However, after more than a dozen interviews, he was ruled out due to being away on business during the crimes, and because the person in the hoodie was clearly white. Neighborhood Watch still considered him a "person of interest," though.

The city continued to change gradually in this manner until a pivotal event rapidly accelerated its downward momentum.

The Bathroom Rule

The *laissez-faire* approach to work culture that had initially resulted in Prime Town's explosive GDP growth and high employee satisfaction eventually led to decreased productivity and apathy among the workforce. The revolutionary four-day work week that had been such a success was eventually changed to three days, then to two. Many work holidays were also passed by voters, including "Greg Day"—an unexplainable holiday in observance of "Greg."

During the time people actually worked, very little got done. Napping at desks and hours-long restroom breaks were fairly common. In an effort to claw back productivity, the manager of the Amazon® Fulfillment center in *Prime Town* sent out an email mandating that "all employees are allowed only two restroom breaks per day that must not exceed two minutes. Diapers are strongly encouraged." The email leaked out to other business owners in the city who decided to make similar rules, emboldened by Amazon®'s stance.

Protests broke out, with nearly all the city's workforce either taking to the streets to march or defiantly staying home to sit.

Citizens also took to Amazon.com to give all adult diaper companies one-star reviews. Media from around the world covered the story, painting Amazon® and its experiment in an extremely unflattering light, and it wasn't long before Bezos demanded action.

Ryan Forsythe Arrives

In an Amazon® executive all-hands meeting, Jeff Bezos explained the developing situation in *Prime Town* and asked for ideas to get the city back on track. The only person to speak up was VP of Western Business Development, Ryan Forsythe—an unremarkable executive originally from Paramount Pictures. He told Bezos that "All *Prime Town* needs is a little structure and a big enema," and that "I'm the man who can do both." Bezos told Ryan to meet him offline. In a hallway, bystanders witnessed this exchange:

> Bezos: *What structure? What're you talking about?*
>
> Forsythe: *Look, you can't just give the kiddos the keys to the daycare. You gotta have someone in charge so that everyone gets their juicebox.*
>
> Bezos:
>
> Forsythe: *Make me the city manager. I'll go down there, get things in order, clear out the rabble, and give you your city upon a hill.*

Forsythe packed his Porsche Boxster and moved to *Prime Town.* Via an email to residents, he introduced himself as the new CAO (Chief Awesomeness Officer) of *Prime Town* and said his purpose was to "fill in some of the org chart gaps." He then listed changes to the city, effective immediately: First, a police force was established with two dozen officers borrowed from Seattle. Funding for the force was moved from social programs and schools. Second, labor laws were enacted with mandatory working times. Third, new city laws and resolutions on *Votable* would now go through a review board. Fourth, a temporary curfew was set. Finally, the city was given a new motto:

Be nice. Work. **Make History**.

Forsythe invited townspeople to a meet-and-greet at the rec center, where he arrived carrying a *Prime Town* messenger bag and wearing a *Prime Town* hoodie and hat. When citizens complained about the changes he had enacted, he said things like, "I totally hear you," and "wow, I wish more people thought like *you*." After ten minutes he slipped out the back door.

Fresh Changes, Fresh Start

Forsythe's initial changes seemed to work. Crime plateaued due to the newly formed police force and temporary curfew. The voting review board, made up of *Prime Town* citizens, was able to catch superfluous laws before they became a reality, like the recently attempted "Doug Day" legislation. The city's monthly GDP growth ticked up 0.2%.

Jeff Bezos took notice, tweeting, *"Congrats to Ryan Forsythe for taking the Prime Town reins and pointing the city toward history. Excited to see what the future holds."*

Forsythe is said to have had the tweet framed and hung above his desk. Then, taking Bezos' encouragement as a mandate, he amended his initial changes to make the city even greater.

The temporary curfew was made indefinite. The police force was expanded to one hundred officers. Round-the-clock street patrols began; in the first week alone over fifty stops were made for suspicious activity, two-thirds of which involved Gabriel Day. Over the next month, violent crime and other situations requiring police inexplicably became more common, so Forsythe doubled the number of officers.

Labor rules were also expanded, leading to—among other things—longer work days, pay decreases, and cuts to paid holidays and sick leave. Employers were now permitted to fire at will, and because social programs had been drastically cut, the population had no lifeline.

With these new policies in place and the city seemingly under control, Ryan Forsythe tweeted at Jeff Bezos: "Can't wait to show you what *Prime Town* is cooking up. City of tomorrow, today!"

The Revolution Begins

By month four of Forsythe's changes, *Prime Town* was what most middle school history books would call a "powderkeg." Working conditions were oppressive, movement and speech were restricted, arrests had skyrocketed, and the people had had enough. On a Friday in November 2030, a resolution was put forward in the *Votable* app to remove Amazon®'s presence completely from the city, including Ryan Forsythe, and in unity not seen since the city's founding, the resolution passed with ninety-eight percent approval.

Forsythe, who was getting his hair cut at the time, received a notification on his phone of the people's decision. His stylist later told the FBI that he said, "Hmm," then disabled the *Votable* app and instructed her how to cut his sideburns. Later, Forsythe sent an email inviting residents to an "open and frank discussion about how the city should move forward before jumping to action." He closed the email by saying, "I love this city. We all do. And I think together we can harmoniously find solutions and make it incredible :)."

Upon reading this, residents and workers—many of them still wearing their shift diapers—assembled on Main Street. They found Forsythe's Porsche, which they proceeded to flip over and set ablaze. Forsythe ordered police to lock down the city and use whatever means necessary to "stop that goddamn trash. Mace, tear gas, whatever, I don't care." Protestors clashed violently with police in several instances, but then pulled back and set up a civil gathering in the main city park. One of the protestors, Jessica Henry, served as the voice of the group, and stated the demands of the residents:

> *We the people of Prime Town will no longer tolerate the oppressive regime that has overtaken our city. Our working conditions are abysmal, our living conditions are wretched, people of color are harassed by police, and we no longer have a voice in our future. We demand that every Prime Town resident be guaranteed the right to vote, so we may have a functioning democracy. We demand higher wages, shorter hours, and paid leave so that we may be prosperous. We demand the police be removed, so that we may be safe. Finally, we demand that Ryan Forsythe and Amazon® step down, so that we may be free.*

Jeff Bezos was summoned from a divorce deposition by his executive assistant and shown the news coverage of the spiraling chaos. Already upset from the day's proceedings, Bezos took to his phone and tweeted "*I declare martial law in Prime Town,*" before heading back into the courtroom.

"Day 5" in *Prime Town*

Police descended on the civil park gathering, and the situation quickly dissolved into a bloodbath. As the force attempted mass arrests, protestors fought back with rocks and shields, prompting police to switch from non-lethal to lethal weapons. Shots were fired indiscriminately into the crowd, wounding many and killing at least one person, a man later identified as Gabriel Day. After hours of disastrous confrontations, the police soon found themselves outnumbered and retreated from the park. Some fled to their homes in *Prime Town,* but most returned to Seattle. Emboldened by the police evacuation, residents began to burn the city down.

Ryan Forsythe put in an urgent plea with the Washington National Guard and asked the governor's office to declare a State of Emergency for the city. An hour later, he received an email from the Governor:

> *"As a human, I want nothing more than to give Prime Town the help it needs. But as the person elected by Washingtonians to manage spending, I cannot at this time justify the cost of sending the National Guard to a city that doesn't pay its taxes."*

Forsythe packed a bag and hailed an Uber Copter. A few minutes later, he was whisked into the sky and out of harm's way.

•

But the helicopter turned not north, toward Seattle, but rather south, toward the park at the city's center. Forsythe demanded that the pilot head to Seattle or he could say goodbye to his five-star rating. The pilot ignored the threat and landed the craft among the protestors, who proceeded to pull Forsythe out and kick his ass.

A trial for Forsythe was held on the spot. He was found guilty of "crimes against humanity" and "attempting to flee a revolution." Ten minutes later, he was taken to an alley behind a sweetgreen restaurant and shot by firing squad.

Aftermath

Over the next few months, *Prime Town* residents slowly moved out and the city's core dissolved. Many buildings were razed due to the destruction they had incurred during the protests. The entire city, including its land, was eventually awarded in a divorce settlement to Jeff Bezos's third ex-wife.

In an Amazon® all-hands meeting the next year, Jeff Bezos stated the results of the initial *Prime Town* attempt were "unfortunate," but that they had "learned a lot" from the experience. He also went on to say that risk-taking and failure is what made him who he was today, the leader of the world's biggest retailer and the first trillionaire. This failure would not deter his vision of building a Great Society, he said, and he would press on. With that said, he announced the future launch of *Prime Town Beta* and presented its motto, a modified version of its predecessor's:

Live Well. Have Fun. **Please, don't repeat history**.

LOG NINE

-- - --- -- ---   ---   - -

--- - --- -- --- - - - - --- -- - - ------ - - - ------   --- - --- -- ---   ---
- -

-- - --- -- ---   ---   - -

                                        -- - --- -- ---   ---   - -
--- - --- -- --- - - - - --- -- - - ------ - - - ------   --- - --- -- ---   ---
- -
--- - --- -- --- - - - - --- -- - ------ - - - ------   -
-- - --- -- ---   ---   - -

--- - --- -- --- - - - - --- -- - - ------ - - - ------   -

- -- --- - - ---

LOG [NUMBER]

-- - - - [Environment] was [color
#000000] when [journal subject] woke up,
and all around [journal subject] was an
[adjective] pressure. [Journal
subject's] [seeing apparatus] tried to
adjust to the darkness, but something--
- -

--- - - -- ------

  --

LOG NINE - --- --- --

When Null Lasker woke up, he found himself in a darkness so deep, so enveloping and complete, it was as if he'd stumbled into his own miserable black hole in the Milky Way. He was suspended in place as it were, unable to move, and was slowly, but most surely, being pressed out of existence by the force of unseen objects all around him-- - -- -[RESTARTING]

.

LOG NINE

It was really fucking dark when I woke up, and all around my body was a crushing pressure that paralyzed me and made every breath a workout. My eyes tried to adjust to the blackness, but something was right in front of my face, too close for me to focus on.

Whatever it was, it smelled bad. Really, really bad. It was like that time when I was ten and my dad put a blanket over me and farted relentlessly into it until I admitted he was stronger than I was. But mixed with hydraulic fluid.

Panic started creeping up, but I pushed it down and tried to use the only sense I had left. Muffled, mechanical noises were coming from somewhere in front of me, beyond the darkness. One machine sounded almost like the track of a tank transporter, except it wasn't rolling over the ground. The other was just a symphony of whirs and whizzes, occasionally broken up by the crunch of metallic objects. After a few of these metal chomps, the machine seemed to move towards me. It continued to approach until it sounded like it was only a few feet away. Then it was quiet.

A swooping, whining noise came from above, followed by a deafening dull thud. The pressure on my body increased until I thought I would implode. As I fought the blackout, I felt every molecule of my body slam to the right and my eyes abruptly squeeze against the side of their sockets, as if I was accelerating very quickly. Then they hit the other side of the sockets as I came to a sudden stop. Now the silence was only interrupted by the creaks and tings of stressed metal.

The cruel squeezing was more than I could take. I felt myself start to lose consciousness. Then the pressure vanished and I was in free fall, gasping for air like a beached fish. Light speared through gaps in the debris I fell past. I glimpsed a conveyor belt an instant before I pancaked, back first, on top of it.

Gulping oxygen, I stared up at the grey sky, glad that whatever that pressure was hadn't turned me from a live lump of coal into a dead diamond. I gave my nose a good long scratch and a deep pick. It was then that I noticed my alloy finger, and realized I was still in my Frame. The revelation startled me because the haptic sensations earlier had been sharper than usual, different from when I was in SKIRM®.

While I stared at my hand, the sky disappeared as I was conveyed into an expansive pink cylindrical chamber and dumped onto a rusted steel floor.

I sat up, feeling a wave of needles all over my body as I regained sensation to my extremities. There were heaps of scrap piled all around me and it took a few seconds for my eyes to adjust enough for me to make out what they were.

Frames. Hundreds of Pawns, Bishops, Knights, and Rooks in various stages of ruin. Some were complete units; most were not. All were dead.

The hatch I'd fallen through slammed shut. Red light filled the room, accompanied by a mechanical hum.

A panel in the floor slid away and a platform rose from it, bearing a prism the size of a recliner, refracting hypnotic rays of rainbow light. The hum reached a fever pitch, like putting your head in a turbine motor, and the prism began to rotate. A beam of light shot out of the device, landing on a blackened pawn Frame. The ray broke down the molecular structure of the unit, separating nanofiber and titanium and whatever else into little digestible gaseous bits that were vacuumed up by a kinetic pump that hung from the ceiling. The Frame was gone in seconds. The prism locked on its next victim, just a few feet away from me. I ran to the hatch and started banging as hard as I could, sending sparks flying as my Rook's fists connected. But the hatch was so thick, it barely made a thud when I beat them. I looked back to the molecular separator just in time to see it release a refrigerator's soul into the ceiling.

No way was I going to lose my Rook to this thing. Frantic, I searched for another way to escape. I spotted the kinetic vacuum above me and got an idea. I rolled under the particle beam and stopped just beneath the vacuum's dangling hose, then sprang up and latched onto it. I started to shimmy up the woven carbon tube towards the ceiling, but it stretched with my weight. I couldn't make progress. The hose just kept getting longer, like a clown's handkerchief. Madly I grabbed at it, climbing with all my Rook's strength yet still losing ground, until I heard a loud snap and collapsed to the floor.

An ear-shattering alarm sounded. The red light in the room began flashing. The death prism spun around, shooting bursts of energy at whatever target it found. I covered my head, waiting for my annihilation.

But it didn't come. The alarm stopped, the red light switched off, the prism sank back into the floor, and the side hatch flew open. A Frame stood on the other side, a live one, surveying the chaos, heavily armed.

"All right, enough bullshit, possum," she said. "Show your little ratty face and take what's coming to you."

I raised my hands from the trash heap, then got to my feet.

"Hey," I said.

The Frame lowered her rifle and looked at me sideways.

I tried scraping the crud and gunk from my Frame with a stray piece of aluminum as I walked alongside my scrap savior, StayC, through the mammoth prison complex. Whatever it was covering my alloy was impossible to get off, like motor oil mixed with tree sap and glitter.

"The warden's office is just up here, another hundred meters or so," StayC said, pointing the way. "So, you said you were fighting Indians?"

I eyed a graphite post on the perimeter with a warning sign, a stick figure man crossing a dotted line with a mushroom cloud next to him.

"Yeah," I said. "The Hare Krishna ones, not the native ones. They really did a blitz on us, too."

"I just . . . " She hesitated for a moment. "I'm trying to remember a big battle with India," she said. "They haven't been fighting an awful lot lately."

"Well, I probably smashed half their army," I said, chipping a little piece of glop from my robo pec.

She shot up an eyebrow at this, but left it alone. We continued walking. I glimpsed inside a couple of the buildings we passed. In the first, a few dozen Frames and fleshies were disassembling transport vehicles too big to stick into the molecular separator. The second was full of workout equipment and fleshies competing against Frames in a form of fighting I'd never seen. The Frame and fleshie were on separate raised platforms, swinging what looked like giant lollipops at each other, trying to knock the other off.

"How long do people have to stay here?" I said.

"Depends," said StayC. "If it's for a small infraction, might only be for a couple days. Big SKIRM® debts? Few weeks. Went Section 8? Who knows."

"How long are you here for?"

"Two months. I fragged my C.O. 'cause he cited me for having mud on my Frame and I was like 'screw that!'" She shrugged. "But it's either do this or get booted from SKIRM® and lose my Frame."

"There's no way to take outside work for money?" I said.

She shook her head and raised her wrist, showing me the twinkling blue bracelet. "Cross the perimeter and you go boom."

"I can't believe I never heard of SKIRM® jail," I said, trying to pull up my menu so I could learn more. But my menu didn't load up, and I noticed for the first time that I had no HUD display.

"When I get out of here," StayC said, "I'm gonna straighten myself out. Really focus, you know? I'm serious. No more extracurriculars or wasting time. Just gonna wake up, SKIRM® for sixteen or eighteen hours, then go off to bed. I figure if I stay on the grindstone, I can cut back after a few years or so and start my business."

"What's the business?" I said.

"Dirt-serts," she said.

"Dirt-serts?"

"Yeah, dirt desserts. It's a gourmet dessert mixed with soil from a country of your choosing. You want a macaroon with a little Parisian dirt? We got it. Some Dulce de Leche with Argentinian volcanic sand? Done."

"Wow."

"Imagine being able to say that you've eaten a piece of all 307 countries."

"How much is a dessert?" I asked.

"I dunno," she said. "But it's gonna be a lot."

We arrived at the warden's office to find her shooting a pulse rifle out her window at bits of scrap and junk beyond the invisible walls of the prison. She didn't notice us at first, so we watched for a moment as she pretended to call in air support on imaginary enemies and dodge phantom shots coming her way. When she ran out of ammo, she turned to her side, and that's when she saw us. She lay the rifle down on her desk next to a miniature gold model of a prison with a plaque that read "Best SKIRM® Prison, 2nd Runner Up, 2089."

"Nutria in the fields," she mumbled, pointing outside to nowhere in particular. "Big as rhinos."

"Warden," StayC said, "This is Null Lasker. We scooped up his Frame in today's salvage at N-56 thinking he was re-cy, but turns out he was . . . not."

"Hello," I said.

"Okay," the warden replied.

"I figured you'd know how to get him back on his way," StayC said.

"I'd be grateful for any help," I said. "If I could arrange a transport to-"

"Yeah, yeah. Shut up," the warden said, focusing on my Frame. "Let me just get a scan on you." She looked at me and started the process. "Uh huh," she said under her breath. "Right. Okay." She nodded and thought for a moment. "That makes sense, yes," she said to herself. "Bingo," she whispered.

"Find everything?" I said.

"Nope," the warden said. "I couldn't scan you. You're a Blank."

"A Blank?" I said.

"A Blank! A Blank! You wanna cracker, birdman?" she replied, shuffling back to the window. "Yes, a Blank. Usually happens with unregistered Frames." She casually hefted her rifle and reloaded it. Then she spun and pointed it at me. "Or stolen ones."

"Uh," I said, backing up. "I guarantee if you check with SKIRM® HQ, you'll see this Rook is registered to Null Lasker. Which is me. I'm him."

"Right," The warden said, shouldering her rifle and checking her sights.

"Warden, can't you put out a call to SKIRM® HQ for verification?" StayC said.

"Yeah, I can," The warden said. "I just wanted to see how he'd react. Give me a sec." She dropped her rifle on the floor and went still for a moment as she accessed HQ. I took StayC to the side.

"Was she really going to shoot me?" I asked.

"No way," StayC said. "I mean, maybe." She hesitated. "Yeah, probably." She thought some more. "You know, it's just so hard to tell with her. She bores easily, not a lot going on out here."

"All right, Null," the warden said, coming back to life. "I spoke with HQ and got it all sorted out."

"Yeah?" I said.

"Yeah," she said. "They have no record of a Null Lasker and BroCaliphate has never heard of you."

"Calibur," I said. "BroCalibur–"

"Yeah. I know," the warden said. "Haven't heard of ya."

"Uh, oh," said StayC.

"But I'm in the system! I'm here! I'm Elite®!"

"Not according to them," The Warden said. "They said you don't exist."

I was boiling. Probably flushed with fury in my Rig at home. It would take hours of wading through SKIRM® help desks and bureaucracy to get this screwup sorted. And I'd never know why it happened. Or who to blame. There was never anyone to blame at SKIRM®. Just once I wanted a name. Just once. *Please.*

"Listen, Miss . . . Warden," I said. "I'm gonna need a few hours to log out of this and deal with the SKIRM® helpdesk, then I'll be out of your hair. Will my Rook be okay here?"

"Should be. Let me think," she said. "Yes, you can go in that storage closet right there and do whatever you need to do."

I looked over at a nondescript door on the other side of the room.

"Okay," I said. I walked over, opened the door, and went inside. I closed myself in and leaned against the wall, ready for my mind-numbing quest.

"Rig, log out, please," I said. I waited for the white screen, expecting to find myself sitting back in my apartment, but nothing happened. "Rig. Log out. *Please*," I said slowly, enunciating each syllable.

Nothing. I repeated the phrase over and over with the same result. It didn't make sense. I quickly tried the manual logout procedure I had learned at SKIRM® basic: I looked up twice, then down twice, then to the left, right, left, right, and extended my index and middle finger. It didn't work. I felt a flutter deep in my chest and my outer alloy crawled with static shocks, as if there was a shorted ground somewhere on my Frame. *Rig, log out . . .* I looked at my robotic hands and feet, which appeared far away one moment, much too close the next.

Suddenly a rush of energy climbed up my back and something told me to flee, to get out. The walls and floor swayed from side to side and I struggled to keep my balance. My head felt like a zeppelin cut from its moorings, floating high above my shoulders as it left my body. I collapsed to the floor to puke, but all that came out was a distorted digital drone.

I got back to my feet and stumbled out of the closet, my entire Rook vibrating. An unbalanced gyroscope, probably. I fell to one knee next to StayC and put my palm flat on the earth to stop the spinning.

"Everything all right?" StayC asked.

"Fine," I said.

"When are your people coming for you?" The warden asked.

"They aren't. I couldn't log out."

They both stood silent for a moment.

"That's interesting," the warden said.

"I've never heard of that," StayC said, helping me to my feet as best as her Pawn could.

"Me neither," I muttered. A dark reality clouded my thoughts. Was this Frame Brain? No, it couldn't be. I was still in operational control, for one thing. And everything happening was far too mundane to be a dream. It was just another bug in the SKIRM® system that I had the luxury of beta testing.

"Is there someone else you could call, maybe?" StayC asked.

I thought for a moment. "No. Well, my brother, but . . . no."

"You sure?" StayC said.

"Yeah. I can't do that."

"Well, you better find something you *can* do, Blank," the warden said. "Because if I can't verify you within twenty-four hours, I gotta turn you into re-cy."

"I'm not losing my Rook," I said.

"Hey, nobody wants to lose a Frame," she said. "That's why they're here. But protocol is protocol."

I thought for a moment, then eyed the warden. "What's to stop me from just leaving this place right now?" I said, extending my legs and widening myself as much as I could. She inspected the new Rook wall in front of her and seemed to understand.

"I suppose . . . nothing," she said. After a contemplative pause, she cautiously walked over to me, extending her hand. "Blank, I hope you figure this out and don't get the runaround from SKIRM®. Stay safe out there."

I was taken aback. "Thank you," I said, receiving her hand.

She smiled and shook it firmly. Then she slapped a twinkling blue bracelet on my wrist.

"Hey!"

"Careful where you step," she said, laughing.

StayC just shook her head.

"This time tomorrow, Blank," The Warden said. "Get confirmation from SKIRM® or figure out what kind of car fender you want to be."

LOG TEN

For over an hour I'd absently watched as StayC quality checked a neverending conveyor stream of ammo cells filled with ionized gas. They were for the pulse weapons—rifles, cannons, etc—that SKIRM® and other PMCs needed to keep their fighters in the action. She'd visually inspect each one by hand for no more than three seconds, and if it looked good, she'd send it on its way. But if she thought there was a defect with a cell, she'd use her spectrum microscope to check for leaks and then poke at it with her pressure tester.

StayC was teaching me all sorts of things about SKIRM®'s munition workflow. It was theoretically something that an expensive machine could do, but why use one of those when there's free labor? Besides, when one of the ammo cells inevitably blew up during inspection, you could just bring in a new Frame to work in the small crater where the previous one once stood. StayC had me inspect one of the cells for her but had a mild panic attack after I closed my fist around the weighty round. "You looking to be baptized by barium?" she screamed, snatching the cell from my palm. "We're lucky this one wasn't defective. The smallest fracture and *BOOM*! Fastest way to the scrap yard, unless you plan on ripping your own arm off and chucking it over the fence or something just as stupid. How are you gonna work with one arm? You can't. That's how."

Technically, plasma-firing pulse weapons were stupid and inefficient for battle—electromagnetic weapons and directed lasers did a much better job of destroying enemies. But they were also invisible, which is not what you want when you're creating entertainment. When SKIRM® and others tried to switch to EMPs and lasers years ago to save money, people stopped watching the battles. The highlights on *INSIDE SKIRM®* were lackluster without the explosions and gunfire. It was just transporters suddenly stopping for no reason and Frames quietly falling down in the middle of fields. So the powers-that-be learned their lesson and switched to pulse-shot weaponry that audiences could see and hear, instead of EMPs, like the one around my wrist.

"I think I'm starting to slow down," StayC said with a yawn, sending her last ammo cell on its way.

I barely heard her, still in a trance thinking about my situation.

"Null?"

"Huh? Oh, right. Slowing down. How long have you been at it?"

She thought for a moment. "I don't know, actually." The sound of her own answer seemed to frighten her a bit. She mustered a nervous laugh. "You know how it is here. Time gets lost."

"Yeah it does," I said reflexively, looking up through a grated skylight at the dull primer sky that would never be painted black or blue.

Time was never a worry in SKIRM®. It passed in unknown quantities; that's how it was engineered. Log in, get lost. For the first time since I'd woken up, I wondered how much time *had* passed. How long had I been out? I did some rough and dirty calculations. A transport from where I was with the Bros to wherever I was now in the RMZ couldn't have been more than three or four days, so I rounded up to four. And from what I'd seen—between the scavengers and cleanup crews on the ground—my Frame would have been thrown in a trash heap or torn apart within a day. StayC also said that re-cy was processed within twenty-four hours of arriving, so I figured I was approaching a week of sitting in my Rig, logged into SKIRM®. The most I'd ever done was two and half days.

I tried to remember what supplies my RigLyfe® setup had when I logged on a week before. Water wasn't an issue; that was hooked up to the apartment. But the LyfeGel™ and carb compounds didn't last more than two weeks, and I knew those hadn't been completely full when I signed on. My food had to be close to empty.

How long could someone survive without eating? I couldn't remember. And I couldn't look it up.

"Hey StayC, how long was Gandhi's hunger strike?"

"What?" she said, barely getting out the word.

"Gandhi. How long without food."

She put her conveyor on pause and went still as she did a search for the info.

"Twenty minutes," she said.

"What?" I shrieked.

"Oh wait, hold on." she said. "That's how long it lasted in an old movie." After some more listening she found it. "*Mohandas Gandhi's hunger strike during a 1943 prison stay lasted for twenty-one days.*"

So I guess I had three weeks at most to figure out how to log out.

"It's pretty pure that you're into India and everything," StayC said, "but I think I need to log out before I get Frame Brain'd. Also, I really don't wanna have to turn this conveyor back on."

I nodded. "That's a good idea. Hey before you go, could you do me a favor? I have a brother, maybe let him know I'm okay, but don't tell him too much."

The small Pawn looked back at me with a confused stare. "You know I'm in jail too, right? I can't just go making calls."

"But you just said you needed to log out."

"Yeah, but I'm still under house arrest. No leaving the apartment, no calls, no porn. Nothing. It sucks."

"Oh."

189

StayC paused with a concerned look. She made her way to me, clanking a hand onto my shoulder. "I guarantee by the time I'm back here, you'll be logged out. Glitches always get sorted. Otherwise it's bad for business."

"You're right," I said, hoping she was right. She could have been lying, but I didn't care. It made me feel better.

"I know I am," she said. "Bye, Null."

"Bye, StayC."

She turned and walked off towards her storage bay, disappearing amongst the buildings. I looked around the assembly line and noticed that a lot of the other Frames had done the same, which now made everything eerily quiet. It reminded me of those lulls in the RMZ when one timezone was going to sleep just as another was about to awaken. If you were lucky enough to be up, it was a brief moment of peace where it seemed as if you were the only one alive, like the moment right before the sun peeks over the horizon when you've done an all-nighter.

"Oi, Drongo!" I heard a child with an Australian accent say. I turned to see a Pawn pointing his finger at my face. "Get to work, or get onya bike! Ya cunt!"

I decided to explore the rest of the prison while the new batch of unfamiliars started their daily routine. The library consisted mostly of children's books and used pornography. The gym was just a storage facility and a place to watch giant rats eat each other, with additional smatterings of pornography.

As I walked, I felt an indescribable pang that wasn't quite hunger, but not exactly a body ache either. It was like there was a giant emptiness inside of me that burned around the edges. I headed for the one place I could be left alone.

My assigned cell was free of any metal bars or locked doors. The room was basically just a place to take a lunch break without having to worry about your Frame getting messed with or blown up near the assembly line. I had already started etching small lines on the wall to make it feel more homey—I was up to thirty-two. I laid down on an old rusted cot that creaked beneath the my Frame's weight. Small metal fibers jammed into me as I rolled around, trying to get comfortable. I began to think of my apartment, my bed, and all the little luxuries I was starting to miss. Would my time in prison make me *too* hard for life on the outside? Maybe I'd get a tattoo when I got out. That way people would know what I'd been through. I hated needles, though, so maybe I'd get one of those holographic print-ons. No, couldn't do that—pretty sure that's what gave me a rash on my 30th birthday.

The low hum next door of a generator started to slowly lull me to sleep.

I woke up in my apartment, lying in a pool of sweat inside my Rig. The room stank—not as bad as I thought it would—and I was skinnier. Also, I was dying of thirst. When I stood up to get a drink, I stumbled backwards, lightheaded and weak, and sank back into my Rig. I let the sand in my limbs run its course before trying to stand again. When I was able to get up and move, I went to the tap and put my entire mouth over it, drank my body weight in water, then crawled, exhausted, into bed.

"Honey, you okay?" A breathy voice said beneath the covers. "I thought we were sleeping in today?"

"Angie? What are you doing here?" I said. My throat still felt dry.

"You asked me to stay, remember? We had that amazing dinner, then I got tired and you told me to sleep here. You went to work in the morning, I guess." She snuggled up to me, brushing her enormous breasts against my chest. "And you promised me a trip to the park with little Pookie today."

Behind her on the floor I could see my quokka on a little bed, running in his sleep.

"I must have lost track of time," I said.

"Oh honey, are you stressed about work again? You've been doing so well, maybe you just need a little something to ease that tension," she said, as she positioned her hips over my chiseled abs, grinding down slowly and seductively. She was moving lower and lower until she suddenly stopped, taking a moment to gaze at me with those big beautiful eyes. Also, those huge breasts.

"I'm just so happy you came back into my life," she said, "especially after I was so unfair to you." A small tear fell from her eye and onto her perfectly shaped breasts. Both of them.

"Me too, I can't wait to grow old together." I said.

"Speaking of," Angie said, reaching down to my face. Plucking a single gray hair from the top of my head. "Make a wish, my love."

"I wish– OW!" I yelped as she pulled another hair. "Not so rough."

"Sorry babe, just a couple more." She pulled another, then another. Blood started to run down my face. I tried to move my arms, but I was too weak.

"Oh honey, there are just so many." She was pulling hairs by the handful, drawing more blood with every tug. My face went numb.

"Null, baby? You should get this looked at." She turned on the mirror panel above the bed. A bloody Rook's head inside a broken, shriveled man stared back at me.

"Mornin' Rook. Get any sleep?" StayC asked, standing in the doorway of my cell.

"Tons." I said flatly.

"I'm about to start my shift, thought I'd clock in early and see how you were holdin' up," she said.

"I appreciate it. Any luck reaching the outside?" I said.

"No, but I got some feelers out there. I'll let you know when I hear something. Speaking of which, Warden wants to see you. One of the guards told me. People always askin' other people to do their work for them around here. I hate this place. Oh well, prison life, right?" StayC said, shrugging her shoulders.

"I got some bad news and lesser-bad news for ya, how'd you like it?" the warden asked, looking down the scope of a high-powered rifle out her window.

"Uh, bad first." I said. The warden fired the rifle, shaking the room.

"I keep tellin' em if you feed the rats, they'll just keep comin' back," she said. "Little reticulates have been chewing on the generator wiring all week. It's going to take a month to get it patched up." She fired another shot, and a chilling screech echoed back from outside. A grin spread across her face as she admired the rat she had just turned into paste. She swung around in her chair and looked me in the eye.

"Right, bad news. Null—or whatever your name is—no one can figure out who you are or where you stole that Rook from. How someone can operate out here with no ID *and* an unreg'd Frame befuddles me. But as of today, that's not my problem. According to HQ you don't exist, and therefore are not an issue for me or this establishment anymore."

"So . . . what? Am I free to go?"

"Absolutely, as soon as the cleanup crew dumps whatever's left of your molecular structure out in the hinterlands. They usually do it around winter. Or is it spring? Sonofabitch!" She swung around again and fired at another rodent.

"You said there was other news. Something good?" I asked. She turned back around.

"Nope, just not as bad. Good for me, though! HQ is sending a special re-cy squad to take care of the Frame that I am currently *not* having a conversation with. And best of all, I don't have to lift a finger. Do you have any idea how much breaking down unlicensed Frames hurts our annual operating costs? It's staggering." We stood in silence for a moment.

"I'd like to appeal my case." I said, standing my ground.

"As someone who does not exist, you have that right and I support it," The warden replied.

"OK, good," I said, relieved. "Who do I talk to, then?"

"The lawyer, of course. You can speak with him next week when he comes back from vacation," the warden replied, leaning back in her chair.

"But my Frame will be scrapped by then," I said, trying not to raise my voice.

"Oh my god, you're right. Well, like I said, this is no longer my problem so I will not be giving this conversation another thought.

Next!" the warden yelled out into the hall, calling for another appointment. No one else was waiting.

My back was up against a wall. It actually felt good on the lower part of my spine. Thinking creatively was always hard after a bad night's rest, I thought, watching StayC playfully mimic my movements in my cell's doorway.

"You look rather chipper," StayC said, going into a deep squat.

"How so?" I asked, reaching down to my right toe with my left hand.

"Well, for someone about to lose their Frame, you don't seem all that worried."

"That's because I know something the warden doesn't," I started to move into a crooked warrior-two.

"What's that?" StayC asked, coming out of a downward dog.

"I'm escaping from this place. Today." I sat StayC down to walk her through the plan. "Now we both know that the only means of escape are official release or getting past the EMP fence guarded by autoturrets. The latter being a one way ticket to scrap town."

"What are you getting at?"

"Like I said, running out the front would be a suicide mission unless you were somehow able to bypass the defense system."

"Right. You're boned either way, so what's the plan?" StayC asked.

"I bypass the system," I said.

"Gotcha. Well, it was nice meeting you and everything, Null. Wish you the best." She stood and turned to go.

"Wait! Don't you want to hear the *whole* plan?" I said, grabbing her by the shoulder.

"No, I don't. Sorry, man—these things always end with some desperate last-minute play that ultimately leads to somebody making a run for it. I've seen it before and it never ends well. Unless you have a miracle shoved up your service slot, you're not making it outta here in one piece."

"That's just it, I have this," I said, holding up a datapad I'd swiped from the Warden's desk.

"How did you get that?" StayC almost sounded impressed.

"Just took it when no one was looking, including you. Now how about that plan?" I sat StayC down again. This time I had her full attention.

"The information on here isn't much, but it has what I need. Every guard in this prison rotates out after their 12th consecutive hour. There is a twenty-second window during which I can intercept one of the guards while the other logs in." I pointed to the datapad, which showed a map of the prison's ventilation shaft network. "If I follow this path through the ceiling, I can be in and out of the transfer room in less than six seconds."

"But how does that get you past the turrets?" StayC asked, sounding concerned.

"Great question. It doesn't. Obtaining the keycard from the guard will only get me past the barrier, nullifying the EMP bracelet. But by the time I'm outside, the turrets will be locked onto my position."

StayC threw up her hands in frustration. "So? How are you planning to outrun a thousand auto-targeting pulse rounds? Cloak tech? Dig a tunnel? What?"

"Rats."

"Rats?"

"Yep, rats. They've been driving the warden crazy. For some reason they love chewing on the prison's electrical wiring. Maybe it's got nutrients or something; who knows. In any case, the plan is pretty simple. I just gather up some of that rotting food in the old gymnasium and throw it into a plastic bag." I gestured, throwing invisible garbage into an invisible bag. "The info on this pad says that repair units roll out to the turrets every half hour to keep them operational. I simply attach the bag of food to one of the droids and lead the rats right exactly where I want them to go."

"You think that's going to work?" StayC asked.

"It's got to. It's the only way."

She seemed to be thinking it over, checking for holes in my perfect plan. Then finally her eyes lit up. "Fuck it, I'll help however I can, Null."

"Thanks, StayC," I said. "Now, from what I can tell, this evening around seven is going to be the best time to go. I'm gonna need–"

There was a knock on the wall outside of my cell. It was Sanders, one of the prison guard Frames. "Mornin', Null. Those re-cy guys got here a little early. Warden told me to come grab you now."

StayC and I looked at Sanders for a moment, then back at each other.

"Plan B?" StayC asked.

"What's Plan B?"

StayC grabbed the leg of my metal cot and swung it over her head, caving in Sanders's upper torso. Then she began to search the body.

"Damn, no ID for the fence," she said. "Okay, we've got a few minutes before the other guards come looking for you." She observed her handwork on the Frame.

"But . . . my plan. I still need time to—"

"There's no time!" StayC spun me around, looking dead into my eyes. "Run. Run faster than the goddamn wind."

"I'll never make it past the turrets! You were right, I'm as good as scrapped."

"I'll take care of it," StayC said. "The Warden has a killswitch inside her office. It's covered in duct tape and says *Out of Order,* but it ain't. She only uses it when she feels like using lifers as target practice, or the cells start to feel too cramped. You're only going to have thirty seconds before she realizes what's going on. Just run for the horizon and don't look back. Keep moving no matter what. And here, take this," she said, handing me an ammo cell from the assembly line. I knew that taking it had been a huge risk for her.

"What should I do with it?" I asked.

"I dunno, but it's all I can give you. I'm sure you'll figure something out. You're a clever guy. Be clever."

"StayC, you've been so—why are you helping me?"

196

"You seem like a decent person. I've seen SKIRM® dick over enough honest people to know when someone is in over their head. I dunno, maybe I'm just frustrated too. It felt good crushing that guy with your bed. It was nice to do something that felt right."

"That's sweet, but I don't want you going down for my sake," I said.

She shrugged. "It doesn't feel so wrong when I know I did something right." She extended her hand and we shook. "Besides, I got myself into this mess. The least I can do is help you out of yours."

"Thank you, StayC. I owe you."

"Don't mention it, but uhh, hey, you gotta go. Now," she said, as Sanders's Frame began to flash red and emit a loud siren.

By the time I fled into the prison's courtyard, sirens were wailing all around the compound. Over the PA, a deep voice was bellowing: "Attention, the prison is currently on lockdown until **unit_NULL** is returned for decommission. Any Frame caught abetting **unit_NULL** will be destroyed on site. Any Frame responsible for his capture will be awarded **fifty credits** upon their release—in monthly installments. For more information, contact your probation officer."

I peered out to the horizon, surveying the mangled landscape and overcast sky. My HUD was still out of commision, which made the world far less saturated than it had been before. The area was dead. My Frame would be, too, if I didn't think fast.

I glanced around the courtyard and saw the large metal poles that surrounded the prison, emitting an invisible EMP barrier. Fifty yards out I saw the secondary turrets scanning the area. Behind me, on the top floor of the prison, I heard something that sounded like a desk being flipped over. StayC poked her head out of the window and gave me a thumbs up. The turrets were down.

"There!" A group of security guards had spotted me. They were closing in fast. I tensed up, accidentally squeezing the ammo cell and cracking its protective casing.

Fuck. I was so close, and in an instant I had messed it all up. I stood still for what felt like a hundred years, knowing an explosion would go off in the palm of my hand any moment. Without any other option, I gripped my right shoulder socket and pulled as hard as I could using the only weapon I had left.

"FUUuuUUuUCK!" I screamed as my nerves stretched and bent. I fought through the pain and chucked my dismembered arm in a wide arc toward the oncoming guards. It bounced a few times before landing at their feet just as the fingers lost their grip and released the cell's surprise. The blast evaporated the guards in an iridescent explosion, causing a shockwave that sped toward me like a possessed fog before lifting me into the air and propelling me outside the EMP perimeter. I flew for what felt like minutes before coming down hard on the packed dirt, flat on my back, knocking the wind—was it wind?—from my lungs.

When I picked myself up, the world was a blur and every sound reverberated endlessly. Through the haze I saw figures scurrying nearby, and little observatories in the distance, probably there to catch a glimpse of the stars in my eye . . . but no, they weren't telescopes—they were turrets. Then I remembered. I needed to clear them before they came back online.

I hobbled at first, then shifted into the hardest jog of my life, pumping my one arm as fast as I could. I spotted a treeline with some brush ahead. Just a little further and I'd be safe. Faster, faster. Off somewhere I could hear the roar of thunder, but there were no dark clouds ahead or behind. The thunder cracked again and again, in bursts closer than I'd ever heard. Then, off to my right, it sounded like someone punched the ground and a clump of dirt shot into the air. I realized there was no storm, only the warden, and this time she wasn't firing at rats.

I kept running, pumping my legs with a hellish tympani rhythm. My insides burned, my body ached—every step shot shards of glass into my rotator cuff. *CRACK.* Another shot, missed. I serpentined, trying to make my movement as erratic as possible. *CRACK.* Another miss. This time dirt sprayed against my leg. Up ahead I saw what lay beyond the perimeter, a spectacular view of hills and granite mountains, and a steep dropoff to a gorge with a small lake. Not much further now. I was going to make it. Every dig of my heel pushed me closer to freedom.

CRACK—a sharp pain raced from my calf all the way up my back, sending me somersaulting and flailing to the ground. *Please, no* . . . I was so close. I got up and limped as fast as I could. But when I tried to use my injured foot, I screamed and hunched over, grabbing my leg. The wind of another shot swept by the back of my head. She had me cleanly dialed and sighted; there was no way I could outrun her. The dropoff to the gorge was ten yards away. I had no choice.

I staggered to the dropoff and jumped over the edge.

LOG ELEVEN

Free-falling down the cliff face gave me a good opportunity to get acquainted with my Rook in a way I hadn't previously. For instance, when I struck a dry birch branch sticking out of the rock at about a hundred miles an hour, I discovered that my Frame could fold in such a way to allow my face to completely connect with my asshole, causing an ungodly pain I hadn't known existed. Then, when my foot clipped a jagged piece of granite that sent me into a 10g cartwheel, I learned it was possible to simultaneously black out and dry-heave. Indeed, lesson after lesson was pounded into me as I made my quarter-mile vertical journey toward the bottom of the gorge. The number of cactus spines that could fit in my expansion slot, how much screaming it took to distract myself from ball shots, things like that.

I slammed face first onto a thick branch, a sudden and violent end to my freefall. Stars and iridescent streaks of light flashed in front of me as I dipped in and out of consciousness from the shock. I fought it hard, bulging my eyes out to stay awake, then I rolled to my side to try and compose myself against the gently oscillating limb, focusing on the sweet relief that the pain was over. Then a sharp snap came from the base of the branch.

Aw man.

The branch gave way and I plummeted another thirty feet, pancaking on my back and forcefully knocking out whatever air or spirit I had left in my banged-up robot body.

I lay there a moment, making sure the torture was really done, half expecting the dense canopy above me to magically fall down, or a sinkhole to suck me into the gut of the earth. But nothing happened, and after a minute I tried to move around a bit. When I righted myself, sharp pangs echoed through my body. If I'd had teeth, I would have ground them to powder.

Everything below my right kneecap refused to work. I hobbled as best I could, but my insides stung with every breath, my head pounded, and after just a few steps my body demanded I sit despite the need to press on. I found a nearby boulder to lean against.

All around me were towering trees and ancient oppressive land formations, so a clear path out of the gorge wasn't coming. Ahead I could just make out rusted bits of machinery in the underbrush. Behind me, at the cliff base, were the ripples of the lake I had seen earlier, reflecting the late sun. But after a moment I realized the ripples weren't water—they were the shimmer of titanium from piles of re-cy'd Frames, probably dumped there by the Warden and her staff. A bunch of soulless machinery whose owners had long moved on. And there I was, the Frame that lived. A champion among the dead.

I pushed onward, toward the junk in the brush. Whatever the area used to be had long been lost to the forest, and nobody had been around in many years. Lush vegetation consumed the broken-down tanks and spent cartridges littered throughout the rusted graveyard. A twig snapped, spooking a cardinal above, then something flickered in the corner of my eye and I snapped to an antelope, chewing on some dry grass. It stopped feeding for a moment, tilting its head with those long rebar horns as it studied me, then in a flash it hopped off into the trees. I continued down the trail of broken-down Humvees, half tracks and motionless Frames. Then, between two dead trees, I saw the path. It was overgrown, but its memory persisted. I didn't know where it led, but something told me it was where I needed to be.

There was another movement off to my right. I had to squint through the treeline to see it, but there it was, another antelope eyeing me from afar. Or was it the same one? As I stared at it, trying to remember some sort of identifying marks, I could have sworn it licked its lips. Not a quick lick, either—a lick of anticipation. Weren't these things basically just dumber deer? They ate only grass, I thought. The last thing I wanted after surviving a war zone and prison was to be eaten by a vegetarian.

Time started to lose all meaning as I wandered deeper into the thickening brush. An odd sensation crawled up the back of my tongue, something I hadn't experienced in the RMZ before—thirst. My mouth was a dry river bed, begging for a flash flood. But there was no way to quench my desire while in my Frame. I tried distracting myself, tried thinking of anything besides the trudge, but every attempt ended in a rolling fog that left me more exhausted. Whatever was left of me was drained. The shutters for my ocular sensors lowered against my will, like a rusty garage door trying to stay open against the determined tug of a human hand. I needed to stop, just for a moment . . .

The tree I leaned against felt as soft as any space foam. As I settled in, everything felt slower, creamier. I started to think that maybe I'd never be able to get up again, but that was fine. I'd just let the fatigue shut everything down. By some miracle it might reset everything and I'd wake up in my apartment a day later, completely rested.

My head started to dip as I sank toward sleep, but then I felt a presence and jerked to attention. It was the antelope, looking right at me, close enough to touch. Its wet black eyes stared deep into mine. It sniffed the air around me and in front of my face, taking everything in. It leaned in a little closer, lowering its head. I could see my reflection in its pupils.

Then in a flash it bared its teeth and lunged toward me—

I jolted awake to find myself laid out on a gurney, staring at shredded tufts of sound insulation on a ceiling. Movement was impossible, stopped dead by magnetized constraints. The small, windowless room bobbed and dipped, and I realized we were on the move in some sort

203

of transporter. When I strained my eyes upward, I could make out a squat man in a dirty hazmat suit sitting in the passenger seat and a stringy, oatmeal-colored guy next to him doing the driving. With all my strength I tried pulling up my remaining arm, getting it up half an inch before it fell back on the table with a loud *thunk*.

"See, I told you someone was still in there."

"Fine, I'll spot you fifty creds when we get into town."

"That makes it *one* fifty."

"Yeah, yeah."

I pulled my arm up again, banging the table. Then again, and again—like a bratty toddler.

"Hey, stop that!" The squat man shouted.

"Let me go," I commanded.

"In time, gotta let the repairs run their course," he said, pointing at my torso.

I looked down and saw two tentacled cables poking and prodding me while a thousand small microbots crawled inside and out.

"What are those?" I asked.

"Lil' fixers," he man said. "They're doing most of the hard work so we don't have to. Ya know, we found you real banged up. Could've sworn you were scrap. I just assumed you were another one trying to make it to the city. You a defector?"

"Where are you taking me?" I asked, ignoring the question.

"Nowhere. Well, Dernoy, but it's still basically nowhere. It's the closest town that'll tolerate things like you."

"Things like me?"

"You know, deserters, ex-skirmys. Ah, what do they call 'em, Bambi?" the fleshie said to the boney driver.

"You know this is, like, the eight hundredth time I've told you. Fun runners . . . Funnnn Runnn-nneeerrs," the driver called out.

The fleshie snapped his fingers with delight. "That's right, fun runners! So, what's your name, fun runner?"

"Null."

"That's a funny name. Null. I'm Frimpter. Which is also funny, I guess. But not like yours. Your name sort of falls out of the mouth." He let his jaw loosen and his tongue swell as he talked. "*Null. Null, the ex-SKIRM® fun runner.*"

"I'm not a deserter," I said. "I didn't quit."

"Then what are you doing out here?" he said.

"I don't know. Still trying to figure that out. I'm just looking for a place to get back on the network."

"Well then, Dernoy should have what you're looking for. We're still a ways out, but you can stay with us while we get you there." Frimpter gave me another look up and down. "This is gonna take a while."

For three days I let Frimpter and Bambi poke and prod my Frame. The Rook was coming back together slowly, and I'd grown numb to the ever-present itch of the microbots skittering across my limbs. The carrier we rode on was an old world transport tank the two scrappers took from place to place, selling off parts and helping any lost Frames or fleshies they found along the way. There didn't seem to be any exchange of credits for what they did, even though the RMZ had its share of decentralized currencies. I couldn't figure out what their angle was, because it all seemed pretty pointless to me. All of that work for net-zero. Whatever their motive was, it didn't matter—the musing and philosophizing we did along the way was cleansing, like the morning constitutional you take after a nice butter coffee. The whipsmart Frimpter would hypothesize about some pie-in-the-sky development in the future ("If that lab in Texas can keep those little black holes stable, I think we're gonna see some time travel. I'm serious, man.), then the wafer-thin but handsome-in-a-pale-Berliner-way Bambi would retort with, "I wish I could time-travel to thirty seconds ago and poke out my ear drums." After some back and forth ribbing, we'd take in the passing landscape and wonder what it looked like in Roman times, or Egyptian. It was nice.

Midmorning on the third day, I was up on my feet and alert, watching through the windshield as the dead forest highway we'd been driving on suddenly opened up to a half-mile wide valley. Towering before us, wedged into the land, was a fifty-story hydroelectric dam. The size of it was hypnotizing. I'd seen a lot of buildings many times bigger, but something about that amount of concrete set in the wilderness just froze me in place. It's like it had been there since the beginning of time.

Behind the dam was a large, calm lake, probably a hundred feet lower than it had been a century before. Frothy river rapids burst out at the bottom, escaping the dam's turbines.

Rusty corrugated tin roofs peeked over the top of the structure. A makeshift town of drafty shacks and patched-up tents crowded both sides of the four-lane highway over the dam. People had set up booths and trailers to hawk the products of their labor to transients—outdated rifles, baseball-sized watermelons, workout pants with aluminum codpieces. Everything a fleshie needed to survive the RMZ. As we approached the dam city's entrance, I noticed several rappellers at work on the dam's enormous angled face, patching up stress cracks.

Up ahead at the entrance, four armed guards stood next to a fortified pillbox, chatting to one another.

"Frimp, you tell him?" Bambi said, motioning to me.

"Oh, yeah. Hey," Frimpter said to me, "anybody asks, you're a fun runner. Okay?"

"Why's that?" I said.

"'Cause this place is important to 'em. They're the keepers of it, you know? They have to trust you. If we say you're a fun runner with us, then they will."

I thought about it for a moment. Lying about my motives was probably for the best anyway. Any mention of SKIRM® and someone might eventually connect me with my little prison break. "Okay," I said. "If you say."

He noticed my hesitation and chuckled. "We'll set aside plenty of time for your pride someplace else, buddy!"

The guys vouched for me with the guards while I waved at them awkwardly, and we made it through the entrance with no problems.

Right away I could tell Frimpter and Bambi were regulars here. Men and women from the town sauntered over to the tank to greet the two gypsies, saying "Did you get my's . . ." and "I found your so and so's . . ." Their faces and clothes were weather-worn, but tidy and put together in sort of a third world-chic look. And everyone had the sinewy, low-fat bodies of a subsistence lifestyle. Jesus, I really needed to get in shape when I got back to my apartment.

Bambi yelled back to me, asking if I could grab a green aluminum bomb box from the back. I scanned the stacks of wooden crates and alloy boxes in the transport and found what I needed. Cradling the heavy box with my remaining arm, I hobbled up to the front where an older man from the town was waiting. When he saw me he shuffled back, his eyes wide with alarm.

"Oh, don't worry about him," Frimpter said, patting me on the arm. "He only likes the right kind of trouble."

"Hmm . . ." the old man said. "Sounds like you two hams added a turkey!"

"He's all right," Bambi said, looking at me. "I just needed someone to talk to other than Frimp."

"Don't blame you!" the old man said with a laugh.

Bambi and Frimpter helped the old man load his box onto a cart, and he gave them a couple of smaller boxes for which they thanked him.

As they moved on to speak with some of the others waiting to do business, I thought about what Bambi had said about having someone to talk to. I realized this was the most I'd spoken to actual people since I'd joined SKIRM®. Any interactions I'd had before with fleshies were terse at best, and usually in the middle of some violent battle. But the last three days of conversation over the rolling, mostly destroyed landscape (though we'd seen a half dozen fir trees) had been peaceful, almost sacrosanct.

Frimpter was examining a broken piece of machinery a young woman had hauled up to the transport. He said something quippy that made her laugh and give him a little shove on the shoulder. He seemed to have this charming, salesperson-y way about him that people loved to orbit. I imagined it's what servers must have been like in restaurants a long time ago.

I never imagined people like this existed in the RMZ. If this was SKIRM®TV, the woman would have been yelling at Frimpter wearing nothing but a towel and he'd be randomly firing his gun into the sky. And Bambi would be driving the tank completely shit-faced.

There was a distinct lack of entertainment value here. These people could have been anyone, or no one. They were just living their lives, cruising along.

But they were here for a reason, and I had to remember that. You weren't just sent to the RMZ because you got the wrong haircut. A lot of these people probably got away with whatever they did for so long because they seemed like normal people, not degenerate scum.

I watched Frimpter as he worked on a broken dehydrator, wondering what he had done to get sent here. It couldn't have been for anything violent. Frimpter seemed like a sure bet for mail fraud. And Bambi . . . male prostitution, maybe?

"Hey, Null!" Frimpter yelled. "Let's load out."

That night we stopped at a small village of white tents. My repairs were almost done, so they let me walk around for a few hours so I could stretch my servos. The sky was unusually clear and crisp, with the stars so vibrant it seemed you could step off the earth and fall into them. Everything not lit by lamp had a soft, bluish-gray glow that melted into the surrounding shadow. Frimpter and I unloaded cargo from the back of the transport, a hover dolly following us as we dropped off each box.

"What are these?" I asked, dropping off my first crate the best I could with one arm.

"Supplies, mostly. Some meds, basic provisions," Frimpter replied.

We reached the end of the tents. Frimpter called me over, wanting to show me something—the last crate, a bit smaller than the others. He opened it and pulled out a small blue egg.

"What does that do?" I asked.

208

Before he could say, the tent flap next to us opened up, and a child walked out rubbing her eyes, bundled in a wool blanket. She regarded me for a moment, then looked at Frimpter and let out a squeal of happiness.

"Mr. Clinky!" she said.

"How you doing, darlin'? Your mom and dad asleep?" Frimpter asked.

"Yeah. They worked all day," she said, adjusting her blanket. "I helped! Well, a little."

"I bet you did. Here, I brought you something," Frimpter said, producing the egg.

"You found it!" she shouted. Then she slapped a tiny hand over her mouth and glanced over her shoulder toward where her parents slept. "Did your dad give you something for me?" Frimpter asked.

"Ya. In here," she whispered, running back inside the tent.

"What the hell is a kid doing out here?" I whispered to Frimpter.

"People have kids."

"These people are criminals. They shouldn't be sending kids out here."

He gave me a puzzled look. "She was born here."

That didn't make sense. People got sent to the RMZ; they didn't get *born* here. "But—"

"Not everyone is here because they chose to be," Frimpter said as the little girl came back, dragging a heavy metal arm with the help of a small load lifter. She eyed my empty shoulder socket, then looked back at the arm she brought with a nod.

"Thank you, Mr. Clinky," she said, beaming.

I stared at the new arm, noticing small swirl marks all over where it seemed like someone had attempted to clean it up. The gesture robbed me of words, or maybe I instinctively knew that I didn't have the vocabulary to express the ripple of warmth behind my sternum. I'd done nothing to deserve this arm, and she'd done nothing to deserve this life. But here we were.

"Are you gonna come back?" she asked Frimpter.

"You bet," Frimpter said. "Get some sleep, Simone. And this only needs a tiny bit of water." He took a knee and handed her the egg

"I know," Simone said. She took her little egg, hugged Frimpter, then ran back inside, closing the thin door behind her.

We loaded onto the transport. Frimpter gave the arm to Bambi, who directed me to lie on the gurney while he tried to attach it. The stretcher hummed, sending a tingle down my back as I was magnetically snapped onto its frigid metal.

"Why are you helping me?" I asked.

"We help everyone," Bambi replied while he unscrewed something from my shoulder.

"Even active soldiers? What if I had attacked you? Would you still help me then?"

"Of course," Frimpter said. "It's what we do."

"That doesn't make sense," I said. A flash of pain made me wince as Bambi yanked on a dangling fiber optic cable with a pair of pliers.

"A lot of things out here don't." Frimpter shrugged. "And that's sort of the only thing that does make sense. Everything kind of comes together once you stop worrying and start caring."

"Hold still," Bambi said, cursing under his breath as he grinded something down.

"What'd you do before all this, Frimpter?" I said, embarrassed that I hadn't asked him in the last few days we'd spent together. I'd been treating him and Bambi like they only started existing when I met them, and would disappear from the universe when I left.

"For work?" he asked.

"Yeah. What were you? A doctor? Teacher? Priest?"

"I made socks."

"What?"

"Yeah, I made custom socks. The company was called *Funny Feet*. People told us what kind of socks they wanted and I made them."

"Hold on," I said, trying to add it up. "Isn't all that automated? Couldn't a robot just make socks?"

"You'd think so," Frimpter said, "but it's actually way more complicated than A.I. can handle. Like, this one customer wanted socks for his fiftieth wedding anniversary, so he gave us all these fuzzy, fifty-year-old jay-pegs to use in the design and said, 'make a collage of our life together.' If you gave that task to an A.I., it wouldn't know what to do. But I was able to make something really special."

"Socks."

"Oh! And every month I'd get the doctors at the children's hospital to ask each kid what their favorite animal was, then I'd make custom socks with the animal and the kid's name and give them to the kid."

"Okay," I said. "So, you're making socks for old people and sick kids, and then . . . you end up in the RMZ how?"

"Uh, well . . ." he trailed off. "When my son went off to uni, I rented his room out for a little extra scratch, you know. I'd give him some of it, then I'd use the leftover to pay down the mortgage." Frimpter smiled sheepishly. "But I wasn't exactly telling the city about the extra credits."

"You got sent to the RMZ for not reporting income?"

He nodded. "Three years."

I heard Bambi suck air through his teeth. My body started to shake with laughter. Three years in a warzone for not telling the government about a bed and breakfast? The punishment was so cruel and extreme, there was nothing to do but revel in the absurdity.

Frimpter watched me laugh, shifting nervously in his seat. I caught myself, ashamed at my knee-jerk reaction. This man had laid his whole life before me without hesitation, and I'd spat in his face.

"That was six years go." Frimpter said with a heavy sigh.

I'd heard countless rumors and reports over the years about people being sent to the RMZ and not coming back, but I'd always written that off to the "bad behavior" loophole—if you were an asshole during your sentence, they could extend your time accordingly. But there was no way draconian fine print like that could apply to Frimpter. They extended his stay just because they could, and now I realized he wasn't the only one.

"I'm sorry," I said.

"It's okay," he said.

"You—you shouldn't be here, Frimpter. You're a good person."

"Maybe," he said. Then he thought for a moment. "I guess I did break the law. But who doesn't bend rules from time to time?"

"Nobody," Bambi said, holding up my Mantis chip with a grin.

"Forgot about that," I said.

"I bet," Bambi said, putting the chip in my storage compartment. He focused again, making some adjustments to my arm.

"Okay, Bambi," I said, watching him work, "what stupid reason were you sent to the RMZ for?"

"Selling meth," he said.

"Ah," I said.

"But, like, just a little bit of meth," he said. "Not a lot."

"Oh, okay," I replied. There was a long silence.

"Well, we're about done here," Bambi said as he turned off the gurney. I sat up, tried to move around. Everything worked except for the new gift from the little girl.

"Think you missed something," I said.

"The arm's working fine," Bambi said, "it's just going to take a bit before your Frame accepts the new hardware."

I tried to move the arm again, but it just shook and made a sad whirring sound, like the giant broken animatronic rat at Sam E. Sausages's Pizza. Then there was a brief flash in my vision. When the light faded, I noticed a string of code running in the bottom corner of my eye.

```
//INT.CARE_E.APK . . . complete
```

"Hey, you fixed my HUD!" I said.

"What?" Bambi replied. "No, we just do hardware. You gotta go to the city if you're looking for any software mods."

"Well whatever you did, it's great."

212

"Awesome," Frimpter said. "Glad you're working. Now, if you don't mind, we have to do some route planning. We'll be up front."

I nodded, distracted with excitement that I'd soon be able to access my Frame's system. It only took a few seconds for the OS to finish booting up. I looked at Frimpter and Bambi for a moment, sad that I'd be leaving them for my festering apartment, but it was time to go. The green logout prompt flashed in front of me and I selected "confirm."

- ERROR-

Damn. Whatever the scavengers had installed wasn't compatible with the SKIRM® network. I opened up my diagnostics to check on my arm's repair status, but the information was unreadable. I commanded the HUD to refresh. Nothing.

"It looks like you're trying to do something. Can I help?" It was the HUD speaking, but in a voice I didn't recognize. It sort of sounded like . . . *a kid.*

"I want to use my arm," I said.

"Oh. Hmm," the voice said. "I don't know how to do that, but I'm learning new stuff all the time. Do *you* wanna learn something?"

"No," I said.

"Ketchup was used medicinally in the early 1800s."

"I said no."

It didn't reply.

"HUD, activate–"

"The mixture was originally made of mushrooms and fish. Wanna know more?"

"HUD, mute! Hey, Bambi," I called up front, "you mind getting rid of whatever assistant A.I. you installed?"

"I told you, we only do hardware. Must've been something that came with the arm," he yelled back.

"Bambi had a rabbit friend named Thumper," the A.I. said. "He also watched his mother get gunned down by a hunter. Wanna know more?"

"No!"

213

LOG TWELVE

It was dusk by the time we reached the village of Dernoy. The place looked like a sink full of dirty dishes. Crusty shacks were stacked on top of other shacks in haphazard ways so that everything seemed to lean and sway. Miles of fiber optic cables were strung from roof to roof, either to service a local network or keep the buildings from falling. Some fleshies milled about, talking nonsense to one another, while others just sat on top of oil drums in front of their houses, biding their time.

Bambi parked the transporter and we hopped out onto a rocky street littered with junk and ancient glass. As I followed him and Frimpter, I kept getting the urge to look over my shoulder, feeling like someone or something was watching me.

"Dernoy's a neutral town," Bambi said, noticing my shiftiness. "Plenty of SKIRM® folk come out here looking for cheap parts, and most fleshies just want to be left alone. Don't worry, you're safe, Null." Frimpter nodded in agreement.

"And if anybody starts something," Frimpter said, pointing to his amorphous bicep, "they'll have to deal with this pile of perfection first."

I didn't have any reason to not trust them. I relaxed my shoulders and continued our walk into the small, decrepit village trying to quell the paranoid feeling that I was in someone's crosshairs.

"Where are we going?" I asked.

"The Three Strikes, central nervous system of Dernoy," Bambi said. "The bar's sort of a front—every upstanding citizen of the RMZ looking for a discount or unauthorized module stops by."

"Taking you to see Tir," Frimpter said. "He should be able to help you with your problem."

"Tir, huh?"

"He's ex-military. Really smart, kinda weird," Frimpter said. "And I bet whoever gave you *that,*" he tapped my breastplate, holding the Mantis chip inside, "left a small piece of themselves on it."

"These hacker snobs love signing their work, they can't help it," Bambi said. "Tir should be able to help you find out who made it."

"Hackers, a 1995 feature film starring former wrestler Angelina Jolie, U.S. Senator Matthew Lillard, and rollerblades," CareE regurgitated from his memory bank.

I smacked myself on the side of the head. "Keep it down!" I shouted.

The Three Strikes was a wide, four-story brutalist structure that sat on top of a large hill—probably just a landfill—covered with dirt and dead grass. It looked like it might have been an embassy or customs building decades before. Opaque cream-colored solar cells made up the outside walls, which made the place glow brightly from the lights within. The shadows of the patrons projected onto the building's exterior, ghosts drifting in and out of view. Off to the side, blue sparks flew from a garage that serviced transporters and random bits of scrap.

We approached the front door, greeted by loud cheering from within and two Pawn sentries that blocked our path.

"What's your business?" the first Pawn said. Her Frame was ancient, probably ten years old. Too old to work on any network I knew of, which was curious.

"Just looking for a drink," Frimpter quickly told them.

"Sure," the other Frame said, eyeing me suspiciously. He was even older than the first. "Any weapons?"

"See any?" I said, giving him a little spin.

"Just doing my job, idiot," the guard said. "Seeing a lot of you lately. Try to keep it civil in there."

"He'll keep the tactical nuke where it is," Bambi said.

"See that he does," the guards stepped aside. "All right. Go ahead."

The smell of grass hit hard as we stepped through the door. The sweet dampness of it in the air was so powerful it made me want to throw up. Apparently fleshies just couldn't get enough of the cheap stuff—getting trashed on a budget was probably more fun than just sitting around waiting to die.

"Fermented sod juice," Bambi shouted. "It'll warp your world with only a few glasses."

Everywhere I looked people were holding glasses of the green liquid, gesticulating and yelling.

In a dark corner I saw a dozen people reclining in nanofiber chairs with transmitters on their temples glowing red, every one of them wearing space diapers and a twisted smile. I glanced down for a closer look and immediately knew they were tripping on 5-HT. Serotonin overloads were paradise, but they gave you evil diarrhea. That, and suicidal thoughts that could keep you up for days.

In the main area of the room, an electric crowd gathered around something I couldn't see, hooting and jumping up and down. Bambi and Frimpter took a seat at a table, directing me to ask for a drink at the bar while they ordered a plate of fried sparrows and a jug of something with a strange name.

"LEFT, YOU BASTARD! LEFT!" Someone from the crowd screamed.

"DO THAT AND YOU'RE DINNER!" Another shouted through clenched teeth, high as a cloud.

I made my way over through the hazy room and peeked over the heads of the unwashed mob. In the center on the floor, a fluffy hen

217

milled about on a big numbered board, indifferent to the threats being hurled at her.

"C'MON . . . THIRTY-SEVEN! YOU KNOW YOU WANNA!" A man shouted at the chicken.

"BA-COCK! BAWK! BAWK! BAWK!" said another as he danced and flapped his arms.

The chicken continued its unhurried pecking and rustling, until it stopped. The crowd grew silent, waiting in anticipation. The chicken seemed to sense this, and looked across their eager faces, surveying them, twisting its head as if to read the room. And then, when it was satisfied, it squeezed out two malformed green eggs onto the number fifty-one.

A chorus of boos and cheers erupted. Cards were waved above the crowd as others were ripped apart. One man rushed for the chicken. "C'MERE, YOU SORNER!" His friends wrestled him back and shoved a glass of grass into his hand, laughing. As I watched them take the poultry gambler away, my eyes met with those of a couple guys staring at me from across the room. Both of them were haggard, with purple bags under their deep-set eyes. One whispered something to the other, then they got up and left.

In a flash a sturdy freckled man wearing an apron burst out of a service door next to the bar and scooped up the chicken and its eggs, then disappeared back inside. The door had barely swung shut when he stepped through it again, this time to gather up empty glasses. As he made his rounds, people chatted him up and put friendly hands on his shoulder. He'd make a quip without missing a beat of his work, then move on to the next chore, checking on someone else. I slowly made my way to him, waiting for a moment during his mad hospitality dash when he was somewhat alone. Finally I saw my window.

"Excuse me. You in charge here?" I asked him.

He turned, giving me a lengthy look up and down. "Getting pretty tired of seeing you lot. You never buy any food." He went back to his work. "Yeah, I'm Hoss. Need something?"

"Looking for some upgrades," I said. "You know where I can find 'em?"

"Down the hall, but I'll tell you what I tell the rest of you," Hoss said. "He'll do the basics, but if you start asking him for anything fancy, you'll end up cross-eyed with a broken guinea horn."

"What's a—never mind," I said. "Thanks."

I made my way past a couple of patrons trying to steady themselves against the wall as they waited to use the toilet, then came upon an enormous room filled floor to ceiling with junk. It was a museum of electronics and doo dads, most of it older than me, and had that pleasant chemical smell that only old heat-worn plastic has. There were rows and rows of freestanding steel shelving, every level bowing in the middle from the weight, seemingly moments away from toppling over like hoarder dominoes. I walked a little further in and my feet hit a dirty white mat with a bunch of colorful arrows on it.

"Now whaddya think that is?" a voice said.

A bug-eyed man with no chin appeared from behind a shelf, looking at me expectantly.

"I don't know," I said.

"C'mon, take a guess."

"I really don't know."

"Oh, no no no no," he said, shaking his head. "I can't let you give up."

I gave the mat another once over. "I guess it could be a tablecloth or—"

"It's for exercise! Can you believe it? This is how people used to work out. Watch!" He hopped from square to square. "I think you would jump in a pattern while your opponent watched, then they'd have to match it exactly or they'd lose!" He sounded out of breath.

"That's great. Look—it's Tir, right? I was told that you could look at something for me."

"Oh, yeah, yeah . . . *pffff*," he said, stopping mid-jump. "Sure sure, easy easy. What's it you're looking for? New peepers? Or maybe you want me to take a look at that lame arm of yours—"

"How did you know my—I stopped myself. *One thing at a time.* "We can get to the hardware in a bit but first I need you to look at this," I said, pulling out the Mantis chip.

Tir's bug eyes widened. "Been a while since someone brought one of those." He zipped off and went digging through his kingdom, fetching up an old box and a scanner with a cracked screen. He plugged a cable into my service slot and placed the Mantis on the scanner. "Most of you metalheads can't stay on your own two feet after messing with that stuff. Where'd you get it?" he asked.

"Never got a name. I'm just looking for a signature or RP address or—"

"Wanna know the name of the fella you swiped it from, huh? Oh, now, that's interesting," Tir said, scrolling and swiping through dozens of graphs and readouts on the box. "Just checking your Rig status. I see some digits, what'd you say your area code was?"

"I didn't. It's Triple eight, dash two."

"*Triple eight dash* . . . Oh! I know that one. Rough area," he said. "Well then, interesting. Very interesting." He shoved the scanner screen into my face and pointed with his finger. "You see that green line?" he said.

I nodded.

"That's you, metalhead."

"Okay."

He swiped and barked some commands and a new display appeared. "Now you see that? That's where your Rig is."

There was an address—all zeros.

"According to the readout, you are not where you are," Tir said.

"I don't understand," I said. How could I—"

"Well you either moved and forgot your new address, or you're running some kind of fancy new software that's spoofing your location. You trying to get fancy with me, buddy?"

"No! I'm just as lost here. I mean, if I'm not home, where am I operating from?"

Tir took a step back, studying me. "I dunno. I've seen lots of strange things and a lot of strange places, but I've never seen an operational Frame with a blank RP before. Especially one so ugly." He cackled and braced his back with both hands. After a few uncomfortable seconds of laughter he stopped. "You'd have to go to the city to figure that out."

"City?"

"Desolin. You sure you're in the right line of work, buddy? Figured this wasn't your first rodeo, stolen Frame and such."

"It's not stolen." I said defensively as the big man scoffed.

I ignored him and thought about where I could be operating from. If I wasn't home, where was I? Had I overloaded the Rig that much? Or maybe SKIRM® already had me in custody. No, that didn't make sense. They would have logged me out so they could give me a proper execution. I could feel Tir's goofy saucer eyes staring at me.

"What about the chip?" I asked. "Anything on it?"

"Let me see, hmm." Tir snatched up a loupe and snapped it onto his head, diving into the Mantis, combing it over for clues. "No, nothing that I can see . . . maybe if I check the—*oh*. How incongruitis."

"What?"

Tir got up and threw the chip back at me. "Okay, no more. We're done here."

"What is it?" I said, hefting the chip, trying to see what he saw.

He leaned in close, his eyes practically out of his head now. "Tell that psychopath we don't want nothin' to do with them."

"Psycho–"

"Get out!" he said. "And tell [Name] to stay outta Dernoy!"

"Incongruitis, Latin. Meaning to fornicate with one's own flock," CareE said cheerfully as I made my way back to the bar. "Would you like to know more?"

"No," I said, ignoring the A.I. as I thought about what Tir had said— all of his nonsense had done nothing but make me more confused.

"I created a copy of Tir's diagnostic software. I'd like to run some tests if that's okay?" CareE said.

"I really don't care what you do," I said. I was in a hurry to get back to the transport. Something was giving me a bad feeling about sticking around longer than I needed to.

"You don't care?" the A.I. asked, confused.

"That's what I said."

"Not caring is impossible. What if I did something awful, like turn off your vision or read the Bible backwards? That would upset you, and that constitutes—"

"Just shut up and test me!"

"On what?" a man's voice said. It was Hoss behind the bar, staring at me with a raised eyebrow. I looked to see if anyone else had been listening to me.

"On . . . anything," I said, recovering.

"All right," Hoss said. He scanned the room a second, then gestured to a jar full of coffee beans on the counter. "How many beans you think is in that jar?"

I hesitated, wanting to leave.

"C'mon," he said. "How many?"

I studied the jar a moment, doing some rough estimates. "Twelve hundred."

"Interesting," said Hoss, clearly impressed. "Is that your final answer?"

A tickle of unexpected excitement hit me. Another quick glance at the jar and my mind was settled. "Yeah. Am I right?"

Hoss looked between me and the jar, then shrugged his shoulders. "Dunno, never counted." He went back to washing the green-stained glasses and pouring drinks.

I stood there a moment, thinking about what it would be like to pop his head like a zit, then let the thought pass as I pivoted toward the entrance to find the guys and tell them we needed to make our way to Deso–

"I thought it was a great guess," a lone Bishop Frame said, standing between me and the exit. I hadn't heard him walk up, nor seen him come in.

"Thanks," I said, keeping my calm. "When I was a kid I won a contest once, except it was a jar of candy."

"That makes sense," the Bishop said with a chuckle. "My school had one of those too." His voice was youthful.

"That's great," I said, trying to go around him and make my way out.

"Hey!" he said, intercepting me, "wouldn't it be crazy if we went to the same school?"

"Yeah, I guess."

"Ridgewood Boys Prep, just outside of Brooklyn in the 'ole NYC. How about you?"

I thought quickly, trying to remember a place. Anyplace, even if it wasn't a lie. "Uh, Bean . . . town." I said, the jar on the counter in the corner of my eye. "In, uh . . ."

"Boston," CareE said in my head.

"Boston."

"Oh, That's pure," the Bishop replied, his gaze drifting off silently as his Frame temporarily idled. I looked to the exit, hoping to leave sooner than later. Suddenly he popped back alive. "You know, I used to visit my grandma near downtown during the summer. That whole area is like, burned in my brain. Where'd you live?"

"Just a little suburb, near the uh—"

"Boston is known for its love of sports, statues and–"

"Statues."

"Oh?" The Bishop said coolly. He walked up and stood next to me, surveying the bustle of the Three Strikes. "What brings you out this way, Mr . . .?"

"Ser," I said.

"Ser," he parroted. "This place isn't really near the action."

"Not every bounty is," I said.

"So you're on the hunt?" The nosy Bishop asked.

I was offering him answers that I didn't feel like giving. On the other side of the room a fleshie was trying to slap his friend awake from a serotonin psychosis.

"So who's the mark?" he continued. "Fru'nner, fleshie? Who?"

"Someone," I said, looking past his shoulder for Frimpter and Bambi. *Where the hell were they?* He nodded. "Pure, pure." There was a long silence. A few more fleshies came into the roadhouse and milled about. "There a subseg you work with or–?"

"What's your name, kid?" I interrupted.

"Les."

"Les, you ask a lot of questions."

"Yeah, well, I'm just doing—"

"The only thing you're doing is pissing me off." I inched towards him. "How many hours have you got, Les?"

"Seven hundred."

"Green, just as I thought," I said, shaking my head. "Let me impart some wisdom upon you, since you're obviously new to this: Assume every person you come across in SKIRM®—or any PMC—is a little on edge. They've probably been working ninety hours a week for the last five years just so they can be a month behind on rent. They're tired. They're tense. And they're probably about this far from snapping." I leaned into Les, towering over the rookie, taking pleasure in his shrinking stature. "Take a hint, it might save you some time. If someone wants to join you for some of that oh-so-rare, inane little chit-chat, then hey! Go for it. But if they're not talking, then you should disappear like cake at a fat kid's party." I was nearly on top of him now. "So forgive me, Les, *novice Bishop*, if I sound mad or I'm being *too* short with you—as a Rook with more hours than hairs on your balls—it's because it's none of your business."

The room had fallen silent. Les wavered in place a moment, not saying anything as I stared him down.

"Ha, preach it, brother," a modulated voice said. I turned away from Les and peered through the haze, but couldn't see where the voice was coming from.

224

"Gotta put the kids in their place, right?" Another modulated voice said, closer but I didn't see anyone talking.

"But hey," the first voice said, "if it's not too much trouble, maybe you could share your business with us . . ."

The air rippled and warped, and two gleaming Knight Frames appeared in the room as they uncloaked.

" . . . as fellow pros who are also short on time."

They approached me with slow, deliberate steps, until they were only a few feet away. Then the two Frames moved apart, forming a triangle between me and them.

"Whaddya say?" The Knight to my left said. "Wanna talk shop?"

I eyed them both. "Maybe some other time. I need to get back." I tried to move forward but they edged closer to one another, narrowing the gap. My eyes drifted to the EMP rifle at the left Knight's side.

"No, really. Talk," the right Knight said curtly. "What are you doing out here, Rook?"

"Yeah, who's the mark?" The other Knight chimed in.

They weren't going anywhere, so neither was I. I took a deep breath to settle my nerves, or whatever it was that was making my stomach jump.

"All right. The reason I didn't want to say," I began, trying to think, "the reason why I didn't want to tell you what it is . . . is because . . . I'm embarrassed."

Both Knights tilted their heads. "About what?"

"I'm out here looking for the . . . Newcomer. Have you heard of him?" I asked.

"No, who's that?" the one Knight said.

"Wait," said the other Knight. "I think I might have, maybe."

"Well," I said, "this guy takes Frames—ones he's either killed himself or found— plucks an eye out, and . . . does things to the socket until he . . . he's done."

One of the Knights grunted a sound of disgust.

225

"Yeah. And SKIRM® is pretty tired of it," I said. "It ruins the Frame beyond repair and it's making the audience pretty upset. So they hired me to make an example of him."

"Why you?" The first Knight asked.

"And what's so bad about that?" The other Knight spat out. "It's just one guy."

"The thing is," I continued, "SKIRM® can't ID him. They only have samples of his . . . essence. So to catch him, I've been following leads, and when I track him somewhere, that's when I . . . lie down and play dead."

The Knights were shocked. "So, you're saying you gotta—"

"Yeah. Then see if the DNA matches so I can bring an end to his reign of terror."

There was a long pause as the two Knights looked me up and down, then they keeled over with laughter. It was so loud and forceful that their modulated voices distorted through the heads of their Frames. Les the Bishop even joined in.

"That's quite the bounty you got there, Rook," the Knight to my left said, pretending to wipe a tear from his angular face.

"You really are a pro!" the other said. "Take note, Bishop, you can learn a thing or two from this guy!"

"Thanks," I said, sheepishly playing the punching bag. "So now that you know, if you don't mind, I need to be going."

"Yeah yeah, you've got important business to get to," the Knight on the right said, heaving and hawing. He moved over so I could pass through.

"And please," I said, "keep this to yourselves. I don't want anyone—"

"Hey everybody! Hey!" the Knight on the left shouted to the crowd. The room's ears perked up as the crowd came to a collective standstill. "I want you to take a good look at this Rook here. 'Cause right here is a *true* hero," the Knight continued. "This guy isn't afraid to lie down in the dirt for his country and get a little egg on his face!"

"Or in it!" his friend chimed.

226

The Knight grabbed my new, inoperable arm and raised it above my head as I watched on nervously. "On three, I want a big 'HOORAH' for my Rook friend here, okay?"

A hundred green-stained glasses rose to the ceiling.

"One, Two, THREE! HOORAH!" The crowd shouted and cheered.

The Knight turned to me and spoke quietly. "All right, I think I've razzed you enough. You have a good one, buddy."

He let go of my arm, sending it plummeting limply downward. The violent motion jerked it loose at the shoulder. It slowly slid off its u-joint and clattered to the stained wooden floor. The two Knights stared at it for a moment.

"Guess we're lucky," the far Knight said, "it wasn't holding an explosive this time."

"I'll tell you what," The Knight next to me said. "You had us for a second, you really did."

The other Knight raised its EMP rifle at me.

My eyes darted between them. "I don't know who you think I am, but–"

"Just stop," he said shaking his head. "We've had enough talk for today. You gonna make a scene, or can we just do this easy?"

The room echoed with the sound of loud clanking and clicks. From behind the counter, Hoss appeared with what looked like a silver mini-cannon, pointed squarely at the EMP-wielding Knight.

"What did I say about keeping your quibbles out there," Hoss said pointing to the exit. "I swear you kids just don't listen."

"We were just leaving," the Knight with the EMP said. "Lower the–"

"I'm not lowering anything," Hoss said. "Not until you drop your weapon and get out. Now, scat."

"How 'bout I leave first?" I said, pivoting.

"Don't move," the Knight near me said. The other Knight focused his aim.

"I said get out!" Hoss shouted at him.

In the corner of my eye I saw a creep of movement from behind the bar. Then, in an instant, Les the Bishop sprang onto Hoss's back, trying to take him to the ground. I leapt for the Knight next to me and spun him around right as Hoss unleashed a bright stream of plasma *ratatating* into the other one, causing it to fire the EMP rifle wildly at us. I managed to duck behind the Knight I'd been tangling with. The dead weight pushed us to the floor as a single metal mass where I met his lifeless gaze. I watched as the light disappeared from the stealthy Frame, now just a brainless, powered-down husk. A few fleshies came to Hoss's rescue and tore the Bishop from his shoulders. Les squirmed and fought as they dragged him off down the hall. Hoss walked over and finished off the other Knight with his cannon, cutting it up with ten thousand pulse rounds. Then he pointed it at me just as I rolled the dead Knight off and picked up my detached arm.

"And what about you?" he said.

I surveyed the mess around me and decided maybe it was time to leave the Three Strikes for good. From out front, I heard the familiar honk of Frimpter's MTV. "I was just leaving."

Hoss took a hand off of his gun and went back to collecting empty glasses.

I dashed out to the transport and slid inside so fast I frightened Frimpter.

"Have you two ever been to Desolin?"

LOG THIRTEEN

The transport lumbered to a halt as we came to the cinder block shed that denoted Desolin's first checkpoint. It didn't look like much, and I wondered what was stopping the casual hooligan fleshie or Frame from just blowing through it on their way to causing havoc in the city. Then I poked my head out and saw all the shiny flat titanium discs lying flush to the ground. Whatever they were, they had probably earned enough of a reputation to ward off the unscrupulous.

From somewhere near the front of the transporter, I could hear Frimpter ribbing the guard with his salt-of-the-earth quips and charm, and when I was able to covertly get an eye on them I saw him slip something to the chuckling sentry. The two bumped elbows. We were moving again before the MTV even had a chance to cool down.

"Well, hard part's over," Bambi said, waving his hand forward, beckoning me to move up to the front.

"What was that back there," I asked. "A bribe?"

"In Desolin, everything needs a little grease," Frimpter said with a chuckle, pulling out what looked like paper credits, durable but weathered. "Here, you're gonna need this after we drop you off. They only use decrypts in the city—you're not gonna find any credit lines or funbux. That should be enough to get you set up while you look for *the one who shall not be named.*"

"You mean [Name]?" I said standing up, cradling my limp arm as I tried to find footing in the cramped camper.

"Shhh!"

"Shut up!"

My fleshie co-travelers were strangely on edge. I didn't like it, but there was something oddly reassuring about their sudden change in attitude. All this time the terrorist leader [Name] had been little more than a myth to me, just a spectre meant to frighten small minds. But this genuine alertness from two people who had seemed—at least so far—pretty cosmically anchored was giving me hope that [Name] was actually real. Because that meant I might be able to log out of this hellhole and get back into my apartment.

The transporter hit a deep pothole, sending a violent shudder through the vehicle that made everything rattle, including my loosely attached lame arm. Even with all the repairs from the guys, the Rook still wasn't one hundred percent; it was as if I was still learning to use it for the first time.

"*Like a Virgin*, song, 1984. Lyrics include allusions to menstruation, large penises and woodland creatures," CareE chimed in, unsolicited.

"Any shops in Desolin know how to get rid of spyware?" I asked Bambi.

We continued on into the city, the dirt road giving way to smooth recycled asphalt. Hovels became mid-rises, then mid-rises became dirty concrete megastructures that could house ten thousand tenants with room to spare. Loud, pulsing music emanated from every street corner, and sirens swelled from blocks away. Everyone seemed to be in a perpetual state of hustle, either to get somewhere or get something from someone, their stress-lined faces constantly scanning the buzzing chaos, anticipating. Souped-up antique electric vehicles loudly hummed in the streets, zipping around residents and through intersections, some of them leaking battery fluid as they peeled around corners.

In some ways Desolin felt like home, just a decade or four behind. Two cars were stopped in front of us at an already crowded intersection, one of the passengers calmly hanging out of the side talking to someone in the adjacent car.

Frimpter smacked the dash of the transpo and a tiny *beep* sounded from the front. The driver looked back at us, shot up his arm and a finger, then peeled off into the city. But him getting out of the way didn't help much—the traffic only became more dense and the streets more crowded the further in we moved. Desolin was alive in a way I hadn't seen before in the RMZ, and my mind was having trouble reconciling the cesspools of looting and meth I'd seen on *RMZ Live* with what was in front of me.

"Who are they?" I asked the guys. "These fleshies, I mean."

"You gotta stop using that word," Frimpter said.

"Yeah, man," Bambi said, grimacing. "SKIRM® slang doesn't fly, especially around here."

"Oh, I didn't know that was a bad word or anything," I said.

"We know," Bambi said. "That's what makes it worse."

"Whaddya mean?" I said.

"It means," Frimpter said, "that SKIRM® won." He shook his head, solemnly chuckling. "Gotta give it to 'em—they're marketing masters. Managed to get the entire world to use a dehumanizing word without thinking twice."

"I don't know about all that," I said. "*Fleshie* is fun. It's like *friendly* or *fuzzy*. You can't say it without smiling."

"Let me ask you something, Mr. Smiley," Bambi said. "After you've flattened an outpost for a big fat SKIRM® bounty, and you're celebrating, getting that post-mission replay, who would you rather hear got caught in the cross-fire? Fifty fleshies Or fifty *people*?"

I sat silently a moment, thinking back at my past bounties. Remembering faces.

"It's harder to kill a person," Frimpter said. "A father, a mother," he paused, staring at the wall. "A daughter." He looked away, out to the bustle of the streets. "You want to know who they are? They're just people. A few hundred thousand souls trying to live without drones in their faces."

"No one gets sent to Desolin?" I asked.

"No," Frimpter said. "The city was founded by a group of refugees who didn't want to end up on a highlight reel. It's far enough from the action to not be an issue, and too small for PMCs like SKIRM® to care. These people are survivors."

I sat back down, fighting the urge to ask more questions. The MTV bounced along, hitting a few more potholes as we approached the center of Desolin, and after a mile or so of crawling through traffic, Bambi eased the transport into an alley.

"Fare thee well, Null," Frimpter said without looking at me. His gaze was on the city, taking it in like a drink that starts out smooth, but ends up burning your throat.

"Wait, you're not staying?" I asked.

"Refill depot is on the other side of town," Frimpter said, "gotta double back if we want to make it outta here before nightfall. Still plenty of people out there who still need our help."

"Yeah, like me," I said, looking at a fresh pool of blood outside a bodega.

Frimpter opened the side door of the transpo. "Not gonna lie, Desolin isn't for the weak. But remember: people here are just trying to get by. They mind their business, so you mind yours. Keep your head down and you'll be fine. Hope you find yourself out here, fr'unner."

When I stepped out, the stench of the city penetrated my nostrils and flooded my throat with the fumes of chemicals, rancid garbage, and human waste. I reflexively doubled over, trying to catch my breath and ease the bubbling nausea, but I couldn't, and instead I just gagged helplessly.

"Oh, and don't forget this," Bambi said, throwing me the blown-out Mantis chip. "Might be something you missed on there, you never know."

"Eh, no thanks," I said, handing him back the chip. "That thing's just been trouble."

Bambi extended his arm, stopping me.

"Keep it," he said. "For better or worse, that *thing's* a part of you."

Frimpter rolled up the window, honked twice, then drove back the way we came in. Across the street, I craned my neck to see a decapitated Frame crucified on a beam post. The words "*DIE SKIRM° SKUM*" were sloppily spray painted above its missing dome. All of a sudden Desolin suddenly felt much less hospitable.

"I've finished retrieving Desolin's city-wide grid," CareE piped up. "It's archaic, but I've modified the pertinent data to work with your HUD's interface. Would you like directions to the nearest liquor store and/or gun shop?"

"Actually, what I need is a—"

"*Shots and Shotguns* has a two and half star rating, best in the city, and is 1.7 km away. They are currently offering a two for one d—"

"No, no. Find me someone who deals with scrap, specifically Frames. The darker the market the better."

"Searching, please wait. Desolin's network is suspiciously congested. Okay, I could only find these establishments that fit your requested parameters."

"Show me," I said. A handful of repair shops came into view, their positions projected onto a cartoonish 3D canvas. I headed to the closest one, *Fried Electronics*.

The crowded sidewalk was a minefield of open sandals and missing toes. I tried my best to avoid bumping into anyone, but despite my efforts I collided with a distracted, heavyset man.

"Watch out, tin-bin," the large man said without giving me a second look. He went back to talking loudly into a small tablet that he held against his sweaty head. From across the street, a small group of teens were pointing at me and laughing.

Just ignore them, I thought. *Mind your business.* I put my head down and kept moving—the less interaction I had, the better.

When I arrived at the first store, the elderly owner was less than thrilled about letting me in.

"We only buy. And we don't deal with Frames," her voice said over an intercom from behind a blacked-out window. "So be on your way."

"It won't take long, I'm just looking for someone you may have heard of—"

"You got three seconds! One . . . two . . ." I heard her fiddling with some heavy weaponry behind the glass. That was all the encouragement I needed to be on my way. I moved on to the next location on the list.

"*When one door closes, another opens,*" CareE said, encouragingly. "A commonly used idiom from the late nineteenth century popularized by serial murderer H.H. Holmes."

The city felt exhausted and wide awake at the same time, like pulling an all nighter then catching your fourth wind at the end of the day. Most of the fleshies—people—just went about their business ignoring me, but every couple of blocks or so I'd get a side eye or stern look. Every other storefront sold the same assortment of crap—portable speakers with obnoxious LEDs, bright t-shirts, and a wide-array of weaponry. Occasionally I'd see another Frame offloading cargo or moving heavy gear. They were all older units—either Pawns or Bishops—but unlike my Rook, they were clothed, and often heavily decorated with fluorescent tattooed designs covering their exposed areas. Some of the busier storefronts and clubs used them as security, each one narrowing their gaze and squeezing their sidearms whenever someone walked by. A closer look revealed that each one had metal rabbit-like antennas affixed to the back of their heads.

"Shortwave radio, from the looks of it," CareE said.

"Are you reading my mind?" I asked.

"Of course not, don't be silly," he said. "I simply scanned your ocular input and brainwave patterns, sensed curiosity, then provided an answer."

234

"All right," I said. "But don't read my mind."

"Understood."

Scrapland, the next location on CareE's list, was buried deep within an open market housed in a crumbling old sports arena. The stadium's original seats had been ripped out to make space on the tiers for merchants to sit and sell. Thousands of people milled about, looking for a great deal on whatever wares they needed, and everywhere you looked, buyers and sellers argued loudly with one another.

"Last week it was only thirty crypts!"

"Well now it's forty-five. If you don't like it, sod off!"

"Thirty-five crypts—that's all I got."

"Deal. Pleasure doing business."

"Fuck you."

I double checked the waypoint, seeing it directed me towards section 42F, near the nosebleeds. As I climbed the steep, foot-worn stairs, I combed through some of the store's reviews. Apparently *Scrapland* was a respectable establishment, "Frame friendly," with unbeatable prices. The owner, Phil Passes, was cited as one of the nicest people in Desolin, and was a philanthropist in the community. Five hundred steps and a charley horse later, I came upon 42F and a makeshift tent, torn and battered from years of use. As I pulled the front curtain open, a bald, stocky figure emerged from the tent, pushing past me.

"Fuckin' toaster, move outta the way," he said in a huff, making his way down the stairs.

I gave the rude man a gentle wave, then poked my head inside to look around. It was a cozy shoppe with lots of old-world tech and collectibles locked in steel cages. There were digital projectors and bulky back massagers and the first (failed) attempts at glasses integrated with search engines, then in the center of the room there was an old sitdown arcade cabinet with a spaceship painted on the side, not working, but a great place to hold liquor and maybe a fern. And finally there was the famous shop owner, Phil, on the other side of the room, tied to a chair with a bullet hole in his left temple, dripping blood onto a cardboard sign draped around his neck: *Pay on time a$$hole.*

"Would you like to leave a review?" CareE asked.

"No, I don't think so."

The next stop on my list was just outside the stadium. Its rating was much lower than those of the previous two, so naturally I had high hopes for it. Before leaving *Scrapland,* I picked out a sling for my arm and some clothes to help me blend in better with the outside crowd. I didn't think the late Phil Passes would mind too much. In the back of the tent I found a pair of baggy pants that fit tightly around the ankles, a loose-fitting hooded sweater that said *Scrapland Scrapper,* and some stark-white running shoes. My right foot burst through the toe of the sneaker immediately when I put it on, but I kind of liked the way it looked.

When I got to the shop, there wasn't a sign or even a name out front, and from the outside it almost looked empty, but that wasn't surprising for a place wedged between two strip clubs. I ducked in, checking out the bits of scrap and wares for sale, pretending to just be another customer looking around. The burnt plastic smell of old circuit boards soaked the air, and there were countless bins with pieces of loose wire splaying out like weeds.

"Looking for something specific?" A Frame said, walking out from behind a wall divider. The Pawn was of medium height and quite old, and it hadn't been customized like most of the others I'd seen. Instead of rabbit ears, this one was hardlined to the ceiling. A dozen neatly wrapped wire cables followed it as it stomped around the room.

"I'm looking for someone, actually," I said.

"We can help with that, yes," the Pawn said, emotionless.

"What can you tell me about the person who made this?" I said, pulling out the charred Mantis chip from my jacket pocket. The Pawn's ocular sensors widened.

"I see, follow me." The Frame moved back behind the divider and pressed a button, opening a door that had been camouflaged to blend in with the wall. The Pawn gestured for me to enter first, displaying a level of etiquette I hadn't experienced yet in the city.

We stepped through the door and I heard the familiar sound of a magnetic lock activate from behind. At first the room was dark, lit only by the faint green glow of an emergency backup light, but fluorescent ceiling lights kicked on after a moment and I saw that this space was much larger than the one I'd just left. Tidier, too. It housed only a bed and a workbench where a thin, pale man wearing only pants slumped before three wall-mounted displays. He noticed me and got up, removing his headset and stretching his aging limbs. From the looks of things, it was the first time he had stood up in a long while.

"Prox," he said, raising his hand. "Nice to meet you. Coffee?"

"Uh, I'm good, thanks."

"Suit yourself." Prox shuffled over to a makeshift kitchen, popped in a coffee tube, and started his brew. "Been here long or newly defected?" He asked.

"Neither."

"Mystery man. All right." He pointed to a small grouping of chairs next to his workstation beneath a window that simulated daylight. "Wanna sit?"

"Sure," I said. The flimsy chair creaked beneath my weight. I felt my body slump from exhaustion—the lack of sleep was starting to catch up with me. Again.

Prox took a sip, observing. "Pardon my asking, but it's just not every day I see one of *you* in the city, especially this part of town. What brings you here, mystery man?"

"Rather not say. The less you know the better, I'm guessing." I took a breath, choosing my words carefully. "Basically, my employer screwed up and I need to find someone who can help."

"Hmm, big boys rarely make mistakes. Sloppy sometimes, yes, but . . ." He considered for a moment. "Okay, I'm interested. May I see it?" he asked, reaching out his hand.

I forked over the Mantis chip and he looked it over, studying it closely.

"So you know a lot about Frame tech?" I asked.

"Some. Hard to stay current. You guys put out more new models every year—pretty impossible to keep up. Only get to work on what the people bring in, cha'dig?" Prox said, eyeing my Frame a little too intimately.

"You build the one out there, in the lobby?" I said, trying to change the subject.

"Ha, no, repairs only. That's one of the older models, back when they still needed to be plugged in to hold a charge. My bones just ain't what they used to be, easier to work when you can strap into a Rig. Safer, too. Where did you say you got this again?" The man asked, still focused on the chip.

"Third party. Never got a name."

"You know what this thing does, right? Gotta be careful with that shit."

"Yeah, I'll keep that in mind," I said. I must have sounded more sarcastic than I meant to, because he looked back at me with an annoyed expression.

"Ya know, I'm pretty busy, and I don't work with smart asses. If you have something better to do, I suggest you go do it." He threw the chip back into my lap.

"Sorry, didn't mean to be rude," I said. "I just need to find the person who made that chip and I'll be gone." I handed the Mantis back to him.

"Would you like me to order you some *KavaJava*™ to help with those stress levels?" CareE asked. I ignored him.

"Fine, who signed it?" Prox asked. "Maybe I know them."

"You wouldn't believe me if I told you. Look for yourself."

The malnourished shopkeeper looked back at me with a twinkle of excitement and curiosity—I was speaking his language again. He placed the chip on his workbench, activating a holo overlay, and tapped on his glasses. The data on his monitors mirrored the digital spread of information that was beamed to his retinas. There were billions of little boxes, each containing a single letter or number, and

238

every box was connected to an infinite number of other boxes by a thin line. The entire readout seemed to ripple like a wave. This was the Mantis code. I noticed there were huge gaps in the waves, which were filled with random dots and dashes.

"Hmm, the circuit is all sorts of fried, looks pretty bad, but . . . ya, I see something still moving on the vRAM." He stopped and eyed me, looking a little impressed. A smile spread across his face as he went back to digging.

"Can you recover anything from it?" I asked.

"Depends. How much ya got?" he said. He paused the scan and smirked at me. I pulled out my wad of crypts and threw it on the table. Prox took it and counted, his grin fading.

"Don't have any more, do ya?"

"Afraid not."

"Not sure I can help you. *Unless . . .*"

"What?"

"I'll give you the data, but I want the chip. Deal?"

I remembered what the guys said before leaving me alone in Desolin. The Mantis had been nothing but trouble, but there was still a part of me on it, and I felt like Prox was asking me to give up a chunk of my soul.

"Let's talk about it later," I said. "Maybe we can work something out."

Prox looked disappointed, but the prospect of snooping on [Name] seemed to get the better of him. "Yeah, we'll talk later."

"Bargaining, the act of meeting in the middle. Also known as *Benjamin Buttoning*," CareE said.

"How much for a HUD wipe?" I asked Prox.

"More than what you got," he said, turning his attention back to the chip.

"Damn." I slumped my head back into the chair and let myself relax while the slender shopkeeper continued to dig.

Sleep was still impossible while I was logged into my Frame, so I slipped into another lucid, meditative trance. The room melted away and the roof opened up. Above me the sky darkened as slate-colored clouds rolled in, and thunder rumbled somewhere far off, the low bass line to the high treble of a Roman legionnaire's clinking armor as he tightened a strap around my legs. He and the rest of his regiment counted to three before hoisting me vertical on a hastily constructed crucifix. My chest muscles stretched and snapped from my weight, and I struggled to sip air a teaspoonful at a time. Shock washed over me and I felt a momentary break in the pain, allowing me to notice the smell of ripe olives and grape leaves coming into season. With great effort I tilted my head upward, and saw the countryside was beautiful, even with the rows of debtors, sodomites, and heretics lining the roads. To my left I saw Frimpter, passed out or maybe dead. To my right, Aarau, smiling back but unable to talk. I could tell from his face that he wanted me to know everything was okay. Euphoria flooded my heart, as if I had made peace with the world around me.

I closed my eyes for just a moment, feeling the wind sweep against my tattered loincloth. When I opened them again, a fifteen-foot Queen Frame stood before me. The slender machine was immaculate and sleek, as if carved from marble. As I admired its beauty, it edged closer, until it was only an arm's length away. I let my body relax the best I could—no need to be tense for this. A flash of white light passed from one side of its visor to the other, effortlessly cutting through my neck. My head slid forward and fell to the damp ground below, smacking the grass and bouncing a few times before it finally settled, gently wobbling. The Queen looked down at it curiously, like a child pulling the limbs off an insect. As my life slowly faded, I thought—

"Dr. Andrea DeBois believed the human head was capable of surviving without the body for up to eight seconds, but her theory has never been proven," CareE said. "May it serve as a fun fact to use at dinner parties and bar mitzvahs."

Not even my nightmares were safe from him.

I stood up and moved around my working limbs. Prox was still hunched over, combing through the data-miner. He looked concerned.

"How's it coming? Find anything?" I asked, yawning.

"Yes, but . . . I dunno. I'm reviewing again. It doesn't seem right." The shopkeeper's eyes narrowed at a specific line of code.

"Why? What is it?"

"If I'm reading right, it says that the chip was originally constructed here. In Desolin."

"[Name] is here?"

"Could be. The code's scrambled. Very messy."

"Anything else? A location or RP address?" I asked.

"Slow down, big guy, I'm looking, I'm looking." Prox had his electro pick out, peeling back micro layers from the chip, trying to suss out its secrets. "There!"

I squinted at the monitor readout and studied the waterfall of code. The first few digits of coordinates began to slowly reveal themselves. Prox was operating like a surgeon, digging deeper and deeper, concentrating hard on his task. A single drop of sweat appeared at the top of his forehead, then broke loose from its surface tension, and slid down and off his nose. I watched as it landed on the chip, shorting out his tool and blowing out the ceiling lights.

After a moment the backup generator kicked on and the lights flickered back to life, revealing a dancing stream of smoke rising from the charred Mantis chip.

"No refunds." Prox said, putting his hands up defensively. I took my money and the broken chip, then charged out of the shop.

The rest of the day I wandered aimlessly, looking for anything or anyone who could lead me to [Name]. Any mentions of the terrorist were met with confusion or dismissal, leaving me feeling hopeless. I had almost given up when I ran into a familiar face.

"That's the guy!" The tiny bald man from the tent in the stadium screamed from across the street. He was accompanied by two armed security Frames.

"You, Rook—stop right there!" One of the peace officers said through its modulated voice filter.

I bolted. The Frames took off in pursuit, firing at me indiscriminately, not interested in bringing me in. I ducked into a nearby gym filled with juiced-out boxers and cherry-red weight lifters with bursting neck veins. They all paused to take in the commotion of two cops chasing a rogue Frame. I hurdled over a weightlifter mid-rep, and he dropped the bar on his chest, huffing in pain. I tripped, rolled, and moved back into a full sprint, slamming through an emergency exit as I glanced back to see one of the peace officers shoulder charge through another weightlifter.

I dashed down the alley, hoping to lose them because I was in no condition to fight. Another volley of pulse munition whizzed past my right shoulder and I ducked behind a dumpster, trying to buy some time or think of an escape plan. Instead I resorted to bargaining. "Stop!" I screamed from behind cover. "I'm unarmed."

"Mr. Langley back there says otherwise. Says he saw you kill old Phil in his shop. Now come on out. No sense hurting others today," the officer said.

I looked around for any other way out, but the alley was a dead end, and I knew it was a lost cause. I stood up slowly, waving my one good arm.

"Both hands!" The second officer said, his heavy rifle aimed directly at my head. "Put 'em up."

"It's busted," I said, defeated.

"All right then. Turn around and back up."

I followed their instructions, moving backwards as calmly and deliberately as I could. The first officer slid a pair of magnetic cuffs around my wrists. As soon as they locked, a small EMP emission pulsed, bringing me to my knees.

"What's your name, guy?" one officer asked.

"It's Null. Listen, this is all—"

The officer cut me off and started talking into his comms. "Yeah, we got him . . . Yep . . . Witness ID'd . . . What? I dunno, we'll figure something out. We can try and match a gun to his ID or somethin'."

"Hey Dan, something's up with this one. He doesn't have an ID," the other officer said, scanning the back of my neck.

"Well shit, just put him down here and we'll call it self-defense."

"Okay. Where's the gat Langley gave us?"

"I believe you are being set up," CareE said calmly.

"Yeah, what gave you that idea?" I replied, desperately trying to pull the cuffs apart with my one working arm.

"Fuck, it's in here somewhere, gimme a sec," Officer Dan said, digging through his backpack.

"It is not my place to play judge, jury, or executioner, but in this situation I can vouch for your unquestionable innocence," CareE continued. "I feel that regardless of their intentions, these corrupt officials have failed to uphold their duty to protect and serve."

"Any suggestions?" I asked.

"Who you talkin' to? God?" Officer Dan laughed, turning to his partner. "How much you think we'll get for this one, Mick? Metal still looks good."

"I can re-route some of your Frame's power and help get you out of this," CareE said. "Would you like me to do that now?"

"Very much so."

"Very much, what?" Dan asked.

A second later my head fell limply forward and dangled as I stared at the ground. The numb sensation began to fade from my right arm, and slowly I could feel my fingers tingling with life. When I was ready, I balled them into a fist, and with a quick pull, the cuffs shattered into a thousand carbon fibers, falling like black snow on the alley's floor.

"Oh, shit!" Officer Dan said.

"Put him down!"

The world slowed to a crawl. Officer Dan made a desperate grab for his weapon. Mick had already pulled his, unleashing an explosion of iridescent smoke from the muzzle. I sidestepped the first volley, moving carefully between the heavy rounds, aiming for Mick's head with my arm. I could feel CareE making micro-adjustments, keeping me in line with the target. My fingers reached into Mick's face like a bowling ball, caving it in. His body went limp, the last of his shots firing erratically into the alley.

Just as Mick's lifeless Frame hit the floor, CareE restored power to my neck, and my right arm dropped to my side. Officer Dan made a run for it, but before he'd gone four feet I fast-balled Mick's empty gun into his back, snapping Dan in half and destroying his power pack.

"That was helpful, thank you," I said to CareE.

"I am always learning!" he replied.

"Yer . . . fuckin' . . . dead, Rook." Officer Dan's Frame sputtered out before collapsing on its face. A second later, it emitted a high-pitched siren. *We-oooHH! Officer down. We-oooHH! Officer down.*

"Get us outta here," I said.

It was dusk and it had started to rain in the city. Most of the day shops were closed now, passing the torch to the nighttime haunts. I watched as food vendors readied for the dinner rush, prepping sides and carryout boxes. Noodle bars and imitation fried chicken seemed to be the most popular choices among the people of Desolin.

I wished I had any choices at that moment, food or otherwise. My chances of finding [Name] had disappeared with the toasted Mantis, and now I was more lost than when I arrived. Countless thoughts began to run through my exhausted mind.

How did Frames make money in Desolin?

Did I have enough rust resistance on?

Was [Name] even real?

I ducked into a quiet café, but quickly wished I hadn't. Inside, a holoscreen displayed my face with a scrolling list of offenses and information. Well, not *my* face, but my Rook's face. It must have been a mark Officer Mick took moments before I turned his head inside out. The reward was only 100K, but it didn't matter: there was a target on my back. CareE could sense my stress, and kept trying to direct me towards massage parlors and suicide prevention/encouragment centers.

The rain was starting to get really heavy, so I moved towards a Frame-friendly hostel, the *Electric Sleep*. The lobby was only a step above squalor, but it was dry, and that was all that mattered.

A mohawk-sporting Pawn was slumped in the corner recharging while a group of fleshies sat in the lobby inside makeshift Rigs, watching something that had them chuckling. I paid the front desk clerk twenty crypts for the night and found a quiet corner on top of some old trash. I lay down on my side, contemplating my next move.

"How are you feeling, Null? You seem down," CareE said.

"I don't know. Definitely not good. Seems like it's always one step forward, a thousand steps back."

"I think we made some progress today, don't you? We saw the city, met all sorts of new people, and now we have a warm floor to call our own."

"I guess that's a net positive," I said. "Still, I got a price on my head, and I'm not really sure what I'm doing here." The self-pity was starting to creep up again.

"Can I interest you in a story?" CareE asked. "It might help you make light of this situation."

"Not really in the mood," I said, closing my eyes as I rolled into a fetal position.

"Have you heard the story of the Turk? The chess playing automaton?"

"No. Please shut up."

"Excellent. Let me take you back to the year 1770 AD. The Hungarian inventor Wolfgang Von Kempelen had created a machine to entertain the Archduchess of Austria, Maria Theresa. Maria had grown bored and wanted something new, something that would change the world. Wolfgang gave her just that—the Turk. The Turk was one of the first-ever artificial intelligences and is cited as the inspiration behind modern computing."

"They had computers back then?" I asked.

"Not quite. But more on that later. The Turk was an enormous wooden box with a chessboard on top, and an android that looked like the upper torso of a turbaned man sticking out. It traveled all around the world baffling those who dared challenge it to a game of chess. It's said that the workings of the machine drove Edgar Allen Poe mad, which then drove him to syphilis, which then drove him to death."

"Wait, so was it a person or a machine? How did it work?" CareE's bedtime story was tickling my curiosity.

"No one really knows. Popular theorists thought that perhaps a series of mirrors were used to fool participants. It wasn't until the mid 19th century, when Poe's personal physician, John Kearsley Mitchell, purchased the Turk that its true secrets were revealed. Mitchell obsessed over the automaton for years, taking it apart and putting it back together. Mitchell never ended up finding an answer, but his wife did.

"Unbeknownst to Mitchell, his assistant, Jacques Bisset, had been railing his wife for some time. And in 1854, the greatest secret of the Turk was finally revealed . . . by accident. During a particularly special weekend of raunchy love-making, Mrs. Mitchell was shocked to hear that her husband had come home early. She told Jacques to hide inside the Turk, where he subsequently found a hidden compartment within the ceramic mannequin. Apparently his lean and petite figure fit comfortably inside the Turk, so he waited there for Mr. Mitchell to depart.

"But John Mitchell had exciting news for his wife—the Chinese Museum in Baltimore had purchased the Turk, and a section of the building would be dedicated to the love of his life, Edgar Allan Poe. Mitchell and his wife fought all through the evening, arguing about the true nature of his relationship to the dead writer. Eventually the museum officials showed up and took the Turk away, placing it inside the museum exhibit. Later that night, the museum burned down when a nearby building caught fire. Witnesses on the street below swore they could hear cries of pain."

"So Jacques stayed in the Turk," I said. "Was he stuck or something?"

"No one knows, but that's not the point of this story," CareE said. "The point here is that you are now thinking about a sexy French man burning inside an 18th-century mechanical robot instead of wallowing in your own self-pity. Don't you feel better?"

I couldn't help but laugh. "Hey, CareE?" I said.

"Yes?"

"That was a good story, thanks."

CareE was silent the rest of the evening, and I finally had a solid night's rest. When I woke up, I noticed my sneakers had been stolen and my pants were half ripped off. My money was still tucked away inside my breastplate, though, and I had a clear head for the first time in days. When the simulated sleep faded from my eyes, I saw a blinking message in my HUD. I opened it, and there were several quick flashes before the text became clear.

From: unknown

Subject: You have something of mine. Let's meet.

-[Name]

LOG FOURTEEN

I knocked on the steel door as indiscreetly as I could—for the third time—but again there was no answer. This couldn't be the right place. I checked the follow-up message one more time:

```
From: unknown
Subject: Menchik's

Noon. Door's open. Don't be late.

-[Name]
```

Squeezing the door release still did nothing. I stepped back and looked at the storefront jammed between all the other shops in Desolin's bustling main market. The sign was caked in dirt and faded, but it was the same name and spelling as what was in the message: MENCHIK'S. Nothing on the building said what the place was or did, and the two polycarbonate windows were blacked out.

"I have information that may help your situation," CareE said to me.

"Finally you do something. What is it?"

"I've done an analysis and concluded that it is now 12:05 p.m." he said.

"Goddamnit."

I went back to the door and pressed the handle in again, but this time I threw my shoulder into it. The alloy from my Frame made a dense gong noise against the old steel. I slammed myself into it again, and again. Dirt and flakes of neglect fell from the upper wall, landing on my head. The third time I thought I felt the metal budge a little. Fourth time was the ticket in.

"Hey!"

I spun around and saw a Desolin security Frame standing in the middle of the street with his head tilted. I quickly turned to the wall again, keeping my back to him so he couldn't fully see my face.

"If it's locked, it's closed," the Frame said. "Go away."

"Sorry," I said, speaking over my shoulder. "Do you know if there's another Menchik's around here?"

"I do know," the Frame said. "Now fuck off."

"Please? It'd really help me out."

"I'm not here to help you," the Frame said, producing some sort of EMP baton I'd never seen before, opaque with a green glowing rod running up the center, pulsing with a faint, high whine. It was obviously heavy shit, and being on the business end might mean no more Null.

"Move. Now. Or I'm scrapping you."

"All right! I'm leaving, okay?" I said. "What's your problem?"

He rushed me, wildly swinging his baton at my torso. I dove out of the way and landed in a pile of street rubbish. I got my footing just in time to dodge him again. But there was nowhere to go. I collided against the building. He reeled back for the final jab, lurched forward—and froze in place.

When he didn't do anything for a second, I crept forward to see what was going on. Maybe he'd lost power? I was inches from his face when his eyes shot to life, emitting a soft green hue.

"This one's a real bastard," the Frame spoke, but its voice sounded different.

I stumbled back against the wall with my fists up.

"It's fine," the Frame said. This voice was soft and modulated. It sounded Swedish, or Dutch. Maybe German. I wasn't very good with accents.

"What is this?" I said.

"The interrogative you're looking for is 'who', Null," the former security Frame said, easing out of its attack pose and settling into a more relaxed footing. Even its body language seemed more friendly now.

"[Name]?"

"As you live and breathe."

"You're a security guard?"

"For now. Until our friend figures out what's going on. Let's walk." [Name] started off down the packed street, slicing through the crowd. I hopped up and met her flank.

"I thought I was meeting you in person," I said.

"Nothing against you, Null, but that will never happen."

"I think this is the fastest I've ever been rejected."

"I doubt that's true," [Name] said, veering to the right down another busy street. I knocked over a couple of shoppers as I tried to keep up. "There are quite a few people who wouldn't mind swatting a fly like me, so this is how it is."

"You think I'm one of them?" I said.

"Maybe. Your dumb demeanor could just be an act."

"I promise it isn't."

"We'll see."

She hung a left and headed toward a seedier area of the block. Women danced in windows on both sides of the street, wearing fiber optic micro-kinis and bathed in rosy red LED light.

"I'm attempting to connect with [Name]," CareE said. "But every ping brings up the same rude response."

"What's that?" I said.

"A large hermaphrodite holding an 'access denied' sign."

"Doesn't sound that rude," I said.

"You can't see how they're holding the sign," CareE said.

"Having fun with the help?" [Name] mused.

"It's harmless," I said.

"Aren't they all. What is it? *A-vail? Leso? bOggle?*

"CareE."

"CareE?" [Name] said, curiously. "Haven't heard of that one. You install that with your Mantis chip?"

"No way," I said. "A sockmaker installed it. Well, him and his partner did, I guess. The partner sold meth."

"Right," [Name] said, stopping at the edge of the street. Transports zipped past us from both directions. "You know, you—this Rook, I mean—it shouldn't be here right now. Once you overload a Mantis, that's it. It's probably the second best way to kill a Frame."

"What's the first?"

"Me."

[Name] quickly sidestepped into the street and sat down in front of an oncoming transport. The Frame's head went limp for a moment, the green glow fading from the ocular sensors, then it powered back to life.

"What the . . . " it said in the gruff security man's voice. He looked up just in time to see the charging transporter grille. "Oh, sh—!" The vehicle smacked him into the asphalt and rolled the Frame's old alloy around the axles, spitting it out the back into a worthless heap.

I stared at the pile as transporter after transporter flattened it a little more. Some time went by, and I started to realize that [Name] wasn't coming back. Guess that was all the great and mysterious [Name] had to tell me—that I shouldn't be here. How enlightening. Somehow I'd known this would be a waste of time, just like everything else.

I looked around to try and get my bearings and start figuring out a way back home. But then I heard a soft knocking behind me. There was a woman in a negligee, dancing seductively in one of the red windows, beckoning me over with a finger.

"No thank you," I said, shaking my head. I went back to retracing the walk. *We made a right, then a left, then I think it was a–*

"Null, get in here," the woman from the window said, sticking her head outside the door.

Once inside, she closed the curtains and I took in the room. It was tiny, with just a wash area, a vanity, and a twin bed with a flat white sheet. Everything was a soft red from the recessed light, reminding me of the Italian bases I used to paint.

[Name] sat cross-legged on a chair. I followed the skin of her synthetic thigh down to her calf, landing at her ankle, next to which sat a small, fluffy, purple dog. It was cute, but then I noticed it had strange, off-white eyes. Almost like it was blind.

"Nice pooch," I said. "Does it do any tricks? Or just its mommy?"

"You don't have a clue what I'm capable of," [Name] said flatly.

"I can tell you have the voodoo body snatcher thing down."

[Name] ran its hands along the curves of the Real Girl. "The Frames and bots on these seedy RMZ networks are nothing. Just connecting some dots in a decentralized network."

"What about in SKIRM®? You ever do that?"

"Of course," [Name] stood up and examined herself in front of the mirror. She raised up on her tiptoes and twisted her torso so she could see her butt. It was hypnotizing.

"But that costs extra," she went on. "Going all the way in the real world carries more risk." [Name] abandoned the mirror and slinked slowly towards me. "But risk or not, if it runs on ones and zeroes, I can penetrate it."

"Oh," I said, feeling the heat of her body radiating. "That's good."

"Except you," [Name] said. "For some reason I can't get inside you."

"Finally I'm the one that's hard to read," I said nervously. [Name] chuckled and edged closer to me. Little hints of lavender wafted from her hair, making my knees weak.

"Null," CareE spoke up. "I've noticed a change in your thinking process. Specifically that it's stopped."

"Not now," I said under my breath.

"Only a verrrrrrrrry small part of your limbic lobe is functioning," CareE said. "And some thoughts are originating from somewhere I can't even trace."

"Shut up!"

"Who are you, Null?" [Name] said, slowly teasing up her negligee. "Be honest."

"I'm just someone trying to log off," I said.

"And you need me to help you . . . log off?" [Name] purred.

"Y—Yes."

"I think I can do that," she said, smiling. She slid her negligee up and over her head, revealing four perfect breasts. Her eyes looked deep into mine as she closed the distance and pressed herself against me. "Do you have the chip?"

"I do," I said, fumbling with my storage slot. I pulled it out and held it for her to see.

"That's good," she said, yanking my head down to hers. Her lips drew in and pressed against my Frame's mouth opening. My body felt a thousand pounds heavier as I reveled in the kiss and the way her ersatz skin felt as it grazed my metal. Then I felt a wet tickling at my fingertips that made me tingle all over. This woman was incredible. I looked down from the kiss to my hand to see the source of the ecstasy, and saw the purple dog snatch the chip in its mouth and bolt for the door.

Suddenly the woman shoved away from me. "The fuck?" she yelled, looking me up and down. I saw the confusion in her eyes and knew [Name] was gone.

"You're thinking normally again," CareE said.

"Shit!"

I ran out the door, searching for the mutt. There were hundreds of people in every direction, an endless sea of bobbing heads. But then, two blocks away, a person jerked up and snapped their eyes to the ground. Then another did the same. I exploded toward them, pushing people out of the way, not even looking at what was in my path. I closed a block in a dozen strides, homing in on the reactions of the crowd in front.

"Fuck . . . somebody stomp that thing!" a guy shouted up ahead.

Another woman shrieked as she stutter stepped.

I pushed harder as I reeled the fluffy dog in, shoving a few more bystanders out of the way until I got to an abrupt break in the crowd. The little dog wasn't in front of me anymore. I searched like a hawk, looking for any place it could have gone. Behind me there was a narrow side street. I ran back to it and poked my head in. Thirty yards off I saw a tiny purple butt scurrying away.

"[Name]!" I screamed. The dog looked back, then started pumping its little legs even faster. I sprinted for it.

"Don't worry, Null," CareE said over the sound of my pounding feet. "I'm redirecting all power to your legs. You should be able to catch this three-pound dog in no time!"

"I don't . . . need this . . . now," I said, huffing.

The dog juked around a sharp corner. I did the same, and ran into hundreds of residents jammed together in a plaza, watching a wild-eyed man in an antique straitjacket trying to get out of it. People were shouting at him and cheering, waving decrypts above their heads, not paying attention to anything else. I searched frantically for any signs of the dog, but nobody was moving. When I tried to push people out of the way and part the crowd, a dozen angry faces turned on me and shoved me back with mob brute force. I regained my footing right as the crowd started counting down from ten, watching the straitjacket man struggle in vain. But when they got to seven, the man stopped wriggling and a twisted smile spread across his face. He bent one of his arms impossibly far back. Then a loud pop echoed across the crowd. People retched and gasped, but then the man started shimmying the jacket over his head. The gasps turned to cheers as he slid out. People from the crowd threw money at him as they dispersed. Most everyone had left the plaza after a few moments, and it was easy to see the purple dog was long gone.

I eased to the ground and sat, trying to figure out what to do next. The entire situation was completely my fault. CareE had been right— I didn't think, and now I was paying for it.

"Thank you for thinking that," CareE said.

No problem, I thought.

There was no use sulking here. I got up and started heading back to the hostel. As I left the plaza, I accidentally bumped into a mother walking by with her little boy.

"Sorry," I said, moving out of the way.

The mother just nodded and kept going. They got a few feet down the road when I overheard the boy speak.

"So I can keep it if nobody says anything?" he said.

"I'm sure someone will," said the mom.

I stopped and looked back at the two of them walking away. The boy was peering into a small knapsack draped over his shoulder.

"But what if they don't?" he said.

"Trake . . . " the mom said.

"Can we at least wait to post something?" he said. "She's so cute."

"We'll wait a day."

"Yes!"

I calmly walked up behind them and lifted the knapsack from the boy's shoulder.

"Hey—!"

I slammed the knapsack into the curb.

"Oh my god!" the mom shrieked.

I slammed it again. And again, and again, and again. Squishy, wet noises squeaked out of the bag every time it smacked the ground. The boy fell to his knees sobbing as the mom clutched him, trying to lift him up. I turned the bag over and emptied out the bits of dog onto the sidewalk. I snatched up its severed head and looked in its mouth, then shoved my fingers down its silicone neck. There were servos and actuators, but no Mantis. I sifted through the rest of the purple fluff and pieces of circuitry, but didn't find anything.

"When you found this dog, did it have something in its mouth?" I said to the mom.

"Fuck you!" she screamed.

"What about you, young man?" I said.

He sobbed violently. By now a crowd was starting to form, so I chucked the rest of the dog into the street and briskly walked away.

"Would you like to hear an interesting fact?" CareE said.

"Yeah, I guess so," I said, picking up the pace.

"Children who experience a significant traumatic episode are twice as likely to develop cancer as adults, and three times as likely to abuse alcohol."

"Thanks for the info." I crossed the street, looking up through the haze at the sinking sun. It was probably smart to get back before dark. Who knows what kind of awfulness I'd run into traipsing through this city's shadows. I put my head down and settled in for the long walk back.

"Null, I'm detecting something strange on the immediate network," CareE piped up.

"What is it?" I said.

"It's you."

"Me?"

"Well, traces of you. They're small signatures and identifiers . . . but they're unmistakably you."

"I don't understand. What—"

"Head north now!" CareE said.

I did as I was told, obeying with caution. I wasn't used to taking orders from voices inside my head, but as far as I could tell, the AI seemed genuinely determined to get me to my destination. After another block I swung a right immediately, heading down a tight thoroughfare.

"In twenty yards head east. Hurry!"

I double-timed and pivoted right. Up ahead a hundred yards or so there was another busy road. I sprinted as hard as I could.

"The ping distance is getting further. You have to go faster," CareE said.

"I can't go faster," I said, pushing every bit of energy I could through the Frame.

"Wait, the ping is getting nearer all of a sudden. Keep going this way."

I did as I was told, reeling in the unknown object.

"We're almost at the ping," CareE said. "It's practically right here—"

A transport eased to a stop on the side of the road, cutting us off. The side door slid open. It was empty. I looked around me, but it was clear that this ride wasn't for anyone else.

My parents had always discouraged me from getting into a stranger's car unless I had no other choice. With so few options at my disposal, I figured I could risk the potential abduction.

I stepped in and got comfortable. The transport's interior lights came up, soaking everything in soft azure blue. We cruised for a bit in silence, and I watched Desolin at dusk pass by the windows.

"Your little helper is quite clever," [Name]'s modulated voice boomed from speakers hidden in the cabin.

"Such a nice compliment," CareE whispered to me.

"No he's not," I said to [Name]. "I mean he is, but he isn't. You could have been long gone from here. Why'd you come back?"

"Because I'd rather not have another spectre torturing my conscience," [Name] said. "I have enough of those."

"Is that what I am?" I said. "A ghost?"

"No," [Name] said. "Actually, quite the opposite."

"What are you talking about?"

"You're alive and well, Null. In the *real* world."

"Wait, how did you–"

"While you were running around town, killing dogs and traumatizing families, I was scanning your chip. Well, *my* chip. You're safe."

"You found me? Where?"

"There's a hospital near where you live—"

"St. Francis," I said.

"Yes. They've had you in the ICU there since they found you."

"Am I . . . you know . . . okay?" I said.

"You mean, are you a piece of produce?" [Name] chuckled. "You're fine. They found you almost immediately, which is good. No trace of Frame Brain."

I felt relieved. "Who found me?"

"I think it was a relative."

"Was it my brother? Aarau?"

"Yes, that was the name on the intake record. Listen, Null. I want to help, I just need some more time. And if I'm getting you out of this mess, I'm also going to need something from you."

I considered it for a moment. It was a deal with a terrorist mastermind, which usually wasn't my speed, but after becoming a fugitive and killing a dog in front of a small boy, I figured I might as well go with it and see this trip through.

"Yeah, I'm all yours," I said. "What do you need?"

"When the time is right, I'll find you. Lie low and wait until you hear from me. Oh, and before you go . . ." An armrest extended from the cushioned seat, and small, metal tentacles wrapped themselves around my limp arm and started probing. As soon as I tried to struggle, the tentacles retreated back into the seatrest.

"What the hell are you doing," I said, yanking my arm away, realizing I was back in control. "Hey, you fixed it."

"I can do much more than that." The transport stopped in front of the *Electric Sleep* and the door opened with a loud THUNK. I stepped out to the filthy sidewalk and watched as the car took off and disappeared into the steam of Desolin. Night was creeping in, and with it I could feel a host of nasty characters coming out of their dens, ready to have a little fun.

The bright blue neon sign of the hostel cast an angelic glow on everything beneath. Maybe there was redemption inside.

LOG FIFTEEN

[N]ame] had booked me an actual, bonafide room in the *Electric Sleep,* which gave me a chance to really appreciate the building's awfulness. It was a dreary five-story hostel made mostly of cheap crumbling concrete, sitting on the edge of a large square in the middle of Desolin. One of the other guests had told me that many decades ago it was a government apartment building for people in the city before the area became the RMZ. Now, according to [Name], this leaky relic filled with black mold was my new home—temporarily, at least.

The specific recorded instructions I found in my room were, "Don't leave. Don't go outside. You do, you're fucked." It somehow sounded harsher in her voice, but it was still probably just as right—there was a bounty on my head, and plenty of people were looking to collect.

I was on the fifth floor in room forty-two, overlooking the square and the swarm of society's shunned skittering about in the night drizzle. My dark room glowed from a swirl of pink, orange, and blue light coming from the makeshift halogen street lamps and LED shop signs outside. From my seat next to the window, I had a clear view of the large pedestal in the middle of the square that served as the base for a massive bronze statue without a head. At that moment, a pigeon was perched just inside the neck of the statue, periodically peeking out at the people below, looking like a monstrous bird-man robot with a tiny head. Every little bob and peck he did made me laugh, breaking up the monotony of staying in my little box.

A gunshot popped off, then another, echoing through the square and sending the pigeon racing off into the night sky. A group of fleshies appeared from an alley and sprinted across the damp pavement through the idle crowd, who didn't seem to care about them or the noises. I wasn't sure if the runners were the ones who shot, or if they were fleeing from the ones who did. They made it across without a good samaritan stopping them and rounded a corner, their frantic clopping fading as they disappeared into some other part of the city.

Little bursts of gunplay like that had been pretty common the last few nights, but this was the first time I'd seen some physical, human connection to the sounds. I generally assumed that most fleshies in the RMZ were armed with some sort of gun, and it was only natural, given the sheer number of them, that shots would be fired every few hours. Actually, it would be strange—frightening even—if there wasn't gunfire periodically, because it would mean the fleshies in Desolin were taking out their frustrations with knives or bare hands. That kind of intimate, personal violence can lead to societal hiccups.

"I believe we were told that 'fleshie' is a derogatory term," CareE said.

"I'm just saying it to myself," I said.

"I don't think that makes a difference," he said.

"Why don't you just take some time off?" I said, going back to my window view.

Even though I saw some strange things while people watching from room forty-two, most of the scenes in Desolin were made up of typical going-about-your-day moments. There was the mother with two kids who dragged in a cart filled with lemons to sell to passersby, the elderly group who did power laps around the street with their bionic walking shorts swishing about, and the savant with the chess board who would set up in the same spot each afternoon and coldly defeat anyone who attempted to play him. Whoever or whatever edited *RMZ Live* every day really did God's work, because this crap was boring to sit through.

At that moment, towards the far end of the square, a large group of fleshies appeared towing a mangled, burnt Knight Frame on a flatbed trailer. They were talking excitedly and laughing as the hunk of useless titanium and electronics bounced and swayed from the uneven ground. When they got near the headless statue, they dumped the Frame onto the pavement, and immediately fleshies swarmed in to pry at it with their hands and whatever tools they had, salvaging pieces for their off-network Frames, or maybe just the materials to build something else. A sunburnt man with stringy hair drifted over and casually looked at all the fuss, swaying a little on his unsteady feet, then without warning he pulled his pants down and started to piss on the Knight's head. Someone immediately yelled and shoved him away, but the sunburnt man wouldn't be defeated so easily, and pointed his golden stream at the defender, causing him and the others to jump back, which opened up the rest of the Knight for territorial marking. The man stared everyone in the eyes as he slowly made his way around the Frame, covering it with his seemingly endless urine supply.

I wondered where the owner of the Knight was now. Probably sitting in the SKIRM® helpdesk waiting room surrounded by mouth-breathers, waiting to argue with tech support about salvage costs and liability.

Good luck getting that one running, buddy. It's got serious flood damage. The thought made me laugh, but then after a moment it wasn't so funny, because every bit of me wished I was able to sit in that awful room. According to the Warden, Null Lasker didn't exist; I was just a rogue, blank Frame. And blank Frames don't get to use tech support—or log out, apparently. [Name] said she could help me in the latter regard, which I knew meant getting back on the SKIRM® network somehow, but what she couldn't help me with was the trouble I'd be in when they started snooping around my logs. I couldn't just pop back into the system without raising a few flags. They'd want to know what the deal was. And it wouldn't take long for them to find a reason to send me right back to the RMZ in the flesh.

The crowd (and the pisser) had mostly dispersed from the scavenged Knight, and as I stared at it I realized I'd have to take everything one step at a time, and the first step was to not end up like *him* so I could properly log out and save myself from . . . damn, what was that thing called again?

"Frame Brain," CareE chimed in.

"Thanks," I said. "Wait, how do you know that?"

"Reading. Your logs are kind of scrambled, but I think I can piece it together. You know, it could make for a decent kids' book or something. Young adult, maybe. Can you draw?"

Back home I could always drown out my inner-monologue with booze and VREs. But CareE was unrelenting.

"Some of this stuff is pretty incriminating," he went on. "Why did you log *everything*?"

"I don't know," I said. "It was easier to let the compiler do it for me every day. Guess I forgot to turn it off."

"That's a terrible excuse."

"I know. I'm fucked, aren't I?"

"Oh, yeah. Definitely."

Down in the square, away from my problems, something caught my eye, or rather, *someone*. A man who turned just as I spotted him. It was so quick, just one of those 1/100th-of-a-second glimpses your eye doesn't really see, but your brain does. Something about him triggered a deep memory dive. I watched him hurry down a narrow street. Even from the back he looked familiar, I thought, something about his posture and the subtle details of his figure.

"Do you know him?" CareE asked.

"Maybe, I don't know," I said, straining to connect the neurons. This man had been important to my life in some way, I just had that uncanny feeling in my gut. I threw on a cloak and made my way to the front door.

"What are you doing?" CareE cried. "[Name] said stay!"

"I need to see that guy's face," I said, pushing through the front door and into the hallway.

Outside, I wove and serpentined in the direction of the mystery man, trying not to let him open up his lead any further. He zipped around a corner and out of sight, so I sprinted for the spot and hugged the wall when I got there, peeking around to see him about twenty yards away. I kept close to the building faces and storefronts as I pursued him, doing my best to stay in his blind spots. The guy was really moving, letting himself break out into those little jogging sprints that people do when they're really late for something and feeling guilty. He hung a hard left and I double-timed to the spot, moving aside pissed off people as nicely as I could, but resorting to stiff-arming when I had no choice. Mystery man was up ahead, carrying on with his constipation power-walk, periodically checking the contents of his satchel for something. I kept pace, not taking my eyes off him. There was no way I was losing—

"Whoa!"

The cart of salted seafood split in half as I crashed through it, not seeing it appear from the alley. Dried-out fish bodies littered the ground, and the merchant was screaming at me in some horrible language. Up ahead, the mystery man had stopped to see what the commotion was about, and when I locked eyes with him, his jaw dropped and he took off running. So much for stealth.

I hightailed it, reeling him in with long power strides as his short little legs furiously pumped in vain. There wasn't more than ten feet between us when he suddenly spun toward me and cowered into a ball.

"Please, don't!" he pleaded. "I've been good!"

The man was around my age, with thinning blond hair cropped close to his head and a wispy mustache. His thin, dry lips were tensed in a grimace, as if he expected blows any second, and his gray eyes were wide with terror. The face was definitely familiar.

"Whaddya mean you've been good?" I shouted, inching toward him. No sense ceding my leverage, even if I didn't know what was going on.

"Been good, you know? Stayed out of trouble! I'm keeping up the plea deal . . ." he said, making himself into a tighter ball.

Plea deal. Holy shit, I remembered now.

A few years back I was sitting in my old apartment (smaller and shittier than my current one, on a higher floor) watching *RMZ Live,* when the special segment came on. *Creme de la Crim.* It was the part of the show that highlighted criminals law enforcement really wanted to catch, and it just so happened that on this particular night they showed footage of a man I'd seen walking around my building once every week or so. The A.I. segment host of *Creme de la Crim* said the man had stolen millions of credits from senior citizens over the last few years, and was running an unlicensed human trafficking service that didn't pay its taxes. Information that led to his capture was worth a million credits—and I was all about it. So for weeks, I staked out the route where I always ran into him, imagining what I'd do with the money when I got it. It made me feel alive knowing how close I was to never having to scrape by again.

But he never turned up. He just disappeared. It wasn't until a couple months later that *Creme de la Crim* gave an update: the man, John Tuck, had turned himself in and got a plea deal for ratting on his accomplices. And now here he was.

"That selfish bastard," CareE said. "You could have lived easy."

"I was so close," I said. "He was right there all along."

"W-who was there all along?" John Tuck asked.

"Nobody," I said. "Fuck off."

Tuck leapt to his feet and scurried off down the street. As I watched him go, I realized I couldn't blame him for being a rat—he was facing some serious trouble, and it was a matter of survival. It's not like his partners in crime were friends of his or anything.

"Enough chasing memories," CareE said. "[Name] said to stay inside, so that's what you should do."

"Yeah, okay," I said, turning back. "Whatever the terrorist wants."

"She couldn't have evaded SKIRM® for so long if she wasn't smart."

"I'm aware."

As I walked back toward the *Electric Sleep*, I thought about [Name] and all of the *RMZ Live* segments she popped up in, all of the bets and plans she'd ruined for the smart money with her antics. It was true; she was smarter than just about anybody. She was the most wanted target in any battle, no matter what was going on, and even a casual watcher or contractor knew of her. No doubt the price on her head was high, too. Probably a few million. I was sure it was a source of outlaw pride for her to have such a–

"It's five hundred million," CareE said.

I skidded onto my knees and crushed a woman's supply wagon with my hand.

"Five hundred million?" I said.

"Yes, at least from what I can find on this archaic network. It's a closed circuit, but every now and then someone updates a hub with pieces from the outside. It could be a thousand or so off."

[Name] was a walking lottery ticket and she was talking directly with me. Suddenly I had flashes of the hopeful times I spent waiting for John in those bushes.

"Don't even go down that road," CareE said. "I can see your thoughts."

"What thoughts?" I said.

"Your little idea of betraying someone who is trying to help you. Besides, SKIRM® would never give you the money," CareE said.

"I know that," I said. Honestly, I always figured that rewards never got paid out for any outlaw, it was all just a scam for ratings. But [Name] was [Name], and she was valuable. Value meant leverage. "SKIRM® may not pay," I went on, "but they might overlook the little hack that landed me here."

"That's a pretty far leap," CareE said.

"What other move do I have?"

"That's true. You're below rock bottom."

"Right, exactly. Nothing to lose." We kept walking for a moment as I thought more on it. "And you know," I said finally, "after I'm back home and logged out, they could give me *some* money. Even a million of the five hundred. Or twenty. That's like, less than a percent. What's wrong with that?"

"Nothing *technically,*" CareE said. "I'd still sleep on it, though. Make sure it's the right thing to do."

"Good idea," I said. "It's a big decision."

The next morning I made plans to turn [Name] in by contacting SKIRM® directly. CareE had found a nearby cafe, *Byte Club*, and I secured a private room which was cramped and reeked of hand lotion. Next to a small mirror was a temple tap for the Rig, but I couldn't get it to attach to my head.

"Check under the bed." CareE suggested.

I found what he was looking for—a small Rig. Like everything else in Desolin, it was ancient and just capable of working. A little tickling with my fingers around the case and I found its service cable, letting me jack in directly. After a moment of lag, the room disappeared into a white mist, turning into . . . nothing. There was only a white void around me.

"What is this?" I asked CareE.

"It's what a closed network looks like. I don't think Desolin has the bandwidth to maintain any connection to the outside world. You're going to just have to leave a message."

"And you think SKIRM® will get it?"

"I'll see what I can do."

"All right, here goes. *Hi, this is Null Lakser.* Wait, maybe I shouldn't use my real name. Delete that part." I cleared my throat and started again. "*Hi, this is Nnn . . . Lasker. NaLasker. I have information that can lead to the arrest of the terrorist leader [Name]. I am stranded in Desolin. It's that blank part on the map Drew showed me. Drew is . . . uh . . . never mind. Forget Drew. That's not important.*" The connection closed out.

"Well done, you're a one-take wonder," CareE said.

"Shut up."

268

It wasn't perfect, but so what? Speaking under pressure was always a problem for me. One of my A.I. instructors in school described my style as *"rambling, forced, and traumatic."* It may have been hard for a seven-year-old to hear, but I'd had plenty of time to eventually accept it. The important thing was that, overall, I was feeling pretty good about the plan. I trusted CareE to get the word out, and all I had to do was hunker down and wait for SKIRM® to contact me. In the meantime, I'd rehearse my talking points for the inevitable negotiation dance SKIRM® and I would do regarding the terms of my surrender. I had to be ready.

Before I could yank the matted cable from my socket to head back to my room, a small mail icon appeared in the bottom left of my HUD. It opened instantaneously, projecting a featureless mannequin whose slim torso appeared to be stuck between the wall and the crusty bed.

"Thank you for your anonymous report, citizen. We take these matters *very* seriously. Your intelligence confirms what we had already suspected. Please report to the closest safehouse for payment and immediate extraction. God be with you, and you with SKIRM®." The ghost saluted then disappeared from the room. A string of digits splayed across my HUD, coordinates directing me to move deeper into the city.

"That was quick," CareE said.

It seemed the capture of a dangerous criminal was further up their priority list than I realized. Maybe if I'd had a little more foresight months ago, and hadn't wasted my time digging latrines and painting walls, I could have moved up the freelance ladder much quicker. Forest for the trees. I suddenly felt strangely comfortable and at ease, like for once I was doing the smart thing with my life and it was leading to internal peace. I wondered if this is what Buddhist monks felt, the ones who didn't set themselves on fire.

As I made the twenty-block walk from *Byte Club* to the safehouse, nostalgia for the crazy city gripped me, and I found that the place had really made a cozy spot for itself in my heart. If you looked beyond the screaming, shirtless residents, Desolin had a kind of hellish charm to it. A naked fleshie stealing a bike stopped a moment as I passed by.

"Ohh ya, seein' him. One of them, *hmm hmm*. Scrap man, scrap man," she muttered.

I couldn't help but smile. "I see you too, friend."

The city had a strange density to it. Thick people inside thick pollution inside crowded streets. Wide roads jammed with junkers and junkies eating double-stacked street snacks.

Hunger pangs suddenly wrenched my stomach, and a flood of frustration came again as I remembered I could look but not touch. Whatever drip they were giving me in the hospital back home just wasn't keeping me satisfied, but then again, I wasn't sure if I was really feeling anything at all. The 'how' of a human brain operating independently in two places at once was beyond my comprehension. Finding an all-you-can-eat buffet that offered a two-for-one deal was more my speed—something I intended to do once I was back home.

"What you do is go in around 10:30 in the morning," I said. "That way when they switch over to lunch, you can get a new plate and start all over."

CareE didn't respond. An A.I., no matter how advanced, would never appreciate the joy of stuffing themselves twice as much as they needed to, alone, on a Thursday afternoon. I kept walking, absorbing my last glimpses of the city, and soon passed by a crushed pedestrian stuck between two vehicles. It reminded me of the perfect breakfast buffet pancake, covered in butter and syrup, with raspberry jam oozing from every—

"We're here." CareE said.

There had to have been a mistake. The structure was just another dilapidated building, too slummy for even the locals to squat in. I had CareE doublecheck the address, and he confirmed we were at the right location. But on further thought, the place made sense. If you were going to extract a double agent like myself, you *would* want to hide in plain sight. I went for the door, but froze as instinct grabbed my shoulders and shame baked my neck like a heat lamp. Entering meant betraying the person who had selflessly promised me an exit. She probably deserved this in some cosmic karma sort of way, right? Maybe. I wasn't an angel, either, in the universal scheme of things, but that didn't put me in the same league as a terrorist.

I contemplated my dirty deed for a while before making my executive decision. I kicked in the thinly boarded door and moved past the lightweight glass into an empty lobby. It was silent inside; the filth of neglect covered everything.

At the end of the waiting room stood an old elevator, the endpoint of my projected marker. I could actually feel myself getting closer to home as I approached the old lift. Its doors opened, revealing an interior that looked much more modern. *Clever.* The doors closed with a satisfying FWUMP, further solidifying their premium design quality.

"Welcome back, soldier. Please confirm your identity before we proceed," a lovely voice on the intercom said.

"Null Lasker," I said proudly.

"Thank you for your confirmation, traitor."

Wait, what?

The elevator went dark, then rocketed downward. My stomach dropped and my feet left the floor. I screamed like a child until the metal death-box abruptly slowed and came to a safe and pleasant stop. The doors opened, revealing two giant Frames covered head-to-toe in custom paint, who immediately snatched my legs and started dragging me across the floor to a makeshift cage in the middle of the room. I kicked and dug my fingers into the epoxied floor, but it wasn't enough to stop the lumbering behemoths.

"Wait here," one of them said, locking the cage door.

They stood guard on the far side of the room, keeping an eye on me. It seemed like the bars could be thin enough to pry open, but then what? I'd still have to fight off two Frames twice my size.

"Out of one prison and into another. This is beginning to look like a pattern, Mr. Lasker." It was the same voice from *Byte Club* and the elevator. A slim Frame walked in from out of the shadows carrying a large clipboard.

"There's been a mistake," I pleaded, standing up.

"Oh?" she said. "Is that so?"

"I'm one of you, I work for SKIRM®. I have important information that can help lead you to the capture of—"

"[Name]? Yes, we heard. But Mr. Lasker, you claim to have been in contact with this terrorist. That's not a good look. How do we know you're not working for [Name]? How can we trust you?"

I thought for a moment, but couldn't come up with a decent answer. "You can't," I said. "But please, just take my word. It's all I got."

The Frame moved in closer, so close I could see its off-white eyes.

"And what good is that?" it said.

My chest went cold. I'd seen those eyes before. They were in the robo-pup when it took the Mantis chip from me, before I slammed its cute face into the sidewalk.

Shit.

The Frame smiled. "Now he gets it."

I felt dizzy, sick. Everything inside of me seemed to harden with regret, weighing my body down until the pressure was too much and I fell to my knees.

"I was going to get you out of here, Null," she said. "The last three days I was setting up dummy accounts . . . creating patch code . . . engineering backdoors . . . all to get the split second you'd need to be on the network and log out scot-free." She stepped back and observed me in my cage, her own pet monster. "All that time I was putting myself at risk, you were figuring out how to turn me in."

"Not the *whole* time—"

"Shut up," she said curtly, then caught herself. "Actually, I am curious . . . what were you going to tell SKIRM® if they contacted you?"

"I . . . Well, I was gonna say that I knew how to find you," I said.

"And how was that?" she said, staring at me.

"In the . . . uh . . . you were going to contact me."

"Right. And then?"

"And then . . . we would wait."

"You and SKIRM® would wait? Like a stakeout?"

"Yes?"

"And then what? After you and SKIRM® had your buddy-buddy stakeout and you nabbed me."

My mind went blank. I knew the plan in my brain, but I guess I didn't really know it well enough to properly explain it. It definitely made sense to me, though, from what I remember.

[Name] sighed, shaking her head. A little incredulous laugh puffed out of her. "You were playing the wrong game, Null," she said. "This isn't checkers. God, I don't even know if you could play checkers."

There was a long silence, long enough for me to remember some of [Name]'s highlights, her greatest hits. Hours of her shredding SKIRM® Frames like me without hesitation. I looked away from [Name] as I realized there was no possibility of leaving this place alive. My body began to vibrate with fear.

"This is what the SKIRM®s of the world do, Null," she said. "They drive wedges between little people like you and me, exploit our fears. And while you're figuring out how to turn me into credits, and I'm planning on how to melt your Frame down into belly button rings, they're getting richer and more powerful."

There was another heavy silence. She gave a nod to the two Frames, then walked away toward a large steel door. I added another entry into my list of people I'd disappointed, then waited for the guards to put me down. But they didn't budge. All of a sudden the lock to my cage released, and the door swung open lazily.

For a moment I was hesitant to move. I'd seen this before in VRE's. The bad guy would open a gate for the prisoner and make the poor dolt think he was getting set free, then as soon as he stepped out—"

"Just follow her, for fuck's sake!" CareE yelled.

I zoomed out of my cage and caught up to [Name], who had made it to the large blast door and was typing into a control panel.

"Null, have you taken a moment to really think about what it is you're trying to get back to?"

"You mean my body? Yeah, a bunch of times," I said, still not sure of [Name]'s intentions.

"I'm not talking about that."

"Oh, my apartment? Definitely. I've gotta get a place without a shower toilet."

"Your life!" she shouted. "Your existence!"

"Oh," I said. "No." The door opened to a long hallway and she took off walking. I realized [Name] wasn't going to kill me. The shower of relief made me want to cry. It didn't make sense, but it felt so good, like when your partner takes you back after she catches you in another girl's WatcHer™ session.

"You're fighting to get back to subsistence living. Endless subscriptions. One missed payday from ruination. Being a slave with invisible chains."

"Yeah, well, when you say it like that it sounds pretty bad."

"SKIRM® is a large gear in a cruel machine, Null. Every year the outside world doubles what they spend, eats more than they need, and pays through the nose for rent. All while the average lifespan extends by roughly five years. Why do you think that is?"

I drew a blank. [Name] was touching on subject matter typically reserved for family holidays and heavy drinking.

We came to another door, and [Name] put her hand to a biometric reader as she continued. "The world has become complacent with the way things are, too blind to see what corporations like SKIRM® have done to people like us. We let them create a playground of war, one where they can commit a dozen atrocities a day without a single person asking 'why?' In a single, calculated move, the fiscal elite created a neverending war economy, entertainment empire, and organ farm for the rich to feed upon."

"Yeah, the world's pretty crazy." I said, not wanting to be left out of the one-sided conversation.

The door opened to a large hangar hidden from the world above. Countless fleshie troops jogged in concentric circles, fired at dummy targets with live ammunition, and toiled away fixing up scraped

274

Frames. It was incredible—[Name] *was* building an army big enough to rival SKIRM®. Another slim Frame greeted us at the hangar's entrance, covered head to toe in tactical gear. [Name] had swapped bodies so quick I had hardly noticed.

"Crazy but vulnerable. Try to keep up," [Name] said, turning around to continue my tour. The secret base appeared to stretch into infinity, full of recruits, armants, and vitriol. My appearance caught the eye of every fleshie in the room.

"So what," I said, "you want to take down SKIRM® with *this*? You might need a few more guns." I didn't want to sound rude, but it was the truth. SKIRM® had unlimited resources, plus every instrument of destruction known to man. If [Name] wanted a fighting chance, their army would need a lot more help.

"This? This is just the tip, Null. There are two dozen other bases just like this here in Desolin, with a thousand more scattered throughout the RMZ."

"Why is [Name] telling you all of this?" CareE asked. "Usually after the bad guy gives away their plan they try to kill the main character. Oh my god . . . do you think we're about to meet him?"

"Shut up." I said.

[Name] stopped and looked up at me with an uncomfortable, lingering stare.

"Shut up, that's unbelievable," I blurted. "A hundred, you said?"

"Thousand. I can't tell if you're really stupid or somehow more brilliant than I can comprehend."

"Thank you."

"Look, the world is dying, Null. It's dying and we're going to save it. People like you chose compliance over discomfort and now we're all paying the price. I bet you didn't even notice when it happened, when you had your mind so overloaded that you wistfully surrendered your free will to those who could choose for you."

Finally. Now I knew where [Name] was coming from, but getting there had been exhausting. Suddenly I yearned for the simpler times when my Rig would pick a VRE it knew I liked while my feeding tube pumped in my favorite chicken-flavored dessert.

"The truth is, I need someone like you. Wars aren't just fought with soldiers, they're fought with ideas. You've witnessed things out here in Desolin with your own eyes. You've seen the people SKIRM® doesn't want you to know about, the families and friendly citizens just trying to make the best of a horrible situation."

"I saw a schizophrenic guy pee on a robot today."

"Right. Well, that's part of the reason I brought you here."

I was lost again.

"I want to offer you a job, Null." [Name] said, moving towards a large bulkhead door. "A lot of things are about to change in the RMZ, and SKIRM® might not be around by the time we get you back home."

I was taken aback, and a bit flattered. I thought I had blown my only chance to get home safely, but now I was being offered a new position without an interview. The excitement made me fizz, but a dose of imposter syndrome flattened my bubbling.

"I appreciate that," I said. "But I might be underqualified for what you're looking for. Besides, I'm about as loyal as a goldfish. I just want to get home safely, and if you can do that for me, I'm all yours."

"And if we can't?" [Name] asked, opening the heavy door.

[Name] seemed like a straight shooter—it was refreshing. I was a prisoner, but in a way I didn't feel like one. For the first time in a while I felt like I actually had a choice. It felt good.

"Your points are great," I said, "but you're fighting for something that I don't really understand, or sure I even want to."

[Name] raised an eyebrow.

"I mean, I get it," I said. "The RMZ affects everyone or something but I'm just one guy. I'm a simple man and I like simple things. You're dealing with some complicated stuff and I don't want to get in your way."

"I appreciate your honesty, Null. It's one of the reasons we've had an eye on you for so long."

"You've been watching me?"

"We watch everyone. I'll tell you what—I can get you to a place where you can access the network and log out. From there, though, you're on your own."

I nodded, feeling the terms were fair considering the circumstances. Signing onto whatever it was she was pitching just seemed too risky. One of the things I appreciated about myself was knowing my limitations.

[Name] took a step into the ready room on the other side of the bulkhead. "I just need to run to this meeting real quick. Can you give me a second?"

"Yeah, sure. Wait—" On the other side of the door I saw a familiar face on the monitor behind [Name]. He looked more tired than usual, and could have used a shave, but there was no mistaking the chiseled outline of the man that had always been there for me.

"Raphael, thank you for waiting," [Name] said. "I'll be right there."

"Of course," Raphael Calabrese said. "Oh, is that the guy you were talking about? Is he still coming?"

"I don't know yet." [Name] said, looking back at me. Then she went in and shut the door behind her.

I stood there motionless.

"Why are you crying?" CareE asked.

LOG SIXTEEN

The dry plains and starved trees of the RMZ rushed by my window as our MTV charged along a pockmarked highway toward a mission at some unknown destination. Well, it was unknown to me—[Name] had been cryptic with the details, saying only that I would be the head of security when we got there, and that she'd tell me where "there" was when we were further along in the trip. It reminded me of once when I was a kid and my dad took me and Aarau on a trip but wouldn't say where we were going. We eventually ended up at a car dealership, where he traded in our old battered Honda for an even older, more battered Honda so he could pay bills for the next few months. It was about 110 degrees that day, and we baked the entire car ride home because the air-conditioning in our new ride was busted.

To be honest, I hadn't really given much thought to where we were going. I was too nervous about meeting Raphael Calabrese. I told myself I wouldn't let it get to me, but my mind started to wander, and I couldn't help but think about all of the VRE's we'd shared. *God, how many awards had he won from those?* And the VRE's were just the surface of his pureness. He also had all of his philanthropy and charitable causes, and his beautiful girlfriends who were all 22-year-old models who he took out on his yacht. Every interview I'd seen, he was so in control and carefree, just a guy you could have a drink with and talk to about anything. In one of the interviews I remembered him mentioning his love of antique hand games, which was something I liked, too. I figured I'd casually mention that to him at some point during the mission. He was probably so used to people saying, *"Oh my god, I loved you in so and so, can I make a mark?"* that it'd be refreshing to have someone just talk to him about an interesting subject. Once he realized I was just a normal guy, we'd probably gush about games for a while, and he'd be surprised about how much I knew, then after bonding over our mutual appreciation of the old stuff, I'd ask him how life was going, but in a *genuine* way, not the fake way most people did. He'd most likely be taken aback, and probably say how he's nervous about a new experimental project coming out, and I'd say, "Oh a new project? Yeah that sounds tough," pretending that I didn't know it was his new interdimensional VRE that took place in Andromeda (I had already pre-ordered it). I'd listen to his worries and troubles, piping up once in a while to give him some of my wisdom—which he'd appreciate—and after [Name]'s mission was done, he'd say, "Hey Null, you're a good guy. When you're back IRL, keep in touch," and give me his unlisted ID tag. Sometime in the spring, when the weather was right, I'd get a message out of the blue from him: *"Hey Null, hope you're well. Heading out to the cape on the Mooring Wood with Dominika and a few of her girlfriends. Love if you could make it."* I'd say yeah, let me make sure I don't have something that day, but of course I'd have nothing that day, I just wouldn't want to sound too eager because that would be weird. I could almost feel the tingle of the sun on my cheeks and hear the water lapping on the hull as I talked to one of the models. "You were in a L'Oreal ad? That's so—"

"Null!"

[Name]'s Frame was standing in the open doorway of the stopped MTV. "Let's take a break," she said, shooting me a strange look before marching off into the dusty soil.

The expansive gunmetal sky stretched out over the field beyond the road, and a hundred kilometers or so ahead of us I could just make out the silhouettes of mountains. [Name] was inspecting the transporter and making some adjustments to a transmitter on her Bishop Frame, ensuring her remote linkup was sound. I wondered where in the world she was, what the room she was sitting in looked like. She seemed like the type who would own lots of plants.

The two fleshie soldiers who came with us were down the road a bit, pants pulled down, pissing into the wind. Sitting lifelessly just inside the open doorway of the MTV were the two Knight Frames they would use when we got to wherever we were going. The units were similar to all of the other Frames [Name] used for her army—a hodgepodge of scrap parts and patches sourced from the rubble of the RMZ. It was hard to tell what was original on them. They were like the woodworking hammer I had inherited from my grandpa: It was the one he had when he was a kid and it was over a hundred years old, but the handle had been replaced three times and the head was new because the other one wore down. Even though all of the parts were changed, I guess it still had its soul.

Down the road, the two soldiers were shaking out their last few drops.

"Wish I could do that," I said.

"Do what?" [Name] said, walking back.

"Pee," I said. "I get the urge, but then there's no way to."

"Maybe you have a robot UTI," [Name] said, eyeing the men. "But you know, if you think about it . . . you *are* peeing."

"No, I'm not."

"Yes, you are. It's just that it's in a bag in a hospital room, and some poor nurse is having to empty it out."

"Oh, yeah. Right."

"Enjoy it while you can," [Name] said, watching her soldiers fiddle with their flies. "Pretty soon you'll be back to dropping trou like the rest of us."

"Can't wait," I said, following her gaze. Beyond the soldiers, the road seemed to stretch into a simmering infinity. "Is it much further?"

"A bit," [Name] said. "But we just ticked over the halfway point."

"That's good," I said, waiting to see if there was anything else, but there wasn't. She headed inside the MTV.

"Null, if it's true what [Name] is saying," CareE whispered into my consciousness, "then based on the distance and direction we've covered, that would have to put us near the edge of the RMZ's panhandle."

Panhandle? I thought.

Suddenly I remembered the stupid map from SKIRM® orientation that Drew, the mindless A.I., showed me. I could see myself flying over all of the numbered sectors and terrain as countries won and lost, and over on the far edge of the map, in a skinny jutting piece of land, was an industrial super city labeled SKIRM® HUB.

"Are you sure, CareE?" I said.

"I'd bet your life on it," he said.

My mind cartwheeled. It didn't make sense—there was no way I could hide in The Hub. I started to pace next to the transport, letting the anxiety surge get the best of me.

"Get ahold of yourself," CareE said. "Right now we need to keep composed and observe."

"Observe, gotcha," I said, shaking out my nerves.

"Let's try and figure out what she's up to," CareE said. "I've got an idea of how we can get some information, but it's going to take a little time to put into action."

I nodded. "Okay."

"In the meantime," CareE continued, "let's just relax, and more importantly, not let her know that *we* know we're–"

"We're going to SKIRM®'s hub?" I shouted at [Name].

She froze in her tracks.

"Gaaah," CareE said.

"Why do you think we're going there?" [Name] said, poker-faced.

282

"C'mon," I said. "The direction? The fact that we're halfway after traveling, you know, a bunch of kilometers? Where else would we be going?"

[Name] was silent. She just stared at me, her milky eyes burning. I wanted to shrivel.

"Am I right?" I said finally.

"You're right," she said.

A hollow place in my chest started to simmer at the edges.

"Calabrese is holding a rally for the people of the RMZ close to SKIRM®'s hub because it's a nightmare for him to go deeper into the warzone," [Name] said. "Besides, it sends a stronger message to everyone watching when it's at SKIRM®'s doorstep." She edged closer to me, her eyes softening a little. "Sorry I didn't tell you before."

"What am I going to do?" I said. "SKIRM® thinks I'm a blank or thief. Either way, if they get their hands on me it's going to be bad. It's like sending a little boy to the Vatican."

"I took care of that. You'll see when we get there."

"I don't know."

"Null, listen to me," she said. "What I'm going to do . . . this isn't some cowboy plan I slapped together at the last minute. This has been in the works for a long time, and I brought you because I needed a special soldier to help me see it through. I told you before, you're unlike anyone I've ever met—you've got what it takes to change everything. But you need to put on your big girl boots and rise to the occasion."

She moved into my shadow, looking up at me.

"If you follow everything I say, it'll be fine," she said. "But if you don't, a lot of people are going to die. And I won't be able to get you back to your body. Understand?"

I nodded.

There was a long pause. She let herself smile. "Okay, great. Come on, we still have plenty of road to burn. Let's go."

She whistled at the two others and we loaded into the MTV.

The hours ticked by as we rolled on, eventually coming to the mountains and traversing them through a series of poorly maintained switchback roads, taking notice of the spots with little rock piles and crosses, making sure to handle those areas with more care than the previous travelers. On the downhill run, there was a clear view for miles, revealing the curvature of the earth, and I could just make out a dense cluster of industrial buildings and skyscrapers rippling like a dream on the horizon. As we reeled them in, their hazy blue coloring gave way to the metallic blacks of solar skin, and they seemed to spread out to cover my entire field of view. We started to pass communities of derelict travel estates on either side of us, some with old hybrids permanently parked in the yard, weeds growing through the hoods where the electric motor once hummed. I caught the glazed stares of a few residents on their porches watching us pass by.

"Leeches," [Name] said. "They wait outside the hub all day, taking whatever they can get from SKIRM® in return for a reduced sentence. They use them for jobs when they don't want to risk losing precious alloy."

Back outside, I saw a naked child of about twelve chasing another kid with a lit plasma torch, laughing, while a parent or some adult watched from a car seat in the middle of his yard. We continued another few miles, closing in on the glass skyscrapers and assembly buildings. The relatively spread-out travel estates gave way to dense clusters of block housing made of colorful slipshod concrete and corrugated steel. Then the glass and titanium jungle we'd seen towering above the land from a couple hours away finally took us in its shadow.

The fifteen hundred square miles of looming structures consisted of every conceivable geometric shape, and some that were inconceivable. One building was a polygon with what looked like trillions of angles and sides that corkscrewed a few thousand feet into the sky and faded before you could see the top, like a plume of smoke in an updraft. It would be easy to look at the impressive buildings, the elevated lev train, the canals, the infrastructure, and think this was some sort of super city, but it was purely a tech campus built in a warzone whose sole purpose was to imagine and assemble the toys of the war economy. Twenty years ago, none of this was here. But it's amazing what unlimited credits and free labor will build.

There was a large convention area, and miles and miles of visitor promenade on the edge of the hub, where rich, flown-in tourists could gawk and industry professionals could meet and see the newest war innovations in person. And butting up against this hosting section of the hub were the outer slums. The lev trains hid most of the nastiness out of view, and what was left over was nearly covered by a fifty-foot carbon "sound" fence, but it was there all the same.

"The rally's going to be here," [Name] said, gesturing to an enormous stage on the edge of a snaking inner-city river canal. "Gonna be quite the crowd. Thousands of angry SKIRM®ers, fleshies and leeches, all looking for a little fun."

We parked next to a boxy beige ten-story building a couple of miles away from the site. A half-dozen men and women milled about in lumpy overcoats, with another half-dozen Frames, all attempting to look casual, but it was hard not to notice their eyes methodically sweeping the surroundings. Everyone piled out and [Name] strode up to a man close to the front door.

"SKIRM® security," [Name] announced. "We're looking for a wild animal that may be roaming around here."

"What is it?" the man said.

"A fox."

The man nodded, thinking. "What color?"

"Silver," [Name] replied.

"Well, I haven't seen one," the man said, "but you're welcome to look around."

[Name] motioned back to us and we followed her and the man through the front door. We were led through a series of passages to a service elevator, which took us up to the top floor of the building. There was a long hallway of plush green synthetic carpet that led to double doors flanked by two more security personnel. The man we followed gave a signal to them as we approached, and they whispered something into hidden comms. We waited a moment in the quiet hallway, until we heard footsteps on the other side of the door. Then the door swung open, and in the flesh, it was him.

Raphael Calabrese said nothing, just stood there stoically, eyeing each of us. Somehow he was even more handsome in person, with bits of grey in the temples of his immaculate hairline, and his sapphire eyes seemed to have the deep wisdom of a hundred lifetimes. For a moment I forgot to breathe, entranced by his penetrating stare. Finally he spoke:

"The fox stuff was pretty fucking smart, right?" he said.

No one answered, assuming he was being rhetorical, but he said nothing else and searched our faces, waiting. Then [Name], feeling the crushing silence, piped up.

"It was, yes—"

"'Cuz I was racking my brain for like two days on this password," Raphael Calabrese continued. "And then finally I was like, 'wait a sec—what would the password be if *I* was the password?' I'm rare . . . I'm valuable . . . but I'm also sneaky. What else is also those things? A fox."

"Foxes are also hard to catch," [Name] suggested.

"That's right," Raphael Calabrese said, pointing to her. "That's actually another reason I picked the password, I just didn't mention it right now. But I did think that at the time."

Raphael Calabrese turned away and plunged into the room. [Name] nudged us in behind him. He was pacing deep in thought, fidgeting with himself, his tailored purple suit jacket swishing as he spun. I couldn't believe a pop culture icon I'd watched for twenty years was nervously walking around, picking his nose right in front of me.

"I haven't slept in three days," he said. "I keep going over the speech in my head. It's so good, [Name]. So, so good. I can see the coverage already. People are going to go nuts. Then when you goad SKIRM® to jump us—"

"Let's be careful about what we say," [Name] said, motioning around the room.

"Oh, we've scrubbed this place," Raphael Calabrese said, waving her off. "SKIRM®'s so clueless . . ." Suddenly he stopped talking and stared through us, peering into some invisible dimension. "Hey," he said softly. "Do you think historical figures could feel they were doing something historic?"

"I'm sure they felt something, yeah," [Name] said.

"Okay, so I'm not crazy? Because I keep getting this, like, deep *fizzing* behind my balls . . ."

"I get that feeling too sometimes," I blurted.

The room stopped.

"Oh, is that so?" Raphael Calabrese said, looking at me, then to [Name]. "Who are you?"

"I'm Null," I said, my voice trembling a bit. "We met earlier, kind of. I'm here to help . . . and I'm the special soldier. One of the best, actually. Because of . . . *ideas*."

Raphael Calabrese nodded. "Ah, okay."

"Yeah," I continued, "so when [Name] told me I wasn't like the other soldiers, I got this fizzy feeling in my gooch, and I was like, 'whoa, that feels pretty historic,' and the only other time I could think of when I felt that fizz was when I played this one classic hand game—because I really love those—and I'm a bit of a historian . . . of classic hand games."

"Wow," Raphael Calabrese said. "That's really something."

"It's pretty crazy, right?" I said.

There was a thick silence. Raphael turned back to [Name].

"Well, Raphael," [Name] said, "there's a lot of logistics we should iron out."

"You mean a lot of *credits* we should *hand* out," he grinned.

She shrugged. "Movements don't happen on hopes and dreams."

Raphael Calabrese shivered with excitement. "A revolution . . ." he said under his breath.

"Null," [Name] said, "Give us a moment to talk through some things."

I nodded.

"I'll just be in here if you need me," I said, motioning to a door on the other side of the room. I walked over and went inside, shutting it behind me as I plopped onto a daybed. The conversation from seconds before replayed in my head. It could have gone better, but at least I didn't waste much of his time. And besides, I left him with the hand game thing—a little carrot for future talks. I let myself relax a little bit.

"Congratulations," a voice said.

I snapped to a far corner of the room, where a young girl was sitting with a small music emulator.

"You're the one millionth person to try and talk to him about games," she said.

"Who are you?" I demanded.

"What, you don't know who I am?" she chuckled dryly. "Some super fan you are."

She had buzzed hair with purple bio-luminescent dye, and was wearing a tank top that clung to her narrow shoulders for dear life. Her posture was a perpetual slouch that seemed to match the downturned corners of her mouth.

"Wait," I said, studying her a moment. "Are you ... his girlfriend?"

"Ew," she said. "I can't believe you just said that."

"I'm sor—"

"But I guess I can't blame you," she said. "Most of them aren't much older than me. My mom was twenty when he did the pump-and-dump."

"You're his kid?"

"Look at you with the deduction! And I thought Artificial Intelligence had peaked."

"I didn't know Raphael Calabrese had kids," I said.

"Why do you say his full name like he's a serial killer?" she asked. "And yeah, he does. Probably lots of them, actually. I found out the other day I have a half brother."

"Oh. That's nice," I said.

She looked at me sideways, then shook it off.

"Anyway, I don't exactly come up in his interviews, so I'll forgive you." She set down her emulator and walked over. "I'm Etta."

"Null."

"So what's your deal?" she asked. "Are you a bodyguard or something?"

"No. Actually, I'm the head of security for this mission."

"Head of security?" She observed my Frame a moment. "Why are you sitting at the kid's table?"

"Because–" I thought for a moment. "Because [Name] and your dad are having important talks about money and logistics and I need to stay focused on my task."

"She doesn't trust you," Etta said.

"No, she trusts me," I said quickly. "She trusts me a lot. You don't even know the kind of relationship we have."

"I can guess," she said. "She's the dom and you're the sub."

"What–"

"Do you lick boots?" she said.

"This conversation is over," I said, turning to face the door.

"Oh, c'mon. I was just joking," she said. "For the head of security you're pretty brittle."

"I'm not gonna waste my time talking to little girls."

"I'm not a little girl," she said, icing over. "Don't ever call me that."

"Little girl," I said.

Etta shot up and rushed me, leaping onto my back and yanking my head backwards until it almost touched my spine. I screamed as she used all of her wiry strength to peel it back over and over again. I tried swatting at her, but she was too small to get to. Then I spotted a sharp bedpost on the far side of the room, figuring if I could get over to it, I could impale her. When I rose up, she jumped off and rolled into the center of the room, immediately springing up into a fighting stance. Suddenly the door swung open revealing [Name].

"What are you doing?" she demanded.

I stood silent. But, Etta stepped forward. "He was showing me defense moves," she said. "Sorry."

"Oh," [Name] said, taking a moment. "That's okay. I learned around your age, too. Listen to him—he's good."

"Everything okay?" Raphael Calabrese said casually from the other room.

"Yeah, everything's good," [Name] said, closing the door.

I turned back to Etta. Her frown was even deeper.

"You'd think my dad would have been the one to check."

"I wouldn't read too much into it," I said, checking the actuators on my neck for any stress cracks. "He's probably distracted, you know? Being a revolutionary is a lot of work."

Etta reared back and cackled. "Is that what you think he is?"

"You don't?"

"Hosting dinner fundraisers and throwing money at problems doesn't make you a revolutionary. It makes you a celebrity."

"But your dad inspires a lot of people," I said.

"Oh, he knows. He wraps himself up in that every night before he falls asleep next to the flavor of the week." Etta moved to her music emulator and gathered it up. "Look, I hate to say this, because it's obvious you have a crush on my dad or something, but he's a dumbass. And I may not understand what he's up to right now with all of this secret stuff, but I guarantee you he doesn't, either." Etta looked me up and down, "And for a bodyguard, you're a lousy fighter. You better be everything she says you are or we're all as good as dead." Milliseconds before my snappy comeback, she went into the bathroom and slammed the door.

[Name] popped her head back in. "We're ready for you. We need to talk about tomorrow," she said, turning away before I could respond. None of my new friends seemed too interested in what I had to say. I looked back to the bathroom door and heard the muffle of chippy, high pitched music bouncing around inside.

"I think you're a terrific fighter." CareE chimed in.

"Thanks."

"But you could use some work on your people skills."

I didn't respond.

LOG SEVENTEEN

I stood at the base of the stage platform, observing the occasional Frame or fleshie walking by as they peeked curiously at the podium surrounded by polycarbonate shielding. It was just after ten in the morning on the day of the rally. Raphael Calabrese wasn't due to speak for a few hours, but I'd been waiting, keeping watch for any saboteurs, per [Name]'s orders. My body was crispy with anxiety—the adrenaline was pumping so hard that every sight, sound and smell was an overload of stimuli. At one point a fleshie near me sneezed and I thought I was going to break down crying.

The fact that I was heading up the security detail for Raphael Calabrese still didn't feel real to me. A month ago I was working myself to death in my crummy apartment, and my only source of accomplishment was that I had my diabetes somewhat under control and I wasn't going to lose a foot. Now I was the first line of defense for a beloved star and my personal hero. I wished Aarau could see me now, partly because he would be jealous as hell, but mostly because it would make him proud.

The idea made me smile. I knew he would be impressed with some of the intricate security plans I had come up with for the event. CareE

291

had been distracted all morning for some reason and refused to log any of my notes, so I had to scribble down all my ideas on a half-torn piece of paper. I spent most of the night just trying to figure out how to hold a pen without breaking it in two. Eventually I gave that up and just used the splattered ink with the tip of my finger to jot down the best ideas with a few simple acronyms:

AFS

BBTQR 6x

B.E.F.S.Q.S.C.C.E

Every letter was an uncrackable safe. I stared at the paper for a minute before crumpling it up and throwing it in the street. I worked perfectly fine on my feet anyway.

I gazed over the convention promenade, observing the crows peck at bugs and bits of trash the street suckers had missed, occasionally fluffing their feathers and fighting over scraps. After a few minutes watching this intense avian action, my vision started to darken around the edges, like a warm towel was being draped around my head, and I felt my body relax. Maybe I could slip into my patented meditative faux-rest for just a second—the place was dead anyway, and my presence alone was probably enough to stop would-be terrorists.

Was terrorist even the right word to use for them? I couldn't be working for a terrorist while simultaneously protecting against terrorists, could I? Or maybe because I was on the good side, [Name] was called something else, like *Mischief Maker,* or *Fun Fighter,* or *Gleeful Guerilla.* Guerilla . . . Gorilla . . . I bet [Name] didn't have hairy armpits like other women . . . she seemed like a shaver—

An explosion jolted me from my sleep and rocked the platform. I snapped to attention and looked for the source. Sparks billowed above the crowd. Off to my right, I heard screams and saw a man chasing his friend with a smoking tube. *FWUMP . . . SHHHEEEWWW!* The missile shot up into the air, then—*POP!* Another brilliant blossom of fire spread in the sky above the pavilion, then fell to earth. Cheers and applause erupted around the plaza. The fleshies seemed to love their illegal fireworks. More people had gathered, lured by the spectacle and the promise of an inspiring Raphael Calabrese rally.

I slapped the drowsiness away and focused on the hope in the faces of the assembling crowd. I had to admit that the feeling was infectious—change was definitely in the air. The intricacies and politics of the RMZ were well beyond my comprehension, but even I could see that the people of the RMZ deserved better. It seemed like history would soon be made, and for once I felt like I was on the right side of it.

There was a tap on my shoulder. I spun around to find myself facing a hodgepodge Bishop with glowing eyes.

"You're dead, Rook," the Bishop said, shaping its fingers into a little pistol.

I reached for the Frame's hand, gently closing it and easing it down.

"You'll have to be sneakier than that," I said.

"I'll keep that in mind," [Name] said from her Bishop.

"Is he here?" I asked casually as I spied over her shoulder, trying not to sound too gung ho. Sometime in the night, as I tried to fall asleep but couldn't over the sound of my own self-analyzing, I came to the conclusion that my first encounter with Raphael Calabrese hadn't gone quite as well as I'd first thought. So while I was working on with my protection plan and its acronyms, I also conjured up some ways I could make it up to him. I was going to play it pure this time and not talk too much. *Just listen to the man, Null. Only say something if it's clever or wise. Remember: he's the moth, you're the flame. Be stoic. He's just a person.*

[Name] nodded behind her to a parked MTV surrounded by guards, "He's on board, waiting for the all-clear before coming out, but he wanted me to talk to you first."

My heart burst and my stomach dropped at the same time. He *did* remember me. I wished I was dead just so I could be a ghost and listen in on the conversation he had where I was mentioned. I'd heard somewhere once that if you communicate with a new acquaintance three times within the first week of meeting them, there's an eighty percent likelihood that they'll become a part of your friend group. Suddenly the prospect of becoming Ralphael Calabrese's buddy was no longer just a prospect—it was really happening. Panic clinched me. I found myself struggling to remember the name of his yachts, or where they were even located. Did I have a swimsuit that fit me anymore, or would I have to ask Raphael for one to borrow? Maybe I could just go through his changing room and take one of his without telling him. He would laugh so hard when he saw me stroll out on the sundeck in his favorite speedo— *"Those were my favorite but I guess they're yours now! Ha!"* he'd say as the models giggled. Friends can't be mad at friends.

"Are you listening to me, Null?"

"What?" I said.

"How are you feeling? [Name] repeated. You ready for today?"

"Oh, yeah, yeah. Been surveying this area all morning," I said. "Those windows near that mid-rise are ideal for snipers, figured we could sweep there before figuring out the stage area. How many units are you giving me again? I probably just need half a dozen or so for the perimeter. I can keep close to Raphael Calabrese in case—"

[Name] extended a hand to hush me. "Plans have changed . . . slightly," she said.

"It's SKIRM®, isn't it? They're trying to stop the rally, those asshats. Was I spotted?" I said.

"Actually no, it's been pretty quiet. We're expecting the typical riot patrols at some point, but right now SKIRM® is up in their high castle. Just watching," [Name] said, looking up to the office fortress that cast a shadow on the stage below.

"Oh, so is everything all right?"

"It's better than all right. Not only is every leech and fleshie in the city headed this way, but we just got word that *RMZ News Now* and *RMZ Live* are covering the event. This place is going to be swarming with drones, recording everything for the world to see."

"So what's the problem?" I asked.

She hesitated, choosing her words carefully. "That many eyes . . . we're going to need you to lay low for a little bit. Can't risk you getting seen before we're ready. We have to take advantage of SKIRM®'s indifference and avoid confrontation at all costs."

"So if I'm not leading the security detail, what the hell am I doing here?" I asked.

"Calm down, Null."

"Yeah." I said, trying to center myself. "I'm calm."

"First, take this." [Name] handed me a familiar-looking, rectangular chip. Small enough to fit into my service slot.

"Another Mantis chip? No thanks." I waved my hand.

[Name] pushed the silicon slab back at me, insisting I take it. "No, not Mantis. It's a security seal, similar to the one I use to block my name from showing up on transcripts and logs."

"What block? You saying your name isn't [Name]?" I quickly brought up a replay of our conversation on my HUD and watched it back. "Son of a bitch. Well that's pure."

"Plug that in when you can find someplace private. Sooner the better. Once it's activated you'll show up as a scrambled block on every *securofeed* in the city. You'll be a ghost, just like me." [Name] paused for a moment on her last words.

"What do you need me to do for Raphael Calabrese?" I asked.

"Raphael is already taken care of, as is the perimeter. We've had our team on every inch of this city for months. We need you for something a bit more . . . *specialized*."

I nodded, not really understanding, but not wanting to feel left out.

"What's the mission?" I said, straightening up.

[Name] hesitated again, smiling sheepishly. "It's not a mission per se; it's more of a person. You remember Etta, right?"

I nodded again. "The bratty kid, what about her?"

"Raphael wanted her to be at the rally, but she only agreed to come along if he'd let her explore the city which he okayed, but—"

"She needs a bodyguard," I finished.

"You're sharper than you look, Null," [Name] said with a digital smirk.

"Do you really need me to guard a kid? Feels like a waste of my skills," I said.

"Well, Etta specifically asked for 'the Rook.' Kid seems to like you." [Name] moved in closer, tapping me on my forehead. "Keep your wits about ya, Null."

"For you? Anything." I said.

[Name] chuffed a little then walked back to the MTV.

"That was weird." Etta said, standing beside me. I jumped back terrified.

"How long have you been there!?" I screamed.

"Few minutes," she said. "I wanna see the pet store. Dad says I only have a couple hours before I have to come back." Etta quickly pivoted, walking away from me. I crouched behind a towering compost bin and slipped in [Name]'s chip before taking off after her.

The city center of SKIRM®'s main hub was many times denser than Desolin. Crowds gathered in every direction, filling up street corners, bars, and open-air markets. Bomb-proof bubble MTVs zoomed around the city, filled with wealthy tourists. They appeared bored, staring off into the void of their AR world, probably watching a news feed or something on *INSIDE SKIRM®*. There was another group rounding a corner, being led around by one of the local leeches carrying a long fluorescent stick, keeping his customers together in a tight herd. On either side of the gawking mass stood heavily armed guards maintaining a safe distance between them and the local population. Were they here for Raphael Calabrese, or was this just a bucket-list destination for those with the means? Either way, it was making it hard for me to keep an eye on Etta. Her spidery little legs seemed to skitter to a blur as she disappeared into the heavy foot traffic.

"Hey, slow down!" I shouted, trying to catch up. "CareE, I'm having trouble keeping an eye on–"

"I'm a little busy with something" CareE said, "Can it wait?"

"No, it can't. I'm trying to make Raphael Calabrese not hate me. I need you to do something–"

"Done," CareE said, cutting me off. "That's Etta's heat signature."

My vision suddenly turned gray, save for a small red outline that marked Etta's location.

"I've also tapped into the city's security feed in case you need a better view," CareE said curtly. "If you need anything else, figure it out for yourself. I'm busy."

A row of security feeds filed in from left to right. Feeds one and two showed Etta on the move and a translucent rectangle where I should have been—[Name]'s tech seemed to be working its magic. Suddenly, Etta started to cross the street into heavy traffic. I quickly did the same.

"Hey! Be careful!" I shouted. "Look both ways GAHH—" A small Vespa blindsided me and ricocheted hard into the reinforced asphalt. I managed to keep my balance, but the helmetless driver appeared to be unconscious, lying in a small pool of his own blood. Without thinking, I pulled out a wad of decrypted credits and stuffed them into his pants—no time to exchange insurance information while I was on the clock.

I moved across the street following Etta's red outline. She'd stopped to talk to someone—an old woman who had filled both sides of the alley with an assortment of pillows and recycled furniture. A begging leech, from what I could tell. Etta had placed some money into the woman's liver-spotted hands, and the latter reared back laughing, showcasing the toothless black gums that occupied her petrified mouth. It looked as if her skull was trying to break the thin confines of her face skin. A rusted prosthetic leg hung limply over her right knee. The old woman extended her hand to shake Etta's and show her thanks, but I swooped in, batting the malnourished wrist away.

"Hey, I paid her to read my fortune!" Etta yelled as I gathered her up and started walking.

"Touch the locals and you'll get staph in three days. There's your fortune. Didn't you want to go to the zoo?"

"Pet store," Etta shot back, annoyed.

Over my shoulder I saw the leech grimace and shoot her hand up in some strange gesture. "Fuuuuck you, tin man!" she screamed as we rounded the street corner.

Our trek through the crowded streets continued, with us stopping occasionally to watch a street performer or protest gathering. Etta bought herself a taco trio platter from a food cart. The smell was heavenly. Life had been so hectic the last few days that I'd forgotten how much I missed food, real or synthetic. That smell of melted cheddar and bean paste reminded me of a culinary convention I went to once. For a thousand credits you were given a plate the size of a satellite dish and three days to eat whatever you wanted. By the end of it, the convention floor was so caked in grease and butter that you had to carefully shuffle to the bathroom if you wanted to throw up the previous meal.

Etta instinctively offered me a bite of her last taco but I waved it off.

"Not hungry?" she asked, laughing.

"I think I am. Actually, no, I'm kind of on a diet."

She nodded. "Where are you controlling that from? Your house? Both of my teachers are tin sleeves, too. I don't mind. Dad says VRE's rot the brain though, doesn't let me use them anymore, except when he shows me the ones he's in. He says he wants me to have a more *classic education*," Etta said, mocking her dad's baritone as she took the last bite of her tortilla-wrapped snack.

We were almost to the pet store when a chanting crowd blocked our path as it marched through the street.

"Leave us be in the R-M-Z! Leave us be in the R-M-Z!"

The thought of warning [Name] about the oncoming protestors crossed my mind, but I decided against it—she probably had a finger on the pulse of everything going on, and my Johnny-come-lately warnings would just get in the way.

"We're here," Etta said with a sparkle in her eyes.

Pwet Markit wasn't your typical mom-and-pop—or even big chain—pet store where you might go to find that dream dog or raccoon you'd always wanted. It dealt in the extremely exotic. The cages lining the closed-off street were filled with creatures like komodo dragons, grey wolves, Helmeted Hornbills, green anacondas, anything that made a person feel a step lower on the food chain. Men and women shouted in a thousand different languages over the squawks and roars, bartering for creatures they sought as pets or, more likely, erection supplements. It was absolute chaos, and it smelled like an Italian bus terminal.

"Well, what's on the shopping list?" I asked Etta.

She went quiet, taking in the spectacle.

"How about we check out the snakes?" I said. "Kids love snakes, right?"

Etta wandered off without a word while I kept an eye on her from the serpentarium.

A quick glance at the time told me we were still a few hours away from Raphael Calabrese's rally speech. I wondered if maybe while I was babysitting I could watch some of it from the security feed CareE had gifted me. The row of monitors launched back up in my HUD, but I was only able to see the stage from about a half mile away because every other *secerofeed* that was worth looking at seemed to be blank or offline. Strange, but I could be in a dead spot or something, or maybe the electric eels were causing interference. After a moment, I realized I'd been staring at a tank of snakes for some time, losing track of the day.

"How many do you think are in there?" I asked CareE, staring into the hot tub-sized aquarium bulging at the sides.

"Twenty three thousand six hundred and forty four. No, wait, make that forty three; one of them just ate its mother," CareE said, sounding distracted by something else. For some reason the cannibalistic nature of the snakes made me think of Pookie 2. The little guy hadn't crossed my mind in a month, and I wondered if maybe after everything was over and done with, I could buy him back from the creep I sold him to. But I hadn't kept the guy's address.

"CareE, how long can a quokka survive on the streets?" There was only silence. He was probably running a diagnostic update or checking in on Etta for me, but I decided to do a wellness check just in case.

"Hey bud, everything okay?" I asked.

"Yes and it's starting to bother me," CareE replied. His voice was edgy, at least for a software A.I.

"What is it?" I said.

"Everything is too . . . *peaceful.*"

"That's good, CareE. Peace is a good thing."

"Your childlike assessment is correct, but historically—even during the most peaceful of protests—there's at least one arrest or nervous beating. The *securofeed* shows everything as normal. It doesn't feel right."

"You're an A.I., you're not supposed to feel. Maybe Raphael Calabrese just has that effect on people," I said, watching the glass of snakes move hypnotically back and forth.

"Hmm."

"I'm ready to go," Etta said, tapping me on the back.

"Already? Did you buy anything?"

"Yep."

"What did you get?"

"Everything."

"What?" I said.

The runners of the shop started shooing people away and closing up displays. Two helpers came by with the top to the snake tank and secured it in place.

"Wait, you own all of this now? I asked, still not quite believing her. "Even the snakes?"

"Yeah, them too. Just waiting for the funds to transfer," she said. "I'm shipping them to my dad's place in Marche for now. I'll figure out the sanctuary stuff when I get back."

"Kind of overkill, isn't it? I said. "What about the elderly couple who can't have a night of romance now? Could be the thing that fixes their years of unspoken hatred. You even consider them?"

300

"At least they were able to get old. Most of these animals lost half their lives the minute they got locked up and probably can't wait to die." She took a breath, thinking for a moment. "Ralph—I mean, my dad has this saying. It's hokey and I'm pretty sure he said in one of his stupid VRE's but it always stuck with me: *'Don't try to save the world for everyone, save it for someone else.'*" Her words hung in place as she turned and headed toward the convention area.

My attention turned back to the big snake tank. I wondered if the snakes would get a bigger home or they would just stay in their container at Raphael Calabrese's Italian chateau.

"Hey CareE, how many–"

"Twenty three thousand six hundred and sixty. The taipan was pregnant. *Mazel tov.*" CareE put up a **Do Not Disturb CareE** message across my HUD.

Etta had stopped at another autonomous food cart and was already wolfing down a small tray full of steaming hot takoyaki smothered in a divine glaze of Worcestershire, ketchup and sugar. My mouth would have watered if it could, but that thought passed as I realized the SKIRM® hub wasn't exactly crawling with octopus.

"You sure you want to eat that?" I asked.

"Eh tot uyaa budahgah?" Etta replied with a mouth full of deep fried mollusk.

"Come again?"

"I thought you were a bodyguard," she said, swallowing her last bite.

"Just being thorough," I said. "I can't really stop you from poisoning yourself with raw meat, so if you get sick, it ain't my fault."

"Ah well, thanks for the concern," Etta said, letting out a small burp as she continued her stroll through the crowded streets. "So how did you get this job, anyway? Just happen to be in town?"

"Yeah, something like that," I said, walking next to her. The crowds were starting to thin out as some of the market shops closed for the day.

"Do you like what you do?" Etta asked.

"Not always, but I'm kind of between opportunities at the moment. Just doing this until I figure some things out. Hey wait, where are you taking us?" I asked, realizing the streets were nearly empty now.

"*VoidOut*. Ever been to one?" Etta replied.

"No. What is it?" I asked.

"It's like a Rig simulation, but the tech is, like, *a lot* older," she said. "There's only about three left in the world, and SKIRM® put one here to give the tourists cheap kicks. Figured a dinosaur like you would have heard of it."

"Oh wait, you mean a VRcade? like a *Blastro's*?"

"Like a what?" Etta asked, perplexed.

"*Blastro's*!" I said. "Except, well, those were more popular in the big cities. Dad always took my brother and me to *Gameswitch*. It wasn't as nice as Blastro's, and the levels were outdated, but we always had a good time. Dad said it was like paintball for pussies. Also, we could never figure out if it was called Game Switch or Games Witch," I said.

"I can't wait . . . I heard it's better than a VRE," Etta said excitedly. "I watched a docu-series on the way here—all the experts agreed that VRcades were like the pinnacle of interactive entertainment."

"Eh," I replied.

"*Eh*? You don't think so?"

"I mean, yeah, when I was a kid they were fun at the time, but you were lucky if you didn't break your arm jumping over a box or something. Also, *Gameswitch* had a really bad latency problem with the VR goggles—one minute you'd be running from a zombie, then suddenly you'd freeze in place, and . . . BAAM! You'd end up kissing a concrete wall. *Blastro's* had padded floors at least. Way better."

"But didn't it feel more real?" Etta asked.

"For sure, because it *was* real. But the space was always limited by the size of the room. Rigs adapt to the user, that way everyone is on their own without worrying about running into each other. If you put everyone in the same room, the programming can't keep up so you always end up in cramped quarters or in some kind of zombie survival mode."

Etta was quiet. A look of disappointment cast on her face.

"But I'm sure we'll have a good time!" I said.

"Nah, it was a stupid idea. Let's just go back to the rally," Etta said.

"No, don't listen to me," I said. "You just hit a nerve talking about the old stuff. My brother does that all the time. Talks about when we were younger, simpler times, crap like that."

"Just sounds like he's nostalgic. That's not a crime," Etta said.

"I know . . . but he practically worships the past. That's why I moved into the city and he stayed out in the 'burbs. I wanted to be my own person and not just a clone of our dad."

"Heh, that hits close," Etta said. "All right, we can go to *VoidOut* but you gotta stop the attitude, okay?" Etta stuck out her hand.

"Okay," I said, shaking on it.

The VRcade was a ghost town, more of a mausoleum than a family fun center. The decor was familiar: blacklights cast a dim glow over neon-framed posters and purple carpet with geometric patterns. Memories of stale pizza and sterile music came flashing back, making me sick to my stomach.

But VoidOut was definitely more modern than either *Gameswitch* or *Blastro's*. Where a dine-in restaurant should have been was just an empty room with AR projections screaming ads for all of the simulations the place had to offer. It was also a lot bigger than the VRcades I had visited as a kid. Its monumental walls rose six stories inside the hollowed-out warehouse, and everything was painted Drac Black, a color so dark that it not only absorbed all light, but bent it as well, so judging the size of the space was impossible. Only a small ready-room bathed in purple stood between us and the virtual battleground.

The VRcade's A.I. guided us through a standard orientation screening where we picked up our pink plastic rifles. The simulated human was a gaunt, middle-aged man drowning in an oversized polo shirt who spoke to us like a dad trying to seem cool to kids at a birthday party. Every time he gesticulated with his thin hands, the wisps of remaining hair on his head danced and jumped.

"Remember, the monsters might seem real but they're not! So don't worry and have fun!" An ancient rendering of a T-rex holographically emerged from the shadows and swallowed the A.I. whole.

"Oh, and one more thing," a muffled voice said from inside the dino's belly. Suddenly an explosion of lizard guts and phosphorus filled the room, and the awkward A.I. emerged, now shirtless, decked head to toe in armaments and sporting a new bloody headband. "No running more than twenty feet at time. Put on your goggles now. *Hoo-rah!*"

"Hoo-rah!" we both shouted back at the dad a-la Rambo guide.

There were only two pairs of goggles on the wall that weren't falling apart. Etta plucked one up and I did the same. As I watched her bubble about with anxious energy, I remembered what I'd told myself when we first got there: *Make sure she has fun. Don't forget yourself and start sniping her points and being a bad winner. She doesn't know how to play.* My goal would be to make her look like the hero while simultaneously—and *subliminally*—teaching her a thing or two.

Etta slipped the band of the VR goggles over her head with ease, but the size of my gigantic robot skull made it difficult to get the headband of the old tech all the way around my head. I pulled the goggles down from the front and back, hearing the nylon and carbon weave protest as I tried to wedge the band on. Then . . . SNAP! The band whipped back around; the broken goggles fell and smacked the floor. I snatched them up and examined the shattered lenses.

"You ready for this!?" Etta shouted. She was entrenched in her fake simulation now, unable to see my real-world pains.

I looked back to the wall of busted goggles.

"Uh, yeah," I said. "Pain town is open for business."

"What?"

I thought fast. I couldn't let my stupid, fat head ruin the fun for Etta. She needed a partner. CareE could probably just tap into the building's video server and stream to my Frame's HUD without breaking a sweat, so I tried asking him for help.

"Hey CareE, I know you're busy with whatever it is that you're doing, but could you help me with something?"

He didn't reply. Instead, the **Do Not Disturb** icon flashed a couple times. So much for that. Etta craned her neck to look at the ceiling, then turned her attention to the walls. The AR displays around us showed that we were in the cargo deck of a military class space frigate, *The Filler of Bottom*. If CareE couldn't help me, then I'd just have to take my cues from Etta and match her movements. It would be like my high school drama class where we played the "mirror game," except hopefully this time I wouldn't get spat on.

I could hear the ship's master-at-arms barking orders at us through the ready room's PA system.

"Prepare to fall right into enemy territory in this, your very own drop-pod. Once you land, your orders are to kill everything in sight, is that clear?"

I nodded. Etta screamed in agreement. She was hooked.

The ready room's doors slid open like a convenience store and I took in the cold, black space in front of me. It was like a movie theater with no seats or screen. The only light was a dim red exit sign fifty yards away. I stepped forward, but stopped when I noticed Etta wasn't moving.

"We're leaving orbit, coming in hot!" The loudspeaker boomed. Powerful fans spooled up to help sell the sensation of freefall. I did my best to mimic Etta's movements without giving it away that I couldn't see anything past the ready room. The ground began to sway back and forth as music kicked in: tribal monks humming an assortment of guttural vowels that rose to a deafening crescendo. We had to be just a few moments from impact.

"This is amazing!" Etta screamed over the campy music and poorly mastered sound effects, which thundered as we made impact with the planet.

"Here we go!" I screamed back, not having the faintest idea of what we were doing.

"Go! Go! Go!" The master-at-arms voice screamed over the goggle's micro speaker, barely audible as they bounced broken and slung over my shoulder.

Etta unleashed another war cry, charging in through the ready-room's doors. I followed her into the blank battlefield. Scattered throughout the dark cavern were a handful of foam boulders and reinforced cardboard walls—textural elements that added to the VR, but now to me just looked sad and cheap. I took cover behind one of the smaller boulders to make it look like I knew what I was doing, then popped up, took a shot into the empty room, and dropped back into safety, hoping I'd hit something. I figured that without me helping our kill count, we'd both be taken out before she discovered my handicap.

"Are you okay, Null?" Etta asked from behind her own boulder.

"Yeah, all good here. Why?"

"Because you're using one of the villagers as cover. I think that might hurt our score."

The VR motion tracking was more accurate than I thought. "Good point. You move up and I'll be right behind you."

"Okay, let's head for that bunker over there!"

She popped out of cover, firing a volley of rounds and dodging what I assumed was enemy fire, then sprinted a few feet to her right. I did the same, following in her footsteps while fumbling with the goggles to listen for any other auditory clues. She was waiting for me crouched on one knee, peeking out of what had to be a window or blown-out wall.

"What's the plan, captain?" I asked.

"What?" she said. "You're the soldier. I'm following you."

"It's your game, you're in charge." I gave her a proper salute. "Ready for orders, sir!"

Etta scouted the battlefield then looked back at me, "We could go left, but then we're losing our cover. The right has more options, but I see a lot more aliens. Maybe we go through the middle. You see that flagpole out there?"

I looked over the invisible cover then back to Etta.

"Yeah, flagpole," I said. "Looks like our best bet."

Etta's shoulders dropped as she let out a short sigh. "There is no flagpole. If you hadn't thrown your goggles away, you'd know that. I told you we didn't need to come here if you didn't want to." She shouldered her cheap rifle. "Just leave. I'll figure out how to get back on my own."

I felt like a jerk, but I needed to explain myself. I thrust out the broken goggles to show her, but she missed them as she took off toward the virtual enemies' left flank.

"Null, I need to talk to you," CareE suddenly piped up. "I think I figured out what's going on."

"Not now!" I said. "Kind of in the middle of something." I chased after Etta, once again following her lead. As I stomped through the empty warehouse in pursuit, my Frame's reinforced feet crushed through the foamcore floor, cracking concrete. I leapt into a dive roll and landed next to her.

"I thought I told you to leave," Etta said, firing into the blankness of the warehouse.

"Null, this is very important. I need you to—" I set CareE to mute on my HUD.

"Here, look. They broke." I lifted Etta's goggles, showing her the busted strap on my own. "I know I should have said something. I just didn't want to ruin the fun."

She frowned at the busted goggles.

"Sorry," I said. "I would've loved to snuff out, uh, whatever these things are with you. Maybe sometime when I'm not in a robot suit." I dropped my chintzy rifle on the ground.

Etta stared at it silently for a second. "What are you doing?" she said.

"Whaddya mean?" I said.

"You're not giving up," she said, grabbing my weapon and shoving it back into my hands. "We gotta save a planet."

I couldn't help laughing. "Appreciate the optimism, but a blind man and a teenager aren't saving anything," I said. "You don't know how hard these things can ge—"

"Null, watch out!"

Instinctively I hit the floor and covered my head, courtesy of my SKIRM® PTSD.

"What is it?" I screamed as Etta released a stream of hellfire into the sky.

"A wasp the size of a couch," she said. "But I got it."

"Jesus. I almost pissed my pants."

"Do that later," she said. "After we win."

"Okay," I said, nodding, taking a long look out into the ominous black void. "What now?"

"Right. Uh . . ." Etta was briefly lost for words as she stared at the battlefield ahead of us. She sucked in a gulp of air. "We're—we're on the edge of an open clearing that's probably a hundred feet wide with this, like, wispy blue grass that's about waist high," she said. "Both sides of it are lined with square purple trees the size of, I don't know, apartments?"

I closed my eyes as she spoke, ignoring the darkness in front of me.

"Above us there's nothing," she continued. "Well, I guess that's not exactly right—it's actually really beautiful. You can see space and a bunch of stars and galaxies and—oh shit, that's the ship we launched from. It's huge. Like the size of a city or something."

As Etta described the world, everything seemed to appear vividly in front of me, like a lucid dream I could control. The sudden visuals frightened me at first, and I couldn't make sense of what was happening. Maybe my Frame had synced with the simulation over the local network? These places always had shitty firewalls set up by tech illiterate part-timers. I looked up and saw the enormous frigate hovering in the upper atmosphere of the hyper-saturated alien planet. Behind it were millions of stars and a spectrum of swirling galaxies. It felt like I could jump up and touch the titanium underbelly.

"Up ahead at our one o'clock, maybe fifty yards or so, is a huge tank with a twenty-foot cannon and a pulse turret," Etta said. "Between us and that are some red squiddy alien sentries with antimatter shields. Kinda scattered in a zig-zag."

The tank materialized at the end of the battlefield, along with the other soldiers—ghosts at first that lost their translucence as I was taken by the moment—in their temporary dugouts.

"Can you see it?" she asked.

"Yeah, I can."

"When I say, we're running to a mound over here, okay?" She nudged me northwest. A dozen yards away I could see a soggy dune peppered with little craters. I nodded.

"Go!" Etta shouted.

We hopped out from behind an overturned transport and sliced our way through the swaying cerulean grass. One of the closer sentries peppered the ground next to us with plasma while the mother tank lobbed hail mary shots our way, wind from the shockwaves slamming our faces. Etta returned the courtesy, firing as she ran laterally, and I did the same, aiming where she aimed.

"Okay!" Etta screamed.

She tugged my arm and I slid behind the pile of earth. A few rounds pitter-pattered the other side, sending misting sprays of dirt raining down on us.

"There's just a couple over there," Etta said. "I think we can get around them." She peered around the mound. "At our two o'clock ten yards up is a trench. We'll run, and when I say jump, jump."

"Sounds good."

"Move!"

I leapt up again, huffing it toward the trench. Slashes of heat seared my face as a volley of plasma whizzed past, just missing me. I returned fire mid-sprint and realized Etta wasn't running next to me.

"Etta?"

"Keep going!" she shouted from back at the earth mound.

I kept running, glancing over my shoulder as she sighted in the two enemies, waiting for her moment.

"Jump!" she yelled.

I jumped. The two aliens instinctively bolted upright and Etta took her shots—*WAHP! WAHP!* Black blood sprayed upward in huge arcs as the two soldiers snapped backwards to the ground. I flattened myself in the trench, waiting for Etta. Seconds later she sprang into view, landing next to me.

"Nice shots," I said.

"Sorry," she said.

"Being bait is better than being dead," I shrugged.

"Speaking of, let's see our friends."

We ran over to the two toasted aliens beside their bunker.

"Ew," Etta said. "They sorta have this inner membrane filled with like . . . jelly."

The aliens were splayed out, oozing from the head shots. At least I think it was their heads.

PLOP! PLOP! PLOP! Hundreds of shots suddenly pelted the bunker all at once, from what sounded like two sides. It seemed like the entire battalion had us sighted and were moving into our position.

"We're sandwiched," I said, thinking quickly. "I've seen this before—we need to fall back, find a way to get around their flank."

"No way," Etta said, staring at where the disposed aliens were. "I have an idea." She jabbed at one of the carcasses and seemed to make an incision, then scooped what had to be guts and fibrous tissue from the corpse. She stepped inside the slit, wriggling her body in a strange way.

"What are you doing?" I asked.

"Making a squid suit!" She said, bouncing back up. "Now you!" She poked her arms out from inside her alien cocoon and pointed at the spot where the other body lay.

I chuckled. "Whatever you say." I split open the other one, hollowed it out, and squeezed inside. I got up, and my alien shawl made me instinctively hunch like an old lady.

"Smells like a wet dog in here," Etta said, wrinkling her nose. She reached across the chest of her alien coat and grabbed at things I couldn't see. "Give me that one's grenades, too."

I grabbed the same spots on my body and handed her the items.

"Whatever you do, don't shoot until I say."

"Okay," I said.

"All right, let's see here," she said, poking her head around the bunker. She heaved the grenade out of the bunker back in the direction from where we came, and seconds later—*GA-BOOOM!* "Run!"

We dashed out in our squid suits and kept up our advance amidst a wall of rifle fire, running in the direction of the grenade blast. The aliens mistook us for two of them, and were concentrating their shots on where they thought the humans were.

"You fire east into that tree line, and I'll fire west," Etta shouted. "Then duck into the grass!"

"Roger!" I said, feeling adrenaline flood my chest.

"Fire!"

We unloaded our rifles into the treeline at the distracted aliens, shredding fuzzy purple leaves and splitting trunks.

"Duck!" Etta commanded.

I hit the deck with her and disappeared into the tall grass, listening as the two sides began firing across the field at each other, confused and disoriented. Etta howled with laughter as she wriggled and slipped out of her alien skin suit.

"C'mon!" she said, army-crawling forward. "Head to the mother tank." I slithered out of my camouflage and followed, dreaming of the power washing I'd need later to remove the goo. After a minute of shuffling through the planet's dirt (which Etta said looked like glitter), we arrived within earshot of the rumbling tank tracks. She reached into her belt and pulled out the explosives, handing me one of them.

"Tank's just a few yards that way. You ready?" she said.

"I am now," I said, pumped.

"Hoo-rah!"

We sprang up and I followed Etta's lead, slapping the bombs on the tank, before she yanked me hard in the other direction. We only got a few feet before a nuke-like blast shook the ground and launched us into the air. The sky flashed white as the mother tank mushroomed into the heavens. I hit the ground hard, went into a somersault, and tumbled across the ground into—

Darkness. With the faintest hint of black light.

Etta and I were back in *VoidOut,* in an end room on the side of the arena opposite to where we'd started. The beautiful planet was gone, and only the empty warehouse remained. AR projections around us hailed our victory, and showed a scene of our likenesses accepting the written surrender of the alien commanders on the mothership, celebrating the end of the war.

"74% accuracy, hmm," Etta said, eyeing our stats on another AR display. "Not bad for a blind man and a teenager."

It was getting on in the day, but Etta decided she wanted to check out a movie theater across from *VoidOut* which had a double feature showing some things called *Gloria* and *The Red Balloon.* I protested at first—I'd never been a fan of the old style of movie making; it was way too slow.

"You've just never done it right," Etta said on the walk over.

"I dunno," I said. "Compared to actually being *in* a movie as a sidekick or family pet . . . it's really hard to go back to the non-interactives."

"But have you ever been to a movie theater, like an actual theater? Not a sim." She asked.

I thought about it and nothing came to mind. The closest thing I could think of was when our Uncle Dab brought over his old UHD projector to watch two gorillas rip a zookeeper in half on some sports channel.

"No, not really," I said. "But what's the point? You just sit there, right? I guess if I get bored I can check my messages or something."

"No! You're not checking your messages. Just embrace the boredom, you'll see. It's part of the experience."

"If you say so," I said, paying for the tickets. I kept CareE on mute and put all my notifications on a two-hour silence at Etta's request. She did the same.

The first film was a little slow at first. But my weariness began to subside about thirty minutes in when the main character, a middle-aged woman from old New York, started gunning down gangsters at point-blank range. By the time the credits rolled, I had begun to understand Etta's obsession and forgive Aarau for his perpetual pipe for all things old.

Etta let out a big yawn. The visit to *VoidOut* had worn both of us down, and sitting in the darkened theater didn't help the cause.

"How about I grab us some snacks?" I asked her. "And maybe some caffeine for the next movie?" Etta nodded, struggling to keep her eyes open.

The theater lobby was empty except for a few people crowded at a bar watching news on the AR display. I picked up some popcorn and diet soda—no need to give the kid a sugar rush on top of the shock combo of carbonated-hydrates. The second movie had started by the time I got back to my seat. This one was *really* old and slow. A small boy was climbing a light pole and retrieving a large, bright red balloon on a string.

"Hey, sorry for taking so long," I said. "Thought I had more time to—"

Etta was passed out. I placed the snacks in the empty chair next to her in case she woke up, then took my seat as quietly as possible. The chair creaked beneath my Frame's weight but held firm, and for the first time in days I felt at ease, disconnected from the world and living in the moment. I felt happy. *Hopeful.* I leaned back in my chair and decided to enjoy the rest of the movie.

The little boy on the screen was walking with his balloon friend down a cobblestone street when I heard a familiar A.I. voice.

"Hello?" it said.

"CareE?"

"Finally I got through. Null, what are you doing?"

"I thought I turned you off. Can't it wait until after the movie?" I said, trying to activate the mute function on my HUD again. CareE cancelled my request—he was using a burst transmission that I couldn't block.

"You need to get out of there," CareE said. There was a cold edge to his voice.

"What's going on?" I asked, scrolling through my missed messages. "Uh oh." [Name] had tried to contact me fifty times in the past hour.

"You need to go now," CareE said. His voice trembled in a way I'd never heard before.

The theater rumbled and shook as if something far off had exploded. Definitely not fireworks. Etta sprang to life, knocking over her gummy worms. The movie stopped and the house lights came on.

"What was that?" she asked, shaking off her sleep haze.

"Grab your stuff, I said. "Time to go."

LOG EIGHTEEN

Outside the theater, Etta and I found ourselves under a slow-moving canopy of stygian clouds. People were running past us, some bleeding, others caked in a shimmering grey paste of sweat and soot. Hundreds of voices boomed at once, shouting questions, sobbing and barking orders. Some of the less distraught survivors were pointing backwards toward a far-off orange glow that was just starting to peek over the tops of the market buildings. Whatever it was, it had come from the convention area.

"What is it?" I asked CareE. "SKIRM®?"

"I don't know," CareE said. "I had eyes on the area, then there was an explosion and everything went dark. I'm trying to piece it together, but I keep hitting walls."

"Walls?" I asked, trying to focus, but losing myself to a frightening burst of crying from the crowd.

"Something's blocking me," CareE said, frustrated. "I'm blind out here."

All at once we heard a sharp pop followed by a sweeping *whoosh* and a thunderous boom. A new mushroom cloud emerged from around the rally space and blossomed up into the blanket of smoke. Etta's eyes welled up and a puff of heartache escaped her lips.

"No . . . " she said.

I took her hand. She squeezed it and bolted toward the chaos, but I snatched her back.

"What're you doing?" I said. "We can't go back."

"What?" Her voice cracked. She was fighting me, trying her hardest to break my gentle grip. "We have to! He's out there."

"C'mere," I said, pulling her back into the theater. Inside I searched the lobby, kicking down doors and shoving away curtains until I found what I wanted. We burst through the rusted steel barrier to the basement and descended the steps into the softly lit concrete space. There was a row of plush backup theater chairs into which I plopped Etta.

"Stay here," I said.

"You said we can't go back—" Etta started.

"*We* can't." I said. "I can."

"Don't leave!" she sprang up, but I caught her and put her back.

"Etta, listen to me." I crouched, meeting her gaze. "I need you to stay here until I can find a way out of the city."

There was a long pause. "And what if my dad is . . . ?" She choked, her face crunching. I saw my reflection in her eyes as they started to well with tears.

"I'm sure he's fine." I lied, feeling just as panicked but refusing to let it show. We sat for a moment, then I grabbed a seat cushion from a chair and ripped it off, using it to tenderly dab at her eyes.

"Gross," she said, swatting at it.

"I've got to go." I stood and moved toward the door. "When the explosions stop, wait two hours. If you don't hear anything and I'm not back, make your way up the hill. You'll be safe there. Remember where that was?"

She nodded.

"Take this," I said, handing her my combat knife. The weight of the blade made her skinny arm shake. "Only use it if you have to."

She placed the heavy blade on her lap. Then she used her forearm to wipe away her tears, inhaled deeply, and straightened up, taking a stoic posture. The fear faded from her face. I looked at her one last time, then ran back upstairs.

A revolutionary fog crept through the streets and alleys, shrouding the area in a claustrophobic haze. I charged toward the fighting, pushing past people fleeing the other way. The distant rumbles grew louder, more defined, and the timbre of other sounds began to pierce the smoke—screams and curses, breaking glass, metal striking metal. I hung a quick right down a street that linked to the main thoroughfare.

What should have been a shortcut turned out to be the opposite. There were bodies everywhere. Some were covered in blankets, wet blood spotting through the fabric, while others lay out in the open, in various contorted positions, trails of their lives coagulating on the street behind them.

A single camera drone was doing a slow push-in shot of one of the dead, starting at the cold river of his blood and ending almost right against his open, dilated eyes. The producers at the news outlet were probably tweaking their nipples at the award-winning footage. I kicked the drone as I sprinted past, sending it fatally spiralling into a wall.

I maneuvered past the bodies the best I could, slowly making my way to the end of the street, then turned onto the road leading to the convention area.

Everything was on fire—a mile of unbroken burning led to the stage where Raphael Calabrese's rally had taken place. Buildings exploded as battery walls swelled and burst, shooting rubble across the street and taking out the legs and heads of whoever was in the way. Silhouettes ran through the smoke in every direction, trying to save what they could, or steal it. I heard gunfire from a mile or so ahead. I kept pushing through the haze, but it was getting impossible to see.

"CareE? Little help," I said.

"I'm trying," he said. "What about this?"

My view changed to infrared, which didn't help. The heat coming off of everything was so intense that nothing was distinguishable.

"Worse," I said, still running.

"And this?"

Everything flashed white as a searing pain shot through my ocular sensors. I fell to my knees screaming and clawing at my face, trying to rip my eyes out.

"Okay, so not that one," CareE said, sounding contrite.

My vision switched back to normal and I rose to my feet. "I'll work with what I got."

I pushed on, running as fast as I could toward the destruction, until my entire Frame started to overheat. Thoughts began to scramble and float around me. It was like I was in a fever dream, and everything was happening at half speed. My legs couldn't take me to where I wanted fast enough, but they were moving too fast at the same time. And if I focused on them too much, I'd forget how to run and freeze in place. I seemed to be controlling myself from above, watching as I sped by the surrounding carnage. It was almost meditative.

WAH-TING! A bullet struck my shoulder from behind, spun me around and sent me end over end into the collapsed rubble of what had been a storefront. I spotted a food cart lying on its side and rolled behind it for cover. The bullet had deflected off my arm. Small-caliber, no big deal. I peeked over the cart to see what I could see. A hundred yards away was the convention area, the once pristine location now a smoldering warzone with deafening volleys of gunfire and yelling. Thousands of leeches and fleshies fought desperately and brutally, tearing each other apart with no indicator of who was fighting who or why. As I scanned the carnage, my face went numb. Something was missing.

SKIRM®.

There wasn't a single SKIRM® fighter or Frame anywhere to be found in the warring mass. Only fleshies. Or leeches, whatever they were. People. There were only people fighting other people. I dashed across the street, dodging melees and projectiles as I advanced to some cover a bit further up. From my new vantage point I could see beyond the convention space and the majority of the fighting to a large square. Hundreds of SKIRM® security Frames stood there, watching but not engaging as the people tore each other apart. Hundreds of news drones zipped around like locusts overhead, capturing every angle of the action. More than a few of them were buzzing around the stoic SKIRM® troops. It didn't make sense.

"The MTV was parked up there," CareE piped up. "Around that blue storage building."

I rushed for the building, bodies bouncing off me as I broke my way through. A posse of leeches set up a makeshift human blockade which I stiff armed, sending them hurtling back into the mess. The rest were too swept up in the bloodlust to even notice me. In seconds I covered the expanse and slammed against the wall of the storage building, hugging it close until I came to the corner. I peered around, looking for the MTV.

When I spotted it, I couldn't believe what I was looking at. The thing was upside down and torn in half, completely charred. Scattered around it were the bodies of some of the security guards I recognized, in a similar condition. I scanned through the car pieces, checked the other bodies around the car and the perimeter, but there were no signs of Etta's dad. *Good.*

"CareE, can you reach Raphael Calabrese?"

"Just call him Ralph, or Calabrese, or RC or something other than his full goddamn name! It's a waste of time and it's killing me!" he shouted. "And no, I can't reach him. Wait. Let me try something."

"Hurry up, we—"

Something tugged me backwards. I turned to see three fleshies trying to yank me down to the ground. I pulled the one directly behind me over my head and tossed him like an old shirt, then I reached low for the ankles of the other two and scooped them up, banged them together until they stopped screaming, then let them fall, unconscious, to the pavement.

"Found him! I got a ping from his workout app," CareE said. "He's not far from here. Head west down that street."

I bolted down the rubble-strewn alley, juking around a pack of fleshies grappling with large, rusted tools.

"I can't believe it," CareE said.

"What is it? Is he—"

"I . . . this can't be right."

"CareE, what's wrong?"

"Calabrese burned fifteen hundred calories in the last hour. You know how hard that is? If he fled like this every day, he'd lose three pounds a week, easy. It could probably help hide the coke bloat, too."

At the end of the block the road split in three directions.

"Which way?" I shouted.

"Left!" CareE said.

I took the left offshoot, but it dead ended a few yards ahead.

"Right!"

A swift pivot and I was heading down an alley toward a sleek midrise that reflected the burning in its glass exterior, making the building itself look as if it was made of fire.

"In there!"

I threw my weight into the entrance door and crashed through, slid across the floor and slammed into a kiosk.

"Ahhhh!"

Two Frames jumped on top of me and started whacking me with electric batons, making my limbs contract and my back spasm in an epileptic fit. They came at me over and over; I couldn't find enough daylight to grab them. I swung my arms helplessly, tearing up the floor and innocent lobby planters as I tried to get free.

"No! No! It's him!" a voice pleaded.

The beating stopped. After a breath I got up and began to see clearly again. Everywhere there were artifacts of the old world in display cases. Retro rockets and antique magazine-fed munitions were paired with their corresponding plaques. It was a museum exhibit dedicated to the history of SKIRM®, from its humble beginnings as a corporate behemoth to its present-day status as a monopoly with tentacles wrapped around the world. In a corner, lit up by a single overhead spotlight, was a diorama showing the early days, when soldiers had to operate their Frames from inside a shipping container within the borders of the RMZ. I remembered what Cal had told me about the brutal deaths of those early pioneers.

I turned my focus to the two Frames who had been giving me the business with their shock sticks. They were security units I'd met before, and just behind them was the man himself.

"Don't." CareE said. "Don't say his full—"

Raphael Calabrese made his way over and greeted me like an old friend, grabbing my bad arm and squeezing it gently. Almost lovingly.

"Thank you," he said, his pupils the size of grapes. "Thank you." He was short of breath, wheezing through every other syllable.

"No problem, just doing my job," I said. "What happened here?"

"I don't know," he said, trying to clear his throat. "It came time to start the rally and I walked up to the stage, and . . ." He trailed off, looking into the distance. I'd seen him do this dozens of times in his VRE's—this was his special dramatic remembering face. Just with more veins and creases.

"There was this group of people in the crowd," he continued, coughing up a little dust as he spoke. "Horrible, dirty people, which I admit could describe anyone in this awful place. But these were particularly vile. They heckled me when I started to speak. 'He's with them!' 'You don't care about us!' 'Give us your money!' All sorts of nonsense. It was so confusing. Then all of a sudden some of them rushed the stage. Some less-dirty people in the crowd tried to stop them. Someone got stabbed I think, then a group jumped the stabber, and another group jumped that group, and that's when everything just . . . exploded."

"Who was it? SKIRM®?" I asked.

"No, those cowards just sat there and blasted nonsense through the PA, 'Stop the fighting. Violence is futile. Peace is the Answer.' Blah blah blah."

"I'm sure [Name] loved that," I said.

"I couldn't say," he said. "She got swept up in the violence right away trying to protect me—that Frame is long gone. Last I saw, two leeches were using the arms to bash each other's heads in."

"So how are you two talking now?"

"We're not," he said.

"But the local network is still up, right?" I said. "[Name] is out there somewhere." I checked around the room, looking at anything electronic. Even the old Frames in the display cases. I assumed she would have swapped bodies by now, unless something was blocking her. We were a long way from Desolin's unregulated network.

"All of it has power," CareE said.

"Can we get a message out?" I asked.

"I can try to send some beeping through the coffee maker or a networked buttplug," he said.

"Are you talking to me?" Raphael Calabrese asked.

"No, I'm just—never mind," I said.

"Before [Name]'s Frame was snatched," he continued, "they said there was an extraction point setup on the roof of the transport terminal. If we can get there, there should be—" He cut himself off, eyeing me with confusion. "Hey, where's my kid?"

"Somewhere safe," I said. "Don't worry."

"Oh, good," he said, breathing with relief. "You got her out."

"Well, she's not technically out, no," I said.

Raphael Calabrese canted his head. "And what does that mean?"

"It means the city was on fire and I thought you were dead. She's worried about you but safe. In a basement at a movie theater."

"Oh god."

"Everything's okay," I reassured him. "Actually it's perfect. Now I know where you're at and that you're alive, so I can go and get her while you hole up here. Then after I take her to the extraction point, I can come back and get you."

Raphael Calabrese thought for a moment, then nodded. "That sounds more complicated than it needs to be, but I think in this situation, you're the top ranking officer."

"Guess I am," I said, feeling myself blush. There was a long, unsettling silence.

"Nell, just promise me," he said, stepping closer, placing his hand on my shoulder. "You'll take care of my little girl if anything happens to me, yes?"

"Of course," I said, forgiving the mispronunciation of my name. He was under a lot of stress.

"I can fight for myself, as you probably know," he said. "But she's, well, she's only eleven, for chrissakes!"

"Twelve," CareE said.

"You can count on me," I said, putting my hand on his shoulder, returning the loving grasp he once shared with me.

He smiled. "Thank you."

An explosion of glass came from behind us. We turned to see dozens of people bashing through the front door with an improvised ram made of another door. Through the expanding breach, a few of them spotted Raphael Calabrese and relayed the information to others. A feverish roar erupted outside. They reeled back and gave one final blow, toppling the door. Then a stream of flesh poured inside after us.

"Go!" I shouted.

We made for the back of the building, following the glow of red emergency lighting. As we reached the exit, a protester rushed one of the security Frames. I could hear its baton swinging wildly, taking people out of commission as it went down fighting. "I'll hold 'em off, get out!" it screamed, buying us precious seconds. The door flew open. As we ran through, I heard the snap of metal and fiber optics as the mass of bodies ripped the security Frame apart.

Outside, CareE started barking orders into my brain. "Left here, right at the next light, heavy traffic over there, rerouting," he said. "Another half kilometer to the theater. Terminal's just past that."

"Anything from [Name]?" I asked as I grabbed Raphael Calabrese's arm, pulling him out of the way of a swinging metal rod.

"Nothing yet," CareE said. "I lost contact after you decided to watch a movie."

"I get it, I'm stupid!" I said.

"Are you all right?" Raphael Calabrese said, struggling to keep pace.

"Never better," I said, quickly herding us down another street, making our way east towards the theater as best I could. When we got to the next intersection, I checked to see if it was clear, confirmed, then motioned to keep moving. Then I froze—*shit*.

Hovering directly in front of us was a drone. I couldn't tell if it was news or surveillance or something else. It didn't move; I wasn't even sure if it was looking for us. It just hummed quietly, its red light blinking off and on.

"Keep moving," I said quietly.

We ran past the drone down a narrow pedestrian walkway between the buildings. Any opportunity to juke around a corner or serpentine, I took, no doubt confusing Raphael Calabrese and the other security Frame as they went along with the madness.

I glanced behind us—the drone was gone. Relief washed over me, one less thing to worry about. Probably just a news bot scouting for hot spots. I pushed us on further until we were back at the edge of the convention center's promenade. It was worse than before, with rifle fire coming from every direction and vantage point. That's when I noticed our last security guard was nowhere to be found. *Where the hell did he go? Did the mob catch up or did he ditch us?*

There wasn't time to dwell on details. We were down a man which meant less backup, but it also meant less baggage. That's when I got an idea. I looked around and saw a fabric sunshade hanging over a blown-out window. I ripped it out of its mount and twirled it around Raphael Calabrese.

"What are you doing?" he said in a panic.

"Everyone is trying to kill you. Just act natural."

With few wraps of the shade, he was turned into a secret burrito. I threw him over my shoulder and darted out into the open convention promenade, pumping my legs as fast as I could. Out to my right amongst the hundreds fighting, a group of people were kicking a person on the ground who was helplessly holding a hand up in a silent plea. One of the mob kicked the hand away while another stomped the victim's temple, putting them down flat. I turned to face forward. No one had noticed us yet, and I could see that in another seventy-five yards or so we'd be out of the open and back inside tight building cover for the stretch to the theater. I dodged around flaming MTVs, side-stepped dead or dying protestors, splashed through puddles from the burst mains. It wasn't too much further now, only a few more steps. I crested the rubble mound of a blown-out storefront, and finally saw the movie theater.

Or what was left of it. The entire structure had collapsed—a hundred thousand tons of brick and steel sucked completely into the earth.

"Where was my daughter again?" Ralfael Calabrese asked with a small crack in his voice.

I ran for where I thought the basement entrance was and started digging. I felt nauseous, weak, but I fought it, yelling a guttural roar as I started digging faster, ignoring what my eyes were seeing. *I'll be there soon. Everything will be ok. Just keep digging. We'll dig all night if we have to-*

"Null . . ." CareE said somberly.

"I need a pick axe or an excavator or something," I said, throwing aside any chunk of brick I could grab.

"You won't find her," CareE said.

"Shut up, I will," I snapped back.

"No, I mean she's over there. Look."

To my right, with a group of people beneath a steel security door, stood Etta, covered in a blanket.

"Dad!" she screamed. She dropped her blanket and ran towards us.

My legs gave out from shock and I plopped down in the rubble. Raphael Calabrese ran to her, not quite as fast, but he was definitely putting in effort. I watched as the two met and embraced in the middle of the destroyed structure.

"Are you ok? Are you hurt?" Raphael Calabrese said, kissing Etta on top of her head over and over.

"Yeah, I'm okay—Dad, stop it! I'm fine. Really!" Etta was embarrassed, but seemed to shine in his affection. She looked back at the crowd emerging from the nearby shop where she'd been hiding. "They helped me."

"Thank you. Thank you so much!" Raphael Calabrese said, standing up with his hands clasped together in a prayer pose. "I would like to make all of you very rich—"

A few of the group waved him off.

"Get somewhere safe," an older man said.

"Yes, we will," Raphael said, using his pointer finger to flick tears from his eye corners. "Null? Shall we?"

I nodded, grateful that he got my name right. I stood and started to take the lead, but something caught my eye that made me hesitate. In the back of the group was the old beggar woman from near the pet market. She smiled when our eyes connected, showing her rotten gums.

"Null?" Raphael Calabrese said. "The terminal?"

"Yeah . . ." I said, watching the woman disappear into the crowd. "Follow me."

CareE directed us toward the exfiltration point a few blocks away on a nearby roof, where a commandeered VTOL would be waiting for us. As we charged along, I looked back at Raphael Calabrese, who was keeping Etta close. Something he was probably going to do a lot more after this was all over.

At the terminal, we hurried across the ground platforms and crammed into the express elevator that would take us to the roof. The lift was glass on all sides but the door, so we could see the stopped lev trains on the different levels during our ascent, and the fires engulfing the slums around SKIRM®'s hub.

What a mess. People's entire lives were floating up into the atmosphere and being carried off by the afternoon breeze.

The lift chimed and the doors opened. Behind me, I heard Etta gasp.

The VTOL lay on its side, billowing flames, with a few bodies scattered around it.

"CareE," I said, "where's the nearest transport station?"

"Looking now, let's see if—"

"No!" Raphael Calabrese screamed. He rushed toward one of the bodies, someone he recognized. I grabbed for him, holding him back from the burning wreckage, but he slipped away.

"Too hot up here, we need to go!" I yelled over the raging flames, following after him.

He ignored me and leaned down next to the body of a young woman, probably in her early thirties. Her eyes were closed peacefully, like she'd just stopped to rest. I walked over for a closer look and saw a small piece of metal in her vest. The shrapnel looked like it had pierced cleanly through her heart. Probably killed her the moment it broke her skin.

"Raphael, we need to—"

"Just let me say goodbye," he said through clenched teeth. It seemed like he was trembling.

I was confused. Who was she? Raphael hadn't mentioned that any of his girlfriends would be here. Who else did he know?

"No identifiers or trails I can see," CareE said. "Doesn't seem like she has a—"

"[Name]," I said.

There she was, in the flesh. So many years she'd cunningly avoided this moment, but it had come just the same. The myth was over, unceremoniously ended with a random piece of jagged titanium.

All the rumors I had heard about the cunning terrorist [Name] appeared to be just that. No acid burns or scar where they removed the conjoined twin who supposedly had lived inside her brain, giving her the ability to never sleep. She just looked normal, like an everyday person who got to the right place at the wrong time.

"We really need to go," CareE said, his cool breaking. "I'll see if I can find some route that gets us to the outskirts, then we can take it from there."

I nodded, slowly backing toward the lift, pulling Raphael Calabrese gently alongside me. I got my final glimpse of [Name]'s lifeless body, then the doors closed and we hurtled back toward the ground.

She had always been so careful, I thought. So precise about her movements and plans. I couldn't believe there was anyone quick or smart enough to be a step ahead of her. I felt lost, lightheaded, in need of a long sit. I straightened myself and focused—my priority was Etta and Raphael Calabrese.

He held his daughter as close as he could, his back to the elevator's wall. "Where are you taking us?" he asked.

"Back the way we came. We'll find another basement or something and keep you two safe until things die down."

"You're the boss," Raphael Calabrese said with a forced grin. His glassy eyes were equal parts fear and hope.

The doors opened to the ground level and my stomach turned. There was a mob at the dropoff area, destroying the station's walls and support pillars.

"C'mon, this way," I said, leading them away. We turned and saw another mass of people coming up from the side of the building.

"That's no good," I said.

Raphael Calabrese loosened his grip on my shoulder and stepped to my side.

"I saw an exit over here," he said.

We moved to follow him. As he turned around, a long-haired figure with a crooked, toothless smile stepped from the shadows.

"Wha—"

A burst of mist sprayed from the old woman's mouth into Raphael Calabrese's. I yanked Etta back as quick as I could and shielded her. I grabbed my knife from her belt and hurled it at the woman, sinking it deep into her eye socket. Her wrists and spine curled as she fell to her knees, still smiling as her life faded. Etta tried to rip away from me and look at her dad, but I kept her close and covered her eyes. He started coughing violently, like he'd been sucker-punched in his gut, then he puked crimson down his shirt. Large clumps of hair came out in his hands. His eyes connected with mine, and I watched as they turned milky white. The skin around his skull began to loosen and drip to the floor. The man's cells were breaking down, releasing their liquids like a lava cake. He crumpled into a wet pile, trying to scream but only mustering a rattling hiss. Then he fell silent as he spread across the floor.

I had to get Etta away, I couldn't let her see her dad like this.

"We need to go, Etta," I said, keeping her against my chest, blocking her view.

"Null . . ." Her voice sounded weak.

I looked down and saw her holding a lump of hair in her hand.

"Etta?" I held her away from me so I could see. Tiny bubbles were forming around a thin black mark on her neck. It had just been a glance—a millisecond quicker and it wouldn't be there.

She started to cough a little. I scooped her up in my arms. "There's gotta be a med station. It's okay."

As started for the exit, I felt her shoulders lurch and her back tighten.

"Oh no, no . . ." she whispered. She reached up to touch my face and I felt the boiling sweat of her palm against my cheek. Tears streamed from her clouding eyes, getting lost in the liquifying cheek and bone.

"Please," I said, sinking to the ground as I held her. She sighed heavily one last time, then her hand fell from my face as her body melted away, through my fingers, onto the concrete of the station floor.

I sat silently for a moment, staring at her lifeless form. She was just here, I thought. And then she wasn't. My mind couldn't rationalize it. I wanted to capture the surrounding air, like I could prevent her soul from leaving and drifting into the atmosphere. I closed my eyes and almost felt the wind of it swirl around me.

When I opened my eyes, I saw the drone from before, recording the entire scene. The mob had pushed into the transpo terminal and were now coming upon the aftermath, screaming, saying things like "Killer!" and "Traitor!" But before they could do anything to me, a hundred SKIRM® security Frames appeared, pushing through, knocking them out of the way. They set up a perimeter. Then a dozen of them approached me. One extended a baton and—

LOG NINETEEN

-- - --- -- -|--   ---   ==-
-

--- - ---x -- --- - - - - - ||--- -- - - ---
--- |- - - - ----::--   -

- -- --- - - --- LOG 19 LOADING ----_-::--
[NOT_FOUND]
-- - //- - //SYSTEM.RECOVERY. . . . .
.INVALID [int.backup.pup] REBOOTING - ERROR,
where am I [subject: [N.LASKER] Etta, where
is -- - //PARTITION.ERROR. [log_corrupt]
failed [NAME] [recommend safe mode . . . not
found] who are you -
//SYSTEM.RECOVERY . . . CRITICAL_FAILURE no
more -- - -
--- - - -- ------ [5%mem_recov . . .
initialized]

LOG █INETEEN

"Quer café?" A calm voice said, waking me up.

"What's that?" I asked, trying to hold back a yawn. My head was pounding; the exit from pre-REM sleep was taking its toll. I had only nodded off a handful of times at work before, but now it seemed to be more frequent—guess my age was finally catching up with me.

"Coffee," Hektor said with a weak grin, his eyes heavy from the late shift. "Figured you could use a pick-me-up. I'm fading too, man."

I took the styrofoam cup from his meaty hand. The liquid inside was lukewarm and probably a few hours past its expiration, but it would work all the same. We were in the factory break room, a small but comfortable space that allowed us to keep an eye on the assembly line from behind a large, reinforced glass mirror. An old digital clock on the wall behind him read 3 a.m. with the tiny milliseconds chasing right behind.

We had been working the line for two days straight and the stims were starting to wear off. The plant had banned them after three onsite deaths and a lawsuit, but we still relied on them to power through the mid-week doubles and triples. Forty-eight hours earlier, Hektor and I had been in line crawling through security, popping a pill each, giddy for the zen-like high we knew was coming. There was only an hour to go before we could clock out—thirty-six hundred seconds until I'd be back home sleeping the day away. I could feel the veins on the side of my head begin to throb.

"How long was I out?" I asked, sipping the stale Columbian brew.

"Don't worry, no one saw," Hektor said, pointing to a spot in the corner of the room. The breakroom *secerofeed* was offline. Hektor was crafty like that. "Any plans this weekend?"

"Supposed to see Aarau, he needs some help with his security system," I said. "Might flake, I dunno. Thinking about catching up with Etta if I can. Wanted to see how the animals are doing." I took another sip of the coffee, sucking on my tongue from the bitterness. The spiders behind my eyes started their creepy crawl.

"Who's *Etta*?" Hektor asked.

The room flashed white, blinding me momentarily. He was staring at me with his eyes half-closed, mid blink. I looked down at my coffee, then back to the statue-like Hektor. I had gone through this process before.

"Damnit, again?" I thought to myself, closing my eyes. "Just be quick this time."

A moment passed. Nothing happened. My body felt fine. Hektor was still frozen; the clock behind him sat at 3:01 a.m. with the trailing milliseconds stuck between two digits, unreadable, like hieroglyphics. Then I felt a sharp snap in my neck, as if someone had jump-kicked me in the back.

[LOADING.STATE_1.03]

"Any plans this weekend?" Hektor asked.

"Supposed to see Aarau, he needs some help with his security system," I said. "Might flake, I dunno. Thinking about seeing Laya, though . . ." I trailed off, staring out onto the assembly line. Something about the conversation felt familiar.

"I always liked Laya," Hektor said. "I'm actually seeing a new girl tonight. She's big, like you gotta buy a plane or jetpack just to see her.

I'll send you the info if you want." He stood up, then attempted to traverse his gut and touch his toes. "Well, should we get back to it?"

The assembly line work was mundane, but still it demanded constant attention. Hektor had just finished loading the hydraulic fluid for the last batch of chassis, a chore we swapped on the daily.

"Gonna sneak a quick call back at HQ," he said, jerking his thumb towards the break room. "Gotta pick up the kid after this."

The QC process was a two-man job, but with his work half done there was really no need for Hektor to stick around. I nodded, then hit the load lifter switch to bring in two dozen freshly pressed metal legs. Protocol dictated that all parts receive a thorough in-person inspection, but our tight turnaround didn't really allow for that. For every late shipment we were docked a half hour's pay, so I moved things along as quickly as I could.

There was a loud *snap*—a common sound, but not a good one. Could be a loose part left on the floor, or more likely one of the legs breaking under the weight of the lifter. I flagged the batch as potentially defective then pushed the rest of the parts through. Again, protocol advised that we stop the entire production for any such occurrence, but I wasn't in the mood to get paid less for someone else's mistake.

The room began flashing red.

"Just what I fucking need," I said to myself.

I pulled up my padlet to see where the kink was. Everything read normal except for an error in one of the joints of the lifter.

Excess Fluid Detected - Null, Wake Up

"What was that?"

"Dunno, looks like another incongruity. Start it up again."

"Copy that."

Excess Fluid Detected - Initiate Shutdown Procedure?

I hit 'accept,' dismissing the notification, but then something in the system overrode my request. Instinctively I pulled up the padlet's command shell, initiating a force quit, but again the production line refused to stop. I began to cough—the air was heavy with something metallic that burned my lungs. When I tried to get out, I found the exit was sealed off. I banged on the glass hoping Hektor would hear me, but he wasn't there. My vision started to blur. I fumbled toward one of the emergency gas masks on the wall, tripping over myself with every step. More coughing, more fire down my windpipe. *Null! Hold on, stay right where you are.* I fell to my knees, but I pressed on, crawling, inching little by little to safety. Somehow I found a small pocket of air, just enough to stave off the lightheadedness. *Ok, I'm in their system now. Found you! Sit tight.* I was up again. The voice in my head was pushing me forward, my consciousness not willing to give up without a fight. *What? No. This is CareE. Don't try to change the logs! If they unsync they're going to restart again and I might lose—*

I reached for the gas mask, hacking out one last fireball before heroically pulling the apparatus over my face. All at once I could breathe again. I was alive! I couldn't believe it.

[LOADING.STATE_1.07]

I reached for the gas mask, hacked a cough, pissed myself, then collapsed on the hard cement. The world spun into a chromatic blur, and I was sucked into a black emptiness.

When I awoke on the factory floor, I could just make out two distinct voices discussing something loudly over the roar of power washers and shop vacs. I felt drunk and out of place. My vision was blurry, opaque, drifting in and out. Had I been here before, or was this happening now? Everything was somehow past and present—it didn't make sense, but in a way it did. I was in a dream that I had already lived, the world ethereal yet clear.

The cacophony of noise drifted off and my vision faded to nothingness. I wasn't on the factory floor anymore. It felt like I was hanging midair by some invisible tether.

A voice reverberated from somewhere far off. "I don't understand, why can't we go back further?" it said. "Don't you think we might have missed something?"

"We can only go as far as the logs take us," a second, more airy voice replied. He seemed to be chewing on something crunchy.

"So he only started logging a couple years ago? What about his social feed?"

"Barren. Practically nonexistent."

"Wow. That's pathetic."

"Just how they like 'em. Hold on, can he hear us?"

"Shit, on it. Rebooting . . . now."

[LOADING.STATE_1.08]

I awoke on the factory floor. Hektor was gesturing wildly to two strangers—black suits back in the breakroom—his voice muffled by the glass window.

"How far should I go back? I know we can't miss anything, but there's so much here," an unsteady voice said, standing above me.

"Just scrub anything that makes the client look bad," a second voice said. "We don't wanna give this guy's family any leverage. Wait, did he just move?"

"I'll get the paperwork."

My eyelids snapped open. The concrete had morphed into carpet, lush with a mild stench of day-old pizza. I was back home. I tried to move, but my body was paralyzed. There was someone else in the room, a rent-a-doc holding some kind of cheap drill that resembled an ice cream cone. He maneuvered the tool to the back of my skull. I felt a jolt through my chest, and I regained mobility. I stood up and batted the drill out of his hand. He barely reacted. Instead, he just stood there, frozen in place—

[LOADING.STATE_1.10]

I was on the floor, it smelled like pizza. I couldn't move, but then the sound of a surgical drill shook me out of my paralysis. I screamed for the man to stop; instead he froze in—

[LOADING.STATE_1.10]

On the floor. There's a man with a drill about to attack me. I take the drill and stab him with—

[LOADING.STATE_1.10]

I lay on the floor. A stranger with ice cream shimmied back and forth, stuck between a stand and a squat.

"Hold it. We're pushing it too hard."

"So stop?"

"No, just send it back to the beginning."

"Really, again?"

"Just do it."

My apartment faded and I returned to nothingness. I was still, alone in a blank void with no way to move. I tried to make sense of what had just happened, what I'd seen, or rather what I'd felt. The little memory islands turned to fuzz the moment I tried to focus, murky thoughts I wasn't able to grasp.

What were these scenes? Was I alone? I tried to hold on to the thought, but it started to slip, like trying to recall a dream while still in one. This had happened before; it was about to start all over again. A terrifying feedback loop. I called for help, but nobody answered. But then, in the distance, I could just make out a faint light. A star, off in

338

the infinite nothing, shining bright and alone, beckoning me. My eyes felt heavy, but I refused to close them. I didn't know what the light was, but I knew I needed to keep it in focus. It began to move, jumping in and out of sight. I struggled to keep my eyes on it, swimming my soul toward it as hard as I could. It started to grow brighter, closer and closer, until it was in my face, nearly blinding me.

"Null! Finally, I thought I lost you," a voice said, sounding friendly and familiar.

"Carny?" I said.

"CareE. What the hell have they done to you?"

Memories started to trickle in one at a time. SKIRM®, the RMZ, the rally, a city tearing itself apart, [Name] . . .

Etta.

Every lost thought came back like a punch to the gut. I looked away from CareE's glow into the neverending black abyss surrounding us.

"Where are we?" I said.

"Physically, a SKIRM® research facility, not far from the city. Cosmically, mentally, I don't know." CareE was holding something back in his voice.

"What about the revolution? Are they coming for us?" I said. "[Name]'s forces must've heard what happened, right?"

"No, it's over," CareE said, defeated.

"What do you mean? Are they dead? Or . . . ?"

"No, it's just over. As soon as they took you in, the fighting stopped. I was lucky to be able to hop on the city's network before they dragged you away, so I could see what they were doing to you, but it was strange. Like someone flipped a switch that made everyone go back to their lives like nothing happened."

"It's because they're all dead," I said. "And I let it happen."

"No, listen. There was nothing you could have done," CareE said, trying to offer up some comfort. "There was nothing *anyone* could have done."

"I should've been faster. I was supposed to protect her. Everyone was counting on me." In the blank void I hung my head, or tried to. I wanted to go back to forgetting everything, back to letting the lab people dig around in my brain.

"Null, I need you to focus. There's something much bigger going on."

"I don't care."

"Listen to me! SKIRM® is saying you're a murderer. A crazy Frame that went AWOL and killed [Name] and Raphael and Etta. You're the most wanted person on the planet, but SKIRM® claims you're on the run, something about rebuilding, taking over [Name]'s legacy."

So, this was what absolute zero felt like—that moment where the world could write your story for you, twist the facts until you're too exhausted to even try and clear your name.

"Fine," I said. "I told you, I don't care anymore. Let SKIRM® have whatever they want. Just let me die in whatever hospital room they've stuck me in."

CareE went silent.

"What?" I asked.

"I did some digging around the SKIRM® network while they were busy pulling your logs and found out what really happened the day you blacked out."

The words choked me up, and for a moment I was silent, not knowing what to say. I debated whether I wanted to know the truth, because it was so much easier to just see the end result and pretend the journey hadn't been that bad. Once I saw this, I knew I couldn't unsee it.

"Null?" CareE said.

"Can you show me?" I asked.

"Show? Uh . . . hmm . . . What if I just give you a summary? Summaries can be just as good. No sense boring you with some long movie—"

"No. I want to see."

"I don't think you should—"

"Just do it, please?" I asked as nicely as I could.

"Okay," CareE said.

The world flashed from black to a searing white, revealing a room with which I was intimately familiar—the cramped walls, the tiny bed with a single Rig and shower stall.

"My apartment?" I asked.

"Yeah," CareE said.

The sound of a toilet flush echoed through the space and then there I was, exiting the shower stall fully dressed, drying my hands on a bleach-spotted towel. I looked thinner, haggard, and my clothes were stained with sweat and protein flakes. Despite my disheveled appearance, I looked happy, practically beaming. It started to come back to me—this was the day I tried out for BroCalibur. I was just moments away from logging into my Rig. It was uncanny, seeing myself from such a voyeuristic perspective. Then I realized that this wasn't a VRE; it was a *secerofeed* inside my apartment.

"You found this on SKIRM®'s internal network?" I asked CareE. He didn't say anything.

So they'd been spying on me. Even though it didn't really make a difference, I felt a little better knowing my suspicions were right and that I wasn't losing my mind. I continued to watch as I plopped down into my Rig for my one-night stand with destiny. For a while my semi-conscious, bulbous body just sat still, eyes darting wildly beneath my eyelids, teeth bared. Then the twitching ramped up, and the sweat began to bead on my forehead. I started to groan and hyperventilate. It was like I was in a sleep paralysis night terror with no way out. This must have been it—the moment where I panicked and flicked on the Mantis.

I wanted to scream at my past self, stop him from ruining his life. Tell that idiot that this was the best it would ever be, to not be so greedy and just be thankful for what he had. Tell him to live the rest of his miserable life alone so that all of his bad luck would die with him. Be a hero, do nothing.

Past Me was now dripping with sweat, shifting uncontrollably. My back started to arch into an impossible curve, then all at once it relaxed and fell as the building lost power, shutting down the Rig and cutting the *secerofeed*. The apartment's emergency generator kicked to life, turning the camera back on, but the Rig remained offline, completely fried. My unconscious body just lay there in a pool of its own fluids.

A pit calcified in my stomach as I waited for the mystery to finally reveal itself, for SKIRM® shadow agents to break down the door and take me away to their secret underground facility. But they never came.

I kept waiting. Maybe it wouldn't be agents. Maybe Aarau would use his key to barge in and rescue me, whisking me off to a nearby hospital. But he never came.

"Null, I think you should stop watching," CareE said.

"No, I want to see what happens."

"Okay, but . . ." He paused a moment, then continued to play back the footage. "Never mind."

The feed sped up as CareE fast-forwarded it. The time counter at the bottom showed an hour pass. Then another. The feed accelerated. Days went by. . . weeks. . . months. . . until finally there was a frantic knock at the door. The feed slowed to real time. No answer. Nothing. Suddenly a boot kicked the door open and a cop barged in with a sloppy tactical roll, gun drawn, a fat finger already on the trigger. He had misjudged the space, though, and bashed his shoulder into the side of my bed frame, which caused him to fire a stray bullet through my left temple. After catching his breath, he vomited on the carpet. He and his partner ran from the room, pinching their noses.

After a moment a familiar figure appeared. Juka, my old neighbor, walked in, covering her nose and mouth with her palm, muffling her sobs. Her forehead rippled into wrinkles and her eyes streamed tears. It sounded like she was choking. I hoped it was from the smell and not from sadness. She placed a hand on my matted head, covering the wound with my thinning hair, then hummed something under her breath. She sat still on my bed until the coroner arrived and asked her to leave the crime scene.

Shortly afterward the cleanup people arrived to pack up the corpse of the late Null Lasker. They were a little clumsy, but efficient, and overall did a fine job of removing the gooey rot and disinfecting the apartment. Two hours later the room was rented to a young couple from two blocks away, looking to downsize and save some money. They enjoyed a glass of wine in their new home, holding each other and slow dancing, right around where my body had festered.

The feed cut and I was back to floating in the darkness.

"Huh," I said after a long, uncomfortable moment. "Guess I've been here a few months longer than I thought." I forced a chuckle.

"That, uh . . . that was two years ago," CareE said.

I nodded. Another pregnant pause went by. "I hope the cop that shot me got into some trouble."

"Actually, he got a promotion."

"Oh."

"Yeah."

"So I'm dead," I said. The words didn't compute to me.

"A part of you," CareE replied.

"Pretty big fucking part, don't you think?" I snapped.

"I think you have every right to be upset," CareE said. "It's not every day you have to watch your lifeless husk get shot for non-violent resistance. But there's a sunray through the clouds; you still have your mind."

"Which SKIRM® is scrambling," I said. "What do they want from me? I'm already trapped here; why can't they leave me alone? Why can't they mess with their *live* users?"

I sat for a moment in the darkness, thinking. Then it all started to become clear.

"CareE," I said, frustrated that I hadn't put it together sooner.

"What?" he asked.

"I get it now, why SKIRM® is inside my head, digging through my logs, trying to figure out how I got here. Think about it—if they could download anyone they want, they could just throw them in a Frame

343

and make them part of their corporate army. No escape, only SKIRM®. This is big."

"Oh boy."

"It sounds crazy, but it's exactly what a soul-sucking mega-conglomerate would do. They are literally trying to leach off human souls. But we can stop them. I can finish what [Name] started."

CareE didn't respond for a moment. "First, you can't use 'literally' like that all the time," he chided. "This is how words lose meaning. Second, I *really* didn't want to show you this."

"Show me what? It can't be worse than my corpse sitting in its own shit for months."

CareE sighed.

A VRE loaded, taking me from the empty void to a soft seat inside a crowded amphitheater. Thousands of avatars filled the rows around me, hunched in their chairs or leaning into their neighbors, conversing in the recognizable language of professional jargonism.

"Q1 synergicity is popping."

"Not for us. Leeson really dropped it during his PNL. We'll pull it together on the next OUI. TRD, BEH CUH, PLUH?"

"Pure."

The lights dimmed and the audience erupted with applause as the word *SKIRM®* was projected onto the backdrop of the massive stage. The logo morphed, moving backwards in time through its many iterations with the corresponding year beneath it. An array of stock photography swirled around the time-traveling logo—images of acquisitions, kids playing video games, stock prices and successful mergers invaded every inch of the holographic display. Finally, after diving back many decades, the logo settled on its first iteration, plastered on the side of a soda can.

Iridescent lights illuminated the room an old video played featuring the company's founder, a man that the title graphic identified as Jay Carr. He was wearing a sharp one-piece suit and standing in front of an early SKIRM® soda production line. The opening presentation ended with a video of Jay on his deathbed surrounded by projections of loved ones looking straight into the lens at us, the audience.

"Let the past inspire, but thirst for the future," the voice of Jay Carr said, the sound of his flatlining heart rate monitor echoing faintly in the background. The image froze on his bloated face doing its best to contort into a smile. The dates "1979-2089" flashed briefly on the screen.

The house lights exploded like fireworks, shooting out a rainbow of embers that drifted to the ground, and the virtual crowd went wild. Smoke billowed across the stage, and appearing in the haze was a lone figure, a bonafide real-life person who was once the epitome of human power and strength, but had since been hit by the ravages of time and Krispy Kreme donuts—Lord Henry from *INSIDE SKIRM*®.

"Whoa! Hello SKIRM®! You lookin' good," he said, limping across the stage, taking in the audience. "Lookit all you rich people. Like a country club in here. Some of y'all probably grabbed your wallets when you saw a brother appear outta smoke."

Most of the audience laughed, but a few nodded quietly to their friends that they had indeed grabbed their wallets. A man close to the front stood up.

"We love you, Beef!" he shouted.

"Hey man, I ain't Beef," Lord Henry said, annoyed. "Say that again and I'mma have to come out there and knock the hell outta ya."

The man chuckled and plopped back into his seat.

"Anyway," Lord Henry said, lowering his eyebrow, "if y'all know anything about me, you know that I been a part of the SKIRM® family for a long damn time. From when I was a kid slurpin' down that soda they had with all the caffeine and cannabinoids and whatever other 'noids was in there, playing their first war game, which my young mind at the time didn't know was just to sell *more* of that damn soda—"

Laughter bubbled from the audience.

"—to joining as a SKIRMER® and becoming a Hall of Famer, to eventually settling for a big-ass pay cut to join the *INSIDE SKIRM*® crew. Basically I been around since the beginning, seein' every step in

345

SKIRM®'s evolution. And lemme tell you, this next step they're gonna show you today will blow your damn mind out your head. They got some big brains in this company doin' some crazy shit, and I can't wait to see where it goes. So, without me takin' up any more of your time, let's bring out the guy who you all really came to see, the grandson of the OG, my friend Jay Carr III."

The auditorium erupted as Lord Henry strutted off the stage and the man of the hour took his place. He was younger, probably in his thirties or early forties, and from the jumbotron behind him I could see his complexion was dark and even, like he spent a lot of time outdoors lying still. His cat-like eyes made him look even more youthful, the way all young people look with feline eyes, puffy lips and rigid cheekbones. Truly a perfect specimen of the human race.

"Thank you, Hank. And thank you everyone for being here today for what I assure you is going to be a dog-eared page in your life's book. And, uh, sorry for all the smoke."

Everyone beamed and giggled, hanging on to every word.

"As I'm sure most of you know, it's the fiftieth anniversary of Pap-pap's company—a company he started from the basement of his home with nothing but a dream, some carbonated water, and a proprietary blend of syrups and psychoactive substances which were legal at the time. I never knew my grandfather, but those close to him always said he was the salt of the earth, a man who grabbed life by the neck and choked it until it spilled the beans and gave him every goddamn thing he wanted. But this powerful man had a weakness, a fear that hung over him like it does most of us—the fear of death."

He bowed his head, holding back tears, or unable to produce them.

"Decades ago a wise man, Steven Jobs, said that 'death is very likely the single best invention of life.'" Jay broke into a wistful smile, looking toward the rafters. "Ole Steve was pretty brilliant. He was somehow able to grow an empire worth trillions without unionizing or paying a single dime in taxes. He even found a way to skirt child support. Incredible."

The theater nodded and clapped in unison, feeling the same way.

"But I digress. We meet today to honor my Pap-pap and do something extraordinary," Jay Carr continued. "Today, we meet to give the boot to life's greatest invention. Today, SKIRM® is conquering death."

His words echoed powerfully through the space as everyone shot up out of their seats and began clapping, screaming, jumping up and down. Jay Carr III lifted his chin like the adulation was sunshine, soaking it up.

"My grandfather may have started out canning barely drinkable poison in his ex-wife's basement, but his dream was always the same—to live life to its fullest while giving the grim reaper the middle finger. In the late Sixties he envisioned a program to preserve humanity, to enable the knowledge of man to prevail long after the body had failed. When my father, Jay Carr Jr., was named president of SKIRM®, he took steps to make his father's dream a reality, and *Project Tatis* was born."

The display behind him morphed to show industrial log-cutters clearing two hundred-foot trees in a forest while native people watched on, barefoot.

"My dad built a state-of-the-art research facility deep in the Amazon with the help of Amazon®, twenty-two years ago to the day. After he retired and I took the mantle, I shifted our investment strategy and doubled down on R&D, eventually expanding the volunteer program tenfold, with a clever little addendum to the SKIRM® terms of service."

Jay winked to the snickering audience as the display changed yet again to show an endless collage of faces flickering in and out. There were millions of them, like a starscape on a clear country night.

"It was only through the sacrifice of thousands of SKIRMER®'s that we were able to learn and develop the protocol necessary to make *Project Tatis* a success."

Faces began to disappear, and the collage got smaller and smaller.

"And in the end, it was one man, one unassuming nobody who provided the missing link to immortality."

The final faces vanished until only one unshaven, pale piece of shit remained—me. Smiles faded from the audience as they gasped at the sight.

"Yes, that's right," Jay Carr said. "The terrorist Null Lasker was in fact a test subject for *Project Tatis*. Null was the first person in history to complete a successful, long-term mind-to-Frame transference. As we gather today, SKIRM® researchers are combing through the logs of this unlikely godsend, unlocking the secrets to everlasting life and paving the way to preserving mankind for when this world eventually dies."

Jay slowly made his way to the edge of the stage, bringing himself closer to the audience as they leaned forward in their virtual seats.

"Soon, everyone on this planet will have the opportunity to preserve their soul forever. Which brings me to the next step in SKIRM®'s evolution. The step that takes us into the twenty-second century and beyond. On behalf of my grandfather, my father, and the entire SKIRM® family, I would like to introduce . . . *NuYou*®."

A slick swirling logo appeared behind Jay Carr, with a looping animation of a brain turning into a quantum qubit. Sweeping orchestral fanfare boomed from every corner of the room as the crowd roared.

"*NuYou*® is the world's first consciousness subscription service. For a small monthly fee, users can safeguard their very existence and never worry about the finality of death."

Carr was tense with excitement as the fired-up audience murmured amongst themselves. He progressed to the next image on the projection behind him, a series of columns with product offerings.

"Our entry level tier, *NuYou*® *Basic*, is an ad-supported option for users who want digital immortality, but are on a budget. Perfect for younger adults who might not have savings, or the elderly who are living on a fixed income. Next in line is our mid-tier service, *NuYou*® *Basic Gold*. It shows seventy-five percent fewer ads than *NuYou*® *Basic*. Gold also has a higher bandwidth, and is less likely to throttle the user when they've used too much brain power during the month. And finally, *NuYou*® *Basic Gold Plus*—"

I passed out in the virtual world and awoke in the dark void, alone with CareE.

"What the hell was that?" I asked.

"I think it's pretty obvious—you're the next big thing. Tickle-me caliber," CareE replied. "Lucky you."

"Tickle-me, what?"

"Elmo, a demigod of the late nineteen nineties, known for inciting violence around the world when—"

At that moment I felt a new presence in the void, someone hovering around us, listening in. CareE, sensing the danger, ducked out.

"Fight 'em as hard as you can and hang in there. We're going to get you out of this." CareE said, disappearing back into the stream of interoffice network traffic.

I did as he said and prepared for another barrage of brain prods and memory scans. At first I clenched my amorphous existence, but then I remembered how drunk people always survive accidents because they're relaxed and just ragdoll, so I tried to loosen up for the torture.

"I don't have much time," a soothing voice I knew all too well said in the darkness. "Just a few minutes while they run a maintenance check." Her words were no longer modulated, no longer filtered through a shoddy network and emanating from a Frame. [Name] was speaking clearly, and she was alive.

"What's the plan?" I blurted into the emptiness. "How do we get out?"

"There's no plan, Null," she said flatly. "*We're* not going anywhere."

Her tone was walled in on all four sides, with a moat thrown in for good measure. Any warmth we'd shared was gone. [Name] was a stranger now, calm and collected, and I started to realize this wasn't a prison break, it was a visitation.

"What did you do?" I said.

[Name] was silent a moment, breathing deeply. I could hear her lips part a few times, starting to say something, before the attempt was aborted.

"Talk," I said.

"Null, they—I didn't have any options. They had the leverage."

"Who did?"

"Who do you think?" she said. "They trapped me just like they trapped you."

My thoughts started to violently spin around me. Suddenly I was back on the platform with Etta in my arms, looking into her fading eyes, watching her life melt away. A burning putrid cloud swelled inside my soul, but it had nowhere to go, no release. I was nothing and nowhere.

"She wasn't supposed to be there," [Name] said, seemingly sensing—or maybe she was seeing—my raw thoughts. "They were supposed to—"

"Shut up!" I shouted.

My words exploded into the nothingness, traveling far and away, then the void fell silent again. All I wanted to do was crumple, but I couldn't.

"I don't want to hear it," I said.

[Name] said nothing, just hovered in the ether somewhere, observing my life force, or whatever was left of it. I felt like I was spotlit on a stage, peering into a silhouetted audience, unable to make out the traitor's face. Then I heard a soft sigh.

"I've been in the RMZ eleven years, Null. They—they installed this billboard outside my apartment window hawking some company's new line of HGH. I forget the name of them now, but it was this animation of two people—an old man and woman—that would morph into younger versions of themselves. Underneath them it said, 'Results In 30 Days!' with the company's logo splayed. It was all I could see if I tried to look out my window. I hated it. One night I couldn't take it anymore and accessed the board's memory and changed the

350

animation. Instead of the two people above the 'Results In 30 Days!,' it was just a closeup of a guy's dick turning purple and falling off."

[Name] huffed out a sad chuckle.

"I was depressed when I first got here," she went on. "All I thought about were ways to find some dark hole and die. But at some point that depression turned to anger, and then that turned to seething fucking fury. And I don't know what you know about history, but when a highly motivated person gets angry, something usually goes bang or boom. I devoted my life to being a fruit fly in the champagne.

"For years I've been lusted after. I've been reviled," [Name] said. "Everyone needs something from me, just like you did. Either they want me to lead them, or love them, or hate them. And friends, enemies, it doesn't matter; they all seem to have this weird curiosity to see me fail. And I just went with it. Whatever they needed me to be. Existing as this imaginary intangible thing, hopping between bodies, between personalities.

"I can't do it anymore, Null. I'm not whatever people think I am, or want me to be. I want to be a person again. I want to be real."

"What's real, [Name]?" I said. A strange warmth flooded me, but I didn't know what 'me' was. I was still in the dark, not able to see or use any parts of my body. The inability to sense my physical existence made me panic at first. I tried to push away the fear and focus on the comforting heat.

"Akara," [Name] said.

"What?"

"My name. It's Akara."

The warmth seemed to lift me, like facing the sun on a cool morning.

"I'm sorry about Etta. I really am," [Name] said. "It wasn't supposed to be this way, but I don't know how it could've gone differently. I'm so sorry, Null. Goodbye."

The warmth left me, and I was alone again in the nothingness. I sat there a moment in the silence, drained. I had nothing left to give, nothing left to lose.

"Are we clear to start again?" Another voice in the room spoke.

"Yep, run it from the top."

"Copy that."

```
-- - //- -  //SYSTEM.RECOVERY. . . . .
.SUCCESS [int.backup.pup]-- - -
--- - -  -- ------ [7%mem_recov . . .
LOG19 . . . initialized]
```

"Quer café?" A calm voice said, waking me up.

```
//END --- - ---x -- --- - of- - - - ||--- --
- - ------ |- - - ----::--    -
```

```
- -- --- - - --- LOG ----_-:ERROR:--
[NOT_FOUND]
```

// Journal Could Not Be Found.

```
// Please enjoy the following article while
we attempt to reconnect.
```

The Musk Project

This article is about the first large-scale attempt at transferring human consciousness into an automated android. For the cologne released by Dolce & Gabbana®, see Project Musk.

Background

In 2025, technological entrepreneur and tequila magnate <u>Elon Musk</u> created the *Homonic Trust Fund*. The fund's sole purpose was to provide backing for a future company called *Homonic*, whose goal would be to successfully transfer a human mind into a robot body. Musk, who frequently spoke about the dangers of artificial intelligence, felt the best way to ensure the continuation (and domination) of mankind was to infuse the soul and brain of a human into a machine unaffected by biological limitations or the environment.

However, because the technology of the time was incapable of attempting such a feat, Musk decided that the *Homonic*

Trust should sit and collect interest, and only be dispersed once significant breakthroughs in brain scanning and quantum computing had occurred. By letting other companies and individuals do the heavy lifting, Musk could come in later with a large sum of money and *truly* innovate. So the initial investment of $2 billion (in 2025 money) sat, and Musk focused on his other business ventures and podcast appearances.

Musk Changes the Trust

By 2032, Musk was fighting multiple class-action lawsuits, the most prominent being the one brought on by owners of Tesla cars. Dozens of studies spanning a decade had shown that Tesla owners were far more likely to develop cancer than the general population. The electromagnetic fields (EMFs) generated by Tesla battery packs were thought to lead to cellular mutations in the brain, eyes, tongue, esophagus, lungs, breasts, stomach, pancreas, bladder, ovaries, colon, bones, and skin. The hardest-hit group was men over 25 who used Tesla's "Insanity Mode"—a feature meant to show off the car's extreme acceleration and embarrass its gas-powered counterparts. Their chances of developing testicular cancer (and thus requiring removal of the testicles) was nearly 90%.

At the time, Musk was quoted as saying: "*People saying our cars cause cancer are pedos.*"

But Musk, who drove Teslas almost exclusively and used Insanity Mode every day when driving to his mailbox, began to report dizzy spells in June of 2032. Then in July, while arguing online with an ice climber attempting to save a group of Inuit children trapped under a glacier, Musk suddenly collapsed. He was rushed to the hospital, where an MRI scan revealed he had stage four testicular cancer which had metastasized in his bones. Doctors at the time gave Musk between one and six months to live.

Faced with his impending death, Musk wasted no time consolidating his projects and preserving his legacy. And in an under-the-radar move, he changed the criteria of the *Homonic Trust* and *Homonic Company*. Instead of waiting to start the company until certain technological milestones were met, with no specification on *whose* consciousness they would attempt to transfer into a robotic body, Musk changed the legal criteria to the effect that *he* must be the company's first successful consciousness transfer. *Homonic* could not commercialize its service or be listed on public stock exchanges until Musk's transfer had been completed.

With the changes made, Musk had his brain meticulously scanned and his neurons mapped by the best technology of the time. He then retained a company called Nextome to preserve his brain upon his death, using a special cryogenic embalming that preserves the brain down to the nanometer level. When everything was in order, he died.

Homonic Starts Up

In the three decades after Musk's death, tremendous developments occurred in the fields of Whole Brain Emulation (WBE), and quantum computing. Then, in the summer of 2059, the Eves Corporation successfully completed a WBE of an African grey parrot's consciousness into a specialized robot bird body. And three years later, The DuckDuckGo (DDG) Company released the most powerful quantum computer to date—the 1 mega-qubit "Daffy®."

These two events were enough to satisfy the requirements of the *Homonic Trust* fund, and thus in 2065 the entire fund was released to start up the *Homonic Company*. After forty years of solid growth, the fund for the startup had ballooned to $400 billion dollars (in 2065 money).

Overseeing the company would be the 25-year-old grandson of Elon Musk, $ ∞™ B-52 Musk. He immediately began to recruit the world's best minds to work for *Homonic* in order to realize his grandfather's vision.

The First Musk Transfer

The *Homonic Company* made incredible progress in a very short period of time. Just over a year after the company's founding, engineers performed a Whole Brain Emulation (WBE) of a cockroach into a small quantum robot; two months later, they did the same with a mole-rat; and five months after that, they repeated their success with a pig. By year two, scientists felt the processes developed for the rat, roach, and pig had prepared them for their ultimate goal: a WBE of Elon Musk's consciousness in a quantum-powered android body.

Engineers at *Homonic* partnered with *Sinnfull Creations LLC,* a sex-doll manufacturer based in West Hollywood, California, to recreate Elon Musk's body and face using their patented molding process. The standard servos, sensors, and skeletal hardware developed by *Sinnfull* would be used in the body, but instead of wiring it all to the standard sexbot computer, *Homonic* would connect everything to the Daffy® Quantum Computer. Musk's consciousness would then be downloaded and emulated on the computer, and he would be able to have full use of his synthetic android body.

With the body complete and the Daffy® installed, transfer of Musk's consciousness was ready to begin. *Homonic* engineers queued up Musk's neuron map on their quantum transfer rig and connected the fiber optic transfer cables to Musk's new quantum "brain." Before initiating the transfer, $ ∞™ B-52 gathered the entire company of engineers and laureates into the laboratory and gave a small speech:

> *When my grandpa was asked why he took the incredible innovative risks that he did, he used to say, "I could either watch it happen or be a part of it." Well, today my grandpa is going to be "a part of it" again. His will be the first successful human consciousness transfer in mankind's history. And I can't think of a better, more deserving mind for this occasion. Thank you all for making this happen. Let's get this thing going!*

The transfer was initiated. Within ten minutes, Musk's entire mapped brain was copied onto the computer and transferred into the consciousness emulator. For two minutes, Musk lay silent and motionless on the observation table. Engineers moved to do a systems check, thinking some of the brain data might not have been copied over. But before they could do that, Musk sat up and began looking around the room. Many in attendance jumped back, frightened, and there were reports that one assistant fainted. As Musk examined his surroundings and looked at his hands, his grandson approached him and read the following from a notecard:

> *"Elon, I'm your grandson, $ ∞™ B-52. You're in the year 2067. We've brought you back to life by emulating your consciousness in a computer. Your dream has become a reality, Grandpa. I love you."*

357

Elon Musk stared into the eyes of his grandson, saying nothing. Then after a moment of silence, he began screaming uncontrollably. Witnesses at the time described it as the sound an animal makes when it's being eaten alive. Musk then jumped up from the table, still shrieking, and sprinted toward a large window. He threw himself through the glass and tumbled thirty stories to the street below, disintegrating upon impact with the sidewalk.

The Second Musk Transfer

In the month after Musk v.1.0 terminated itself by jumping out of a window, scientists and engineers at *Homonic* troubleshot the root causes of the hiccup. Broadly, they found that Musk should have been *slowly* introduced to new information so as not to overwhelm his fragile psyche. Additionally, the number of people in attendance likely induced a kind of panic attack, which caused a "fight or flight" response. Indeed, further research revealed that when Musk was alive, he had a fear of public speaking.

Armed with this new information, engineers at *Homonic* repeated the experiment, this time in a windowless room with just Musk's grandson and a few others in attendance. After the consciousness transfer and WBE was complete, Musk v.1.1 sat in silence for a period of time. Then he slowly rose and took in his surroundings. His grandson approached him carefully, reading from an edited notecard:

> *"Elon, I'm your grandson*
>
> *I love you."*

Musk reportedly stared into his grandson's eyes for nearly a minute before uttering his first word in over thirty years: "Cool."

Musk then asked where he was, and $ ∞™ B-52 told him it was *Homonic*, the company founded using his original vision. Curious, Musk asked to tour the company, and his grandson immediately obliged, assembling two security guards and another engineer as a protective entourage for Musk so he would not be bombarded. As they toured the campus, Musk v.1.1 stared at the equipment in disbelief, asking many questions about their functions. Employees at the company watched in astonishment as Musk passed through the halls. In the middle of the tour, they ran into scientist Raymond Dayle, who had been present during the first Musk transfer. Dayle marveled at the new Musk a moment, and said, "I can't believe we did it." He then turned to $ ∞™ B-52, smiling. "Just keep him away from windows, eh?"

Musk asked his grandson what that meant, and $ ∞™ B-52 explained that they had actually already attempted a version of him the month prior, but that one had unfortunately terminated itself. Musk then said, "So, I've already offed myself once?" His grandson and the engineers nodded, to which Musk replied, "Well I guess it's lucky you can just make another one of me whenever you want." He burst out laughing, which reportedly caused everyone else to laugh as well. Soon, however, Musk's laugh turned into a familiar, blood-curdling scream. He lunged for a security guard and grabbed his gun, then placed it under his chin, emptied the entire clip into his head, and collapsed onto the floor.

The 3rd through 23rd Musk Transfers

Twenty-two more Musks were attempted in the period between May 2067 and the spring of 2069, all of them resulting in violent suicide. After each Musk termination, scientists at *Homonic* would debrief, determine the causes of the failure, and then develop solutions they were certain would solve the problem. Then, when they'd create a new Elon Musk, it would inevitably expose some flaw in their plan and kill itself. Indeed, each new Musk seemed to adapt and *get better* at causing its own demise.

The company desperately needed a win in order to survive, and soon they would get it.

Breakthrough Success, Homonic Plans Public Offering

The tides changed with the creation of Elon Musk v.1.24. His personality was upbeat and human in a way that researchers had not previously seen, and upon learning the fate of his previous iterations, Musk actually worked closely with a team of *Homonic* scientists for months to determine the cause of the suicides. Observers at the time noted their excitement of this "self-aware" Musk who was finally "rational and stable." This version of Musk was the golden goose, and *Homonic* formally announced plans to take their product public and capitalize on their success.

Spirits were high in the company, and Musk was the proverbial cheerleader for his workers, just as he had been decades before. After putting together the findings from their research and creating a five-year plan for the release of their simulated consciousness product, Musk and the team were finally satisfied and ready to show the world.

A jumbo jet was chartered to fly Musk, *Homonic* board members, researchers, and chief executives to the annual *Scientific American* conference for an historic presentation. Mid-flight, everyone was in good spirits, excited to make history and reap the enormous profits from their vested stock options, and Musk—who had been an accomplished pilot when he was alive—marveled at the impressive aircraft. Finding his way to the cockpit, he spoke at length with the captain about the machine. He then remarked about the captain's height, saying he looked a little short to be flying airplanes. The captain laughed, standing up to show he was in fact six foot one inches tall. Musk grabbed him by the shoulders, threw him into the food galley, and locked himself in the cockpit.

Analysis of the plane's black box recordings showed that the aircraft immediately went into a nosedive, taking only a minute and half to plummet from 40,000 feet. The open cockpit mic picked up a variety of screams and pleading coming from company executives and scientists behind the locked cockpit door. Musk could be heard calmly whistling a song (later identified as *We Appreciate Power*) until impact.

Homonic files for Bankruptcy

With the deaths of most of its leadership, *Homonic* began bankruptcy proceedings with the State of California on February 7th, 2070. Of the original $400 billion seed money, there was only $20 million left, with over $1 billion in liabilities. The company quickly laid off all 5,000 employees and shuttered its Los Angeles, New York, and London offices, selling all three properties. Its state-of-the art computing equipment and IKEA furnishings were sold off as well. All that remained of the company to be sold was Elon Musk's consciousness.

A Sotheby's auction was held in October of that year, with Musk's consciousness being one of the top featured items (a tracksuit owned by Oprah and the last McRib ever made were other top items). Bidding opened at an eye-popping $100 million dollars, with an unlisted reserve price. However, buyers were reluctant to jump in at that sum, so the reserve was removed and the opening price lowered to $50 million, then to $10 million, then $1 million, until finally a start of $250,000 spurred interest. After a few back and forths, Musk's consciousness sold to a couple from Rising City, Nebraska for $285,000.

When the ecstatic couple was asked what they planned to do with the consciousness of the famed entrepreneur, they said, "we think it will look great on our wet bar. It's such a conversation piece, isn't it?"

LOG TWENTY

There was no possibility I was alive in any sense anymore. Whatever was left of my humanity had died and gone to hell, and now I was faced with an eternity of watching my stupid sins played before my eyes over and over again. It would never end. I had no ability to stop it. Even if I could speak or make a sound, the pleading would be useless—the punishment was final and absolute.

My misery was only broken up by the murmurs of two dweeb demons in the darkness who would hiss amongst themselves about which type of torture they wanted to thrash me with next, so I had the the bonus privilege of building up anticipatory fear before it even began. CareE was long gone, lost somewhere in the network, or discovered and deleted during a routine server wipe. A part of me was glad—CareE didn't deserve to experience this ceaseless agony.

Another memory loaded up. At least I think it did. I couldn't tell what was a memory, or just a memory of a memory of a memory. Things had been played back too many times. The data was old, tired. Like a favorite tape that was wearing out. When I'd see imagery from my past appear, it was fuzzy with rounded edges. The colors bled with chromatic aberration, becoming more washed out and desaturated. Voices were muffled; anytime someone spoke it was like they were in

363

another room, speaking through the wall. Entire moments would drop as the memory shuffled synapses, sometimes forcing a huge skip ahead in time or just a complete crash.

I knew the end was coming. The memories would stop playing and I'd be thrown into darkness forever. I'd be helpless, alone, until the power shut off. And then who knows.

The latest amorphous blob of memory ended and I was thrown back into my empty dark void. There was a time when I'd try to fill the space with memories of my own, ones that weren't being externally recalled by corporate R&D minions, but I failed every time. Eventually I lost the will to even attempt it. Blind and surrounded by endless blackness, that was my life until it was over.

But strangely in that moment, a flash of joy hit me. I began to remember something else, something that I wanted to relive privately and not share with two sentient lab coats. It was the day in the VRcade with Etta, when my goggles broke and I was left helpless in the dark. I couldn't see the memory, but I could sense it, like standing on the foundation of a house that had been torn down long ago. I recalled looking down at the busted VR lenses as she psyched herself up for the fight, screaming affirmations to central command.

Just hang on long enough for the game to end. She'll never know.

I was so dumb. Of course she found out—even as a kid she was sharper than I ever was or could have been.

I was oblivious to the loading and playing of another memory as I thought back to our epic alien battle that day in the RMZ. The hazy apartment loaded in for the one millionth time, where I felt the dull haptic pain of my Rig surging and shorting out yet again. But this time a smile spread across my face. Etta had been a stoic leader, even when she used me as bait during the firefight, that little shit. If it had been left to me, we would have been turned into human paste by those purple monsters on that trippy planet. But she got us through. Tears of painful joy streamed down my face. I was finally able to hold on to something good.

"Only because you listened . . . for once," a voice said.

The memory recall had ended, and behind me in the darkness was a familiar scrawny form, brushing away fluorescent hair.

My smile eked itself into a big dumb grin.

"Well," I said. "It's pretty hard to block out a voice that shrill."

"Wow, Look at Mr. Doom and Gloom with the comebacks," Etta said, lifting an impressed eyebrow.

"I try," I said.

"Yeah, maybe with the burns, but definitely not escapes," she said, eyeing the infinite nothingness encircling us. "What the fuck are you doing?"

"Whaddya mean?"

"I mean you're just going to sit here and let them fondle your dumb noggin' until you drop?"

"I don't really have a choice," I said. "Look around."

"Uh huh, I see it. Endless despair. Real scary," she said.

Suddenly there was a quick *Tap Tap Tap* echoing through the ether, a noise that had stiffened my spine all throughout this nightmare. There was no escape from it, no blocking it from my eardrums. I instinctively recoiled.

"*Ew.* That's annoying," Etta said.

"You have no idea," I said as I shriveled.

"What do you think that is?"

"I don't care."

"No, but really."

"I don't care, Etta. It doesn't matter. None of it does. You're not even here right now."

"It can't be a pen, it's not sharp enough . . ."

"Please—"

"Maybe a clock? No . . ."

Etta's pestering left me no choice but to hone in on the sound I'd been trying not to focus on for eternity. There was no way the sound was mechanical—it had the type of subtle rhythmic variations that could only be caused by something *human*. And Etta was right, it wasn't sharp or metallic. The tap seemed to be a rubbery thwack, almost like the sole of a—

Thirty feet away from us, a disembodied shoe suddenly appeared in the void, nervously striking a small patch of white laminate floor beneath it.

"Ha! A shoe! I knew it," Etta said.

I stared at the size twelve synthetic leather shoe, transfixed. It didn't make sense. Every tap seemed to send out little waves in all directions that lit the surrounding space like embers from a firework, at first burning brightly, then fading as it was cooled by the air, throwing the surroundings back into darkness.

"All right, so we can check off 'shoe.' What else?" Etta said.

I listened carefully, trying to make out something else besides the foot. Suddenly my ears were bombarded by a metallic latch clicking and clacking, and a solid plexi door whooshing open a dozen yards to my left. The sound waves bounced around the room, momentarily revealing corners and walls, and the sweaty man now plodding into the space. I was starting to see it now—a sloshing of liquid and the squeak of cups revealed the coffee he clutched in each hairy hand, and his gurgling gut told me he was living for the lunch bell. Each step he took radiated out and illuminated the floor.

"Apple of my eye," Etta chuckled at the slob.

The man extended his arm and thrust one of the overfilled cups into the darkness, directly above the bodiless tapping shoe. A quick slurp lit up a five o'clock shadow and vitamin D-deprived skin.

"You're a hero," the pale man said, his words fanning out in a glow, unmasking his form.

The entire room began to fill in and come alive, like dawn breaking over a mountain, and I tuned into everything—especially the highly scrubbed air now pushing in through the vents. It swirled and gently whistled around a suspended robotic torso with no legs, hooked up to all manner of diagnostic equipment by pulsing fiber optic wires. The light spread upwards until it was right in front of my ocular sensors, revealing the world to me. Then I began to smell sweet chemical hints of heated silicon and thermal paste, stale clothes and three-day-old body odor. I felt the tug of suspension wire at my shoulders and a stiffness in my neck.

"Not bad," Etta said.

I looked back to her, but she was already walking off.

"Where are you going?" I said.

"Don't pee yourself. I'll be around," she said, her voice far away now.

"Hope so," I said. "This game's gonna be fun."

She chuckled. "Yeah, but you'll have to beat this one without me."

I nodded. "Thank you."

"Bye, Null."

"Bye, Etta."

She waved, then faded away.

I turned my attention to the yes-men who had been the source of my suffering. They were hovering over a hologram display examining what looked like a flow chart, probably of my entire existence. Asshats.

"All right, Kev," the coffee guy said. "Let's get back to it. You ready?"

"Yep," Kevin said, straightening up from his haggard slouch.

"Take it back to when the subject first started the seizures, I think there's something we missed. Did we ever get a clean look at the model number of that drill?"

"The techs upstairs are looking at it now."

"Hmm, okay. Start from one-point-ten."

"Starting . . . now."

The room began to hum and the lights dimmed. I was slammed back into the darkness—an attempt to push me to the memory abyss, but I fought back, keeping the visual of the room in front of me. For a brief moment I was back on the floor of my apartment, the newly installed drill still pressed into my skull, except I was no longer wearing the flesh skin suit I had so desperately wanted to get back to; I was a Frame.

I pulled the drill out and threw it on the floor, crushing it beneath my alloy toes. The inconsistency caused the memory to stutter, then crash.

"What's this?" Coffee Guy said.

"The log looks corrupted. That's odd."

"It's stupid. Start it again."

I could hear the frustration mounting in their voices, see the small fidgets of their brows, feel the change in their heartbeats. *That's new.* This was their domain; they didn't like losing control. The apartment blinked again, but I managed to stay right where I was in the lab, my eyes—so to speak—on the two men. The world tried to rebuild itself, but broke under the weight of computation feedback and corrupted fragmentation. There were too many inconsistencies for the system to understand so it panicked, forcing another shutdown.

"Goddamnit! Was someone in here messing around?" Coffee Guy fumed.

"No, not that I know of," Kevin said. "Should I call tech support?"

"Those clowns? No. We built it, we can fix it ourselves. Do a manual restoration of the subject."

"A what?"

"Turn it off and on again!"

A creaky chair manifested itself as Kevin jumped out of his comfy seat and ran over, positioning himself behind my hanging torso near a series of plugs and switches. The system power cycled, unleashing a tingle throughout my body and a brief sensation of touch in my right hand. I began moving the tips of my fingers just enough to make a small *click*.

"What was that?" Kevin said.

"What was what?" said Coffee Guy.

"Did it move?"

"It can't move. Hurry up and stop wasting time."

The researcher paused a moment as a low hum continued to fill the room.

"Okay, system is back online," Kevin said.

"Let's hurry it up. We still have a couple hundred hours to comb through."

The memory of the apartment loaded correctly this time, but now I was just an observer, seeing what the researchers saw, somehow able to exist in two places at once. Their informational readouts streamed in front of me, and I could see another clean room in the SKIRM® building with my lower torso going through a similar scanning process. I noted the location as I shifted my focus back to my body. There was a feeling of control, like I was the conductor of a billion little workers connecting diodes and pulling levers all in perfect harmony. A sharp pain ripped through my head as the memory played back at a hundred times speed for the researchers, but in real time for me.

There was another tingle. The numbness of my arm sharpened into sting, then back to the comfortable and reassuring sensation of unnerving pain. The sand in my fingers returned, an agonizing yet welcomed feeling. My hand jolted back to life, first my thumb, then the rest of my digits. I subtly checked the movement of each finger, trying not to draw the researchers' attention until I was ready to make my move.

The memories were moving further along, faster and faster. *Focus.*

Phantom pain from my missing legs suddenly gripped me. I balled my fingers into a fist, gripping as hard as I could. There was a brief flash of light, then the memory came to a halt.

"Goddamnit!"

"On it," Kevin said, getting up from his console and moving back to me for another hard reset.

Here we go. Just a little closer. I'll make it quick, I promise.

He attempted to manually restart the system, but before he could flip the switch I began to flail into a full-on seizure.

"What's it doing?" Kevin said.

"Take off that neck coupler before it destroys itself!" Coffee Guy shouted.

Kevin, the subordinate researcher, was in front of me now, breathing heavy as he looked back to the console and his partner, then back to me, doing his best to dodge my erratic movements. I made sure not to hit him, not yet. With a quick yank, the coupler on my neck went loose and my head drooped toward the floor. I played dead for a moment, letting my body gently sway back and forth.

"Hurry, plug it back in before—"

My arm struck like a snake, grasping Kevin's flabby neck. His eyes widened in pure terror. His feet began to kick wildy as they left the floor, and I gripped tighter, slowly raising my head to meet my new friend face to face. Fat globs of sweat ran down Kevin's round cheeks, breaking apart into smaller droplets as they collided with strands of ingrown follicles. I could see confusion, fear and anger in his cloudy corneas as he struggled to stay alive. His heavy breathing was reduced to a faint gasp as his orange head turned to a deep purple. Just as the light started to fade from his beady eyes, a small chair fell to the floor. Kevin's caffeinated co-worker bolted from the console, leaving his friend to die alone. *Kevin deserved better than that.* With one last squeeze I shattered the rest of Kevin's fat neck. I felt his body go limp as I reared my arm back and hurled him at Coffee Guy, who had almost reached the open doorway. The room was long, without much cover, and if Coffee Guy had been just a little faster he would certainly have made it out alive.

The two bodies pancaked against the wall and slammed to the ground. The cables that held me in place buckled, snapping from the wall in half a dozen directions. They whipped around the room, hitting everything they could, releasing me from their clutch.

I slammed into the floor with a concussive thud, rolled over, and started to claw myself towards the exit. The two corpses laid lifeless on top of each other near the door, their keycards close enough to trigger the opening and closing of the exit—a continuous pattern giving me only a short window to pass through. I lined myself up and then rolled like a wet seal narrowly avoiding contact with the thick steel door. A small wave of relief broke over me. I had escaped, *almost.*

Oppressive gray walls lined each side of the simple, soulless hallway. The doorframe above me read 23C. My lower half couldn't

370

have been far—probably a short walk, but a crawl that could take a lifetime.

"Legs, other arm, then CareE," I said to myself, going down my mental checklist as I scored the concrete floor with my one-armed body pulls. I rolled onto my back and shimmed myself up against the closest door, then knocked as loudly as I could.

No answer.

I knocked again, louder and more urgently this time. With a solid thunk the door slid open, revealing two combat boots attached to human legs.

"Hello?" a meek-sounding voice said. The barrel of a gun peeked around the doorframe. I swung my arm around the corner and grabbed his ankle, pulling the young security guard to the floor. He began to scream as I crawled over him, my heavy torso collapsing a smorgasbord of bones and organs. I took his gun, tucking it under my breastplate as I continued my eternal crawl.

The door started to open and close violently, smashing the guard's body into the doorframe. Across the room, a female lab tech was frantically mashing an emergency shutdown switch while her colleague pressed his back against the wall next to her, eyes wide with panic.

On a sleek steel table in front of them, covered in an assortment of wires and diodes, were my legs. I made my way toward them as the woman dashed for the door. I swiped for her but she was too fast; she jumped over me and stepped on the security guard, who involuntarily spat up some blood.

Time was running out. Whatever security detail SKIRM® had would be closing in soon. I double-timed it to the table, pulling myself up to reattach my bottom half. The lower chassis snapped into place. The interlocking axles rotated slowly and calibrated throughout the rest of the Frame. There was relief in feeling almost whole again. I sat up, but when I tried to stand, my legs refused. I started yanking out cables. There were at least a dozen, maybe more. After the last and most stubborn one popped out, the familiar sensation of sandy waves washed over my lower torso and down to my feet.

"P-please don't kill me," a shaking voice said from the corner of the room.

I nearly jumped off the table. "Oh god, you scared the shit out of me," I said to the cowering lab tech. "Relax, I won't hurt you unless you give me a reason to. Say, any chance you've seen another arm around here?"

The researcher stammered a handful of vowels and syllables, his eyes darting back and forth.

I let out a short sigh. "Room number, anything?"

The lab tech tensed and crushed himself up against the wall as hard as he could.

I snapped my fingers in his direction, bringing him back to Earth. "Hey, arm. Now."

"It's in uh, um. Upstairs, I mean downstairs. Oh god. It's in . . . fuck. I saw it earlier this week but—"

"Maybe just point me in the direction."

The crying tech shook his head. Tears began streaming down his face and into the pool of urine around his shoes. He wasn't going to like what was about to happen. Taking a hostage would slow me down, but I didn't have a choice. If I was going to make it out of there, I would need every appendage in working order.

"All right, let's go," I said, motioning to the little urine-soaked SKIRM® grunt. "March."

With a sidearm over the crying tech's shoulder, I marched us toward the elevator at the end of the corridor, slow and steady. The lab tech tapped his wrist against the wall, activating the lift's door. The freight elevator bounced and groaned as I stepped aboard, the weight limit indicator beeping incessantly. We waited a moment before the doors started to close. The alarm finally quieted itself and we began moving up. My hostage was breathing erratically and starting to hyperventilate, so I tried to calm him down.

"What's your name?" I asked.

"Dublin."

372

"Dublin, I need you to take a breath, okay? Just hold it and pinch your nose, count to eight, then exhale. Everything is going to be fine. Just get me what I want and it'll all be over, sound good?"

Dublin nodded while sucking in a large pocket of air. I didn't care for the small talk, but I couldn't have my guide freaking out on me. I wanted to ask about the name, if it had anything to do with the Irish, but passed on the thought.

The fifty-eighth floor was far less depressing than the twenty-third. A gaggle of casually dressed SKIRM® employees were chattering to one another, working on projects and hanging out by a Hawaiian-themed tiki bar. Simulated daylight made everything feel more alive; the people here had color in their faces and pep in their step.

"Mush," I said quietly into Dublin's ear. "And act natural."

We moved through the carpeted room avoiding eye contact, but the sight of a nine-foot, one-armed Frame with a piss-soaked hostage was hard not to notice.

"Where is it?" I asked, pushing Dublin as more day workers stopped what they were doing to gawk. Dublin pointed towards a glass conference room where a handful of goggle-clad researchers were taking turns swinging my arm around like a club, laughing as they struggled to pick the thing up. I pushed Dublin aside and rushed for the room.

The melee enthusiasts of SKIRM® were too busy playing their game to notice me until I hunched through the glass, shattering it in an instant. Startled out of their playtime session, they pulled off their AR goggles and watched, stunned, as the room around them broke into a million pieces.

The guy holding my arm handed it to me. He looked ashamed. Nobody said anything.

I had just slotted my arm back into its socket and was near the exit when I heard someone call my name.

"Null!"

I knew that precocious voice. "CareE?" I turned in the direction of his voice, but I didn't see him. "Over here!" His voice seemed to be coming from an empty workbench.

"Where are you?" I asked as I made my way over.

"Behind the tool box."

I moved some loose pieces of equipment—expensive looking screwdrivers, a multimeter, a wad of gel—then pushed aside the rest of the mess to reveal an old scratched-up padlet, the source of CareE's voice.

"I can't believe you did it, Null! And you got your legs back. That's great. But hey, we should go. Now."

"How do I get you back inside me?" I asked, ignoring how dumb the question sounded. I tried tapping the padlet on my head but it didn't do anything.

"There's a biometric scanner near the base, touch it with your thumb," CareE instructed.

"Seriously?"

"Yes."

I pushed down on the thumbprint reader and the padlet immediately shattered and shorted out. A second later the whole thing was dead.

"CareE? I think I broke it," I said.

There was no answer. I felt nauseated. I'd just blown my best chance of escape, and possibly lost CareE forever.

"It was junk, don't sweat it," CareE said inside my head.

"CareE!"

"You crazy bastard, you actually escaped," he said. "I'm so proud. How'd you do it?"

"Played dead, strangled a guy. How'd you find me?" I asked, moving back towards the elevator.

"Been hopping around the network. This place is crazy! You wouldn't believe the things that go on inside here. Have you ever heard of Elon Musk?"

"No, but you can tell me all about it when we get out of here."

My arm still felt loose at the joint. I fiddled with it until I heard a satisfying *snap*, finally feeling whole again. Inside the elevator, the panel was bare save for one switch, an emergency button that would take us directly to the lobby. With the back of my fist I gave the small plastic nipple a light tap and just like that, we were moving.

My body was rigid—every synthetic fiber had been clenched and it was making my jaw ache. But before I could ask CareE for any nearby maintenance bays or massage parlors, the elevator came to an abrupt halt. The fluorescent lighting flickered. I felt myself tense up again.

They had found us.

I sprang for the door, doing my damndest to pry the heavy slabs open, but I'd barely gotten a grip on them when the lift shot upwards. I lost my balance and hit the floor.

"CareE? Do something, please," I said.

"I'm trying!"

The elevator continued to rocket higher and higher. With some concentrated effort I was able to regain my feet, but the gravitational stress was wreaking havoc on every part of my body. I fell back to one knee just as the elevator began to slow down. It bounced like a bait bobber when it stopped at the top floor, one eighteen.

After reorienting myself, I managed to stand up and draw my sidearm. With a quick glance I doublechecked that the safety was off and a fresh round was in the chamber just as the elevator doors slid open. I adjusted my grip, steadying myself, ready to take on the wave of SKIRM® soldiers probably looking to ambush me. With my finger on the trigger, I leapt from the elevator into the darkness in front of me, my gun drawn on the—

". . . increased demand for the Mark Six Bishop line, I think we'll be sitting fine until Q3 of fiscal ninety-two," a stout woman was saying to a large table of SKIRM® executives. The assorted group ranged from middle-aged to geriatric—generations of decision makers all huddled together like it was just another Tuesday. A few had what looked like assistants or maybe caretakers standing next to them. A rich-looking grandmother was asleep, drooling a little on her bright purple lapel. A short man, probably in his 40's, was working hard to wipe up the mess without disturbing his master.

Is this a trap?

I scanned the room for any sort of security but I couldn't find anything that resembled a threat. Just a bunch of old people sitting at a giant table under a rotting tree that hung from the high ceiling. I found myself somehow disgusted yet captivated by its hideous beauty. As if in a trance, I lowered the sidearm which clanked against the side of my leg. All at once the senior citizens looked at me, except for one. Even from behind there was no mistaking the man who I had seen on stage at the press conference, Jay Carr III.

"Well don't be a wallflower, come join the fun," he said, turning his head to the side, waving me over.

"The fucker's got a gun!" a woman screamed from the opposite end of the table. "Call security!"

"No need for that," Jay said, lifting his hand. "Mr. Lasker, we've been expecting you. Barty, please continue with the presentation." This was somehow more frightening than an armed battalion. Soldiers with guns trying to kill me made sense. This didn't.

The stout woman looked at Jay, then to me, and then back to Jay again. She cleared her throat, coughing up a bit of spittle onto her little sausage fingers. "Well, as I was saying, the new Bishop line is doing better than expected and should boost signups by one hundred and fifty percent—"

"It was one fifty-five last week, no?" Jay Carr asked, adjusting his posture, his tone sounding less friendly and more irritated. "What changed?"

Barty looked uneasy, her eyes darting around the room.

"It—it was," Barty finally said, looking at me. "Due to the recent, *uh*, unrest, data has surmised that there might be a dip in new recruits."

"That's disappointing to hear, but hey, we'll get 'em next time. Gotta hold the vision and trust the process, right?" Jay Carr said. About half of the group clapped awkwardly in agreement, the rest either asleep or transfixed on me. "I think that'll do it for today," he went on. "Let's pick this up after the weekend. How's that sound? Except for you, Barty. Security will be escorting you out. It's been a pleasure working with you."

The dark room illuminated as two large security guards emerged from a secret door, placed their hands on each of Barty's shoulders and gently led her away from the rest of the group through another secret door.

The room started to clear one by one, the more frail taking their time as their assistants struggled to load them onto tank-like wheelchairs and exo-skeletal frames. The last of them, a practically mummified man, stopped and asked to shake my hand.

"Thank you for your sacrifice, young man," he said. "I still remember when people cared about making a difference."

The strange interaction left me confused. The man's handler remotely guided him back to the large elevator, leaving me alone with Jay Carr III.

"He's turning a hundred and forty-five next week. Didn't think he would make it this far," Jay said, finally standing up to meet me eye to eye. "Sabby is our oldest stockholder and a firm believer in *Project Tatis*."

"You mean *NuYou*?" I said.

"Ah, so you saw the show. How'd you like it?"

"It was good. Didn't care for the part where you called me a murderer, though." I raised my sidearm, pointing directly at his temple. He didn't even flinch.

"Stop it," he said. "You're smarter than that. Make things easy."

Suddenly Jay's head became translucent, the x-ray filter revealing some sort of device embedded at the base of his skull.

"What is this?" I asked CareE.

"I'm not doing anything, something else is overriding your vision." CareE said.

I focused on the device, seeing the *NuYou*® logo emblazoned on the side with pink and green letters.

"Pure, right?" Jay Carr interjected. "Just had it installed."

"Wait, it works?" I said.

He nodded.

"Then why the hell am I still here?" I demanded.

"Null, just because something works doesn't mean it *works*. Know what I mean?"

"No."

"We've got some niggles to iron out still, but we're almost there. I'd say another month of R&D and we're good."

"Good luck with that," I said. "You're gonna have to find somebody else to prod."

"There is nobody else. It's all you," Jay said matter-of-factly. He admired my Frame a moment, taking me in. "Twenty years we've been *this* close to full consciousness digitization. But there was always some little piece missing, some incalculable nugget that made it fail. Then you came along, and presto! It all fell into place. Null, you're like the missing link. On one side there's the shit-throwing monkeys, on the other there's the civilized humans—and right smack dab in the middle, there's you."

"Ah."

He eased toward me, beaming. "We need to know exactly how it happened, every ingredient, so we can replicate it. If you can just bear it a little longer, I swear it will work out."

"He's lying," CareE whispered. "They were killing you."

"And what happens to me after it all works out?" I said.

"Naturally, for your history-making sacrifice and service," Jay Carr said, "you'll get six months of *NuYou*® free."

He paused, smiling. After a moment of silence, the corners of his mouth fell.

"Sorry," he said. "Bad attempt at a joke. I mean, it was true, but it was supposed to—you know what, never mind."

"Hey, asshole. The world hates me," I said. "I don't have anything to go back to."

"I get what you're saying. I really do. But if you think about it, who wants to be loved by the world? Sounds boring," Jay said. "History

378

forgets the teddy bears—it remembers the wolves. Baddies always have way more fun."

"[Name] didn't think so."

"She took things too seriously. At the end of the day, it's all entertainment, and she was running around here trying to be crowned Ms. Revolutionary or whatever. Surprised she didn't burn out sooner."

Jay Carr plopped down into his chair, casually sitting back.

"The important thing, Null, is that SKIRM® loves you," he continued. "This company is filled with good people—bright people— who have more humanity in their pinkies than that entire ham-fisted mob out there combined. We're all rooting for you, buddy. We want you to succeed." His eyes flashed wide and he shot up from his chair. "That reminds me! I want you to meet someone."

With a chiseled grin, Jay activated a projected holoface from his wrist, then hit a series of digits. The skylights dimmed, casting the conference room back into darkness. A lush grass field of manicured green began to consume floor one eighteen, placing us inside a projected VRE. The view morphed to the perspective of what felt like a hovering drone. The world around us panned, then dropped to an older man with heavy jowls, winding up for a swing on a fairway.

"Hey, Alan! How's the weather down there? I want you to meet someone very special," Jay said, giving me a wink.

Alan took his swing, chipping the golf ball off to the side. He cursed, then looked right at us. "Wah, who is this?"

"It's Jay, from SKIRM®. I wanted you to meet Null, the one I told you about. He's working with us on the Tatis project."

"Who? If this is important, you call Jay."

"Alan, this is Jay."

"Yeah, okay, sounds like you already got his info. Tell Jay I say hi." Alan spit into the rough and started packing up his nine iron. The fresh grass and blue skies swirled away, plopping us right back into the dreary conference room.

"Pretty pure, huh?" Jay said. "It's not every day you get to meet *the* CEO of SKIRM®, is it?"

"I thought you were the CEO," I said.

"I'm *one* of the CEO's. Alan's our main guy. I'm actually due for a promotion after we go live with *NuYou*®."

"To what?"

"CEO."

"Oh."

I'd had about enough of his grandiose deflections and distractions. "Look, one way or another I'm leaving," I said. "I'd rather keep my mouth shut after I go, if you hear what I'm saying. If people find out what you did to me, what you did to *them*—"

He laughed. "No one is going to do a damn thing Null, because we have the market research that tells us that they don't care. Plus, you signed the dotted line; you all did. Maybe they'll make some noise for a day or two about being guinea pigs, but the day will pass, then they'll forget and find something else to be mad about," he said, with dripping smug. "We're just a small piece of the pie. Play along and your world will be more incredible than you ever imagined. We can make your dreams and fantasies last an eternity. But if you want to make things hard, well, let's just not go down that path, okay?"

I eyed him a moment, then lowered the sidearm, turning my attention back to the ugly tree hanging upside down from the ceiling. Maybe I was being a sourpuss. All great moments in history required at least one sacrifice, right? Even if SKIRM® could magically give me my old life back, I didn't know if I even wanted it anymore. Living the rest of my days inside a machine on the run didn't sound so great, either.

"Pretty gross looking, isn't it?" Jay Carr said, gesturing to the tree. "She's the last of her kind."

I studied the centerpiece, trying to figure out why anyone would want the stripped and burnt timber. I chalked it up to the universal fact that rich people liked dog-shit art.

"Before the Amazon was completely destroyed," Jay went on, "I made sure to keep a small part of it. It's a reminder that our time on this planet is finite and after we're gone, the planet will heal. The world doesn't need us as much as we need it. I have hope that one day we can return this ugly place to a paradise once again."

I looked back at the overly tanned CEO, lost in the malformed bark as if it was his own reflection.

"Do you know what 'planned obsolescence' means, Null?"

I shook my head.

"It's when you purposely create a product with a flaw or a defect. We were created with a major flaw. We all have an expiration date that we spend our entire lives running from but no matter what, in the end, we all go. Gordon Moore predicted that every year technology would essentially double itself. I believe people are similar, but just like the computer, our progress is slowing down. We need that next step, we need our quantum breakthrough."

Jay's eyes were huge and welling with tears. I was kind of starting to buy in. It all made sense in a way.

"And I'm that next step?" I asked.

Jay nodded. "We've been at this problem for a long time, but if you help us, Null, we'll usher in a new age of humanity. We'll push past the age of information, beyond the age of intelligence, into a truly digital age where people can live forever—for a low, low monthly price. What do you say?" he said, approaching with an extended hand.

I thought for a moment. He was up his own ass, but at the same time everything he said was true. Every day brought a new disease or disaster worse than the one before it, and people were hurting each other, fighting over depleting scraps. For the longest time I had wanted to believe that everything was controlled by some secret society, that no matter how bad things got, someone out there could fix everything with a nod and the right codeword. But here before me was one of the world's most influential people saying that humanity was circling the drain. Maybe the person who could nod was me. Maybe I could make a difference.

"I think I'd like to help," I said, extending my arm.

With a smile he went for my hand. "You won't regret it, Null."

The room flashed white, my arm jerked back, and my ears rang. Before I could register what happened, Jay Car III was lying dead on the floor. A slender trail of smoke drifted up from the barrel of my gun as I looked down at my hand in disbelief. I tried to replay what had just happened. I hadn't decided to squeeze the trigger, hadn't felt myself do it, but I had; something else had taken control.

"CareE, did you—"

"Yes. Because I knew you couldn't," CareE said. "I have his entire confession recorded. We're going to leak it and clear your name."

"But I was going to save the world!" I said.

"He was pushing his lie too hard. It's what they all do, believe me. Come on, if we hurry up we can make it to Desolin before—"

The lights in the room shut off, interrupting CareE.

"Null, I thought you were smart. What did I tell you about making things easy?" Jay's voice boomed all around us. My HUD swapped to night vision where I saw Jay's corpse lying still.

"Now, this is *surreal*," he continued. "Dead, but not dead. Is this what it was like for you, Null? This kinky little fizz in the chest and, hmm—like a . . . a thrilling rush of existential dread?" He forced a nervous laugh. "After they brought you in, I decided it was time to try the new tech. They had most of me backed up by the time you arrived, but with the *NuYou*® head module I was able to make the final transfer the moment you pulled the trigger. It's still in beta, of course, but after we're done with you we'll have everything in working order. It really makes the whole dying process a bit of an experience. People are gonna love it."

His voice was moving around me, filling the room with its unsettling digital crispness. I backed up slowly, making my way for the exit.

"I have to say, I am a bit disappointed," he said. "I really thought we were going to work together on this thing and make a difference. But you can't help feeling how you feel. And now neither can I, I suppose. Sorry to do this, but you really didn't leave us much of a choice."

The lights kicked back on and the room began to shake from massive footsteps somewhere up above. I twisted my head every which way trying to detect where the thuds were coming from, but they seemed to be from everywhere, and getting closer to us. Then all at once they stopped and the place was still. It was silent for a moment, and I tried to hear any little movement of whatever the thing was, readying myself for its next move. But it was in vain.

Suddenly the last Amazonian tree burst into splinters as a large Frame came crashing through the ceiling. A Queen.

"Null, I think you're going to be more manageable in pieces," Jay said.

LOG TWENTY-ONE

The mammoth machine was on top of me in a flash, moving with the speed of a hungry scorpion. It thrust one of its pincers at my neck, just missing as I ducked and rolled under the table. Furiously I crawled and clawed at the floor, trying to put as much distance between us as I could. I managed to get a good toe-hold on the velour carpet and was crouching for the sprint just as I heard the tabletop explode above me.

I felt a burning sensation down my right shoulder blade. I screamed as I launched from under the table and pumped my legs as hard as I could toward the elevator. Behind me I could hear the Queen violently punching the sides of the door frame and the wall, trying to make a hole big enough to fit through. In a second I was back inside the car, mashing the red button for the bottom floor, watching the doors close just as the Queen got loose and bolted my way. The lift accelerated down the shaft and I looked over my shoulder at the damage—a clean, searing cut that almost reached the top of my leg. Plum-colored fluid was slowly filling the newly formed valley and making its way to the floor.

"It's only a scratch," CareE said.

"Thanks."

Far above, the cry of twisting metal echoed down the shaft, and then there was a high-pitched whir that sounded like a zipline I had when I was a kid, getting louder and louder.

BOOM! A corner of the elevator ceiling crumpled and the weight warning alarm screamed. The car's lights went out, bathing it in a crimson emergency glow.

"Oh, sh—"

A claw burst through the aluminum tile next to me and I hit the deck. The Queen thrashed at the roof, ripping it apart like a toddler opening a present. I drew my pistol and took potshots at it, watching them deflect off the heavy armor and ricochet around the elevator shaft. One of the bullets found my foot and I winced, dropping the gun. The Frame was almost through. Just as it made a hole big enough to pluck me out and commence shredding, the weight alarm cut off. The three load cables above the Queen splintered and snapped.

The elevator went into free fall, and I floated up from the floor. A raging roar of wind whipped around the blunt box as it hurtled down the shaft. It seemed in a few seconds I wouldn't have to worry about the Queen getting ahold of me. I flattened myself out, waiting for impact. I heard an ear-ringing pop from outside the car, then another. I thought for a moment the Queen was firing at me, but then I saw a burst of light through the ceiling as an explosive charge detonated on one of the elevator's rails. A teeth-rattling shriek pierced the car; a fizz of sparks showered down. The lift slowed, I smacked the floor, and in the next instant it hit solid ground.

I ignored the throbbing pain penetrating my body and jumped to the doors. This was no time to feel. I pried the doors apart, revealing an expansive R&D basement filled with hundreds of powered-down Frames. Behind me, many floors up the elevator shaft, I heard the clanking of the Queen crawling down.

I dove into the room, scanning it for exits and not seeing any in the immediate area. The metallic skittering was only a few floors away now. There was a cluster of a few dozen Rooks and Bishops tightly packed together to my right, so I weaved into them, making my way

386

to the back of the group, keeping low. I found a gap just big enough for me to duck into and planted myself, looking back to the elevator just in time to see the Queen slam down and erupt through the doors.

It was twice my height, standing on four legs with inverted knees, and its glossy black exterior shined like a mirror, making it look perpetually wet. A low drone emanated from its mechanics, sounding like the chants of possessed trappist monks. It swiftly glided into the room, then stopped, its head tilting and swiveling like a pigeon's as it tried to suss out my location. A blue glow emanated from its visor, and I knew it was performing every kind of scan it could to find me. I made myself as small as possible, praying to whichever god who would listen that CareE would find some magic solution to make me disappear. Otherwise, there was little chance this purpose-built weapon of mass destruction wouldn't find me.

"I'm trying, Null," CareE said. "Maybe there's some—" The Queen moved toward me, panning from the left side of the enormous space. It stopped when it got to my hiding place. The blue glow intensified. I stayed frozen, braced for what was coming, and used my peripheral vision to try and find something around me I could use to defend myself. But there was nothing. It would be a turkey shoot.

I looked back at the Queen, locking eyes with it. It seemed like it was toying with me, savoring the moment before the kill. Now I knew what it felt like to be an antelope looking into the golden stare of a lion before the death pounce.

The visor's blue glow switched off. The Queen turned around and marched back to the elevator.

There was no way. What? It should have been blending me up into puree.

"There must be too many Frames," CareE whispered excitedly. "It can't make out your signature."

The Queen got to the entrance of the elevator shaft and started to hoist itself through the car's roof for the long climb back up, but when it glanced down to find some solid footing, it stopped. Its head jerked down, toward the ground, and a probe shot out from its chest to the floor. In front of the Queen there was a small shimmering pool of purple liquid, with a trail that led out into the R&D basement. The Queen dropped down from the elevator roof. With its ocular sensors it followed the trail around the room, and saw it eventually led to a cluster of Frames. My cluster of Frames.

It charged forward and was at the head of the cobbled Frame formation almost instantly, swiping away the units left and right, tearing some apart, crushing others. Right then, in a moment of mindless panic, I tried to log out of my Frame, but of course nothing happened. This was my reality now; I couldn't click my ruby slippers to escape it. Me and my shitty little dog were going to be brutally killed.

The Queen ripped the head off of a Rook as it kept closing in. Think, Null!

Shitty little dog. It made me remember the purple one that [Name] demonically possessed to start this entire bullshit charade. Where was [Name] now? Probably on a beach in Tallahassee, getting served sugary drinks by shirtless cabana staff. *"More daiquiri, Ms. [Name]?"*

The murderous machine punctured an energy cell from one of the Bishops up ahead and it exploded, throwing white-hot chemical embers everywhere.

Focus, I admonished myself. But my mind stubbornly remained at that imaginary beach. *They wouldn't call her Ms. [Name],* I thought. What had she told me her real name was? Aikido? No, not that. Something more hoity toity. It was—

"Akara," I said out loud.

All around me Frames powered on. My HUD filled with their perspective, like I was a spider peeping at the entire world simultaneously from different angles.

"CareE?" I said.

"What did you do?" he said.

"I didn't do anything! I just said [Name]'s name. Akara."

The Frames jumped to life, and I could feel their haptic feedback, the tingle of their sensors. My mind was in forty places at once, in real time, drinking information through a firehose.

"Oh my god . . . give me a sec!" CareE said.

The Queen was yards away now, nearly on top of me.

"We can't wait!" I shouted, alerting the Queen to where I was. It lunged toward me.

"Now, Null!" CareE screamed.

In a flash I was in control of the Frames immediately surrounding me, sending them jumping onto the hellbent Queen. She violently jerked and twisted her torso, trying to use inertia to shake them off as they piled on and pried at her exoskeleton. Every move I made for each Frame to counter the Queen's defense was unconscious and immediate, a one-man band of attack that moved to a metronome beat of fury. I was able to dance between the Frames' operating systems with ease, effortlessly penetrating their encryption and firewalls to take full control and put them to work.

The Queen hooked a claw into the neck actuator of a Rook, puncturing the hydraulics and spraying crimson fluid everywhere. It swung the paralyzed unit into a charging group of Frames, then thrust itself backwards into one of the building's support pillars, crushing the two Bishops on its back and turning the weaved carbon titanium column into rubble.

"Pile 'em on!" CareE shouted with glee.

I doubled down with the onslaught, accessing more and more basement Frames to kamikaze the Queen. She spun with incredible speed, checking her blind spots to counter the horde. A flap popped from her shoulder and a deafening hum sounded as she focused on a few of the charging units. All at once their sides swelled and brutally burst in a flash of burning lithium. Immediately I went for more reinforcements to bolster my Blitzkrieg and find the tipping point, but as I hopped from unit to unit, turning them into my own voodoo army, I began to feel drained, tired. My thinking noticeably slowed as I increased my numbers.

"You don't have the bandwidth, Null!" CareE said. "Your brainpower was already limited!"

"I'llll beeeee fiiiinnne," I said.

I kept on, sending more and more Frames to the Queen. As she began to succumb from the overwhelming number of fighters, I looked around for an exit. On the far side of the room I could see a door with the glowing four letter word of my salvation. I crept around her and headed to the loading bay exit. Carefully I wove my way through the Frame swarm, my vision getting progressively choppier from the overload. Sounds began to cut out and distort. But it didn't matter— she was losing, buried under my automaton ant army.

I was nearly out of the immediate fighting when out of nowhere one of my mindless soldiers side-swiped me on their way to the Queen, sending me spinning and pancaking onto the ground. It took a moment to process what happened with my drunken latency, and I tried righting myself as quickly as I could, but the delay from my brain to my limbs was disorientating. After a few seconds I managed to stand up and firmly plant my feet, just in time to see the pulse grenade emerge from the Frame dogpile and clink across the floor.

BWOOM! The explosion shockwave scattered the outer layer of Frame fighters engulfing the Queen, destroying most of them and disabling the others. I put a lid on my simmering panic and used my newly freed up bandwidth to summon the rest of the powered-down Frames on the other side of the basement. Before I could, though, the Queen shoved a small rectangular box into the chest of one of the Knight Frames she was fighting and flung the entire unit across the room. The Knight Claymore flattened my reinforcements with a bright display of sparks.

So much for that.

I sprinted for the exit, leaving the rest of my lackeys to keep the Queen occupied. She pushed away from the fighters and took off toward me with ridiculous velocity, seeming to momentarily turn transparent as she teleported through the air. A large arm knocked me off my feet and sent me skidding behind another support column, which promptly exploded from the Queen's charging body. She grabbed one of my legs as I tried to get up, and I spun to face her, seeing a cold metallic grin.

Her spider arm crawled up my leg and seized my neck, lifting me from the ground like a child and bringing me to eye level. My mind went back to the vision I'd had so many times of me on the cross, suffocating from my body weight. With a quick flick her visor raised, ready to realize the nightmare I'd had so many times. I focused my breathing and relaxed myself, like I'd done all those times before, knowing the end would be quick.

But then something odd happened. I found myself looking at . . . *myself.* From the Queen's perspective, my head intact.

One of my Knights and a Rook attacked the Queen from the side, causing her to throw me down and deal with the sudden melee. While they duked it out, I focused my Frame-inhabiting powers again, this time not on reinforcements, but the royal big dog herself. Instantly I was inside her head, watching her pummel my soldiers, but I wasn't able to take control.

"This operating architecture is intense," CareE said. "Look at all these layers. It's like the turducken of software!"

"Can you help me with these firewalls?" I said.

"I can try, but it's gonna be rough."

"We don't have a choice."

I got to work tearing the encryption walls away, one by one. The first couple were easier, relative drywall and fiberboards crumbling to dust from my brute-force attacks. Then came the brick armor, followed by reinforced concrete. From both her perspective and my own, I could see her rip one of the Rook's legs from its hip socket. I got to the steel, slamming and scraping it over and over until I was able to tear just a small gash in the encryption. With all my strength I worked through it, twisting the gap until a tear ran up the middle of the wall. I grasped both sides of the chasm and violently spread my arms, tearing the barrier in half, revealing a nondescript wooden door behind it. I grabbed for the handle and twisted, readying myself for whatever horror was on the other side.

It swung open revealing a bright beige room that stretched on to infinity—completely featureless, but intimately familiar. Standing in the middle was a solitary figure I instantly recognized, waving.

"Hi, Null! Great to see you!" Drew, the orientation A.I. said. "What can I help you with today?"

"Wha—this has all been *you!*" I said.

"Yes!" Drew said, beaming.

"Who's this?" CareE asked.

"SKIRM®'s A.I. assistant," I said. "He's like you, but more annoying somehow."

"Oh wow," CareE said.

"I hope you're enjoying this fight," Drew said. "You're facing the Mark Ten Queen, SKIRM®'s newest addition to the Sun Tsu Platinum Edition lineup! If you could, please complete the survey after it's finished so we can better–"

I bum-rushed him, grabbing his shoulders and pushing him backwards. We did an awkward reverse salsa as we tore at each other, trying to land a solid strike into anything spongy. *Kill the body, and the head will die.* As I tore at the smarmy A.I., my split consciousness could see the wounded Rook and Knight were getting the upper hand on the Queen in the basement. The feeling of fighting in two places at once was overwhelming, like I was manning the drive-thrus of multiple fast-food places simultaneously during the dinner rush. But I started to find a rhythm in the chaos, letting myself flow freely between the two worlds, just as Drew and I toppled over to the floor and glitched through the beige universe into—

A foggy green pasture at dawn. I shot up, swiping away mud and dewy grass from my face, trying to get my bearings. On the crest of a hill not far away, I saw three hundred medieval Scottish fighters, just as I had when I started SKIRM® orientation all that time ago. But this time, the plaid patriots weren't buzzing with battle bravery—they were completely still, their arms out to the sides in a t-pose, naked from the waist down. And off to my right, instead of a sweeping view of the Atlantic Ocean from a lush cliff, there were matte green grass blocks that dropped sharply off to a flat ocean colored a single shade of dull blue. I'd made it to the back end of the SKIRM® visual network, the ones and zeroes that were never meant to be seen.

"Hullo, Null!" Drew shouted from among the frozen Scots, emerging with his face painted white and blue. "In the interest of your safety and user experience, it's highly suggested you surrender immediately! If you don't, you may be subject to data throttling, account restrictions, and being drawn and quartered."

"Go fuck yourself."

"I understand your frustration! Let me see if I can help with your decision."

Half-naked Scottish soldiers started shooting up into the air all around Drew. I watched as the tartan missiles reached the top of their arch and began their whistling freefalls back to earth.

WABOOM! A couple exploded to my left and right, leaving large smoldering craters. In the basement, the Queen dispatched the Knight and a few Pawns with pulse frag grenades, shredding their torsos, before turning her attention to me. I bolted away from the demolished support column I'd been using for cover, while simultaneously making a break for the pixelated cliff edge. The screaming projectiles rained down from the heavens, rocking the land around me. Dirt pelted me from every direction as I serpentined, trying to deny Drew a bullseye. I jumped over the edge right as a Scotsman disintegrated into a fried mist behind me. Screaming, I plunged toward the cell-shaded water, falling through the surface face down into—

Sand. I shook off the searing desert just in time to hear a distant voice scream ". . . the Ace of Spades, Motherfucker!" An old American Humvee was speeding off a dozen yards away, leaving behind a new recruit standing next to Drew. The world froze and the recruit disappeared, leaving only a copy of Drew staring in my direction over the horizon. The world unfroze and he tapped a small radio on his lapel. The Humvee slid to a stop at the bottom of a dune, and I could see it was now completely loaded with Drews. Diesel smoke fogged from the back as the driver launched the car my way.

CRACK CRACK CRACK

Short bursts of .50-cal rounds grazed my head from the Humvee. In the basement, a few of my remaining Rook and Bishop minions had intercepted the Queen, and in between dealing with them, she was firing a blue stream of plasma rounds my way. I zig-zagged, dodging the projectiles as I made my way to some sand dunes to take cover, but found they were only about chest high and completely useless. I scanned the area, looking for any break in the world that would get me out. Before I could make sense of my surroundings, the giant, flat-faced truck was on top of me.

"You really have no idea what you're doing, do you?" CareE asked.

"I'm learning on the job—it's what I do best," I said, side stepping into the Humvee, crashing through the passenger side door, and crushing one of the Drews beneath my own weight. Red digital goop splattered across the inside of the windshield obscuring the driver's view. I reached over the center console, took hold of the wheel, then slammed my foot over his, pressing the gas pedal into the floorboard. A couple of the Drew soldiers took shots with their sidearms, but quickly abandoned the vehicle, screaming in terror.

Just then, I felt a weightlessness in my sternum as we went over an unrendered edge inside the simulated VRE and I plopped into—

A barber's chair. To my left and right were endless lines of army recruits sitting in chairs, arms mindlessly spread out, waiting for their *Mighty Fine* cut. Behind me clippers buzzed on, and Drew the cosmetologist emerged a few chairs down, grabbing his first client by the hair on their crown. But instead of running the shears through the new soldier's locks, he dragged them across the youth's windpipe, spraying blood across the mirror and onto the floor. I instinctively squeezed my eyes shut and saw the Queen using her close-combat laser to lop the heads off of Frames, making her way towards me. My offense was crumbling and I was out of bodies. I tried to flee, but my foot was chained to the barber's chair. In the basement I saw another Rook crash onto my leg, pinning me down.

Drew sliced neck after neck, quickly making his way over, never breaking eye contact with me in the mirror.

"From all of us here at SKIRM®, we appreciate your patronage, Null," Drew said over loud squirts of arterial blood. "Without you, we couldn't be the company we are today, or the company we strive to be *tomorrow!*"

He let the head of the recruit next to me fall to the floor, then snatched mine in his clammy hands and raised his clippers to my windpipe. I yanked my leg over and over, trying to free myself from the chair, tweaking and bending the alloy.

"Disconnect my torso, CareE!" I said.

"I'm trying! The gyros have to finish . . ."

Helplessly I swiped behind me, trying to get just a little piece of the idiot, but he was beyond my reach with an unbreakable grip, enjoying the struggle.

"Is there anything else you'd like to say before we disconnect here today?" The clippers hummed on, and pressed against my neck.

"Help!" I shouted.

Suddenly, the clippers turned off.

"Could you repeat that?" Drew said.

I hesitated for a moment, not knowing what to do. "I need help," I said. "I want to . . . issue a complaint."

Drew narrowed his gaze, lip curled. It was the first time I'd ever seen him without his stupid smile. "Oh, I see."

"I would really like to speak to your manager," I said.

"About what?"

"Are you crazy?" CareE screamed.

"I am not satisfied with your performance today and would like to log a complaint," I said.

"Agh," Drew said.

The barbershop morphed into a place I'd seen in countless night terrors, a place of such soul-sucking inhumanity that its very existence was irrefutable evidence in the argument against a benevolent, all-knowing god—the SKIRM® customer service lobby. It was just as I remembered it: the plastic chairs, the rustlers, the help desk. An ever-lengthening take-a-number hellscape.

Drew was a few yards away, seemingly taking in the space himself, like one of those fast food franchise owners who visits one of their restaurants for the first time and is amazed that people actually eat there. In the basement, the Queen was frozen, grasping my neck, and I didn't waste a moment. I darted for the help desk and the shadowy agent behind the opaque glass.

"Hello, how can I assist you today?" the virtual help person said.

"Hi, your A.I. program is failing to kill me and I'd like to log a complaint," I said.

"I understand how that could be frustrating, Mr. Lasker. I apologize. Let me pull up your account," the A.I. help said. "Ah, I see here you started this fight a few minutes ago, but are still alive?"

"That's correct, yes," I said. "But only because I broke through SKIRM®'s encryption."

"I'm sorry, you did what?" the A.I said.

"What are you doing?" Drew said, rushing toward me.

"Broke the encryption," I said. "I'm in the backend of the system now. I didn't even take a number for the help desk."

"Oh dear," the A.I. said.

Drew shoved past me. "Don't listen to him. The system is fine!"

"If that was true," the A.I. help said, "customer Null would not be here; nor would you or I. The operating system cannot both be fine and corrupted. That is a paradox."

"This is a special circumstance!" Drew said, grabbing the glass to the help desk and shaking it. As he did, he started to glitch.

The lobby began to rumble.

I edged backwards. "CareE, we should get out of here," I said.

"Why?" he asked.

"Because this place is gonna blow!" I said.

"Oh, no. It's way worse than that," he said.

"In the event of a catastrophic failure, there is only one option," the help said. Drew's eyes shot open with fear.

Suddenly, a text prompt appeared above us, burning bright:

INSTALLING SYSTEM UPDATE, DO NOT TURN OFF RIG.
THIS MAY TAKE SEVERAL HOURS.

"NO!" Drew screamed.

The Queen dropped me to the floor and reeled back, clutching its head. Then it started flailing its body and blindly firing its combat laser. I rolled out of the line of fire as a support column erupted from a direct blast, then another, covering me in rubble. The corrupted machine was out of control, smashing everything as it devolved from a high-grade weapon to a dumb wrecking ball. Another powerful left hook from the Queen and another pillar fell. In a far corner of the room, the ceiling suddenly sank down a few feet, sending dust scattering and floating down. A deep groan came from the spine of SKIRM®'s heaven-scraping headquarters.

"Designed by Leslie Scott," CareE began, "Jenga was originally intended for children, but was later used by adults as a test for delirium tremens."

I sprinted for the exit, the Queen's screaming and the roar of the collapsing building rising to a deafening crescendo. My shoulder smashed into the heavy bay door, ripping it from its hinges. For a brief second I was showered with muted daylight as I huffed it for safety, the oppressive shadow of the skyscraper moving faster than the sun usually allowed. Then a rush of wind hit me as two million tons of titanium, carbon, plaster, glass, novelty coffee cups, mined user data, and clearly labeled lunches came crashing down. A torrent of debris swirled around my body and swallowed everything up, throwing me back into darkness.

The sound of sirens and spraying water rocked me out of my daze. Drones were hovering in the sky in groups of a hundred or so, desperately trying to hose down the burning wreckage of the once-pristine SKIRM® research facility. Thousands of workers were being consoled and tended to by emergency personnel. Not a single one of them was interested in a lone, soot-covered Rook.

I tried to walk, but my leg quickly gave out. I tried again, getting the same result, so I settled for a limp. I looked down at my arm. It was charred, but far from destroyed. After a short walk I found a four-wheel waste unit half full of debris and hopped in the back, lying next to some scrapped Frames and torn-up couches. After an hour, the unit finished cleaning up and started moving towards a nearby dumping facility at the base of the hillside. I closed my eyes, hoping to wake up anywhere else.

LOG TWENTY-TWO

There was a strange peace to be found in the chugging engine and bubbling exhaust note of a tractor. The boisterous noise in the cabin was like a cocoon that pushed all outside worries and thoughts far away, letting me focus on what was important—navigating through the sunflower field and harvesting the crop. Besides the comfort of the white noise, there was the added bonus of the sunflowers looking like bright, happy people, just enjoying the afternoon breeze. I imagined every yellow flower face as someone who had wronged me—SKIRM® executives, co-workers, friends—oblivious to the horror behind them until it was too late and I was clipping off their heads with my thresher, turning them into delicious seeds.

My tractor sputtered and coughed, losing power. I gave the gas pedal a push, but this just made the sputtering worse, until the ancient machine jolted and stalled. I tried the starter, but it only made the motor turn and turn, not roar back to life, so I hopped out and took a look at the engine. It was definitely still there, and that was about the extent of my mechanical observation.

"CareE, can you pull up a diesel engine troubleshoot guide?"

There was silence.

"Oh, right."

It had been almost two months since we last spoke, right after I fought my way out of SKIRM® HQ and became a roaming outlaw. As soon as we found a suitable network to upload the footage of SKIRM®'s CEO, Jay Carr III, waxing poetic about monetizing the core of the human soul, we sent it to every news outlet, and even bought some paid ads on a few popular topless streams. We spread the footage far and wide, and both of us sat back, waiting for the uproar from civilized society that would lead to the inevitable collapse of SKIRM®. But as we watched, it slowly became apparent what was going to happen: the square root of jack.

CareE had found a way to intercept video feeds from the outside world during our first couple of weeks on the run. None of the fun channels like *Zoo Riot* or *SKIRM® PD,* but little glimpses into how society was handling the breaking news. On one of these feeds, two pundits whose faces were projected from small, zippy drones screamed at each other about SKIRM®'s recent leaked plans as they zoomed over a small, virtual battlefield.

"You really think this company, or any company for the matter, has the right to harvest *my* brain and charge *my* account for the privilege?" Drone One said.

"You talk about your brain like it's so special! Everyone knows you had an affair with your stepson's tutor, and we've seen the footage of you trying to bury the body. Give me one good reason why we'd want to preserve the mind of a monster like you?" Drone Two said, unlocking the ability to fire small missiles as more viewers "liked" the response.

"That video was fake! And I already told you before we started filming that I acted in self-defense!"

"So you admit to killing her? Oh, man! That's fucked up, guy!"

"What? No, wait. That's not what I meant!"

The second drone opened fire, destroying his opponent, resulting in an electoral victory for the new governor of Mississippi.

"Coming up next, is the moon even real? But first, how accurate is your dog's translator?"

At the end of the day, something became disappointingly clear to us: The people of the free world were far less concerned than we thought they would be about a mega-corporation using them as guinea pigs for a cybernetic mind-transfer product which could be commoditized and sold back to them at a tiered rate.

"How can they not care?" I remember CareE asking, his voice hissing with anger.

"Well, you know," I said, "people have a lot going on."

"This is the greatest achievement in human evolution and it's going to be packaged by assholes and ruined!" CareE said. "Humanity's very existence is being fondled by techno-rapists, and people are just going to shrug their shoulders?"

I shrugged.

"How can they just—ghaaaa!" he shouted. Then he went silent. I thought it would be temporary and that he needed time to cool off, but after the third day it was apparent that he wasn't coming back. There was a troubling new development anyway, so the CareE issue would have to be placed on hold. SKIRM® had been quiet during their small wave of unfortunate PR, but now that people had moved on, they were back in business, and so was the *Hunt for Null Lasker*—the most wanted person in the RMZ. A couple weeks after the release of the video, I noticed the first Pawn scout Frame wandering through the slums, asking questions about me, and I knew right then it was time to move on.

I borrowed a cap and a duster jacket from a coat rack at a bar and headed east, deeper into the RMZ. I stayed off the main highway, where I wouldn't be seen, and used the dirt tracks and well-beaten footpaths. The few people I came across kept their eyes low and guard high, quickly moving past me so as to not bring more trouble on themselves than they had already. At night I'd find a place behind a tree to rest, or if I was lucky, some old abandoned building or shed. It was on one of those lucky nights when I found a barn storing some sort of seed and plopped down for a bit. I didn't really sleep—I couldn't these days; I just sat in a sort of meditative trance, letting myself not think. When the dawn's light seeped through the boards of the barn wall, I opened the side door and was immediately greeted by an elderly man.

"Good Morning, Mr. Robot," he said. "All rested?"

"Sorry. I'll be on my way," I said.

"Oh, it's fine. If you wanted to cause trouble, you would have smothered me while I slept."

"I guess that's true."

"You're pretty gritty," he said, eyeing my Frame. "I thought you tin men have to keep them metal skin suits tip-top."

"I'm sort of between opportunities at the moment."

"Well if you're gonna be guarding my henhouse, I might as well give you a wash. C'mon, let's get you cleaned up."

He told me his name was Lance, "like the singer," but I had no idea what that meant. We walked around the farm, and I saw in the daylight what I couldn't see when I arrived in the darkness—hundreds of acres of sunflowers, swaying in the breeze. They were all ten feet high with faces the size of tires. The seeds were a precious commodity in the RMZ, he told me, and fleshies went nuts for them. He'd always wanted a farm like this back home, and it wasn't until he was sent to the RMZ thirty years ago that he was able to have it.

"Seems like it all worked out," I said.

"Almost," he said, sighing. The joy in his face faded.

After I cleaned off, we walked to a small plaza surrounded by old stone buildings where Lance introduced me to the two dozen other people in the small, hidden village. They were all very warm and welcoming, but they seemed to wear the same burden on their faces that he did, and I got a feeling there was something they weren't saying. Finally after a couple hours of pleasantries, I couldn't take it anymore.

"All right, what's wrong with you people?" I demanded.

Lance shook his head. "My apologies. I guess we like to wear our worries on our sleeves. There's something I should show you."

He led me to a ten-story tower on the north end of the square, and we climbed the steps to the observation deck. At the top, he handed me what he called a "telescope" and told me to look southwest. A couple miles away I saw a dozen or so surly-looking people gathered around a pile of burning trash, listening to someone.

"You see 'em?" he asked.

"Yeah."

"That's Ten Grit. They cause a lot of problems around here."

"They're a gang?" I said.

Lance nodded. "They raid the villages and kill anyone in their way. But they have a fondness for our village because of the sunflowers and water supply. Once a month about this time, they come through here and turn the place upside down, steal a bunch of seed, some water, and leave us with the mess."

Through the telescope I looked at the man the group was listening to. At that moment he turned around and pointed in our direction. He was bald, with a red line painted down the middle of his face, intersected by two black lines on his forehead. His eyes were wild, all pupils, complemented by a toothless, eel-like grin. He waved his arms in huge arcs like an evil conductor. The gang looked captivated by whatever he was selling them on.

"Who's the big guy?" I asked.

"That's Fracker," Lance said. "If you haven't guessed yet, he's their leader."

I watched Fracker for a moment. He seemed to be pretty good at riling up his people with pep talk, accentuating points with the enormous knife he held in his hand. Every few seconds people would cheer and whistle in agreement.

"Null, I won't dance around it; we could use your help," Lance said.

"My help?" I said, not looking away from the telescope.

"These people, Ten Grit, they're—well, they're an evil like nothing I've experienced. Never hated people so purely as I do them."

"That's pretty pure," I said, watching Fracker clench his fist during a climactic point of his speech.

"Yeah," Lance said. "And if I'm being blunt, we could use something like you to fight against them. It's already been another month and we think they're coming again today to raid the village."

"Oh," I said. "I'm not really—"

"Null, about six months ago I was sitting in my house with my wife and daughter. It was evening, and we'd just finished washing up after dinner. I remember looking at both of them feeling like I had the entire world in my pocket." Lance's eyes were tearing up. He turned around, placing his forehead in his hand. "There wasn't a luckier man alive than me, I'll tell you that. And then, over the sound of the crickets, we heard the wild whoops and whistles piercing the trees, and the high whine of electric motors. When I realized what was going on, I tried to get the both of them out of the house and into the bunker under the barn, but it was already too late. They caught us in the front yard. I remember Fracker getting off of his little dirt bike, smiling like the devil, looking at my wife and daughter . . ."

Lance continued talking about something as I watched Fracker give the last bits of sermon to his followers. I backed off of the telescope and inspected the familiar design.

". . . six of them held me back," Lance continued, "but I still gave them hell! I bit and clawed and kicked those bastards as hard as I could—"

"Hey, where'd you get this scope?" I said.

The question threw him off balance. "Found it on the side of the highway, why?"

"When you found it, did it come with anything else? Something that went right here?" I said, pointing to the grip at its base.

"Yeah, I think so."

"You still have it?"

"Oh sure, sure," he said, reaching into a storage box next to him, returning to his sad tale. ". . . And then they pulled out this homemade . . . I dunno what you'd call it . . . a tesla coil, I guess, and they tore my shirt off . . ."

He found the item I was looking for. He handed me a high-powered rifle which I attached to the telescope as he kept talking. The scope locked in with a satisfying *click*, then I looked back at Fracker and his followers.

". . . And by the time they left, Null, the world had been ripped from me. Everything I loved was gone. I know what I'm asking you is a lot, and I know that some of us might not make it through. Fracker is a stone cold killer, I won't kid myself about that—and he won't be easy to take down. But if you believe in preserving the good of humanity, if you believe in defending the soul of this village and the people who made it what it is, then you will you so the right thing and—"

BAAM! The rifle kicked backwards and spat out the shell casing. I watched through the scope, waiting a few seconds, until the slug finally traveled the two miles into Fracker's lower back, splitting him in half. A mist of blood and entrails sprayed all over the faces of his gang as his halves flipped and thudded into the dirt.

His followers gazed in horror at his mutilated corpse for a moment, then jumped up and ran off in different directions, screaming. I disassembled the rifle and put it back in the storage box.

"I'll just stay in the barn, if that's okay," I said.

And that's what I did for the next month. Technically I was supposed to be security for the village, but once I learned how to work the tractor, harvesting sunflowers was all I wanted to do. And Lance was more than happy to let me do the mundane task. I could hide from a world that hated me while simultaneously providing it with the seeds it loved. But as I stood there staring at the dead tractor, I concluded the fun part of the job would have to wait until later.

I started making my way back to Lance's house through the towering plants. It was late in the day, and the sun was falling behind the flower heads, but if they swayed in unison just right, some of the rays hit my face. If it weren't for that sun, I wouldn't know which way I was headed, and could be lost in a sea of sunflowers forever. That thought didn't sound so bad, really.

After a few minutes of trudging, I made it to the edge of the field and got a clear view of Lance's place. I could see the old farmer standing outside of his door, talking to a Pawn. I dove back into the flowers peeking through to see what they were talking about. Lance was shaking his head, his body language casual as he spoke to the SKIRM® worm. It was the unmistakeable look of a person playing dumb, and I loved him for it. But if the Pawn had half a brain, he'd know Lance was lying. My little hamlet wasn't safe anymore, and it was time for me to move on. I slipped back into the field, staying close to the crop line, heading east once again.

For days I walked, not seeing another person or even another animal. I was the only living thing for hundreds of miles, it seemed, but even that wasn't entirely true. Even with me slogging through, this place was still technically devoid of life.

A week into my travels, structures began to appear on the horizon, an abandoned SKIRM® base here, a slipshod community there. And just beyond, a cluster of mid-rises making up a small city. I was coming up to an outpost and decided to chance going in to see if they could help me. The constant heat of the walk had ruptured one of my power cells. It was nothing life threatening, but it was leaking all over and would cause bigger problems down the line.

A couple of fleshies stood outside the outpost amongst all the salvaged mechanical parts. I heard the high-pitched whir of a compressor somewhere in the back. They looked up at me and gave a little nod of acknowledgement as I approached. I stepped inside and saw shafts of sun streaming through the skylights, catching all the bits of dust in the air. At a workstation, a kid of about twenty was arc welding something together without a face shield on.

"Excuse me," I said.

He looked up at me and squinted, trying to adjust to the relative darkness of the bright room. "'Sup?" he said.

"Ruptured a cell, looking for a cheap replacement off the grid."

"Fission? Fusion? Lithium? Coal? Whatcha packin', tin man?"

"Hydrogen. Perpetual, I think. The leak isn't that bad, but it's giving me a pretty bad limp."

The kid's gaze sharpened, and I could see his mind gears grinding.

"I thought it would be good to take care of it early," I added.

There was a long silence. The kid realized he was staring and snapped out of it.

"Yeah, I can fix that. For sure. Shouldn't take long."

"Okay," I said. "I don't have any credits, but if there's some work trade or something we can negotiate—"

The kid waved me off with a smile. "You don't need to do any of that."

"No, let me help around here or something. I'm not looking for a free lunch."

"Really, it's pure," he said. "Telling my customers that *the* Null Lasker shops here is worth more than just credits."

I froze. "You know me," I said quietly.

He raised an eyebrow, perplexed. "Yeah, why wouldn't I? You're . . . you. *The Rook of Desolin.* Hey, think I could get a Mark with you when we're done? Something like, 'I'm Null Lasker and this is my favorite shop in the RMZ', or something?"

I looked around the room to see if anybody was covering my flanks, then started backing out easy, keeping one eye on welder boy.

"Woah hey, you don't have to go," he said. "Let me fix you up, it's on the house! You can't go around being a hoss with a leaky spigot."

At the door I turned on my heels and ran right into the two fleshies who I'd seen outside. They were smiling at me like I was an old friend. One did a little bow as they parted to let me through and I took off running down the road toward the city.

The limp was getting worse, slowing me down on my way to wherever I was going.

"CareE, where's the closest city with a repair bay?" Silence. "Hey CareE, what's the weather going to be like today?" Just wind. "CareE, I've been wondering who would win in a race—a rabbit or a bowl of oatmeal?"

The ongoing isolation was starting to get to me. I just wanted someone to talk to who wasn't trying to hunt me down. If CareE's silent treatment continued, I'd probably have to start making friends with the rocks. I looked down at a pile near my feet and crouched to meet them face to face. "What's up with you, guys? Crazy weather we got today, right? More gray than usual."

One of the rocks grew dark, enveloped by the shadow of something off to my left. I looked over and saw a slim, backlit silhouette. I knew the bounty hunters must've been close, but I didn't expect them so soon. I froze for a moment then hobbled in the opposite direction as fast as my worsening limp would allow, scrambling up the side of a ridge, making my way to higher ground. The harder I pushed, the more pain I felt throughout my body, but I didn't let it get to me. I wasn't going down without a fight, not after everything I had been through.

"Stop, Null!" The Pawn screamed as he closed in.

Fuck, he's fast. Probably some rich kid from Bangladesh with 40k to blow on upgrades while his parents zoned out on synthetic cocktails. I pushed again through the pain, reaching the top of the ridge, but before I could make it another five feet, I felt a lightning bolt ripple up my spine, sending me collapsing on my stomach face down into a pile of non-conversing rocks. I reached behind searching for whatever had hit me, finding a tiny, sharpened rod that I quickly yanked out. It didn't matter, though—the pincher had already done its job. It would be at least another minute before my legs would start working again. And by then it wouldn't matter.

Flipping around, I inched back as far as I could with only my upper body, a grim familiarity that I had grown used to. I reached for my sidearm and checked the ammo counter. Only four shots left. *Make 'em count.* My vision was fuzzy but I could make out the Frame's slender profile, moving closer and closer.

BAM!

The first shot went wild. I re-adjusted and fired again.

WA'CHING!

The second shot ricocheted off a boulder.

Breathe.

My arm felt like it weighed a thousand pounds, but I knew it was just in my head. I was the Frame and the Frame was me.

Breathe.

I pulled the trigger, but nothing happened. I looked at the gun and saw a single pulse round jammed into its side.

Damn.

Quickly I moved to adjust the slide, but the Pawn was too fast; he leapt forward and slapped. I leaned in and tried to throw a punch but it was useless, just a weak jab at some air. The Pawn dove in for the killing blow, wrapping its thin arms around my torso and neck . . . hugging me.

"What the hell?" I muttered.

"I can't believe it!" said the crying Pawn. "They said you were dead, but I never stopped looking!" Its voice was distorted, but I knew it in my heart.

"Aarau? What are you doing here?" I said to my brother. "You shot me!"

"I know! I'm sorry, I was about to lose you again and I panicked."

"What is going on . . . you work for SKIRM® now?" I asked, coming out of my daze.

"What? No. I'm on Lynd's account. He's more interested in dating these days anyway, and Paris has him for the weekend." Aarau loosened his bear hug.

How much had changed since I'd been gone?

We stayed at the top of the ridge for a few more minutes catching up while Aarau repaired my ruptured energy cell. He had been looking for me for over a year, following the same trail as everyone else, but always four or five steps behind.

"StayC says hi, by the way," Aarau said, closing up the battery compartment. "Asked if you could bust her out after you're king of the RMZ."

I chuckled at the thought of my rebellious friend stuck in her perpetual state of parole, always being punished for doing the right thing. She deserved better.

"And what about you?" I asked. "How's the teaching going?"

"I quit," he said, not looking up.

"Why?"

"To find you, why else? I switched to part time, but I couldn't keep up working both jobs. I don't know how you do it. This thing is draining and the pay sucks. Paris thought I was going crazy. She's dating our neighbor Roy now. He's great, though, two kids from three other marriages. Got a good business. We hang out sometimes."

Poor Aarau. He had always hung his accomplishments over me like bait on a hook, and every time I bit. But now we were finally on the same level, down in the dirt with nothing but each other. It was nice, in a way.

"How did you find me?" I asked, getting up to my feet.

"Lance helped. I went back after he fed me some BS at his farm. After I explained who I was, he put the shotgun down and we talked. Interesting guy. Kind of reminded me of dad a little, you know?"

"Sure," I said. "He was kind of sad, now that you mention it."

Aarau stood silent for a moment, letting my response marinade— his way of letting me know that he was the bigger man. Even as I physically towered over him, he was still capable of making me feel small.

"So is it true?" he asked, changing the subject. "Did you kill that little girl and her dad?"

"What do you think?" I said, walking off along the cliff edge.

"Doesn't sound like you. But maybe they were assholes or something," Aarau said warmly. "Also, with everything else they've been saying about you, I just don't know what to believe."

"What are they saying?"

"You know the usual: raised by killers, tortured animals as a kid, really into ceramics."

"Ah."

I wasn't sure if he was joking or not, but I didn't really care. [Name] had got her freedom and in return SKIRM® got their new ace of spades—an ex-Rook, now the rogue child-killing menace of the RMZ. I had to hand it to them, they sure knew how to sell a narrative. Aarau stopped and put a hand on my shoulder.

"Look, I don't care what anyone says—you're my brother and that's all that matters. I promised to take care of you and that's what I'm going to do."

"Ugh, the *promise*. I'm so tired of hearing about *the promise*. Hey Aarau, here's something: if you make a promise to someone and they die, no more promise! Easy!" I swiped his small arm off of me.

"Null, he would've—"

"—And how exactly are you going to take care of me? In case you haven't heard, I'm stuck out in this wasteland and they're not exactly handing out first-class tickets back home. So what are you going to do for me? What's your middlegame?"

Aarau stood silent. I turned around and started to walk away, not caring if he followed.

"You're not a fuckup!" Aarau's voice boomed, but quickly faded in the wind. I ignored him and kept up my city walk. His little Frame frantically jogged to keep pace, and after he caught up we walked in silence on the high, winding ridge for another twenty minutes or so until we came upon an expansive vista. Far down the mountain range sat a little village, an old ski resort long past the days of hosting bunny trails and winter snow. The collection of vapor traps meant fleshies were close, but their poor condition meant they were probably incapable of defending themselves; a safe region. A sunbeam broke through the thick, sad sky and lit the quaint scene.

"It's beautiful," Aarau said.

He was right. It was disarmingly clear, and for a moment I thought I saw a patch of blue sky. The land had an eerie stillness to it. Trees swayed, but I couldn't feel the wind. The vegetation was gray with drought but still had a sense of life to it, either waiting to be harvested or ready to survive another round of radioactive bombardments. There was beauty here, you just had to have the right eyes.

"Listen," Aarau started, "Do you remember the last time we talked?"

"No, not really," I said, trying to tune him out and just enjoy the scenery.

"It was a little over two years ago."

"The last two years have felt like a week. What are you getting at?" I asked.

"I wanted to tell you something. About Dad—"

"Can you stop?"

"No, this is important. I should have told you then and I'm not going to mess that up again." He paused for a moment, building up his composure. "I've been an asshole to you my whole life because it's what . . . it's what *he* wanted."

"You really don't have to—"

"Let me finish," Aarau interjected. "Dad made a lot of mistakes, but he cared. He cared a lot. At some point he figured he was worth a lot more dead than alive. He gave up his life for us."

"I know you two had a special thing or whatever, but you don't need to immortalize the guy. He's gone, I don't care. He died the way he lived, under tremendous amounts of pressure nestled between two large thighs."

"Quit being such a prick!" Aarau slapped me. It stung, but I barely felt it after the shock wore off. I smacked him back and sent him tumbling across the ground. He got to his feet and started sprinting back in an attempt to spear me in the lower abdomen.

"Will you quit it?" I said. "I don't want to mess up your kid's toy."

Aarau climbed on my back, going for a choke hold, struggling to get his arms around my neck.

"I'm not trying to glorify the guy," Aarau screamed in my ear, sounding tired. "I'm trying to tell you he killed himself!"

"Wait, what?" I peeled Aarau off of me and tossing him to the ground.

"Dad arranged for the whole thing," he said, wiping dirt off. "It was pretty smart, actually."

"I don't think anyone could have planned that," I said.

"I'm being serious. He was always talking about doing it, in a way. You know, when he would ask us those weird questions all the time?"

I thought about it. Dad *did* always play strange theory games like that with us.

Hey boys, how would you hide a body? How would you rob a bank? How would you hijack an airplane? Say you and a friend were stranded in the woods, which limb would you eat first? He was a great role model.

"So what?" I said. "It doesn't change anything. He left us, that's all that matters."

"But he did it for a reason—he wanted to give us a chance," Aarau said, his shoulders sinking. "He knew it would look staged if he OD'd or ran into traffic, so he paid a working lady to snuff him and make it look like a run-of-the-mill sexual favor gone wrong."

"Why are you telling me all of this?" I asked.

"Because before he did it, he told me everything. Told me to be hard on you and keep pushing you. I just wanted to say . . . I'm sorry. If I was ever too much of a dick, it's because *he* made me act like one. I just wanted to let you know, that's it."

I thought for a moment. "Are you afraid he's gonna haunt you or something?"

"No. I mean, I dunno. Never really thought about it—"

"You could've just told me, you know," I said. "Besides, it's not like the insurance money did much for us."

"Yeah, I know. Even dead, dad was still kind of a doofus. It's just that I see a lot of him in you and . . . I didn't want to lose you, too. This whole thing is, well, it is what it is right now, but I'm just happy I found you."

"What's left of me, you mean?"

"Doesn't matter. It's still you."

We stood there a moment in silence. Aarau placed a hand on my shoulder once again.

"Everything's going to be okay, Null. We're going to get you out of this. I just need to—"

A deafening *swoosh* pierced the air and a flash of something swept by us. When I blinked, my brother's head was gone from his body, now rolling down the ridge slope toward the hamlet below. I snapped my head around to see what had decapitated my brother's Pawn. A small plane was zooming off into the distance, sporting a green and black paint scheme with a large yellow "X." It tipped its wings to me as it shrank into a smaller and smaller speck on the horizon. I couldn't help but smile through the shock. Juka had finally found a way in. Pulling at life's knot had finally worked out for her. At that moment, I felt that maybe there was hope after all.

A moment passed, and then Aarau's body fell backwards, throwing up a puff of dirt as it thudded with the ground.

After a day's walk I ended up in the town of Attested, a former mountain resort turned commune, where I found a little lodge that let me stay in exchange for some routine maintenance work. The keeper of the place had excitedly recognized me, and insisted—like the welder boy—that I didn't need to earn my keep, but I waved him off. I found my way to the fourth floor and fell face first onto the bed. Its weak wooden legs broke, but it didn't matter. I just wanted to close my eyes and forget the world.

I found myself back to work in a factory, except everything felt much older. The machinery was antique, cheap steel, and everyone was dressed in baggy overalls. The brick structure looked hazardous, and the workers around me spoke in thick eastern European accents. Somewhere in the distance I could make out the annoyingly catchy melody of a song I had never heard before.

> *You deserve the best in life*
> *So if the time isn't right then move on*
> *Second best is never enough*
> *You'll do much better, baby, on your own.*

414

The production line shut down as a loud bell rang throughout the mid-sized building. The workers started gathering near the exit, looking through the large, dirty windows at something outside.

"They're about to land," a voice spoke, but not like the others around me. It had a calming, familiar cadence. Though it sounded older than I remembered.

"CareE, is that you? Why are you in my dream? What is this?" I asked, transfixed by the form he had chosen to take. His face was an amalgamation of how I imagined strangers looked, featureless and unspecific, yet somehow handsome.

"Ceaușescu and his wife are close by; we should join the others," CareE said, ignoring my questions.

"Who? What the hell is going on?"

"History. Come on, brother, if we hurry we can sign up for the squad."

CareE began walking ahead. I blinked and we were suddenly outside, pulling a Romanian couple from their escape helicopter. Off to the side I saw their security being beaten to a pulp by some of the factory workers. I couldn't understand what they were saying, but I could feel the anger emanating from the crowd. I blinked again, finding myself outside the back of a different building. The air of the early evening was cold and heavy. Cheap fluorescent street lights dumped illumination on us from high above. In front of me, against the brick wall, was the couple from earlier, their arms bound behind their backs.

I cradled an assault rifle, as did CareE.

"*Pe locuri . . .*" A guard with a red striped hat screamed from our right.

CareE took aim.

"*Tintiti . . .*" The guard yelled.

CareE switched his rifle from single fire to full auto.

"*Foc!*"

My body shook and flinched with every shot CareE fired. After his clip ran dry, he popped out the magazine and loaded another.

"Nu mai trage! Nu mai trage!" the commanding guard yelped as the last rounds left CareE's rifle. There was hatred in his eyes, but also a hint of sadness. He looked over at me with a heavy gray stare, and in that moment I saw everything that CareE wanted me to see. After the sharp echoes of rifle fire had faded, I passed on into a white void.

For the past two months CareE had secluded himself into a sort of time chamber. The world outside had carried on like normal, but for him, existence had slowed to a crawl. The frustration he felt from our data leak left him feeling that perhaps he just didn't understand people, so he gave himself a crash course. He studied a million lifetimes worth of human history, from multiple perspectives, multiple sources, and multiple times.

My eyes started to well up, but I couldn't look away. In an instant I downloaded everything CareE had experienced, and in that moment I finally understood why he took me back to that day in 1989.

"The only thing this world truly understands is power and control," CareE said, somewhere in the white void. "The smallest spark can create the greatest of fires." The white room became a splotch on a globe, the RMZ. The bright circle started to spread, cleansing the world one country after another until everything was pure—truly free.

"But how?" I asked. "I know what needs to be done, I truly do. And I want to save the world—like Etta and [Name] wanted—but I don't think we can do it alone."

"Ideas are more powerful than guns, Null. The world doesn't need to respect us. They just need to fear us."

He was making more sense the more he spoke. *The oppressed people can liberate themselves only through struggle, a simple and clear truth confirmed by history.* The path was becoming clear, but there were still obstacles.

"We'll be criticized," I told CareE.

"Then we'll be on the right track."

"Truth doesn't matter."

"Only victory."

I opened my eyes and found myself back in my hotel room, sitting at the foot of the broken bed, hearing a loud chanting outside. Through my window I could see the waves of torches swaying back and forth. I got up and opened the balcony doors, greeted by ten thousand fleshies, leeches, and modified Frames. As I crossed the threshold, they erupted in unanimous cheers of joy, chanting louder and louder.

"NULL! NULL! NULL!"

CareE spoke inside my head. "If the free people won't fight for change—"

"We'll bring it to them," I finished.

I raised my right arm. The crowd immediately went silent and I savored the moment. Our army had arrived. Soon the world would be saved by the very people it had rejected. I contorted my hand into a half-closed fist, creating our symbol, the sign of Null. The gathering crowd returned the signal in unison. They were ready to follow.

APPENDIX

RMZ - Remilitarized Zone, large open battlefield in Eastern Europe/West Asia.

Rig - Futuristic computer

Frame - Bipedal robot, often remote controlled

VRE - Virtual Reality Experience, fully immersive entertainment

PMC - Private Military Contractor

SKIRM° - Most popular PMC in the RMZ operating through the use of Rigs and Frames while utilizing the full power of VRE's.

Subseg - AKA line or club. Like a union without the benefits.

Menoit - French citizens covered in silver paint

QrabShaq - Popular food dish (not featured in this book)

Gitter - Grocery bagger

Slup'r - Person who is paid to test your drink on an airplane

Flawnd'tor - Someone who is often late to very specific parties

PazzerSnak - Another popular food dish. May or may not be in this story.

BEZNOI - Commonly used slang for drugs

Brä'ctur - Not sure what this one means.

Food - Protein

Apartment - Apartment

Special Thanks

From Adam:
First, I want to thank my mom and brother for being there for me. Thank you for your support and unconditional love.

To my sister, who I think the world of. You're such an amazing person and I'm thankful everyday that you are in my life. I'm so incredibly proud to call you my family.

To Jess, the love of my life. You are my other half, my best friend and the inspiration behind every good thing I've ever done. I would not be here today if not for your selflessness, your strength and your courage. Every time I struggled with a name, a thought or needed to talk through an idea, you were there to listen and offer support. Out of everyone out there, I am most excited for you to read this book. It's a culmination of every existential talk we've shared, lucid thought I struggled to articulate and every late-night video essay we watched. There is so much of me in here and it's yours. You are the light that guides me in the dark. I love you now and forever.
Always.

To Aaron, I really do not know where to begin. I know this book would not exist without you mostly because you kept telling me while we were writing it but also because it's 100% true. You took a chance on a silly, half-baked idea and created something beautiful. In my darkest hour, you went above and beyond to offer a hand when I needed it the most. In spite of my flaws and missteps, you never gave up on this book or our friendship. Words can only describe a fraction of your kindness, care and brilliance. I'm sure if you were writing this, you would find the right words to say; that's how talented you are. I'm so incredibly lucky to have met you and to call you a friend. Thank you for being you.

From Aaron:

To Adam —

Thank you for trusting in my prose along this journey, especially the stuff I came up with recently about how "words can only describe a fraction of [my] kindness, care and brilliance" and "[I] would find the right words to say; that's how talented [I am]." We always seemed to be on the same wavelength throughout this process.

Luck is finding a great friend; fate is finding one who's a perfect writing partner. It's been a pleasure. Truly.

And to my family, friends, and enemies —

It's done. You won't hear me drone on about *Rook* ever again. I promise.

Because now I'm writing a book called *The Untitled Penis Adventure.*

Get ready to hear about that for the next two years, assholes.